"OH, ZACK, PLEASE ..."

The "no" that would have completed her sentence lodged in her throat as his moist lips searched down her neck to her breasts and found the nipple they sought, peaked and ready to be taken.

White fire flashed through her body, and she arched to meet him, thrusting with her hips. She hardly noticed when he dragged her camisole and petticoats down, finally shoving them away with one foot. All she knew was that explosions of desire were igniting deep inside her. Shaking her. Pounding her. Turning her from a woman of flesh and blood into a trembling mass of molten longing ...

BECKY LEE WEYRICH'S *GYPSY MOON*
WINNER OF A *ROMANTIC TIMES*
REVIEWER'S CHOICE AWARD

D1457269

HOT WINDS FROM BOMBAY

Becky Lee Weyrich

FAWCETT GOLD MEDAL • NEW YORK

For VINCENT—The next author in the family.

PART ONE

1837

CHAPTER ONE

SILVER birch logs with bark like thin, dry parchment crackled and hissed in the delft-tiled fireplace. No other sounds, save the occasional rustle of paper, disturbed the morning quiet of the sun-drenched blue breakfast room.

Persia Whiddington's mother and older sister, Europa, had excused themselves from the table some while before. Persia, too, was impatient to be up and about on such a crisp, white morning. But still she held her place, sipping absently at the cold dregs of chocolate in her Manila-patterned blue china cup and tormenting a congealed lump of egg with her coin-silver fork, anxious for her father to finish reading. He seemed to be taking an agonizingly long time over the newspaper today.

No one in the Whiddington household was allowed to lay a finger to the *Portland Transcript* until Captain Asa Whiddington had completed his long, thorough perusal of its contents. He claimed that what he had missed most in his many years at sea—besides his beautiful wife, Victoria, and their two lovely daughters, of course—

was fresh news. He still bemoaned the fact that he had been at sea for almost a year before learning of Andrew Jackson's election, which had taken place back in 1829. Eight years later, now that he had retired to the big white house on Gay Street in Quoddy Cove, Maine, he spent hours devouring newspapers the way a starving man might attack a long awaited banquet.

Only Persia begrudged the captain this luxury. She craved the news with his own brand of hunger. Perched now on the very edge of her chair, she watched puffs of blue-gray pipe smoke issue forth from behind the *Transcript* like signals from one of the newfangled steamship's stacks.

Suddenly, his voice made her jump. "Ayah, she'll be putting in today just as I reckoned."

Persia made no reply to her father's statement. She knew he wasn't addressing her. In all likelihood he was not even aware of her presence in the room. He was merely commenting to himself—a habit ships' captains acquired from long, lonely years at sea when, owing to the loftiness of their positions, they were forced to keep their own council.

Still, Persia knew her father and his habits of speech well enough to be able to decode his cryptic words. He was reading the Marine Journal, her own favorite part of the paper, which told of the arrivals and departures of ships and of those "spoke at sea"—in laymen's terms, sighted and hailed through megaphones when they passed close enough to another vessel. The "she" referred to a ship that would be putting in at Quoddy Cove today.

The news set Persia's pulses racing. She left off toying with her cold breakfast and leaned forward in her eagerness to hear more, her chair legs scraping on the floor as she did so.

The sound of the chair disturbing his calm, Asa Whiddington flipped one edge of the paper aside and peered at her over the tops of his wire-rimmed spectacles, his face stern and hard at the interruption of his sacred morning ritual.

"Aye, I might have known it was you, girl. Your

mother's long been about her household duties, direct-
ing her crew and getting the place shipshape. And
your sister's undoubtedly stowed herself in her room,
making ready for the skating party tonight or doing some
other such ladylike thing. But here you sit, Persia
Whiddington, watching my paper with the same greedi-
ness that a gull eyes a fat mackerel."

"I only thought when you were finished, Father . . ."

His gray eyes danced with merriment and the twitch
of a smile tugged at the corner of his mouth opposite the
stem of his meerschaum pipe.

"If it's the ladies' gossip news you're so eager for,
you may have it. There's nothing much there anyway
except that Mr. Benoit of Kennebunkport has asked for
the hand of Mistress Shute of Peake's Island, Mrs. Stowe
of Brunswick is visiting in Poland Springs with her ailing
sister, and Mrs. St. Onge of Skowhegan entertained the
ladies of that town with a quilting bee on Thursday
last."

He knew Persia wasn't the least bit interested in such
frivolous fare and was not at all surprised when the
gleam in his younger daughter's china-blue eyes dulled.
She shook her head, making the bright sunshine that
streamed in through tall windows dance in her red-gold
hair.

"No, thank you, Father. I'll wait."

She sighed a bit wearily and folded her hands—itching
for the Marine Journal. Her eyes were downcast, staring
vacantly at the white on white of the Irish damask
tablecloth with its pattern of hounds and harps so that
she didn't see the broad smile break over her father's
sea- and salt-chiseled face or the quiver of his full gray
side whiskers that always betrayed his amusement.

A long silence followed before the captain said, "She's
been out three years, eight months, and eleven days."

Persia's head shot up and she felt a rush of excitement
sweep through her. She didn't have to beg her father for
more information. He could see the eagerness in her eyes
and would comply, all in his own good and thrifty time.

"One would think you were waiting for a lover coming home from sea, the way you watch the ships, Persia."

"It's not that, Father." She blushed at his teasing. When the ship in the news had left its homeport, Persia had been only twelve or thereabouts—far too young to be interested in the opposite sex. "It's just that the ships, the sailors, have been *everywhere,* have seen *so much* of the world. I've never been anywhere."

"You've been to Paris, Lisbon, Norway," he pointed out, a sly grin curving his lips.

"And not a one of them out of the state of Maine," she replied with an unamused huff. "I want to see the rest of the world. You've told me all about it, but I'm restless to go to all those exotic ports myself."

Captain Whiddington laughed softly, but Persia knew he wasn't making fun of her. He admired her curiosity and her sense of adventure. He always had and had made no secret of it, from the moment she'd learned to crawl and claimed his sextant as her favorite teething toy.

"Ah, my cunning child, you should have been a son. Then we'd have made a stout seaman of you. Ayah."

She felt a little stab of regret. How often she'd wished . . . But wishing and a penny would buy her a stick of hoarhound candy. She would have to learn to be content with her lot as a female. Still, she could live the sailor's life vicariously, thanks to her father and the seamen who passed through. They were always eager to share their tales of adventure with a willing audience.

"What ship is it, Father, and where has she sailed?"

"The *Tongolese* out of Boston, under Captain Bartholemew." Whiddington chuckled and lifted a shaggy gray brow at his daughter. "Ayah! He'll retire a rich man after this voyage. He took Maine timber down to New Orleans, sold it, and purchased bales of cotton. Stopping off in the West Indies, he loaded sugar. These goods he sold in England, acting as his own supercargo to deal with the merchants. From there, carrying salt meat, he sailed to West Africa for palm oil and white pepper. Tallow from Madagascar, dried fruit and wines from the Mediterranean, coffee and spices from the Far East. Finally, to Bombay and Calcutta, trading these goods for Indian cotton, which he sold at a profit in China, investing there in a cargo of tea, silk, and chinaware. That will bring another fortune when it's auctioned at Central Wharf to the Boston market.''

Persia's head was spinning. So many places, such exotic goods. If only she could go and see it all for herself.

"If she was blessed with fair winds and following seas, the *Tongolese* should be making port before noon today, I'd guess."

Persia didn't wait to hear another word. Glancing up at the ship's clock on the mantelpiece, she saw that its brass hands were nearing south and nor'west—ten-thirty, almost five bells. She voiced a hasty "Excuse me, please, Father," and was up and away.

She raced out of the room and headed up the stairs. Her mother attempted to put a halt to her flight in the second-floor hallway, and Europa tried to detain her with chatter about the skating party as Persia dashed to her room for shawl, bonnet, and gloves. But she would not be deterred from her mission.

Hurrying on to the attic, she threaded her way through trunks of old clothes, tarnished brass birdcages, packing crates filled with straw—the accumulated trash and treasures of half a dozen generations of Whiddingtons and Forsyths, her mother's family. She found her spyglass on the shelf where she always kept it and headed topside.

A ladder led the way to the very peak of the three-story house. She hoisted her green woolen skirts above her booted ankles and mounted the steps like an able seaman, shoving the trapdoor up with her head and shoulders when she reached the top rung.

With one gloved hand, Persia gripped the sturdy, turned railing of the widow's walk, hoisting herself up through the narrow opening. The door banged shut behind her. The dim interior of the house was closed away. She had entered another, brighter but more private realm.

Below her and to every point of the compass, the

landscape glistened with a fresh blanket of snow that had fallen silently during the long winter night, turning the Maine coast into a crystal fairyland. She shaded her blue eyes with one hand and faced toward the sea. The wind, rising with the tide, whipped her cheeks to a rosy hue and fluttered the lace edge of her flannel petticoats like the froth of a wave beneath the sea green of her skirt.

"A spice wind from the Orient," she whispered, in spite of the fact that its icy bite made her chest ache when she breathed too deeply.

She let her mind stray to warmer climes—to exotic, palm-fringed lands, where brown-skinned natives danced on white sands and bright birds cried as they swooped through tropical rain forests. She had read about all these things in her father's books and the logs he'd kept when he captained his ships to Barbados and around the Horn. He had spun his fantastic tales for her on a thousand snowy New England nights as they sat before the fire in his library, tracing his journeys on charts spread about the floor.

The cold wind freshened, teasing a wisp of Persia's flame-colored hair from under her bonnet. The feathery touch on her cheek was like a light kiss. She closed her eyes and her smile glowed. Like many a down-east woman, born and bred, she firmly believed the tales that ghosts of long-lost seamen rode the winds, stealing kisses from pretty girls. Such a phamtom kiss brought good luck. She touched her face. Her flesh felt warm even through her glove.

Opening her eyes, she looked out over the village toward the water. From the rooftop of the house on Gay Street, she could see the tall masts of the ships anchored off Quoddy Cove, like so many leafless trees in a watery gray-green forest. Bright spots of sunlight danced over the waves, shifting and changing from moment to moment. The sight made her ache with longing. What would it be like to ride those sparkling seas southward and around the Cape of Good Hope to India? She could only imagine it in her dreams. And she dreamed those dreams every single night.

"Someday," she whispered wistfully.

She scanned the water once more and was not disappointed. A tall ship, well sailed, rode the tide, her topgallants puffed with the brisk wind. Putting the glass to her eye, she quickly focused in on the vessel. She could just make out the scroll on the transom that read *TONGOLESE*.

Persia stood very still, her spyglass trained on the figures on deck. There was no mistaking her father's old friend, Captain Bartholemew, on the quarterdeck, his feet firmly planted and hands behind his back as he passed on orders for the crew to the first mate. Persia took her time, observing each of the dozen or so sailors on deck in his turn. Some she recognized as coming from foreign lands by their swarthy darkness and odd clothing. At each port a ship lost sailors to the lure of the land and signed on others to take their places. Perhaps these men were Greek or Italian or even Indian.

Suddenly, the crystal eye of her glass focused on a giant of a man. He was no foreigner, even though his skin was almost the color of the teakwood table her father had brought back from the Orient on his final voyage. The seaman's brown, wind-ravaged hair was streaked with lighter hues by the same fierce rays that had darkened his body. He sported a full beard that curled upward over his cheeks—rampant, golden, satyrlike.

Persia laughed softly, thinking how horrified her mother would be if she knew her daughter was staring at such a sight. The man was as nearly naked as any she had ever seen. His broad chest was bare except for a gleaming forest of bristling man-hair that spread from side to side, tapering down in a funnel shape to his belly. Canvas britches, cut off at the knee, rode low on his trim hips. She shivered and drew her shawl more closely about her shoulders. How could he bear the cold?

As the man bent at the capstan, making ready to drop anchor, she watched the hard muscles of his back and shoulders strain at the task. The sight sent another shiver through her, but this one had nothing to do with the briskness of the morning air or the bite of the north wind.

And it was accompanied by an unfamiliar ache in some secret, hidden part of her. The sensation was new . . . alarming . . . entrancing.

She turned away suddenly, rubbing a hand over her eyes. She felt so strange, almost as if she had seen too much all at one time. Clinging to the railing, she forced herself to breathe slowly, evenly, but the feeling refused to pass completely.

When she was calm enough, she looked again. The brawny giant was obscured from her view. Even though her heart sank, she tried to put him out of her thoughts. She forced herself to concentrate on the sleek lines of the vessel—her clean hull, painted stark black, relieved only by a white band at its waist, the gilt figurehead, the tall, square-rigged masts—and the masterful manner in which captain and helmsman were handling her.

How she would love to slip away and hurry down to the dock to mix and mingle with the crew and the people welcoming them home! But, of course, such a thing was unthinkable. If she was lucky, her father might invite an acquaintance or two on board home to dinner. Then she would sit in total thrall, hearing firsthand of the places she longed to see.

"Persia, are you up there?" Victoria Whiddington's voice came through the closed trapdoor.

"Yes, Mother." Persia felt desperately embarrassed suddenly, as if she had been caught at some nefarious crime. Quickly she hid her spyglass behind her skirts, even though she knew full well her mother never trusted the ladder enough to climb to the widow's walk herself.

"Well, do come down. *This minute!* I won't have you looking wind-whipped tonight at your first social outing."

"Coming, Mother."

Persia cast one last, longing look at the incoming ship. Then, tucking the rebellious lock of hair back under her bonnet, she lifted the hem of her long woolen skirt. She raised the trap and started down the ladder at a much slower pace than before. She hated leaving her vantage point high up on the widow's walk. But even without the ship in sight, this promised to be an exciting day and night—her first skating party. She must start getting ready.

Suddenly, a new thought struck her, causing a quiver of excitement and a feeling of keen anticipation to run through her. Perhaps some of the sailors off the *Tongolese* would be at the skating pond this evening. It would be perfectly proper for her to talk with them there, under the watchful eye of the chaperones. The very idea quickened her pace, giving a new purpose to the tiresome hours of preparation ahead.

But for the rest of the day, every time she thought of the *Tongolese*, she remembered the near naked sailor with the strong tanned body and the mane of gold-streaked hair. What would such a man be like?

"No doubt a rough, uncivilized brute, Lady Guinevere!" she said to the bisque doll propped against the pillows of her bed. "No gentleman at all!"

Lady Guinevere, of course, lay quietly on the crisp white candlewicking of the spread, staring out of unblinking, painted eyes, the same bright blue as Persia's.

"Never mind," she continued. "You don't have to say a word. I know by your silence what you're thinking. But you are wrong—*totally*! I haven't given him a second thought, nor do I intend to."

Persia could invest Lady Guinevere with fabrications all she liked, but she couldn't lie to herself. The sight of that sailor had changed her somehow. Even as she talked on to her favorite childhood confidante, for the first time in her life she felt rather foolish doing so.

Perhaps it was time to put away the childhood things. Perhaps it was time for Persia Whiddington to become a woman.

CHAPTER TWO

*T*HE greenish-yellow glow of the aurora borealis shimmered its luminous arc in the black heavens. November was late in the year for such an arresting phenomenon. Perhaps it bode well for a mild winter and an early greening in the spring. All over the village, citizens of Quoddy Cove commented upon this hopeful possibility, nodding sagely and punctuating their laconic statements to one another with the ubiquitous "ayah."

From the Federal-style house on Gay Street, Persia, in the final stages of preparing for the skating party, glanced out her bedroom window and uttered a cry of wonderment that carried to the farthest reaches of the second story.

"Come quick, everybody! Look at the sky! I never in all my life saw anything like it."

All of her life was not that long. The younger Whiddington daughter had passed her sixteenth birthday the previous week. The day had been celebrated quietly at home with only Captain and Mrs. Whiddington, Europa, and the servants in attendance since a November snowstorm had chosen the night before to close its chilling hand over coastal Maine. Still, the wintry blast had done little to cool Persia's enthusiasm at being sixteen and on the very brink of everything wonderful in life, or so she assumed.

And tonight her life seemed almost *too* wonderful. The arrival of the *Tongolese,* her first skating party, and now *this*! The fabulous light show above had to be a good omen. Watching the colors shift in the night sky gave her the same pleasant, queasy feeling she had experienced while staring at the bronzed sailor a few hours earlier. For some unknown reason, she was unable to shake the man from her thoughts, though, in truth, she hadn't tried very hard.

Holding a delicately wrought, gold-on-brass whale-oil lamp, Persia shaded her eyes against its glare and peered heavenward through the dimpled glass of the windowpane, all the while murmuring her delight at the shifting drapes of color glowing in the black sky.

"You sound like a silly child, Persia! For heaven's sake, I don't know what's to get so excited about. It's only the northern lights."

Europa Whiddington's tone conveyed the superior, pseudosophisticated air that set eighteen-year-olds apart from their younger siblings. She swept across the room and, pushing her sister aside, yanked the window sash down.

"What did you do that for?" Persia demanded. The angry toss of her head captured the lamp's light, making golden sparks dance in her long auburn hair and gleam in her blue eyes.

"My dear little sister, you aren't even dressed. And here you stand, gaping out the window for any passerby to see. Why, I'd die of shame!"

Europa, of course, was fully dressed. She looked breathtaking in her mauve velvet skating costume, trimmed in silver fox fur. Every glossy black curl was in place. Her cheeks had been pinched to bring forth a rosy glow. Persia could tell that Europa had sucked and bitten her lips to make them full and red. And she guessed that her sister had employed a broomstraw up the chimney to extract soot from the flue to darken her brows and eyelashes. Europa had been preparing all day and had long since been ready to leave for the skating pond.

Europa's perfection caused Persia a twinge of envy. The older girl was every bit as fragile and elegant as their mother. Her features were finely sculpted, resembling those carved in the cameo brooches their father had brought back from the little town of Torre del Greco in Italy, where skilled craftsmen wrought delicate jewelry from the shells of the Mediterranean. Europa's skin was just as white as the patrician lady's portrayed in the delicate gold frame pinned at her breast. The only difference was that Europa's shell-pale features were framed in the luxuriant darkness of her onyx-black hair.

Persia often bemoaned the fact that she herself had inherited nothing of their mother's beauty except her eyes. She possessed her father's sturdy frame and adventurous temperament—not wonderful attributes for a young woman. As for her red hair, she hated it! Once, when she was a tiny girl, Europa had told her that fiery curls were the devil's brand. Although she had learned through the years to ignore her sister's taunts, those early pronouncements had left their mark on Persia. She was ever wary that Lucifer in some guise or another might one day present himself and trick her into giving him his due.

"Well, are you going to get ready or not?" Europa snapped. "I'm not really delighted at the prospect of taking you along anyway. And if you keep up this dawdling, I'll have a fine excuse to go without you."

"Go on, if you want to," Persia answered, peeved. "I'd just as soon not be seen in your company?"

"Afraid of the competition?" Europa asked, bestowing a sarcastic smile on her little sister.

"Hardly! But you're the worst skater in York County! It's embarrassing the way you have to hold on to that stupid chair to keep from falling on the ice. It seems to me you would have learned how to skate after all this time."

"That just shows what you know! Every time I fall, some handsome man comes rushing to help me up. You might try it, Persia. There's something to be said for weak ankles. You'll never get anywhere racing all the boys and *beating* them. Why, one would think you don't know how to act like a lady!"

"I know how to act, but I'm not going to make a blasted fool of myself on the ice just to get attention from a man."

"You'll learn, little sister. Or you'll find yourself an old maid one of these days. Mark my words!"

"Well, I'll certainly never stoop to tricking a man to get his attention!"

Europa moved to the mirror, admiring her perfect features as she answered in a knowing tone, "Every woman who aims to marry has to use some tricks to get the man she wants."

"Europa Whiddington! How can you say such a thing? Are you suggesting that Mother tricked Father?"

The sisterly argument carried down the hall to their parents' bedroom, bringing their mother immediately to the door.

"Young ladies!" Victoria Whiddington's voice, though quiet, held a certain undeniable authority that none of their father's stentorian harangues could equal. Both girls fell silent and lowered their faces in shame. "If either of you wants to go to the skating pond tonight, there will be no more bickering, I'm sure. Am I understood?"

"Yes, Mother," they chorused in muffled tones.

"Very well, then. Persia, finish dressing."

Europa turned to her sister with a pleased, haughty smile.

"Europa, go to your room and find something to occupy yourself until the rest of us are ready to go."

"But Mother, I was only—"

"Never mind! Go work on your sampler."

Now it was Persia's turn to flash a momentary triumphant look before Europa fled the room.

Mrs. Whiddington started for the door, then turned

for a moment and measured her lovely younger daughter with a gaze of sudden awareness. Persia's full breasts were straining at the fragile smocking of her camisole. The pleasing plumpness of her baby fat had melted, reshaping itself into comely curves. When had Persia grown into a woman? And how could she have been too busy to notice the new ripeness of her daughter's figure and the enchanting beauty of her bold features—her full, slightly pouting lips, the delicate arch of her dark brows, and the glitter of golden, featherlike lashes framing her large, sapphire-brilliant eyes? Persia looked every bit as mature as Europa. And furthermore she possessed the ripe, voluptuous beauty that men had found most difficult to deny themselves.

All of a sudden, Victoria Whiddington felt something like a blizzard assault her heart. Tonight her little Persia would be thrust into a woman's world for the first time. Could her youngest handle it? She prayed so.

"Persia," she said, 'you will be careful tonight?"

Her daughter looked up, her eyes sparkling suddenly and a lovely smile lighting her face. "Careful, Mother? You know I skate well. I've never had an accident."

"That's not what I mean." The older woman's tone and demeanor were serious.

Persia's smile faded and a small frown took its place. "What then, Mother?"

Victoria couldn't bring herself to put her cautions into words. How could a decent Christian woman voice the shocking dangers unscrupulous men presented to innocent young women? How could she explain the demands of lovers on their sweethearts? How could she tell her daughter of the intimacies husbands exacted from their wives? She couldn't! The words refused to come. She could only pray for the best and live with the nagging little coldness that had taken up residence in her heart.

"Oh, never mind. Just be sure you keep your curtains closed until you're dressed, dear. One never knows who might pass by and glance up at you."

*   *   *

Victoria's caution came too late. Already the moth had been drawn to the flame, where it lingered, feeling the smoldering, tantalizing heat.

Seaman Zachariah Hazzard, down in the street below, hadn't meant to stare. Following the bright skaters' lanterns—like a river of fireflies—he had been on his way to the pond with everyone else in town when he paused to look up at the curious lights in the sky. Only by chance did Persia peer out of her window at that exact moment. Zack's gaze had quickly shifted from one wondrous sight to the other.

A gentleman, of course, would have averted his eyes. But never had Zack Hazzard been accused of being a gentleman. And he wasn't about to choose this moment to start correcting bad habits.

He couldn't see the woman's face, but he knew her hair was red. The light in the upstairs room cast its glow behind her, making her long tresses shimmer like a fiery aura. And he could see her tempting silhouette, dark against the bright room—soft shoulders, full breasts, and a becomingly slim waist. Even after the drapes were drawn shut, Zack stood his ground, still staring up, still trying to imagine what she must look like in the flesh. A warm, delicious woman—smelling of lavender and powder and fancy French soap.

He swiped at his brow and gave himself a good shake. He'd been a long time at sea on the *Tongolese. Too long,* when a distant silhouette could cast such a spell over him.

Most of the crew had gone on to Boston, the ship's homeport, where families waited to welcome their world-wandering loved ones back. But something had made Zack stay. Maybe, he thought grimly, he simply didn't want to see all those joyous, tearful homecomings. He had no relatives expecting him to rush back to them. For all his family knew, he was long since dead.

When he had cursed his father, kissed his mother, and run away to sea at the age of twelve, he'd known that he could never return to the fold. Many a time he had lain

awake in his hammock aboard ship, seeing his mother's
face in the dark and wondering how she was.

After turning twenty-one—a *man*, salted and cured at
sea—he had taken his one and only sentimental journey
back to Salem, Massachusetts. He could still remember
his light heart and his lively step as he greeted sights he
knew so well. In his mind even now he watched the
younger, unsuspecting version of himself as he neared
home.

Swaggering up Derby Street, his sea bag filled with
gewgaws of ivory, ebony, and gold to delight his mother
and younger sisters, he spied the old house. But a crowd
was gathered about the place. His eyes were drawn to a
woman in black who looked strangely familiar. She stood
on the front stoop, holding a solemn-faced little boy by
the hand and dabbing at red eyes with her handkerchief. Zack stood stock still, trying to figure out what
was going on.

"Pardon me, sir. Do you know that woman?" he
asked of a passing stranger. "It seems I should recall
her name."

The grim-visaged passerby looked the young sailing
man up and down before he answered. "You wouldn't
be knowing Miss Mary unless you was from around
these parts."

"Mary? You mean that's Mary Hazzard?" He squinted
hard, trying to make himself believe that the woman in
black with features drawn and careworn was the same
bright, winsome sister he had kissed good-bye as she
slept clutching her ragdoll so many years ago.

"Not Hazzard any longer. Not these seven years past.
She married old Doc Goodlow. But even he couldn't
save Mary's poor mother."

At that moment, Zack had understood what was happening. There was a funeral in progress at the old
homeplace. Cold dread filled him. He felt like a small
boy again, crying in the night for his mother when a
nightmare marred his sleep.

"You mean, Mrs. Hazzard's passed away?"

"Passed away, bah! She was pushed into her grave.

Murdered by that bastard husband of hers. Beat her to a bloody pulp, he did, in a drunken rage.''

Zack had felt a sickness rising within him at the stranger's words. He had known his father's cruelty. He had run away because he hadn't been able to take it any longer. He'd had to stand by and watch the old man slap his mother more than once. Still, the real brutality had been directed toward Zack himself, the only other male member of the family. And now, Zack relived the same awful guilt he had experienced the night he ran away. His mother had found out he was leaving. But instead of trying to keep him from going, she had given him what little money she could and had wished him a tearful farewell.

"You'll never grow up to be a man in this house, son. He won't let you," she had whispered. "Go! Find a life for yourself."

"But what about you and the girls, Mama?" he'd asked, his determination to leave faltering at the last moment.

"You mustn't worry about us, Zachariah. He won't harm your sisters. And I've lived with him long enough to know how to deal with him."

But in the end, she hadn't been able to cope. He had dealt her a killing blow, with an axe handle, the stranger told Zack, crushing her skull and releasing her from the hell she had lived on earth.

Zack had wanted to go over and speak to his sister Mary, to see if there was any way he could help. But what could he do now? He should have stayed at home with them instead of running away. Maybe if he had, his mother would still be alive. He had known at that moment that he would have to live with his awful guilt to the end of his days.

"Her husband?" He caught the stranger by the sleeve as he tried to hurry off. "What's become of Mr. Hazzard?"

"Killed his own self once he'd done for his poor woman. Saved the hangman an honest day's work. Good riddance!"

Zack felt numb at the words and muttered in answer, "Aye, good riddance."

He'd gone to the burying ground and watched his mother's funeral from a distance. But he'd been unable to go to his sisters with consolation afterward. Since that day nearly six years ago, he had stayed away from Salem and his remaining family. Better for them to think he was dead, too, he told himself. After all, what good could he do them now?

So, even though it felt fine to be ashore after his long voyage, he was at loose ends. He was sure neither where to go nor what to do with himself until he signed on for the next voyage. His future lay at sea . . . not in Salem, not in Boston, not in Quoddy Cove, Maine.

He glanced up at the window and saw her once more—a dark, bewitching silhouette against the closed drapes.

"Then again, Quoddy Cove might not be so bad," he observed, stroking the wild gold of his beard.

Suddenly, he remembered something his good friend Jehu, the carpenter on the *Tongolese,* had said to him that afternoon as they were departing the ship. "Well, Zack boy, it's shore leave for me . . . for the rest of my life. And I'm more than ready."

"You'll be back," Zack had told him, laughing, because Jehu always claimed each trip was his last. Then invariably he shipped out again.

"Not this time! I got me a wife I hardly remember how to make love to and a son nigh on to four years old that I've yet to lay eyes on. No, laddie! You take the sea for your mistress, if you like. Me, I want a real woman with warm lips to kiss, soft arms to hold me, and a need that won't have to wait for years at a stretch. You better think about that, too. You're not a bad sort. You're no beauty, I'll admit. Hawk nose, shaggy brow, and a temper about as sweet as a harpooned whale's. Still, there's some women likes the rough, hard-bit sort. Mark my words, there's one for you out there somewhere. You're not getting any younger. You'd best go find her before someone else steals her out from under you. Then you'll kiss the sea good-bye. It's no decent life for man nor beast."

Zack shoved his thick fingers through the shock of sun-streaked brown hair tumbling over his forehead. Remembering Jehu's words just after seeing the woman in the window gave him a strange, squeamish feeling in the pit of his stomach.

He needed a woman all right, but not one who lived in a fancy white mansion. Not one who was going to tie him down to home and hearth in exchange for her meager favors. The kind of woman he wanted right now would most likely be found in a room over some local tavern, and she'd know all there was to know about taking the ache out of a man's gut while leaving his heart in one piece. Never mind love and wedding bells and forevermores. Who the hell needed all that?

At twenty-six years of age, Zachariah Hazzard considered himself a confirmed bachelor. If he belonged to any female, it was to the daughter of Neptune. He was happy with his sailor's life, and it promised a bright future. He had spent years climbing the ladder, from cabin boy to apprentice, and finally to able seaman. Now he was making the staggering sum of twelve dollars a month. He patted the bulging pouch at his waist. Almost five hundred dollars in honest wages. He was a rich man after his four years before the mast. But better still, the promotion he'd worked for all these years would be his once he signed on again. Captain Bartholemew promised a second mate's billet for him his next time out. And someday Zack would captain his own ship.

That was happiness! *That* was true love!

Still, he lingered outside the house on Gay Street. *Idle curiosity*, he told himself. He wanted to see if the woman's hair was really as bright as copper, the way it had looked from a distance.

But the blood surging hot in his groin and the film of sweat on his brow bore out the full truth.

He wanted more . . . he wanted *her!*

* * *

Persia dressed quickly once her mother and Europa left the room. Her father had bought her two presents for her birthday, her own copy of Dr. Nathaniel Bowditch's book called *Practical Navigation* and a new skating outfit—neither of which her mother found acceptable.

"A book on navigation?" Victoria had said shrilly. "I apologize profusely for not supplying you with a son, Captain Whiddington. But I will not allow you to turn our youngest into a male child. We will exchange this for a nice book on cookery."

Of course, the book had not been exchanged.

As for the costume, the soft cashmere was the same brilliant blue as Persia's eyes, and the fox fur trim and muff matched the color of her hair. A long, fur-lined cape of a deeper hue completed the ensemble. Her mother had claimed that the bright color was fit only for peacocks and brazen women, certainly not a young girl. But Asa Whiddington had countered that the color of Persia's eyes and hair were nature's own doing and if the good Lord had seen fit to paint his daughter with such a bold brush, there was no reason he shouldn't be allowed to adorn her just as vividly.

Persia stood back a moment to admire the cut of her costume with its trim bodice and skirt that fitted neatly over her hips before flaring from the knees to the ankles. There was no denying the fact that her father had excellent taste.

Victoria Whiddington had lost the argument almost before she'd gotten started. Finally, with a little sigh of resignation, she'd said, "At least it will be dark at the pond. Maybe no one will notice Persia."

Persia smiled. They would notice her. They always noticed her when she was on the ice. She was the best skater in three counties, even if she was a girl.

"Persia, are you ready?" came her father's voice from the other side of the door. She hurried to open it, anxious for him to see her wearing his gift.

"Yes, Father!" She whirled for his inspection. "What do you think?"

Asa Whiddington's granite-gray eyes glittered and a

smile twitched at one corner of his mouth, making his silver side whiskers quiver the way they always did when he was about to laugh aloud.

"By God, Persia, you look like one of those fancy ladies I saw in the Tuileries in Paris, France!"

"*Captain Whiddington!*" His wife's horrified cry came from the hallway. "I won't have you telling the girls about *fancy women*. You shouldn't know about them yourself. And I certainly don't want one of my daughters looking like one!"

Asa cleared his throat and gave Persia a wink. "I was only teasing, my dear."

"Well, that's highly improper talk for *teasing*! You spent too many years at sea. I'll thank you to remember that you are in a Christian home now, not on board some godless ship, and that you are among *ladies,* not rough sailors."

"Yes, my dear." His reply was meek, but he winked at Persia once more and gave her a secretive smile.

To Persia, her father seemed the only truly understanding person in her family. Of course, anyone as lovely as Europa had a right to act a bit high and mighty, lording it over lesser beings. As for her mother, Persia knew her life had been hard with her husband always at sea and the two girls to raise alone. Still, she thought perhaps if her mother didn't lace her corset quite so tightly, she might have a different, more relaxed view of life.

"Come along now, girls," Mrs. Whiddington called. "Fletcher has brought the sleigh around front."

"Please, Mother, may Europa and I walk to the pond with the others instead of riding in the pung?" Persia begged.

"I think not."

"Oh, come now, Victoria. Let the girls have their fun. After all, this is Persia's very first skating party," their father pleaded on behalf of his favorite daughter.

Victoria held her tongue for several moments while Persia held her breath. Half the fun, according to Europa, was walking, lantern in hand, to the pond and meeting friends along the way. But if their mother said no, there would be no further discussion of the matter. Her word was law in the Whiddington household. Victoria was captain of her Gay Street ship.

Finally, giving a curt nod, she agreed. As Persia hurried down the hallway to fetch Europa, she heard her mother scold, "Captain Whiddington, I wish you would not side with the girls against me. You would brook no such interference with command of your ship. I expect the same respect in my home."

"Yes, dear," Asa answered, and Persia knew that he was melting his wife's anger with that special smile he saved only for his Victoria.

Zachariah's hands and feet were getting cold in spite of his fur-lined gloves and heavy boots. It was one thing to strip down while working on deck in the winter, but quite another to stand about idle. A man could endure extreme cold, he'd learned in the iceberg-infested North Atlantic, but only if he kept moving. To remain too long in one place, motionless, could be painful, even fatal. He stamped his numb feet and blew into his palms. Maybe the young woman in the house wasn't going to the pond with everyone else.

But just then, a shiny black sleigh came jingling around from the back of the house. On the front seat holding the reins sat a smartly dressed native servant—from one of the South Pacific islands, Zack guessed by his big frame, erect bearing, and the blue patterns of tattooing on his cheeks and forehead. He gave a husky command in his own dialect, and the matched pair of dapple grays pranced to a halt, stamping the packed snow under their hooves.

A moment later, the front door opened. Two bright skaters' lamps glowed golden in the dark. For an instant, the hallway light outlined a pair of women.

"Ah, my own aurora borealis," Zack murmured, feeling his hopes and the heat in his groin rise once again.

The pair shrieked with laughter as they slipped and skittered along the icy walk toward the sleigh. The driver hopped down and offered in oddly stilted English, "Allow me please to assist you in, Miss Europa? Miss Persia?"

"No, thank you, Fletcher. We'll walk to the pond." The one who spoke, Zack could see by the glow from her lamp, was the red-haired beauty, dressed in blue. She was "Miss Persia," he noted.

"Please do have a good evening, misses." The driver bowed grandly to them and climbed back up to the driver's seat of the sleigh.

Without a moment's hesitation, Zachariah stepped boldly toward them. "Going to the pond to skate, ladies?"

The woman dressed in smoky pink whirled away from him and sniped, "I don't see that that's any of your business, sir!"

When her sister answered, "Yes. Are you?" Europa tugged her sleeve and whispered, "Persia, *really*! He's a perfect stranger."

But he wasn't a perfect stranger to Persia. He was wearing more clothes now, but the untamed beard was the same and she knew that his hair, hidden under a black stocking cap, was just as wild and sun-streaked . . . the tight curls on his bronzed chest as well.

She heard a ringing in her ears, and although the temperature was below freezing and the mercury dropping fast, she felt a hot flush tinge her cheeks and an unexplainable heat rise beneath her peacock skirts.

Even as Persia hesitated, staring up into the tall man's smoldering brown eyes—a detail she had not been able to ascertain through her spyglass—Europa was tugging her away.

Zack was not to be put off so easily. He hurried after them.

"I see by the black stacks on your house, ladies, that a seafaring man lives there. The smut-colored bands on your chimney are supposed to signal an offer of welcome to all who sail the seven seas. I'm just off the *Tongolese.* I've been 'round the Horn and back again. I'm still walking on sea legs this very minute. Don't I qualify for some of your hospitality?"

Persia was being dragged along by her sister, but she

stole a chance to look back at the friendly giant. Her lamp cast its pool of flickering light over him. She could see the bronze hue of his skin and his thick, sun-marked hair escaping from under his cap. He wore a pea coat and canvas trousers. She imagined that she could smell the salt and tar about him.

Again her gaze traveled back to his deep-set brown eyes. They gleamed with a sharpness honed from many hours of squinting into the tropical sun and staring heavenward to navigate by the stars. And beneath their bold challenge, she saw in their depths the sadness of a man many times his age—the look of one who had sailed the oceans of the world and beheld its miseries as well as its wonders.

How she would love to talk to him about the places he'd been and the things he'd seen! But all she had time to do, with Europa pulling her away, was offer him a hasty smile. He returned it to her in his own crooked way.

"Honestly, Persia! If you can't behave yourself, the next time I'll send you along in the pung with Mother and Father. You can't imagine how you've embarrassed me. What if some of my friends saw me talking to a common seaman on the street?"

"I thought he was nice, Europa. And I think you were downright rude. He's right about the homes of seamen offering hospitality to other sailing men."

"That hospitality, my foolish girl, does not extend to captains' daughters taking up with any riffraff off the docks!"

"He wasn't riffraff!" Persia insisted hotly.

"And just how would you know? Hurry along now. We don't want to be the last ones there."

Persia wasn't sure how she knew that the man was made of better stuff than most of the common sailors fresh from the sea. Maybe it was that look in his eyes or the husky timbre of his voice. But one thing she knew for sure: she *would* talk with him before the night was done.

CHAPTER THREE

ZACK watched the two women hurry away, the red-haired beauty—Miss Persia— stealing a glance over her shoulder at him from time to time. Soon she would be out of sight. He knew he couldn't let that happen. With determination guiding his steps, he started off down the path they had taken, his lurching, shipboard walk veering him from starboard to port in a rolling gait.

At the top of the hill above the pond, he stopped. The sight nearly took his breath. Although he'd spent many a night at sea with the starry heavens a bright canopy overhead, he had never witnessed such a scene as this. Above in the black sky, the curtains of yellow, green, and violet of the aurora borealis folded and unfolded themselves in an ever-shifting pattern of brilliance, reflecting softly on the irregular circle of ice in the little hollow below. And on all sides, streaming down from the wooded paths like sparks shot from above, the skaters' lanterns pinpricked the night a thousand times over. The townspeople sang as they moved toward their destination, and their voices carried, crystal clear and sweet, on the cold air. He felt the old ballad tingle through him, making his heart ache with a strange, dark loneliness.

His vision misted for a moment, and the whale-oil-burning lamps turned to fire flows down the hills. He remembered another place, another time, when chanting filled the sultry air and singers of a faraway isle presented a similar picture. There had been a beautiful woman in that place, too. He closed his eyes and sighed, remembering.

It had been his first voyage to the South Seas. He would always remember it as the best time of his young life.

Aye, he had been young then, but no virgin. Already he had taken a dark-skinned woman with soft black eyes in New Orleans as his first, and others in Boston, Charleston, and Savannah after that. But those meetings had been dimly lit assignations, arrived at down dark alleys in the dead of night. A password through a door, an exchange of gold, and then a hurried half hour of strange flesh pressed to his on a hard mattress in a stuffy, dingy room. The women's faces, bodies, techniques, all blurred and ran together in his mind. They had no names.

But Mahianna—the tender beauty on that South Pacific isle—had been a different matter entirely. He remembered his shipmates laughing, joking, slapping him on the back as they approached the sheltered, ginger-scented cove.

"Aye, lad, you'll be wanting to jump ship here and that's no lie. Four women to a man, and every one of them a delicate jungle flower. Just mind you take it slow and easy. Don't drink too much of their coconut beer and take a nap *alone* in the heat of the day. Otherwise that fine young dick of yours will be turning blue and falling right off from sheer exhaustion before we leave this paradise."

The others who had been to the islands before regaled him with wild tales of exotic delights. The women were the most beautiful, the most willing and expert at giving pleasure. He didn't believe a word of it . . . until he met Mahianna.

"Mahianna," he sighed aloud on the cold Maine air.

He'd left ship with the others in one of the long boats. As they rowed ashore, the women swam out to meet them, tossing orchids, hibiscus, and plumeria blossoms into their boat. Some of the sailors tore their clothes off and dived overboard, making love to their passionate partners in the salty aqua sea. Zack remembered his own desire rising as he'd watched. But he'd kept his seat, not sure how to deal with women so eager to give themselves to strangers from strange lands.

He walked the shore alone for a time, trying to recover his land legs. At the edge of the forest, he sat down on the sand and watched his shipmates groping, fondling, and mounting their women. He was aching to have one of them, but they didn't speak English. Since he seemed less than willing, the girls had left him to himself to take their pleasures with more eager partners. He was sitting under a banana tree, feeling lonely and sorry for himself, when she stepped out of the green foliage. His breath froze in his throat at the sight of her.

She stood before him, smiling shyly. Her hair was long, falling past her slim, bare waist. Her eyes were as black as a starless night, and they seemed to be staring into him, caressing him gently. She stood very still for several moments, allowing him to take her full measure with his gaze. Her skin was smooth and firm—the color of the petals of almond flowers. Her lips were wide, sensuous, and as bright a coral as the hibiscus blossom she wore in her ebony hair.

At first, because of her cascading tresses and the lei of purple orchids about her shoulders, he didn't notice that she wore nothing above her waist. But when she bent toward him, removing the flowers to place them around his neck, Zack saw her beautiful, bare breasts—full and tanned with large, erect nipples.

He was sitting on the sand. She was leaning over him, placing the flowers, kissing his forehead, his salty hair, his sunburned cheeks. But her breasts—those wondrously

soft, warm globes of pulsing flesh—held his full attention, fascinating him with the rich copper brown of their
crinkling crests. His hand came up. He hesitated. She
looked into his eyes, smiling, took his hand to hers, and
guided it to where she sensed he wanted it to be.

Her skin was every bit as silky as it looked. He held
her warmth in his palm, feeling a pulse against his flesh.
She was kneeling beside him now, brushing her long hair
back over her bare shoulders, offering him what seemed
to entice him most. He rubbed a callused thumb over
her nipple. A delicious little shudder shivered through
her, and the taut skin shrank from his touch, growing
hard as a pebble.

He was aware of his own hardness and the heat rising
within him to an unbearable fever pitch. Still, she seemed
in no hurry. She knelt there, smiling and making soft
cooing sounds to let him know his caresses pleased her.
He forced himself to take his time. There would be no
hurried, sweaty pounding of flesh with this woman. She
would not allow it. She came from a hotter clime, a
people who lived at a slower pace and took their pleasure in long, refreshing drafts.

Smoothing the satiny hair over her bare shoulders, he
spoke to her. "I am Zack," he said, emphasizing each
word and speaking too loudly as if that might make her
understand.

She frowned and shook her head slightly. Reaching
up, she took his hands from her shoulders and brought
them back to her breasts.

"No, no." He shook his head and drew his hands
away, using one to pound his chest. "Zack!" he repeated.

She seemed to understand this time and tried his name.
"Zaa." Smiling, she reached out and took his hand from
his chest, placing it between her breasts. "Mahianna,"
she said. Then, putting his hand back to his chest, she
repeated, "Zaa." For several moments she played her
hand game, saying each name at the appropriate time.

Soon they were both laughing and chanting the names
together. And moments later they were tumbling in the
sand, playing like children on a picnic at the beach. She

fought with him, tickling and jabbing, until he pinned her on her back beneath him. Lying atop her, laughing down into her flushed face, he watched a change come over her. Her smile turned from the playful teasing of a child to the sensual invitation of a woman. Slowly, beneath him, her body began to move. He felt her warmth thrust up against his groin and he moaned softly.

Mahianna let him know with the veiled look in her eyes and soft words in her own tongue that the time was upon them.

He rose from her, staring down at her lovely naked torso, covered only about the hips with a swath of brightly colored material that was knotted low on one hip. Her long, shapely legs looked dark against the white sand. She raised her arms to him and he pulled her up, clinging to her, reveling in the feel of her breasts against his bare chest.

Moments later, she had led him a short way through the rain forest to a hut beside a secluded lagoon. A mat bed made of the fibers from coconut palms awaited them in one corner. But first Mahianna went to the rough table and poured a milky liquid from a hollow gourd into a coconut shell. She offered it to him. This was the sweet, burning ambrosia his shipmates had told him about—coconut beer, they called it.

The concoction scalded his mouth and throat but soon brought a soothing pleasure to his whole body. He imagined he could feel its milky fire streaming through every vein. Mahianna, too, drank of the magic potion. When her cup was empty, she went to her "Zaa" and led him to the mat, indicating with sign language and soft sounds that he should lie down. He did, feeling his head swim with a delicious lightness while the rest of his body pulsed with desire.

Slowly, deliberately, Mahianna stripped away his clothes, stroking his body with long, cool fingers as she undressed him. Zack could still remember the way he'd writhed and moaned under her knowing touch.

When she had finished with him, Mahianna stood. He stared up at her, not knowing what would come next.

She went again to the gourd and poured more of the potent liquor into the coconut shell. Then, dipping her fingers into the milky drink, she rubbed it over her breasts with slow deliberation. Finished with that task, she untied the knot that held the bright sarong about her hips. It fell away, giving Zack his first look at the rest of her—a smooth, taut belly, narrow hips, and ebony fur dividing her thighs. He caught his breath at the sight of such beauty and felt as if he might strangle on his own need.

Still standing over him, Mahianna proceeded to rub the rest of her body with the sweet liquor. When her copper-gold skin was glistening with the sugary substance, she knelt down and put the coconut shell to his lips. Zack drained the fiery contents thirstily. A new buzz sounded in his brain and he felt his manhood seize itself and shudder, straining to its fullest erection. There could be no more waiting. He must have her *now*!

Mahianna, her peaked breasts glistening with the sweetness of the dried liquor, went into his eager arms. Zack leaned down to touch his tongue to one nipple. The taste was of sugar and wine and woman. His lips covered her, drawing her into his mouth. Now he knew the task she had set for him. He must drink the aphrodisiac film from her flesh before taking her. He went at it with a lusty thirst that only served to feed his hunger for her. Nipples, belly, the tender insides of her thighs. She moaned and cried and keened for him. She stroked him and clawed him, kissed him and bit him.

And finally, when he had sipped the last drop of sweetness from her willing flesh, he sought out the sweetest spot of all. Wild now with desire, Zack plunged into his Mahianna, certain that he would die in the next instant if he was forced to wait any longer.

She made no sound as he battered through her maidenhead, possessing her as no man ever had before. He drew back for a moment, staring down at her face in disbelief. He had never taken a virgin before. But when he saw no pain in her eyes . . . when she smiled up at

him and drew his mouth on hers, he thrust anew, feeling
his desire rising with every new depth he conquered.

When his body-shattering, soul-jarring, earth-shaking
climax came at last, Mahianna shared it. So total was
their exertion and their repletion that they fell asleep in
each other's arms almost immediately afterward. But
during the coming sun-drenched, breeze-softened days in
that island paradise, he had laughed and loved often—
taking his Mahianna to the heights with him a dozen
dozen times. Then he had sailed away, never to lay eyes
on her again.

"Hello there!"

The woman's voice wrenched Zachariah out of his
erotic musings. He found he was sweating, trembling,
and sporting a full erection from communing with his
lusty memories of Mahianna's love. And, with a jolt, he
realized that he was looking not into the black eyes of
his pagan lover, but into eyes as blue and bright as an
untroubled South Pacific sky. However, far from dimin-
ishing the desire his memories of his island lover had
fostered, he realized that the beautiful face and form
before him only heightened his need. He wanted to lash
out at her for tempting him so.

"You came back, Persia." His words were an accusation.

How could this fire-haired temptress have presented
herself to him at such an untimely moment? Did she
know the dangerous position she had placed herself in?
He needed a woman desperately. And it made damn
little difference to him if she was an innocent New
England maiden or a well-ridden professional.

They came together on a sheltered part of the path.
The other skaters had reached the pond, leaving the two
of them all alone, far from chaperones and prying eyes.
Blood pulsed hotly through his body. Granted, he had
not been without a woman during the entire voyage of
the *Tongolese,* but it had been over four months since
they'd put into a port until this very day. This beautiful,
eager-faced young woman had no idea the shaky ground

she was treading. On half a dare, he would drag her into the nearby woods and shower her with the full breadth and depths of his passion. It would serve her right, he told himself.

Zack rubbed a gloved hand over his face to wipe away the perspiration and to try to get hold of himself.

She gave him a momentarily surprised look, then smiled. "How do you know my name? I don't know yours."

"Easily taken care of." His voice was gravelly, his throat dry. "Zachariah Hazzard. My friends call me Zack."

She curtsied and laughed softly. "Well, Zack, I'm very happy to meet you. But I still don't understand how you know my name."

He started to tell her that he'd heard the driver address her, but measuring her in a quick glance, he decided that this young woman would be intrigued by the mystery of not knowing for sure.

He glanced over one shoulder and then the other, as if making sure no one would overhear their conversation, then leaned so close he could smell her lilac cologne and whispered, "It came to me in a dream last night. I saw you standing at a window, your red hair glowing as you stared up at the sky, and a voice kept repeating, 'Persia, Persia, Persia.' "

Persia didn't believe a word of it, but she loved his wild imagination and the way his lips pursed as if he might kiss her every time he said her name.

Suddenly she frowned. Why had he mentioned seeing her at a window? Had he been watching her from the street before Europa snatched the curtains closed? One hand went to her breast as she thought of the thin camisole she'd been wearing. No! That was silly. He'd simply made the whole thing up.

"I'm sorry my sister was rude to you, Zack."

"Sister? Rude? I didn't notice anyone but you when we met a while ago."

He was handling himself well—breathing normally now, remembering his manners, making small talk as if he'd never had a thought in the world of forcing himself upon her.

She laughed softly, a sound like gentle raindrops kissing a meadow of wild flowers on a summer afternoon.

"Why, Miss Persia, how could I have eyes for anyone else with you before me?" His tone was slightly mocking, but his words amused her.

Oh, he was a charmer! Imagine telling such a wonderful lie to impress her. There wasn't a man alive who could help but notice the exquisite Europa Whiddington.

She leaned close, putting a gloved hand beside her mouth, and whispered, her breath teasing his beard, "Whatever you do, Zack, don't let on to Europa that you didn't notice her. She's not used to being ignored. She'd pout for days."

Persia watched an intense, smoldering mist descend over the seaman's eyes. Suddenly, realizing that they were alone on the path, she felt a nervous shiver pass through her. She took a step back, but he caught her wrist.

"Don't go!"

He had tried his best, but a man had his limits. Her warm, mint-scented breath on his cheek had put all his senses into action once more. A man deserved *something* in the way of a welcome on his return from sea. And this red-haired beauty seemed just right for the welcoming-home ceremonies.

Seizing Persia about the waist in a strong grip, Zack propelled her off the path into the deep woods.

"What are you doing?"

He didn't answer. And he didn't allow Persia to ask any more questions. When they were behind a large fir tree, he swept her into his arms, pulling her fast against him. Her struggle was instinctive, but it lasted only moments.

Zack felt her body give in to his demands. He poised over her—eager for her touch, hungry for her lips, thirsty for the taste of a woman after so long. But not just any woman . . . *this woman*.

Persia was stunned. Never had she dreamed of finding

herself in such circumstances. What was she supposed to do? What would Europa do if she found herself in such a position? Faint, in all likelihood.

But Persia was not one to take shelter in such feminine weakness. Her curiosity, her sense of adventure, and her budding womanhood were too strong. The man's breath on her cheek was too caressing. The heat at the junction where his hips pressed hers was too tantalizing. And the feeling of his hard muscles even through the heavy clothing he wore brought back visions of him as he had appeared through her spyglass—almost naked, sweating even in the cold, teasing her senses to play tricks upon her ripe, virgin body.

She felt the moist, demanding pressure of his stranger's lips, urging her to submit. She was conscious of him, totally—the odors of salt and tar just as she had imagined earlier and the heat and rigidity surging from his loins. His hands were hard on her back, kneading the soft cashmere and fur even as his lips and tongue caressed her mouth. Soon her arms stole around him and she clung to him, wondering what in life had ever given her this much pleasure.

She had never been kissed before, and her head went light and muddled. Confusion took possession of her brain. She should fight him, of course. After all, he was a stranger and a brash one at that. Europa, she knew, would swoon under these circumstances. But Persia was not like her sister.

When he released her at last, Persia stood very still, staring at the serious lines of his face. She had half expected that he was making fun of her, taking advantage of a "silly child," as her sister called her. But there was no mockery in Zachariah Hazzard's expression, only an intense, burning look of desire. An expression that made her body tense and pulse with a mingling of dread and wanton longing.

"You shouldn't be here with me." His voice was hard, edged with contained rage.

Her own answer was little more than a whisper of breath from her swollen lips. "I know, Zack."

"Then why don't you run away? I won't stop you."

Persia hung her head for a moment, trying to sort out her confused feelings. She should go . . . yes! It was the only proper thing to do. But she didn't want to go. She had enjoyed his kiss. Even now, she was experiencing the most delicious fires torching her whole body. She had never felt so alive . . . so much a woman.

Why must everything wonderful be forbidden? she raged silently.

"Last chance," he said darkly. "Go now or . . ."

Persia's confusion fled. She looked up, gazing directly into the smoldering eyes trained on her face. Slowly, her hand came up and she twined for fingertips through the wrought-gold beard.

"I don't want to go, Zack."

CHAPTER FOUR

*S*o this was the secret wonder of being a woman. This was what it was all about. How marvelous!

Persia's head was still spinning and her blood pounding, but her mind was made up. She wanted to know *everything*! Until tonight, she had known almost nothing of life and love. But she had always been a bright pupil, and Zack was an extraordinary teacher.

His hands were on her shoulders now, tightening and relaxing his hold rhythmically as he took deep, steadying breaths. All the while, his eyes searched hers, seeming to probe the very depths of her soul. His gaze made her wonderfully weak. She felt as if she were standing naked and defenseless before him. There was something utterly alluring about being so totally under this man's spell. She wanted him to kiss her again. *Desperately!*

"Zack, please . . ." she began, not knowing exactly what she meant to say.

"Sh-h-h. Don't break the spell. I've been a long time waiting for this moment."

He leaned down toward her, and his warm breath

singed her flesh. She quivered. She sighed. She closed her eyes and waited.

He touched her cheeks with gentle fingers, letting his thumbs brush over the trembling line of her mouth. Then, slowly, his hands slid inside her hood, forcing it to fall away. His fingers twined through her thick red hair—tugging, massaging, sending fire to her brain before it surged through the rest of her.

Tenderly this time, he took her lips. Although he had been almost brutal in his hunger before, now he soothed her burning flesh, gliding the moist tip of his tongue over her full lips until she quaked and shuddered in his arms. She felt as if her body were melting where she stood. In the morning, the citizens of the village would come looking for her, but they would find nothing more than a smoldering pool of bright blue liquid here behind the fir tree where Zack had kissed her. She was sure of it!

His tongue grew bolder, urging her to imitate his actions. Persia felt as if some other being held control over her body. Surely she was not the one allowing her fingers to steal through the coarse hair at the nape of his neck. And no proper New England lady would press her breasts so firmly to a stranger's chest or feel such pleasure from the sweetly aching contact. Nor could Persia Whiddington's delicate pink tongue be boldly gliding between his lips, searching the mysterious cavern of his mouth for its delicious hidden treasures. But he urged her on with his kiss, his touch, his very masculine nearness.

When Zack released her from their second kiss, Persia felt the glowing night spinning around her. Her emotions seemed as bright and swirling as the aurora borealis still draping the night sky. She stared down at her body, amazed to find that it appeared exactly the same as before. She was sure she had changed in some way.

He smiled suddenly and cupped her chin with one big hand. "We'd better join the others. I'm not sure these woods are safe, Persia."

Not understanding what he meant, she replied, "There's

no danger. There hasn't been a panther seen in these parts in some years."

He took her face in his hands and looked into her eyes, unsmiling. "It's not panthers *you* need to fear, my love. As for me, I'm sure the man in your life would dispatch me in short order, if he found me with you here."

Without another word, Zack took her arm in a gentlemanly fashion and guided her toward the skating pond.

As much as she enjoyed skating, Persia had no desire now to join the others. She wanted more time with Zack. Hoping to slow his progress, she said, "There's no other man in my life, Zack."

He stopped dead still and looked down at her. "You mean such a beauty isn't spoken for?"

She shook her head.

"Are all men in York County blind, or has your family kept you locked in the attic your entire life?"

"Neither," she answered, suppressing a giggle. "I simply haven't received any proposals."

"Well, we'll soon fix that," he replied in a voice half-teasing, half-serious. Persia couldn't decide which, but she hoped he meant it. "There's a man in your life now, Miss Persia. You can consider yourself spoken for. I won't rush you, of course. I know that certain amenities are required. I must meet your parents, flatter your sister, and bide my time until I'm accepted by one and all. I plan to court you good and proper." He seemed to be talking to himself as much as to her.

She looked up but couldn't read his expression in the darkness. Now she was more confused than ever. Was he mocking her or proposing to her?

Seeing her staring up at him, Zack broke into a broad smile, his teeth even and startlingly white against his dark skin.

"Aye, it's a lucky man who comes home from the sea to find a good wife waiting for him, so I've been told. When I marry, my bride will have treasures from around the world. And during the lonely years away, I'll write to her faithfully—long love letters to make her weep with wanting me. I'll make her a scrimshaw pie crimper out of a whale's tooth. Mrs. Zachariah Hazzard will never want for fine silks or surprises.''

Persia believed him totally. He seemed to be a man much like her own father—thoughtful, loving, born to the sea. He would make a wonderful, exciting husband. As for the surprises he promised, she had known him scarcely an hour and he had given her the greatest surprise of her life—first his kisses, and then his promise to court her. She could hardly wait to experience all the others he promised. If marriage followed, that was fine, too.

Suddenly, she was frightened. What would her parents say? How would she explain to them that she was perfectly willing to marry a stranger who had literally accosted her on the front stoop and swept her off her feet and into the woods, where he had stolen her heart with a kiss?

Never mind, she thought. He had promised to court her. Obviously Zack was a man of the world who knew the right way to go about things. She would trust him to win her parents over just as he had won her—instantly, totally, and forevermore.

They reached the log near the bonfire where Persia had left her skates. She sat down, and Zack knelt before her in the hard-packed snow.

"Here, let me help you," he offered.

Gently, he took her foot in his hand. Even through the leather of her boot, she could feel the warmth of his touch. He caressed her ankle, toe, and instep before carefully fitting the metal footplate with its wooden runner to the sole. Still holding her, he tied the leather thongs tightly in place.

She would have blushed had she known what Zachariah Hazzard was thinking at the moment. He was trying to imagine how her bare foot would feel in his ungloved hand . . . how she would react if he suddenly stripped off her boots and stockings and ran his hot tongue between the toes and over the sensitive arch. The thought pumped new desire through his body. But the desire this time was not for his own pleasure. Suddenly, he wanted desperately to please this lovely, trusting woman.

"Aye, you're a dainty one, Persia love."

She covered a pleased smile with her hand. He was a gallant liar! *Never* had anyone called her *dainty*. But the way he said it and the look he gave her made her feel as if she were exactly that. And compared to Zachariah's height and breadth, she was a mere feminine slip of a being.

Zack borrowed skates from a young man just coming off the ice and quickly strapped them on. Then, offering his hand to Persia, he said, "Shall we have a turn at it?"

She stumbled slightly as they plowed through the deep snow to the edge of the pond. But once she put blade to ice, it was as if she had wings. Her strong ankles held her erect, and she moved with speed and grace. Zack matched her expertise, all the while holding her in the skaters' embrace, his left arm about her waist and his right clasping hers.

Persia experienced new thrills tingling through her. Never before had she skated with a male partner. Until tonight, she had spent her time at the pond racing the boys or taking her place on one of the teams for a raucous game of ice ball, to her mother's extreme horror. Persia had always felt competent on skates. Tonight she felt graceful and feminine for the first time. She leaned on Zack's strong, supporting arm and let him guide her as if they were on a ballroom floor.

"Are you up to a bit of show for the folks?" he said close to her ear over the whisper of their skates scoring the ice.

She nodded and a gleam caught in her bright eyes from the lights overhead.

Immediately, Zack whipped her away from him with a quick tug on her waist. Still holding her other hand, he skated in position while she zoomed backward, making a circle around him. Figure eights, spirals, and sweeps. They covered the pond, forcing the less accomplished skaters out of their path. Persia felt breathless, and her cheeks glowed with cold and delight. She thought she could skate all night and well past the dawn with Zack beside her.

She stared up at him, hardly able to believe her good fortune. Always, Europa was the one who attracted male attention; Persia was only tossed the crumbs reserved for younger sisters. But here was a man who seemed to feel differently, who looked at her as if she were the only woman in the world, who kissed her with unmistakable passion.

Where had he come from? And how had she managed to attract him so quickly and surely? Trying to find answers seemed a fruitless task at this point. All she knew was that this was a man she could love and belong to for the rest of her life. And wonder of wonders, he seemed every bit as attracted to her as she was to him.

They skated on, oblivious to all the others about them, caught up in a crystal world inhabited only by the two of them and their sudden, unfathomable attachment for each other.

There were few at the pond who failed to take note of the charming and graceful pair. But some watched more closely than others.

Victoria Whiddington, seated next to her husband in their sleigh, set aside her cup of steaming tea laced strongly with lemon and honey to keep the cold from her throat. A frown marred her exquisite features.

"Who is that man with Persia?" she demanded.

Captain Whiddington cleared his throat, aware of feeling a curious hostility toward the young man who skated every bit as well as the pretty girl in his arms, and who stared at her with undisguised desire etched into the hard planes of his bearded face.

"I can't make him out from here, Victoria. I'm sure he's one of the boys she used to beat when they raced. He has undoubtedly noticed tonight for the first time that she's quite an attractive creature."

"Well, I'd rather she were still racing him!"

The captain took his wife's hand and patted it understandingly. "We can't keep her a little girl forever, my dear. She's a beautiful, spirited young woman."

"*Young* is what bothers me, Captain. Our Persia is *too* young to be in a man's arms that way. And he's *no* boy!"

"They're only skating, Victoria."

"For now, at least," she replied in a weary voice. "But so it begins, and where will it lead?"

Just then Europa hurried up, interrupting their conversation. Her face was flushed with fury as much as with the cold. How dare Persia upstage her this way?

"Mother, she's making a spectacle of herself again. I'm so embarrassed I could die," Europa wailed. "Everyone is staring! Do make her come off the ice."

Asa Whiddington said exactly the wrong thing. "They're staring in admiration, Europa. Your sister and her young man cut a fine figure together."

Ignoring her father, Europa once again pleaded with her mother. "Do you know that man is a sailor fresh home from sea? He tried to impose his attentions on *me* earlier this evening, but I could see he was no fit escort, much less a skating partner. He couldn't have me, so he went after poor naive Persia instead. And now there she is—even after I warned her to keep her distance from him—languishing in the man's arms as if they were sweethearts."

"Europa!" her mother cried. "That will be quite enough! Do you want everyone to hear you? I won't survive this evening if both my daughters forget they are ladies."

Europa sank down into the chair she had been using on the ice to keep her balance, her lovely face a mask of misery. She had managed to fall eight times this evening. But all she had to show for it were bruises. Not once had anyone interesting come to her aid. And now her little sister was taking the spotlight with a devastatingly mysterious stranger. Granted, she had tossed him off earlier, but she certainly hadn't meant for him to land in Persia's waiting arms.

The night was nearing disaster proportions. It was

almost more than a body could endure! Europa's mind turned to scheming. Surely there was some way she could salvage the evening and turn it to her advantage.

"Captain and Mrs. Whiddington!" A voice cracked with age and dripping with accusation announced the arrival of Quoddy Cove's self-appointed moralizer and purveyor of gossip.

"Oh, God, preserve us!" Asa moaned under his breath before his wife could shush him.

"Birdie, dear, what are you doing out on such a cold night?" said Victoria. "Do come and have a cup of tea with us before you're chilled through."

An ancient crone all swathed in black motioned the two servants carrying her chair to set her down. She snarled at one and cracked the other across his shoulders with her cane when one leg of the chair sank into a soft patch of snow, nearly tipping her over. Then she clutched at her heart, feigning the fatal attack half the town would have welcomed.

"Ah, Victoria, decent help these days is impossible to find. Get away from me, the both of you!" she screeched at her pair of menservants.

"I believe that was entirely an accident, Miss Blackwell," Asa said in defense of the men.

"Ayah," she replied sarcastically. "And I suppose it was an accident, too, the last time they tipped my chair and I nearly tumbled down the stairwell to my death!" She stabbed the air with a bony finger, squinting hard at Asa. "Nay! They're out to do me in, I tell you. If only my dear brother were here to protect me. But, alas, he feels it his due to serve God even at the expense of being here to take care of this poor, ailing wretch who gave up her whole life to raise him. Mind you, I'm not faulting Cyrus. A fine man!" Her wrinkled features contorted into a self-satisfied smile, threatening to crack her face like old plaster. "A missionary, you know."

Asa offered her a weary nod. Who didn't know? Birdie Blackwell never started or ended one of her tiresome bouts of gossip without reference to her saintly brother. Somehow Asa found this transformation of the man hard to explain and harder to visualize. The Reverend Cyrus Blackwell remained in his memory as a troublesome and sometimes vicious youngster who had stolen merchandise from his father's general store on Main Street and tortured the town's population of cats, dogs, and birds. There was even some talk that as a young man he had torched the home of a woman who refused him. The girl and her aging mother had died in the flames. The fire was never explained. Soon afterward, Cyrus Blackwell left the area to enter the seminary. Since that time, he had never returned to Quoddy Cove. But even if the man were innocent of that crime, with a sister like Birdie, Asa could understand why he stayed away.

"Now, mind you, I'm not one to cast dispersions," Birdie went on, "but you know how the people hereabouts will talk. If Miss Persia were mine to bring up, I'd haul her off the pond this minute, take her home for a good strapping, and lock her in her room with only her Bible for company until she's old enough to know how to act properly in public."

Victoria, who had been thinking that just such a course of action might be wise, took exception to someone else voicing such an opinion.

"Birdie dear, they're only skating, and in broad view of everyone in town. I can't see that it's so scandalous."

Miss Blackwell made a disapproving, clicking sound with her whale-ivory teeth. "Of course *you're* her mother, Victoria, but no daughter of mine would make such a display of herself with a man. Mark my words, the girl wants discipline—a strong hand, well placed. Or the next thing you know, she'll be sneaking out to meet men and doing you know what behind your backs."

Europa snickered softly. Her father gave her a scathing look. His temper was nearing its limits.

"Please explain exactly *what* you assume our Persia will be doing in the event she decides to start *sneaking out,* as you put it, Miss Blackwell. I'd like to hear it in so many words!"

"Captain!" Victoria gasped softly, placing a restraining hand on her husband's arm. Miss Birdie Blackwell, the town gossip, was not one to be goaded without retaliating in the meanest fashion.

"*That* sort of thing doesn't need explaining to any man, Asa Whiddington! How dare you try to embarrass a poor spinster lady who's dedicated her whole life only to God and her dear, devout brother?" She shook a warning finger at the captain once more. "You just mind that red-haired wanton you've raised up. I'm warning you, she's one of the devil's own!"

Before Asa Whiddington could calm himself enough to frame a suitable reply, Birdie Blackwell summoned her servants with an angry howl and was off to sow her seeds of discontent elsewhere.

"The bloody old bitch!" Asa mumbled, clenching his fingers, which he very much wished were around the woman's wrinkled throat.

"Asa, please," Victoria whispered. "Europa will hear you."

But their elder daughter was no longer beside them.

Zack whirled Persia about and soon had her in his arms, facing him as if she were a dancing partner. Immediately, she saw his intent. He moved them into the figures of an ice waltz that set her skirts swaying and her head reeling. So precise were his movements that she could almost imagine the accompanying music as their blades sliced neat patterns in the coldness beneath their skates.

"Watch yourself," he warned, steering her away from an area marked with a hand-painted sign that read THIN ICE.

"I've heard of ladies wearing through their dancing slippers in an evening, Zack, but I may be the first to wear out a pair of skates."

"Do you want to stop?"

Persia threw back her head so suddenly that her hood fell away, releasing her shining, fire-colored hair to whip in the cold wind. "Never!" she cried. "I want to go on and on. I've never felt so wonderful!"

His hand tightened on her waist and he drew her

closer, whispering into her free-blowing hair, "You certainly do, Persia, more wonderful than you can imagine."

At that moment, a scream pierced the night air. Zack whirled them to an ice-shaving stop, his brown eyes giving up their lock on his partner to scan the pond. Shouts went up from the shore, and in a moment he saw what had happened. Leaving Persia where she stood, he put wings to his skates, flying over the ice toward the warning sign they had passed moments before.

"Help! Please, save me!" came the strangled cry.

A woman had fallen through. Zack could see her arms waving. She went under—once, twice, a third time. People were rushing out onto the ice. He had to reach her and try to pull her out of the frigid water before the crowd converged around the broken place in the ice. Otherwise, their massed weight might cause a larger break and draw dozens of would-be rescuers down into the icy depths. A real disaster was in the making, and only Zachariah could avert it.

"Try to grab hold of the ice!" he yelled. "I'm coming!"

"I can't. Help me, oh, please, I . . ."

The weak voice trailed off. Zack saw a gloved hand clutching the edge. Slowly, it slipped away, leaving long scratch marks in the death-white ice. He plunged forward, diving for the edge.

Persia waited only a stunned moment after Zack left her. She recognized the first cry for help and knew who had fallen through the ice. A coldness gripped her heart like none a Maine winter could produce. Europa's life was in the hands of the man she had called "riffraff" —the man she herself *loved,* Persia realized suddenly. And he might well lose his own life attempting to save her sister.

Skating quickly after Zack, Persia arrived at the broken ice only an instant after he reached the jagged edge of the hole. She saw her drowning, half-frozen sister go under once more and then watched, stricken, as Zack plunged into the black water.

Persia's heart was pounding. She could barely hear

anything for the rush of blood in her ears. The shouts of the others on the pond came only as a dull roar from far away. She must remain calm, do whatever she could to help. That was difficult, however, with the dark patch of water yawning empty before her. Both Europa and Zack were under the surface now. If they stayed down much longer, neither of them would survive. But she couldn't think about that.

Acting with a calm reason she was far from feeling, Persia lay down on her stomach on the ice, reaching as far out over the opening as she could. She scanned the black surface with keen eyes, alert to any movement. The reflection of the northern lights played over the water, mocking her with its beauty. Now other skaters moved closer in, ringing the broken ice to light the area with their flickering lanterns. Persia was uncomfortably aware of the cold dampness seeping through her woolen gown, but she held her prone position, ready to lend a saving hand to Zack and to her sister the moment they surfaced . . . *if* they surfaced.

Suddenly, the water stirred. At first, Persia thought her hopes were causing her eyes to play tricks on her. Then Zack's head burst above the water. He spewed icy spray and shook the clinging ice crystals from his hair. A moment later, he hoisted Europa up. Her face was blue and still.

"Give us a hand here," he called through chattering teeth.

The hand he requested was there already. He caught it, not even realizing it belonged to Persia. Together they eased Europa up over the edge of the ice. Others were there to pick the unconscious woman up and to help Zack out of the water. Persia whisked off her cape and covered his shoulders. Already Europa was wrapped in a heavy carriage robe from the Whiddington sleigh.

In moments, Persia, Zack, and Europa were in the back of the sleigh, speeding up the trail toward the house on Gay Street. Persia chafed her sister's icy wrists while Zack held the blanket securely around Europa's trembling shoulders with a strong arm.

"Faster, Fletcher, faster!" Asa Whiddington urged.

"You saved me. How can I ever repay you?" Europa's voice, although shaky, held an undercurrent unmistakably dripping with feminine allure.

"I just thank God you're alive, Miss Europa," Zack replied.

The horses roared to a halt outside the house. Scooping Europa up in his arms Zack made for the front door, leaving Persia to see herself out of the sleigh and into the house. She refused to acknowledge the little stab of jealousy his actions caused. After all, her sister was in serious condition. Europa must be everyone's first concern.

But she couldn't ignore the pain a half hour later when she entered the sitting room, bringing a tray of hot broth and tea. Europa, warmed to glowing health and swathed in a lush velvet robe of emerald green, looked fetchingly petite and vulnerable reclining on the chaise lounge. Because of an error in Mrs. Whiddington's planning, the usual decorum of the carefully run household had broken down and Europa and Zack had been left alone momentarily. Persia walked in just in time to catch her sister taking advantage of the private interlude by bestowing a kiss of gratitude squarely on Zack's mouth.

"Oh, I beg your pardon," Persia said, flustered and furious, sure that she was blushing all over.

Zack quickly pulled away but avoided meeting her eyes.

"Your sister's much better," he said.

"So I see." Persia knew her voice sounded cold, but she couldn't help herself.

"Persia dear," Europa cooed, "how sweet of you to bring us tea. Poor Zack has had quite a night of it—first being monopolized by you all evening and then having to risk his life to save me. Why, the dear man is an exhausted saint!"

Persia's lips tightened into a grim line. "Saint" was a far cry from what Europa had called Zack earlier.

"It was nothing, Europa. I only did what any other man would have done under the circumstances. I just happened to be the closest one to you when the accident occurred.''

Persia watched their eyes meet and felt her blood rising. She hated herself for suspecting that Europa's plunge was no accident. But as her sister preened and simpered for the man, Persia realized that her suspicions were a devastating reality. Europa would go to any lengths to get what she wanted. And at the moment, it looked as if she wanted Zachariah Hazzard.

What did Europa have in mind? She had a dozen men dangling on her silken strings. Why was she flirting so with Persia's beau, whom she had earlier labeled "unsuitable"?

Persia watched as Europa reached out a pale hand and placed it on Zack's arm, at the same time lowering her long dark lashes to offer him a veiled and sensual look. "You know what my father says the Chinese believe?"

"What?" The word came out of Zack's mouth in a husky whisper. His gaze was locked on Europa's mesmerizing eyes.

"They say that when one person saves another's life, the two are bound together for eternity."

Persia had had all she could take. Slamming the tea tray down on the table, she rushed from the room. She tore for the attic stairs and the little ladder up to the widow's walk, where she always escaped when she was upset or wanted to be alone.

The northern lights had faded and the stars in the velvet night sky blurred as she gazed up through her tears. She gripped the railing, not feeling the numbness creeping into her ungloved hands.

"Why, Europa, why?" she cried. "You can have any man. *Why Zack?*"

But she knew why. It had been so between them all their lives. Whatever Persia got, her sister must have the same whether she honestly desired it or not. Suddenly Persia remembered the black-and-white puppy, and tears flooded her eyes.

She had found the half-starved mutt wandering down Main Street. Some rough boys were throwing stones at the poor creature. Europa had stood on the sidelines, urging them on in their meanness. Persia's heart had nearly broken at the sad, helpless look in the little dog's eyes. Throwing caution and fear for her own safety to the wind, she had rushed out into the street and shielded the mongrel pup with her own body. For her efforts, she had received a nasty cut on her forehead from a stone and a bruise on her arm from a stick Europa herself had hurled. But she had claimed the dog for her own and received his affectionate licks of gratitude.

When she took him home, her mother had grudgingly agreed to let him stay. Persia had immediately named him Salty, fed him a bowl of milk and meat scraps, and made him a bed behind the kitchen stove.

When Europa arrived home, her eyes held that hard glitter Persia had learned to read so well.

"That's *my* dog!" Europa had told their mother. "I found him and Persia stole him from me."

Victoria Whiddington had looked surprised. "But my dear, you don't care at all for animals. Why would you collect such a poor stray?"

"Just because," Europa had answered in that high-and-mighty tone of hers.

"Well, he'll be our *family* pet," Victoria had answered, playing the role of peacemaker.

"Very well, I'll share," Europa had answered smugly. "Persia, you may feed Fido, bathe him, and take care of him. But just remember, he's really *my* dog!"

"His name's not Fido! It's Salty!" Persia had raged.

"Girls, girls! If this animal is going to cause trouble, we'll just get rid of him this minute."

For the time being, Europa had held her peace and the dog stayed. Persia had taken great pains to care for her Salty; she'd loved him dearly. She'd taken him for walks, bathed him in the wooden tub, and smuggled him choice cuts of meat from the dining room table. Dog and child were inseparable.

Then one morning when Persia had hurried down to the kitchen, she'd found Salty's box empty. Frantically, she'd dashed about the house and then the yard, calling him by both his names, but there'd been no sign of him. She'd ran up to Europa's room to enlist her aid in the search and found her sister still abed.

"Get up quickly! Salty's gone!"

Europa had stretched, yawned, and bestowed a condescending smile on her. "If you are referring to Fido, I know. And there's no need searching for him. I gave him away."

"Gave him away?" Persia had stood at the foot of her sister's sleigh bed, stricken, feeling her heart crumble. "How could you?"

Europa had answered her with a shrug. "He wasn't a very good dog. I never liked him that much. So I traded him to a peddler passing through town yesterday for a new pink hair ribbon. He's long gone by now. If you don't mind, I'd like to get some more sleep, Persia. Please close the door on your way out."

Persia could still feel that emptiness in her heart—the place where love had been before it was snatched away. But it wasn't a black-and-white-spotted pup in question this time. It was a man—the man Persia wanted.

Drying her tears with a furious swipe of her cold hand, Persia whirled toward the ladder. There would be no more sighing and crying in dark corners. Her sister had taken from her for the last time.

"Europa wants battle? Then battle it will be!"

By the time she reached the hallway, Persia was ready. She squared her shoulders, took a deep breath, and headed for the parlor.

"Not this time, sister dear!"

CHAPTER FIVE

PERSIA ran full tilt into Fletcher in the hallway, almost upsetting the tea tray in his hands and definitely ruffling his usually stilted and correct bearing.

Fletcher, so named because he claimed his father was the leader of the *Bounty* mutineers, did carry himself with a first mate's dignity. But as to whether the poor, abandoned child Persia's father had rescued from a sinking boat off Pitcairn Island back in 1810 was Fletcher Christian's son or came from the seed of any of the other eight mutineers could never be proved. The brown-skinned boy, once he was taken on board Captain Whiddington's ship, attached himself to the man like a leech. He begged not to be put ashore at Pitcairn or any of the other Oeno islands along the South Pacific shipping route between Panama and New Zealand. Thus, he became Asa Whiddington's cabin boy and later his faithful retainer. His age was somewhere in the neighborhood of thirty, although no one, including Fletcher himself, could be certain.

"Please to pardon me, Miss Persia." The well-trained

servant, collecting himself immediately, took full blame for the collision even though they both knew she was at fault.

"Fletcher, didn't Mother tell you to remain in the parlor with my sister and Mr. Hazzard?"

"I was exactly there, Miss Persia, just as the mistress instructed, until Miss Europa directed me down to the kitchen to bring up tea and cakes for herself and the gentleman."

Persia bit the inside of her lower lip and her eyes narrowed in annoyance. So, Europa had connived to get Zack alone. She might have guessed!

"I've just taken them a tray, Fletcher. You may carry all that back to the kitchen."

"But Miss Persia, do you not think someone had better go in there? It is hardly proper for the young mistress and that strange man—brave though he is—to be left all alone."

"It most certainly isn't, Fletcher. You should have considered that before you went to the kitchen. But I'll go in now and see that they're properly chaperoned. You can count on it!"

She whirled away and hurried through the door to the sitting room. But she didn't interrupt anything this time, even though it was evident from the frown marring her sister's lovely face that Europa wished she had.

"Do come over here closer, Zack," Persia heard Europa say. "Why, you're miles away!"

Zack's big frame was perched in an ungainly manner on the very edge of a dainty, brocade-covered ladies' chair, his cake plate balanced precariously on one knee while he tried to manage the fragile china cup and saucer and a silver spoon with hands more used to tin plates and grog mugs.

He looked up when Persia came in. She could almost swear she detected a hint of relief flicker in his brown eyes when he saw her.

"Persia darling, you're back." Europa spoke the words with less than delight in her tone.

"Back to stay!" Persia answered, bestowing a triumphant smile on her sister.

"That won't be necessary, dear." Europa's "dear" dripped contempt from *d* to *r*. "I'm sure you must be exhausted after exerting yourself so athletically on the ice this evening. Why don't you just run along to bed now? I'm completely recovered and perfectly capable of entertaining our guest."

"Oh, I'm sure you are, Europa. But while I was out of the room for a few minutes I did some thinking."

"Thinking?" The tone suggested that Persia hadn't wits enough for such strenuous mental activity. "Whatever about, little sister?"

"About *dogs* . . . one in particular, a black-and-white puppy."

Zack was sipping his tea slowly, his head turning from one sister to the other, trying to follow their conversation. But it was obvious that he was not meant to understand their meaning.

"A *puppy*?"

"Yes," Persia replied. "My Salty. Surely you remember him. I've just been thinking how this situation is very similar to that one. However, I don't intend for the outcome to be the same this time. I won't allow it!"

Europa's eyes narrowed and she shot a quick glance at Zack before she looked back to Persia and smiled. "My, my! Is that a threat, sister?"

Persia smiled back. "No. A *promise*!"

Just then, Asa Whiddington came into the room. "Well, it's been a trying night, but you all look hail and hearty now. Maybe I should take a spot of that tea. Your mother is finally asleep, worn out by the terror of the evening. But I still feel rather shaky—gray about the gills, so to speak." He nodded his thanks as he accepted the cup Persia offered him. "Europa, you gave us all quite a scare tonight."

"I'll agree with you there, sir," Zack added. "Me most of all."

"Yet you went in to save her. Commendable, young

man, highly commendable. I don't know how we can ever thank you."

"Father, we could invite Mr. Hazzard to Sunday dinner tomorrow," Persia suggested.

The captain frowned and glanced toward Europa, who suddenly had a stricken look on her lovely face. He guessed the cause. She had already invited a young attorney, Seton Holloway, to dine with the family. Even the charming Europa could hardly juggle two men at one meal. He smiled, thinking it might add a touch of humor to a long, dull Sunday afternoon.

Yes, it would be highly entertaining to see two young men vying with each other for his daughter's favors. He could tell already that Seaman Hazzard was smitten. And, too, perhaps the presence of another suitor at table would prompt the shy barrister to make his long-awaited proposal. After all, Europa wasn't getting any younger. At eighteen, it was high time she found a husband. And there was Persia to think of, too. Although she was still too young to be seriously considering such a matter, she couldn't even think of marriage until her older sister was wed.

"What do you say, Mr. Hazzard?" Asa asked. "It's the least we can do after what you've done for us. I'm sure you're ready for a home-cooked meal after almost four years of subsisting on salt horse, weevil biscuits, and brackish water to wash it down."

Zack broke into a broad smile that brought his heavy beard almost up to his eyes. "I'd be more than happy to break bread with you, Captain Whiddington. It has been some time since I've sat down to a real family dinner."

"Fine! Then, we'll look for you around one. By the way, where are you staying?"

Zack shrugged slightly. "I stowed my gear at Jefferd's Tavern when I came ashore, sir. I suppose it's as good a place as any."

Persia's heart took a sudden leap. For a moment she thought her father meant to invite Zack to take their guest room. She envisioned staying up all night before

the fire in the parlor, listening to the sailor's tales of
adventure on the high seas.

But instead, the captain said, "Jefferd's is first rate.
The rooms are clean and the prices reasonable. And it's
only a short walk up Main Street to Tavern Hill. Of
course, I could have Fletcher drive you up there."

"Thank you just the same, Captain Whiddington. But
I'd as soon walk. I'm still trying to get the hang of
having my feet on steady ground again."

Zack realized that Asa Whiddington was not simply
making a polite suggestion, he was also giving a gentle
hint that it was time Zack was leaving.

"Well, Miss Europa, Miss Persia, Captain, I'd better
be going now. Thank you for the tea and the invitation
for tomorrow."

"It's we who thank you, Mr. Hazzard," replied the
girls' father.

"I'll see you out, Zack." Even as Persia made the
offer, she was aware of Europa's gaze shooting daggers
her way.

The entrance downstairs lay in guttering half darkness. The gilt-draped bronze nymph who adorned the
newel-post stared up at a well-trimmed wick inside the
cranberry glass globe she held high in her right hand.
Fletcher had been about his work of turning down lamps
all about the house. Usually at this hour everyone in the
Whiddington family was in bed already, although a few
lamps always burned low since the captain had a habit
of slipping down for a sip and a read once his wife was
asleep.

The soft rose glow in the hallway made the familiar
seem strange to Persia. The Adam-green wallpaper looked
black, while the white lilies in the pattern turned a
shocking pink and seemed to stand away from the wall.
The heart-pine floors shone like marble, and the Indian
rug before the door took on exotic hues she could not
name. Even the air in that part of the house seemed
thick and warm and rosy.

She looked up at Zack. He, too, had been transformed

merely by walking downstairs. The golden tangle of his hair and beard glowed bronze in this light. And his eyes smoldered darker and were more mysterious than ever. He was still wearing the clothes he had borrowed from her father after taking off his wet things. Although the captain was a good-sized man, he was not nearly so broad or tall as Zachariah. Zack's muscles bulged at the seams, and his hard thighs strained every fiber of the trousers to their limits. Persia felt herself blush as her eyes strayed downward at the obvious artifacts of his manhood, outlined through the coarse wool.

He reached out and touched her cheek, letting one strong finger glide along her high cheekbone, leaving a little shudder of sensation in its wake. He was smiling at her, a touch of irony deep in his eyes.

"Well, Persia, it's been quite a night."

"Yes, a lovely night," she said softly.

He laughed. "I rather gathered that you'd just as soon I'd let your sister sink to the bottom to await the spring thaw."

"Oh, no!" Persia cried, horrified that Zack had read the animosity between them and misinterpreted her words. "I meant that meeting you . . . skating with you . . . was lovely. Certainly not what happened to Europa. I'd never wish *that* on her."

"You don't have to explain to me," he said in his husky voice that now carried a touch of melancholy. "I have sisters, too. I remember how, from time to time, I wanted to sell them to gypsies, even though I loved them well."

Persia laughed softly. "I'm not sure even gypsies would take Europa."

"I wouldn't be so certain. She's a lovely woman."

Persia felt the hair at the nape of her neck bristle with anger. Granted, Zack's words were true. But she certainly didn't relish hearing them from the same lips that had tantalized her with their kisses this very night. And, too, if he was stating that Europa was lovely, wasn't that only pointing up that he did not consider Persia the same?

"Don't frown," he ordered, rubbing a rough thumb over her lips. "Your smile is bewitching. I want you always to bewitch me, Persia Whiddington. Just as you have done tonight."

His words caused such a sudden rush of joy and relief that her heart raced and her head felt light. Maybe he hadn't been leading her down a primrose path. Perhaps he did feel something for her, and nothing for Europa.

His next action seemed to prove that. Glancing first up the stairs to make sure no one was watching, Zack grasped Persia to his chest and took her lips. Willing lips, aching to be kissed.

She felt the silkiness of his tongue caressing her and responded in appropriate fashion, aware of a burning in her blood that threatened to consume her. His hands slipped down from her shoulders to glide along her arms. He spanned her waist and squeezed gently, but she felt as if he were pressing the breath from her. When his fingers moved up her ribs to her breasts, stroking her boldly, she gasped.

Zack released his hold on her only a moment. In that instant, as their eyes met—touching souls, linking hearts, promising eternities—Persia knew.

"I love you, Zack," she whispered. Her heart exalted in hearing the truth spoken aloud.

He made no answer but captured her lips once more in a fever of passion and need. She answered him in kind, making no move to escape from his strong grasp.

"Ahem!"

The sound from above was startlingly loud. They wrenched apart, and Persia felt her face burning along with the rest of her body.

An uncomfortable silence followed. Zack shuffled his feet. Persia smoothed her damp palms down over the front of her gown. He nodded toward the stairs.

"Well, good night, Miss Persia, Captain." Zack offered a nervous salute to the man standing at the top of the stairs, arms crossed over his chest and side whiskers twitching, but not in amusement. "I suppose I'll see you tomorrow?'' Caught, he was making sure his invitation still held.

"Yes, tomorrow at one, Mr. Hazzard.''

Persia watched Zack disappear through the door. The last thing she wanted to have to do was meet her father face to face. Taking her time in turning, she steeled herself for the well-deserved lecture to come. But when she looked up, the captain was gone. He could no more deal with chastising her over a kiss than she could deal with his disapproval.

Jefferd's Tavern was only a brisk walk away from the Whiddington house. Zack welcomed the cold bite of the air and the silent solitude of midnight. He needed to clear his head and his senses. He needed to think. What the devil had he gotten himself into?

"Never let a sailor loose ashore,'' he muttered to himself. "He's only safe with the sky overhead and the sea beneath his feet. Chee-*rist,* but I'm in the soup!''

He trudged on, thinking of Persia—how sweet and willing and innocent her kisses were. But that was not to say they weren't tempting. And it could get mighty dangerous for a man when he felt as tempted as Zack did at the moment. Maybe Jehu was right. Maybe a man needed to stay ashore with one woman all the time. At least then, when you itched you could scratch! And Zachariah was itching right now as he had never itched before.

He wondered what tomorrow would bring. It was bound to be interesting with both sisters there.

That Europa was something. Even as he'd been hauling her out of the icy water—both of them freezing half to death—he'd felt her turn her body in his arms so that her breasts snuggled right up to his chest, begging to be fondled. But damn, his hands had been too numb with the cold to feel a thing. Still, he'd hardly needed the fire in the Whiddington parlor to warm him up! Her kiss might have been brief, but it promised a world of passion. He'd met her kind before—"Venus flowers,'' he called them. They'd attract a man with their sweetness, only to devour him when he got too close. Yes, he had Miss Europa pegged all right. Still, there wasn't a man alive who could resist such a woman's sensuous invitation.

But Persia, now there was another matter. The girl—*woman*, he corrected in his mind, for she was all of that—the woman had no guile about her. She was honest and open with her feelings, almost *too* open. Jesus, hadn't her mother taught her anything about men? Didn't she know from observing Europa that a woman was supposed to cozy up to a fellow, keep him dangling, play the game by the rules? He'd never met a woman who just came right out with it: "I love you, Zack!" No pretty this and that . . . no stalling, no teasing, no flattering, no flaunting. Just the words, plain and simple and honest and *terrifying!*

Christ, it was enough to scare a man out of his wits!

He shook his head and jammed his hands farther down into his pockets. No, sir, he'd never met one like her!

Suddenly, he came to a skidding stop on the icy street, a memory bright in his thoughts. He had met another, yes indeed. Mahianna. Except that her coloring was different and she wore more clothes, Persia could be his native lover all over again.

He groaned aloud at the thought. How the hell was he supposed to act toward her now? A man couldn't compare a bare-breasted native woman to a proper New England maiden and come up with anything but trouble. Maybe his best bet was just not to show up at the Whiddington house for dinner. He'd clear out first thing tomorrow . . . take the cars down to Boston and never look back.

He hurried on toward the tavern, feeling the cold gnawing at his bones. Yes, that was his best bet—*stay clear altogether!*

The hot, smoky atmosphere of Jefferd's taproom engulfed him as soon as he opened the door of the tavern. The essence of the place, thick with malt and body sweat, made him feel at home. The subject of women and how to handle them might be beyond his grasp, but he understood his own kind. There was something so right and comfortable about men gathering in a hospitable tavern to bend elbows together, swap brags, and tell lies.

"Hallo there, Hazzard!" hailed a familiar voice from across the layers of blue smoke hanging in the air. "Hey, barkeep, a mug for the hero of the hour."

"Sorrentino, is that you, man?" Hazzard called back, knowing full well it was indeed his shipmate.

"*Sí*, as big as life and twice as ugly." The swarthy, wine vat–chested Italian, who had signed on in Naples, clamped a bear-paw hand on Zack's shoulder and made an expansive gesture toward the other men at the bar with his free arm. "You see, I told you he was my *amico*! Would a Napolitano lie?"

"I thought you were off to Boston with the others."

"I decided to stay and see what this skating on ice was like. *Mama mía!*" Enrico Sorrentino rubbed his backside and grimaced. "I am more sore than when my *bella* Angelina kicked me out of the house! That ice, she is hard!"

All the men at the bar laughed at the little Italian's mournful tale.

"But you, *amico*, you fly like a ship under full sail over the ice. I never saw nothing like it. And when you dived in to save the beautiful *signorina* . . . ah-h-h!" He turned a knowing conspirator's smile on Zack. "It is love at first sight, no?"

Zack threw back his head and laughed. "Always the romantic, aren't you, Enrico?"

The man shrugged and grinned. "It is my blood. But who wouldn't fall in love with such a dark-haired beauty? Ah, she reminds me of my own dear Angelina. The sweetest woman God ever created."

"I thought you said she kicked you out."

"*Sí, sí!* But I deserved it. She caught me with her delicious cousin Luisa. I was *stupido*! A man may need more than one woman, but he does not take his wife's cousin to his own bed, if he is wise. I should have found some other woman and set her up in a little place on the far side of Vesuvio. That would have been the smart thing." He grinned, shrugged, and turned his hands palms up. "But it was a sultry August afternoon, the kind when a man sweats and pants for love. My wife was visiting her mama, and Luisa was tending our *bambino*. She was so lovely, so . . ." Unable to think of the word in English, Enrico made open-handed gestures before his chest, indicating the fullness of Luisa's breasts. "So *available!*"

"And you got caught."

"Si" the Italian said miserably.

"Ah, my friend, you should never tamper with two women in the same family at the same time." Zack's words stopped abruptly when he realized he might be warning himself as well as Enrico.

A glint kindled in the Italian's obsidian eyes. "Was the beautiful one with hair like fire not the sister of the one in the water, my friend?"

"Yes, but—"

"Oh, ho-ho!" A thick finger wagged under Zack's nose. "Heed your own words of wisdom, Zack boy. And listen, too, to one who knows: Choose one of the two, or you will end up with neither."

"What does that little *Eye*-talian know?" broke in a bearded logger, well in his cups, who was farther down the bar. Abe Cushing was his name. "A big strapping fellow like you could handle half a dozen women at once if he set his damn mind to it! What say you, mates?"

The others all voiced their agreement.

"See, I told you," Abe said. "Give him a bottle on me. We got plans to lay, friend."

"Do not listen to him, Zack. He is drunk. Would your old friend Enrico tell you other than the truth? If you value your life, you will pick one or the other. But *two sisters*? *Mama mía,* is big trouble!"

Zack, of course, agreed with his shipmate. But with each free drink, his self-esteem grew. In little over an hour, Zachariah Hazzard was larger than life and every woman's dream. Why couldn't he have both the pure and innocent Persia and her provocative sister Europa?

They were so different. They would make his life wonderful. When he wanted reality and love, he would choose Persia. When the need of fantasy and raw lust fired him, he would seek out Europa.

As the alcohol bubbled through his blood to his brain, he began to visualize himself as a sultan, calling one woman or another from his harem at his whim. He saw himself stretched out naked on scarlet satin cushions with Europa, wearing only a transparent mauve drape, purring in his arms. Persia stood by, her own slim, delectable form visible through the folds of her thin gown, waving a peacock feather fan to cool the lovers, begging intermittently to be allowed to join in the pleasuring of the master.

"In a minute, Persia. I'll take you next," he mumbled.

Someone was shaking him. "Zack, *amico*! Snap out of it! You're raving like a crazy man. Two women . . . bah! Better one good one for the rest of your life. Here, drink this."

Enrico held a scalding mug of coffee to Zack's lips. It burned like hell going down, but it chased away the craziness in his head.

"You're right, my friend," Hazzard agreed. "One woman . . . only one."

"But which one?" demanded Abe, the bearded drunk. "And could you even *get* one of the Whiddington sisters, if you wanted to? My money says that the old captain would have that trained savage of his, Fletcher by name, skin the hide off you and shrink your head for his collection before he'd let you even call on one of his beauties, much less marry either of them."

"That just shows what you know, mate!" Zack fired back at his tormentor. "It so happens I'm invited to call tomorrow . . . for dinner."

The others in the bar exchanged looks, low whistles, and lewd comments.

"That don't mean a thing," Abe said. "You're talking one call. I'm talking forever after!"

"I could marry either one I wanted to."

Abe slammed a leather pouch down on the bar. "Then

put your money where your mouth is, Zachariah Hazzard!''

Zack reached down for his own purse, which contained every cent of his wages for the past four years at sea. Enrico caught his hand. "Zack, no! Don't be crazy!"

"Leave me be, Sorrentino," he growled. "By damn, I'll match his bet, and I'll win it all!"

He slapped the full pouch down on the bar.

A hush fell over the barroom. Men whispered among themselves, but no one spoke aloud. Never had any of them seen so much wagered over such unusual stakes.

"Which sister you planning to marry?" asked the grining logger.

Zack rose grandly, if a bit unsteadily. "I'll let you know when I decide."

Abe Cushing scooped up the two pouches and shoved them across the bar to the tavernkeeper. "You hold the bets. I'll be back to collect within the week."

"Like hell you will!" Zack roared. The next instant, he sank to the floor.

"Zack, *amico*, what have you done?"

They were the last words he heard until he awoke the next morning, his head throbbing, the same words gnawing at his frazzled brain.

CHAPTER SIX

*A*s usual, the Whiddington family set out early to walk the short distance up Main Street to the white, steepled church. This ritual had been observed every Sunday of Persia's life. While the laws forcing New Englanders to attend regular services had been abolished, it would have been frowned upon for any church member to forgo the opportunity to worship each and every Sunday.

They always walked, whether the air was fine and mild or blustering with hurricane winds. Victoria, on her husband's arm, led the way, with Europa and Persia following along behind, their faces hidden demurely by ruffled bonnets and their gloved hands folded at their waists. Nothing was really different on this November morning. The same friends greeted them. The same bells called the citizens of Quoddy Cove to worship from the same white steeple. The same tap-tap of her father's scrimshandered, whale-ivory walking stick rapped out their progress along the way.

But something seemed different this morning. Persia was different. She looked on the snowbound world with brighter eyes and a lighter heart than ever before. There seemed to be a new awareness about her. She could almost feel her body growing and changing from the flesh her soul had worn as a girl into the more shapely human garb of a woman. And so had her mind turned, too, from childish thoughts to mature needs and desires. Of course, her main desires centered around Zachariah Hazzard.

It seemed to Persia that she was wedded to him already in spirit. Their parting kiss the night before and her admission that she loved him sealed the vows in her mind. Now her thoughts were focused on how she might accomplish a like oneness of the flesh.

"Do hurry along, girls," urged their mother. "I can't abide the thought of heads turning as we enter church. After being the center of all attention last night, I want to be early this morning. We must be in our pew before everyone else is seated."

"Poor Mother," Europa whispered. "Always so concerned about what other people will think and say."

"And you couldn't care in the least, I suppose?" Persia asked.

"Certainly not! I do as my conscience dictates. And from your performance last night, I'd say you do the same, sister dear."

"I certainly do not! I'd never do anything to upset Mother and Father, if I could help it. I owe them my respect. And so do you!"

"But we don't owe them our lives. Not if it means sacrificing our happiness to satisfy them. You're so young and naive, Persia. But I suppose you'll grow up *someday*."

"I can't imagine that they would ever want us to make such sacrifices for them."

Europa made no reply but cocked one sooty eyebrow at her younger sister, as if unwilling to explain further to such a dull child.

Persia was still smarting under Europa's taunts as they entered the church and moved down the aisle to their pew, second from the front.

Although the hour was early, quite a few members of the congregation were seated already. Apparently, their mother was right. There were those anxious to ogle the Whiddington clan after last night's activities at the pond. Among them was Miss Birdie Blackwell, dressed as always in vulture black, her beady eyes trained on them and her wrinkled neck craning to overhear any word they might say. Persia felt the woman's eyes on the back of her head and turned slightly, catching her staring. When Persia smiled, Miss Blackwell, with an upward tilt of her sharp nose, quickly looked away.

Undaunted by the old gossip's curiosity, Persia settled herself into her usual prayerful position. The Reverend Osgood had often commented to Captain and Mrs. Whiddington on the piety of their younger daughter. "She's as still as a nun in church, her eyes fixed on the cross, her hands folded in prayer. And she pays the closest attention to every word of my sermons. If only all young people were so meek and attentive. She must be a blessing to you."

Persia felt guilty whenever her parents mentioned the minister's remarks about her. She never admitted to anyone that she grasped very little of what the good reverend said as he droned on and on every Sunday. Her attention instead was focused on the beautifully crafted pulpit, fashioned by ships' joiners. She loved the romantic story behind its creation. The remarkable pulpit was made of one huge mahogany log that had been found floating in the Gulf of Mexico by down-east seamen. Since the log was too enormous to be hauled aboard their ship, the men had tied it securely and towed it all the way back to Maine. She loved sitting in church and staring at the pulpit, all the while making up tales about pirates and handsome sea captains and faraway lands. She often dreamed of the stories the rich red-brown wood might tell, if only . . .

Suddenly, Reverend Osgood's voice boomed out over his congregation, jolting Persia in her seat.

"Let us pray," commanded the white-bearded cleric.

Persia bowed her head and closed her eyes. But she

heard not a word of the prayer, nor did any visions of
heaven enlighten her soul. With her eyes tightly shut,
she watched great ships sail through her mind. And on
the deck of every one stood Zack Hazzard, his chest
bare, his beard and hair rampant in the wind, a smile on
his face . . . and smoldering desire in his brown eyes
only for her.

Zack sat on the side of his bed, his aching head
clutched in his hands. Each peal of the distant church
bell resounded painfully, as if the clapper were inside his
brain.

"Oh, God," he groaned, but he wasn't praying. Or
perhaps he was . . . for death to free him from the pain.
Suddenly, he remembered the events of the night before
and evoked the name of his Maker louder still. *"Oh,
God!"*

He seemed to remember making love to two women
. . . he remembered a barroom celebration . . . an outrageous wager. He moaned. Maybe it was all a dream, an
hallucination drunk from a mug in the tavern.

Rising with some difficulty, he stumbled about the
room. He dumped his sea bag, digging with trembling
fingers through shirts, trousers, and linen, searching for
his money pouch.

"Not there," he muttered.

He kicked aside the strewn clothes and searched the
room—pulling out empty drawers, slamming the closet
door, searching under the mattress—frantic now. All his
wages from four long years at sea, every cent he had in
the world. Surely he hadn't . . .

"But I must have," he said at last, sinking back down
to the bed.

He had let a stranger con him into an impossible
wager. Now he must convince one of the Whiddington
sisters to marry him or lose the fortune he had worked
so hard to earn.

"Enrico, my friend, why didn't you stop me?" he
moaned. Then he remembered that his shipmate had
tried. But grog was a formidable opponent against reason.

Suddenly, he brightened. The tavern owner was holding his money. Surely the man would understand that
what Zack had committed himself to last night while in
the clutches of demon rum was only the purest form of
insanity in the bright light of a Sunday morning. No one
could hold him to it. He would simply go downstairs and
reason with the man, explaining that all bets were off
and he would like his purse returned.

Zack started down the stairs at a dash, but vertigo and
a throbbing pain in the back of his head soon slowed his
tread. There was no need to kill himself. His pouch
would still be there when he reached the taproom. He
felt a wave of relief when he spied the familiar face of
the barkeep, polishing the empty bar.

"Morning, Mr. Hazzard," the man said with a smile.

But Zack was in no mood for pleasantries. "You have
my money?" he asked of the round-faced, balding man
he remembered only slightly from the previous evening.

"Yessiree! Safe and sound. Locked away for the time
being. And in a lot better shape than you this morning,
I'd say. Ayah!"

"Give it to me, please."

The man's grin was literally blinding. The morning sun
came through the window and shot off a gold front tooth
directly into Zack's aching eyes.

"Sorry, sir. But a bet's a bet. I'll have both pouches,
ready for the proper disbursement, here in the taproom
next Saturday night. I believe that's the time and place
you and Abe Cushing agreed upon." He flashed his
eye-shattering grin once more. "Ayah! Be expectin' a
big turnout come Saturday. Whole town's going to want
to know the outcome."

"But I didn't know what I was doing last night."

The barkeep shrugged apologetically. "I doubt old
Abe did, either. But we got at least two sober witnesses,
one of 'em being your little Eye-talian shipmate, the
other being me. Makes it a honest bet. Ayah. Good as
gold and bindin' as roughage!"

Zack turned away. He felt sick. It was obvious that he
would get nowhere with this man. He was probably in

on the con and would receive a cut of Zack's purse when the time came and no bride was presented.

Cursing himself for a damn fool, Zack turned and climbed the stairs slowly. Where could he go? What could he do? He didn't even have the money to pay for his room. Enrico? No! It would be too degrading to go to him begging for a loan after last night. Maybe he could pick up a few odd jobs around town to see him through until he could sign on with a new ship. But that would only solve his immediate need for money. He had wagered almost four years of his life. He couldn't allow himself to throw all that away.

Damn! He had no choice. He would *have* to convince Miss Whiddington to marry him. But *which* Miss Whiddington?

Even the beautifully crafted pulpit failed to hold Persia's attention on this particular Sunday morning. As Reverend Osgood stretched his sermon beyond its usual limits, she found herself fidgeting in her seat. Her hands worried one another in her lap, twisting her linen handkerchief until it was little better than a limp rag. All she could think about was getting out and dashing home to wait for Zack.

She had scanned the congregation upon arrival, hoping to see him in church. But, of course, most sailors attended only the obligatory services on the Sunday before setting out to sea. They were not known as a group for their piety. Apparently, the man she loved was no different from the rest. Still, in a way she was relieved that he wasn't in church. How much more difficult it would have been to sit still and make even a pretense of paying attention to the sermon if Zack had been there, staring at the back of her head and sending shivers through her simply by being under the same roof.

Careful to hold a properly devout expression on her face, Persia whiled away the time by planning what she would wear to dinner. She had several new dresses, recently arrived from her mother's dressmaker in Boston. There was a dove-gray flannelette trimmed in cotton lace, a blush-pink taffeta, and a new highland plaid from Scotland. But none seemed quite right for the occasion.

"And the meek shall inherit the earth!" boomed Reverend Osgood, noting with satisfaction that even as he pronounced the words, Miss Persia Whiddington colored demurely and cast her gaze down before him. Ah, she was a pious girl!

But piety had nothing whatsoever to do with the high color in Persia's cheeks or the downward cast of her eyes. That both had come at that precise point in the sermon was purest coincidence.

Persia blushed at her own private thoughts. She had decided what she would wear . . . *if she dared*.

She remembered well the day that Europa had cast the gown from her closet, saying, "Here, Persia, take this old thing. You can use it to play dress-up. The colors have never been right for me. Yellow turns me sallow. And that particular shade of blue clashes with my eyes."

Persia had murmured her thanks, being careful not to give away the joy she felt at the acquisition of this cast-off for fear her sister would reconsider and take it back. For some time, Europa had been allowed to wear the latest fashions with their high waists, low bodices, and long, narrow skirts. Although Persia's wardrobe was filled with gowns of the richest fabrics from Europe and the Orient, they all appeared to be cut for a child. Never was she permitted to display a hint of bosom or a length of shapely arm. But now, at sixteen, she was old enough, she decided.

Secretly, she had altered Europa's gown to a perfect fit. She had been saving it to surprise everyone on some special occasion. What better time than this to spring her surprise?

"Persia, for heaven's sake, are you asleep?" Europa was poking at her. Reverend Osgood had finally run out of pious platitudes, and everyone else had risen to leave the church.

She flashed her older sister a wide, confident smile. "No, Europa. Not sleeping, just dreaming."

Resigned to his fate, Zack spent the rest of his morning nursing his hangover. While doing that, he bathed as best he could in the small metal hat tub the innkeeper provided. He glanced in the mirror and was suddenly struck by how sensible it was for human beings to do this sort of thing in absolute private. What would a bride do—Persia or Europa Whiddington, for instance—if she came upon her naked husband jammed in the tub as he was at this minute with his long legs folded up practically to his chin and all his maleness lying there shrunken and far from inviting in the cold light of day?

"Probably take me for a great hairy spider, scream, and run for her life," he observed wryly.

No, he was not a pretty sight this way. But what man was? He could only hope that the proper clothes would successfully hide the naked animal and help lure his ladylove into believing him handsome and of the proper material for a husband.

"Persia or Europa? Europa or Persia?" he mused aloud while washing a foot.

Although this was not an easy situation, it would be so much simpler if there were only one woman to consider. And with seven short days to pay his court and win himself a wife, there was precious little time to be spent pondering the matter. He must move right in and ply his strategy from the moment he arrived at the Whiddington house.

Suddenly he brightened. Maybe he didn't have to choose one or the other right now. He could pay equal attention to *both* sisters, bide his time, and see which one seemed the more likely to accept his proposal. Yes, that would not only be the smart thing to do, but it would be a damn interesting experience! He'd sensed the competition between the pair. If neither of them knew which one he was courting, they would both be more aggressive, making his task much easier.

His decision made not to make one at this time, he set

about bathing in earnest. The scalding water turned his salt-cured skin red bronze. He scrubbed himself hard, feeling as if he were scraping away four years' accumulation of the grime of the whole world. For longer than he cared to remember, his bathtub had been the briny ocean. Soap, even the caustic cake provided by the tavernkeeper, was a luxury. He lathered, scrubbed, rinsed, then lathered again. And by the time he finished his bath, he felt half-alive again.

For once in his life, he had not squandered his spending money on trinkets but had gone to a tailor in London a few months back for a proper suit of clothes—something he had never owned before. Now, carefully and with no small measure of delight, he folded back the layers of brown paper and tissue that had protected the fabric these past months. It was all there, and in the latest fashion. The tight fawn trousers were tapered the full length of his legs, with loops to fit snugly under the instep. The bottle-green coat was cut shorter and with a closer fit at the waist than the style of a few years ago. It sported tails. The burgundy brocade waistcoat was also cut low to show his beruffled shirt to its best advantage. And a crisp stock would grace his throat. Top that with the new gray beaver hat and a scarlet greatcoat with several capes to make his shoulders look even broader, and what woman could resist him?

He smiled and ran a finger over the fine linen of the shirt. It would feel good against his skin. Or against a woman's soft cheek, he mused.

Still naked, his sleek body glowing from his vigorous scrubbing, Zack strode to the shaving stand in the corner and took up his straight-edge razor. He held the instrument poised for several moments while he stared at the wild tangle of beard and hair in the oval mirror. It was impossible to tell where one left off and the other began. Perhaps he should shave it all away. But he'd worn the beard too long. His cheeks would be as tender and vulnerable as a baby's bottom if exposed. He decided merely to tame the thatch.

With careful strokes, he brought forth more face than

he had seen in many months, leaving a mustache and full side whiskers for protection against the snow glare and winter wind. After more than an hour spent at the task, he nodded his approval to the image before him.

The next time he got Persia—or Europa—alone, there would be more of him to kiss. He grinned.

Persia waited in her room, watching out the window for any sign of Zack. Her sister's most persistent suitor, Seton Holloway, had strolled up the front walk nearly half an hour before, looking his usual self—preoccupied, rumpled, and a bit too eager. Europa was no doubt furious that he had come so early. That meant she had to entertain him until their other guest arrived. Any other day, she might have accomplished this by playing the piano and singing. But, of course, singing was strictly out of the question on a Sunday. Persia almost felt sorry for Europa . . . but not quite.

She glanced out again and then looked toward the door. The wait would be much easier if she were downstairs with the others. But she dared not put in an appearance below before Zack arrived for fear she would be sent immediately back up to change. She cast an uncertain look at the mirror and watched as color flooded her cheeks. The change in her was shocking, she had to admit. Would Zack even recognize her? She hardly knew herself!

The gauzy silk grenadine of Europa's cast-off gown fit Persia as if it had never known the curves of any other woman's body. Narrow stripes of palest blue traversed the cream-yellow background in perfect vertical lines. The demure poufed sleeves only served to accentuate the daring dip of the bodice. Had it not been for the straw embroidery on the sleeves and tight-fitting top—featherlike in design—Persia was sure the darker flesh of her nipples would have peeked through the thin material. The same decorative pattern—made by splitting ordinary wheat and applying it with an embroidery stitch—was repeated at the hemline.

The long narrow skirt fell from just beneath Persia's

high, full breasts. When she walked, the barest hint of the rest of her lovely figure—slim waist and rounded hips—was given away to the eye of the beholder by the soft contours of the material.

Persia had changed her hairstyle, too. Her long hair was swept up and fixed in place at the back of her head with ivory combs. Only a few flame-colored wisps trailed down in back, while a curl on either side framed her perfect oval face. A blue ribbon, pinned with her cameo, circled her slender neck—simple, but exquisite.

She paced the room, pretending that she was practicing walking in the narrow skirt and shaped-heel slippers. But eventually, her measured steps took her back to the window to search the distance for Zack. Still no sign of him. There was a man coming down Gay Street from the direction of Main, but she didn't recognize him. He was certainly a fashion plate, though, in his gray beaver hat and caped scarlet greatcoat.

He turned in their walk, and her curiosity grew. Suddenly, he paused just below, glanced up at her window, and swept the hat from his golden-brown hair. He smiled up, then offered her a bow.

Persia's heart seemed to stop for an instant before it raced to catch up with the blood coursing through her veins.

She gave a nervous laugh. "It can't be! *Zack?*" If she had transformed herself, he had performed an even greater miracle.

Taking up her silk-fringed shawl and draping it becomingly about her shoulders, Persia went to her door and opened it just far enough to hear voices from the entranceway below.

"Well, Mr. Hazzard," boomed her father, "you've made it."

"I hope I'm not late, sir." Zack's voice made Persia's pulse quicken once more.

"Oh, certainly not. At any rate, we wouldn't have started without you. In fact, you aren't the last to arrive. Persia is taking her own sweet time today."

"Hello, Mr. Hazzard," Persia heard her mother say. "Welcome to our home once again."

"Thank you, Mrs. Whiddington. It is all my pleasure to be here."

"Captain, perhaps you had better go and fetch our youngest."

"I'm sure she'll be down in a moment, my dear."

"A young lady must have time to dress properly, Mother." Europa, with her sugary voice, had joined the others. "Why, Zachariah, how handsome you look this afternoon! Seton, do take his coat; I believe Fletcher is occupied in the kitchen."

"Of course, Miss Europa," came a thin, male voice, and Persia could almost see Seton Holloway's Adam's apple bobbing.

"Zack, come along with me to the parlor," said Europa. "I have something there that might interest you. There's time before dinner, I'm sure."

Zack's voiced agreement propelled Persia from her room without further delay. She posed at the head of the stairs and, summoning her most seductive voice, said, "Hello, Zack. I'm so glad you could come."

All eyes in the hallway below stared up. Her mother's face paled, and her hand flew to her lace-covered throat. The captain's lips twitched in surprise, then turned up in an appreciative smile. Seton Holloway, still holding Zack's scarlet coat as if he had been frozen where he stood, gaped at her with his mouth wide open.

Europa already had possession of Zack's arm but had not yet managed to smuggle him off to the parlor. Gowned in nutmeg and cinnamon bombazett with cream lace at her bosom, she made a striking picture. But, as Persia watched, her face contorted into a grimace of rage.

"My dress!" Persia heard her say in a strangled tone.

Persia only smiled. Not at her sister, but at Zack. He had extracted himself from Europa's grasp and was making his way up the stairs, one strong brown hand extended toward Persia.

His eyes devoured her as he came, caressing her face, her hair, and her thinly clad breasts until her nipples stiffened beneath the shiny straw stitching. His expression mingled desire with amazement. He gazed at her as if seeing some new wonder of the world for the first time.

Persia felt as if she were drowning in the flood of sensations washing over her. All the others at the foot of the stairs dissolved into a hazy half-light, a halo that was only the backdrop for the man coming toward her. He was everything she needed, wanted, and must have in the world. She could not live without his touch, and she would not.

"Persia." Her name upon his lips was a loving demand that made her quiver in the same manner she would have if he had reached out and fondled her aching breasts.

"Hello, Zack," she whispered.

One side of his mouth quirked up in a quasi smile, and he reached out toward her hand. "That's all? Just *hello*?"

She smiled back and answered, still in the barest of whispers so that the others wouldn't hear, "Hello, and I still love you."

"Even in broad daylight?" he challenged.

"Even under the blazing eye of noon."

He gave a low, tantalizing laugh just before he brought her hand to his lips and brushed her tender flesh with the rough silk of his mustache.

CHAPTER SEVEN

"*D*INNER is served, Captain and Mrs. Whiddington."
Fletcher, dressed in knee britches and jacket of the
same Prussian blue as the tattooing on his cheeks, captured everyone's immediate attention. His voice boomed
like cannon fire in the shocked stillness of the entrance
hall. All eyes turned from Persia and Zack to the tall
servant.

Europa fumed silently. She had been on the verge of
maneuvering Zachariah away from the others so that
they would be automatically paired as dinner partners
when Persia had made her entrance and spoiled it all.
Now he was on the steps with her, even at this moment
tucking her hand into his elbow to escort her to the
table.

The dark-haired beauty's eyes flashed a warning, and
the smallest of smiles touched her rose-petal lips. The
day wasn't over yet, and neither was this battle of wills
with her sister. Persia had yet to win out against her.
Europa certainly didn't mean for this to be the first time.

Persia, oblivious to her sister's hard gaze, had eyes

only for the man beside her. She had thought Zack was wonderful—witty, devastatingly masculine, and decidedly passionate—last night. But how much more of all of these he was by daylight, decked out in his fashionable clothes and best company manners. And he seemed just as taken with her. She never even considered the thought that he might have intended to escort Europa into the dining room. After all, Zack was *hers*!

Europa, deciding to make the best of a nearly hopeless situation, moved toward her own beau, the ever-present, ever-reticent Mr. Holloway. She would concentrate on using Seton to make Zack jealous. But she had wasted too much time indulging her anger.

"My dear." The captain offered him arm to his wife.

"Oh, please, sir," Europa's lawyer beau broke in. "Allow me. Mrs. Whiddington, may I escort you?"

"That's dear of you, Seton. Thank you."

So, Europa was ushered in on her father's arm, her cheeks flaming with indignation and her mind calculating revenge.

The three couples moved through the wide doorway into the dining room. Suddenly Persia was aware that the room, her mother's decorating pièce de résistance, had captured Zack's full attention. He paused in midstep and gave a quiet gasp.

"I never saw anything like it."

"And probably you never will again," Persia told him. "Mother hired an itinerate artist to paint the walls."

It was, indeed, a striking room. Victoria Whiddington had given the traveling artist specific instructions, and he had carried them out to the letter, even adding a few imaginative flourishes of his own. The walls depicted the shipbuilding yards at Quoddy Cove, with tall ships riding at anchor beyond in the water. Another section featured the exotic ports Captain Whiddington had visited in his travels—the West Indies with Carib indians in their canoes, fishing the palm-sheltered waters of a turquoise lagoon; the Cape of Good Hope with a storm tossing a square-rigged ship; Madagascar, Bombay, Tahiti, Shanghai. And finally, there was Gay Street, showing in every

vivid detail the white, Federal-style house with its porti-
coed front and widow's walk high above. A woman and
two girls stood in the yard, welcoming a sea captain
home, while a black-and-white-spotted dog—Persia's own
contribution to the mural—yapped and cavorted beside
the girl with burnt-sienna hair.

The long table gleamed with white lace, brilliant blue
Chinese export dinnerware of the finest grade, crystal
from Ireland, and the company best pearl-handled silver
flatware. Mrs. Whiddington was not one to let anything
go lacking when it came time to entertain, especially if
her guests were possible husbands for her daughters.

As they all took their places, she glanced at the two
young men before her. Seton Holloway was everything
she wanted in a son-in-law. He was learned, mannerly,
attentive at all times to Europa, and best of all, he possessed no longing to go to sea. The absence of such a
desire was a unique quality in down-east men, and one
to be much sought after in Victoria's opinion.

She loved her husband dearly. She had from the first
moment she'd laid eyes on him over twenty years before.
But that love, warring for the upper hand over his love
of the sea, had cost her much through the years.

He had been thousands of miles away when Europa,
their first, was born. He never saw her until she was
three years old. Again, when Victoria's next labor pains
started, Asa was half a world away. He had planned to
be home for this birth, but their second daughter came
early and lived only a few hours. He was there to attend
the baby's funeral, however, since she was born and
died in the dead of winter. By the spring thaw, when
earth could be turned and the tiny white coffin lowered to
its final rest, the captain had sailed his ship home. But
as they had stood together in the greening burial ground,
holding hands and weeping quietly, she had known that
she could never again bear a child alone. There was an
ache in one dark part of her heart, put there on that
lonely blizzard-wild night when she had given birth and
cradled her tiny daughter in her arms as she died, that
would never go away again.

She could no more stand the thought of one of her daughters going through that than she could have allowed her husband to sail off when she found she was in her third pregnancy. She had insisted that Asa stay ashore from that time until Persia was two years old. This was the reason, she felt sure, that their youngest daughter had always been the captain's favorite.

And now that favorite, that child the father had taught to love the sea and all its glamour and adventure, was gazing up at another seafaring man—one who could bring her nothing but pain, in Victoria's estimation.

Yes, it was good that Europa must marry first, Victoria told herself silently. For she could see in Persia's eyes a deep emotion and desire that mirrored her own twenty-odd years ago when she'd looked at Asa Whiddington. Victoria ached for her daughter, knowing that pain was ahead for her. If she wanted him—and it was plain that she did—but could not have him, she would be distraught. On the other hand, if by some outside chance they should marry someday, Persia would know a far deeper and more lasting pain. There was nothing so terrible as seeing your man sail away, not knowing when or *if* he would return.

Before grace was said and the first course served, Persia's mother had made up her mind. *Never* would she allow her youngest to marry a man of the sea!

Persia meanwhile was thinking thoughts quite to the contrary.

For a time after Fletcher served the meal, the silence grew as thick as Mrs. Whiddington's pot roast gravy. Even Persia, lost in her romantic reflections of following her husband to sea, paid close attention to the richly browned beef, potatoes, carrots, and boiled cabbage. She, like other down-east women, possessed a stout appetite that guarded the body and soul against Maine's freezing winter breath. She had heard that women in the warmer, southern climes ate like birds and were thought unladylike if they ever finished an entire meal. But such delicate belles would never survive outside their hot-house climates. *Fuel your body against the cold,* her mother had always told her. And Persia was at all times obedient.

But once the plates were cleared and coffee and a steaming plum pudding served, the diners relaxed and took up polite conversation.

"Seton, what do you think is the answer to this present financial panic sweeping the country?" the captain asked.

The lawyer looked slightly embarrassed at being singled out for such a difficult question. He had no answer. No one did.

"It's come as a hard blow to the whole country, sir. I hear in Boston the harbor is crowded with ships unable to sail because markets have dried up for lack of funds to purchase cargoes and supplies. I see no end in sight."

"Aye," the captain replied, frowning. "It will get worse before it gets better, I'm afraid. I've been thinking of investing as part owner of a ship out of Boston. But with times what they are, I'm not sure I want to risk it."

Persia's eyes lit up. "You're going to buy your own ship, Father? Why haven't you told us?"

He smiled and shook his head. "Calm yourself, little sailor. The deal's not set, and as I said, I'm not sure it ever will be with times what they are."

"But Father, you're a wealthy man. Surely—"

"Persia," her mother said in a warning tone. "We don't discuss finances at the table."

"But a *ship*, Mother! Did you know?"

Victoria did not, but she wasn't about to admit it in company. In answer, she only smiled and looked at her husband, letting him know that she would speak to him later.

"Sir, if I might make a comment? . . ."

"Please, Mr. Hazzard. I'd welcome your opinion."

"This panic, as I see it, is a passing thing. The United States is too strong economically to stay long in its grip. I would be willing to wager all I own in the world"—Zack paused and cleared his throat, remembering suddenly

that he had done exactly that on the previous evening—
"little as that is, that in a few months we'll be coming
out of this financial slump. If a man owned a ship and
was willing to send it out to trade among the foreign
ports at this time, in two or three years when the ship
returned, he would make a fortune. Money will be plenti-
ful by then, but foreign goods scarce because of the
cutback in shipping activity at the present time."

Captain Whiddington was nodding his agreement.
"You've a good head for business on those broad shoulders of yours, Hazzard. Have you ever thought of seeking an assignment as supercargo on one of our mer-
chantmen?"

Zack matched his host's smile, answering, "Oh, I'd
like that, sir. But I want more. I've been all but guaran-
teed a promotion to second mate the next time I ship
out. I figure in another few years I should be ready to
take command myself. Then I'll act as my own supercargo."

Zack pressed the knee next to his under the table and
offered Persia a sidelong glance. She smiled, unaware
that he was rubbing her sister's ankle with the toe of his
boot at the same time. She welcomed his attention but
longed for it to come somewhere besides at the dining
room table with her whole family in attendance.

"I congratulate you, Mr. Hazzard," said the captain.
"It's not every young man these days who knows what
he wants and has the ambition to go after it. You'll do
well, I'm sure."

Zack chuckled softly and found Persia's hand beneath
the table. He pressed it to his thigh. "Well, I'd like to
think that I'll realize my goals, Captain, but at times I
wonder. Right now, I need to get back to sea as quickly
as possible. Would you know of a crew needing a second mate, by any chance?"

Persia turned to stare at the man who was holding her
hand, caressing the soft flesh of her palm with his thumb
and making her quiver inside and out. He couldn't mean
what he was saying! They had only just found each
other. How could he possibly leave her so soon?

Europa voiced Persia's own disappointment. "Zack, you can't go yet! Why, I simply forbid it!"

Persia seethed and her eyes flashed blue sparks at her sister. *Forbid it indeed!* Who did Europa think she was to approve or forbid anything that had to do with Zachariah Hazzard? In her anger, she dug her nails into Zack's hand, making him wince.

"Mr. Hazzard is quite right, my dear," the captain said to Europa. "A man must be about his work if he ever hopes to realize his goals. And I might be able to say a word or two to friends in Boston to speed you on your way, Zack."

"Bless you, Captain," Victoria said under her breath. She hadn't missed the byplay between her younger daughter and the rugged seafarer all through dinner. Although she had no idea what was going on beneath the pristine lace of the tablecloth, from what she could see, the situation was apparently more serious than she had imagined.

"I would be most obliged, Captain Whiddington. I'm afraid thrift is not one of my virtues. I seem to be in rather straightened circumstances at the moment."

The captain's eyebrow cocked at this. Good Lord, the man had only made port the day before! He must have been paid a small fortune at that time. What could have become of his wages? Had he spent them in advance by borrowing from his shipmates? Or possibly he had been gambling . . . and losing . . . while at sea. However he had spent all his money, it was a foolish thing to do in such uncertain times. Suddenly, the captain wondered if Seaman Hazzard was officer material after all. But Zack had continued explaining while the captain's mind whirled with uncertainties.

"I should have been planning for this all my adult life, but somehow I never imagined that it would happen to me. Now I realize that I want a home ashore, some anchor to the land. I'd like to give up rented rooms and tavern cooking for all time. But plans like mine take cash. I want to buy some land, build a house, and then perhaps . . ." Zack let his words trail off but looked

meaningfully at Persia and then Europa, flattering each
with the intimacy of his unspoken words.

"Ayah! I know the feeling well," the captain said. "I
remember exactly when it struck me. The first time I set
eyes on the lovely Victoria Forsyth. I had to fight my
way through a pack of suitors, any one of them a more
likely catch than I was at the time. But, mark my words,
both of you young men, persistence will win out in the
end. And hard work will pay off. Isn't that right, my
dear?"

He nodded toward his blushing wife.

"And I'll tell you another thing, Mr. Hazzard, you
have the right idea. Put your money into land. Make a
home before you make a family. You'll be happy for it
later on."

This remark from the captain, although addressed to
Zack, seemed directed at Seton Holloway. The man
knew it and squirmed in his seat. For some time now,
Europa had been putting Seton off by telling him that
she could only consider marrying a man who was well
established in his career and financially stable. Holloway,
as the junior partner in a small law practice, was neither
of these. And because of Europa's protests, he had not
felt secure enough to approach her father and ask for her
hand, even though he knew that Mrs. Whiddington was
all in favor of the match.

"Please tell me if I'm out of bounds in asking, Mr.
Hazzard . . . but might there be a young lady who has
prompted these domestic designs of yours?" the captain
asked.

Both Persia and Europa leaned slightly forward, staring at Zack. The silence that followed, although brief,
seemed interminable to the pair. Zack, aware of their
reactions, squeezed Persia's hand under the table and
offered Europa a smile that promised much.

"Aye, Captain. There is."

"And have you spoken for her already, lad?"

Zack cast his eyes down and shook his head, smiling
sheepishly. "I'm afraid I haven't worked up the courage
yet. You see, we've only known each other a short time.

I fear she'd turn me down flat, and her family would probably cast me out and order me never to return again. There are certain manners to courting, as I'm sure you know.''

"That's very decent of you, Mr. Hazzard, to take the family into consideration,'' Mrs. Whiddington said. She was feeling much relieved, assuming that he spoke of a Boston girl. But she added, just in case, "I would certainly not take kindly to any man who tried to sweep one of my daughters off her feet without the proper amenities being seen to first.''

"Exactly my point, Mrs. Whiddington. But it's difficult for a seafaring man to court a lady properly. We haven't long ashore.''

"You certainly haven't,'' Persia put in. "And I think that we've spent enough of it over Sunday dinner. Mother, do you mind if we go out for a walk?''

Before Mrs. Whiddington could answer, Europa piped up, "Seton and I will join you.''

"I suppose that will be all right, as long as you girls wrap up warmly. Seton, you and Mr. Hazzard bring them back home well before dark.''

"Of course, Mrs. Whiddington,'' Zack answered for the other man.

Bundled and mufflered, the four young people set out for a brisk walk. The afternoon was fine, with a bright sun making the snowbanks gleam as if diamonds were buried in their depths. Many other townspeople were out for their Sunday-afternoon constitutionals. But Persia barely noticed them. The man whose arm held hers consumed her full attention.

"Are you really planning to buy land and build a house, Zack?'' she asked.

"Yes. I am.''

"Here in Quoddy Cove?''

"Possibly.''

She paused a moment before working up the nerve to ask her next question. "For *us*?''

When he looked down into her upturned face, his dark

eyes made contact with such an impact that it jolted her almost as sharply as his first kiss had.

"Now what would make you think a thing like that, Miss Whiddington?" His voice was husky, playful.

She forced her gaze away. She didn't want teasing. She wanted serious discussion.

"It's just that, as you said, you don't have long ashore. I think we should be direct with each other. I have been. But I'm not sure about you."

He covered her hand with his, stroking gently. "Persia, my sweet, you can't imagine how I feel . . ."

"Zack!" Europa hailed from right behind them, interrupting. "I'm freezing. Seton has come up with a grand idea. We'll stop off at Jefferd's for a mug of hot cider. Hurry along now, both of you."

Persia saw a frown crease Zack's brow as he replied, "I don't think that's a good idea."

"It's perfectly acceptable, if that's what you're worried about," Persia told him.

That wasn't what was bothering him. He was afraid that someone at the tavern would say something to the girls about his wager. Then he decided that it might not be a bad idea after all. He would show those land pirates that he was well on his way to winning the bet. And he'd let them guess which woman would soon be his bride.

"That's fine," he said. "Some hot cider will taste good about now."

The tavernkeeper, giving Zack a sly wink, showed them to a rough-hewn table in the back corner near the fireplace, where great logs of oak crackled and hissed on the hearth.

"Spiced cider all around," Zack ordered.

"Yes, sir, four mugs of sweet apple." He moved off to fill the order.

"Well, isn't this nice!" Europa enthused. "Now, Zack, you must tell us all about yourself. Father kept you so occupied all through dinner that I felt like you were *his* guest instead of *mine*."

Zack felt Persia bristle beside him and touched her hand under the table.

"What would you like to know, Europa? I'm twenty-six years old. I was born in Salem, Massachusetts, and ran away to sea when I was twelve. I've been shipwrecked twice and barely escaped being eaten by cannibals on the isle of Borneo. That's about it."

A general gasp went up around the table. Europa reached over and took his hand. "You poor, brave man! However did you escape?"

He smiled, wondering what Europa would say if he told her he bedded the chief's daughter and thus enlisted her aid in escaping the tribe's big black pot. No, he decided, he'd better keep that story to himself.

"I managed to slip past their guards and steal one of their boats. Luckily, I spoke a ship out of New Bedford after two days on the open sea. I was sunburned, thirsty, hungry, but I still had my head on my shoulders."

The young lawyer across from Zack was wide-eyed. "I can't even conceive of living such a dangerous life, Mr. Hazzard."

"Please, it's Zack. And I think your life here is every bit as dangerous as mine, Seton."

The man blushed and laughed. "Sure it is! I could get captured by Aroostook Indians walking to my office some morning!"

Zack leaned across the table and lowered his voice to a whisper as if he didn't want Europa and Persia to hear. "It's not Indians a man has to watch out for in the woods around here, my friend." He glanced at one sister and then the other and said hoarsely to Seton, "*Women!* The woods are fairly crawling with them. And they jump out and grab you on dark nights."

Seton chortled loudly, causing heads in the pub to turn toward their table. "I wish you'd tell me what woods you've been walking in after dark, Zack. I've been out beating the bushes and I can't scare any up."

"*Beating the bushes,* Mr. Holloway?" Although she refused to commit herself to Seton, Europa considered him her own private property. That he would even joke about such a thing as trying to interest other women was an affront to her pride.

"A figure of speech," he said apologetically. "I'm sorry, my dear. I simply forgot myself for a moment."

"You two are planning to be married, aren't you?" Zack inquired.

Suddenly, Europa and Seton looked at each other. At the same instant, he answered, "Yes," while she said, "No." Zack looked from one to the other, waiting to hear the true answer.

"Well, I suppose the idea has crossed our minds," Europa finally admitted. "But there's plenty of time for us to decide. We'll both be here. Seton never goes *anywhere*."

The way she said it wounded Seton deeply. He started to rise from his chair.

"Where are you going?" she demanded.

"I'm going *somewhere,* Europa!"

"Sit down! You can't leave me like this."

"Oh, but I can. And I intend to. I certainly wouldn't want to bore you any further."

He was up and moving away from the table as the barkeep brought their steaming mugs and set them in place.

"Seton, for heaven's sake," Europa whined. "You're being silly!"

Seton took a step back toward the table and grabbed her arm, his fair face suddenly dark with anger. "Don't ever call me *silly*! Do you hear me, Europa?"

"Yes, Seton," she answered in a submissive whisper. "I'm sorry. Truly I am."

But he was not finished with her yet. He had spent years courting the fair Miss Europa and had taken all the indifference and abuse he could stand. He should just walk away, but, God help him, he loved her. Maybe it was meeting a man like Zachariah Hazzard that brought out his more assertive side, or maybe Europa had simply gone too far this time. Whatever the case, he meant to have his say and settle the issue of their marriage once and for all, here and now. He faced her squarely, his face hard.

"Seton, whatever has come over you?" Europa asked, almost thrilled by this sudden change in her beau.

"Just hold your tongue, woman, and listen to what I have to say to you!"

Persia and Zack were all ears, immensely enjoying Europa's distress and Seton's sudden show of male dominance.

"I have been very patient with you, Europa. For over three years now I have waited and watched, fetched and carried, been mocked and maligned by you. *No more!* I will not have a wife who plans to use me as a doormat. *I am a man!* I intend to marry you, Europa Whiddington. You will agree this moment, and you will be happy with me. I may not lead an exciting, adventurous life, but I know how to love a woman and love her well."

Both Europa and Persia caught their breath at Seton's sudden outspokenness. Zack laughed and said, "Well spoken, friend."

But Seton didn't seem to see or hear any of these reactions. He plunged on. "Now, Europa, I demand an answer! Will you marry me?"

Europa was close to swooning. Never had Seton or any other man addressed her so harshly. If he was this forceful now, what would he be like on their wedding night? A delicious shudder trembled through her whole body.

"Well?" He gripped her shoulders, refusing to allow her to turn away from him.

"Yes, Seton. Oh, yes, I will marry you!"

Zack and Persia voiced their congratulations and toasted the newly engaged couple. Everyone in the tavern had heard, and a cheer rang out.

The barkeep brought another round of cider, on the house. When he set down the mugs, the man leaned down and whispered for Zack's ears alone, "One sister down, one to go, Mr. Hazzard."

Zack turned and smiled at Persia, who was all dreamy-eyed with happiness for her sister. "Yes," he said to the man who was holding his pouch. "One to go."

"What are you murmuring about, Zack?" Persia asked.

"Oh, nothing, my sweet. I was just thinking how crowded it is in here. I'd hoped we might have some time alone together."

She was drowning in his eyes and never wanted to come up for air. "Yes. I had, too."

"I have a room upstairs. It would be quieter."

The very thought of going to a man's room shocked her. "We can't leave Europa and Seton." But even as she voiced her weak protest, the other couple were excusing themselves. They, too, wanted privacy.

"You don't have to be frightened, Persia. I won't try to take advantage of you. I promise."

"Oh, I'm not frightened," she said with a weak laugh. Actually, she was quaking in her fur-lined boots. "It's just that if anyone should see us . . . Mother would die!"

"There's a back way. No one will see us."

Persia had run out of excuses, and her resolve was crumbling fast. Besides, Zack had said he would be leaving soon. She wanted a commitment from him every bit as much as Seton had wanted it from Europa. This might be her only chance.

"I understand," Zack murmured in a disappointed voice. "I won't press you, Persia."

Without a word, she stood and offered her arm for him to lead the way. She was nervous, uncertain, terrified of being alone with him. But at the same time, she wanted him with everything in her. And she had promised herself that she would never keep a man dangling and wondering while she manipulated him the way Europa had done Seton.

"You're sure?" he asked.

She answered him boldly. "Very sure!"

CHAPTER EIGHT

PERSIA'S heart was in her mouth by the time they reached Zack's room on the second floor. In spite of what he'd promised her, someone had seen them climbing the narrow stairway from the pantry. The man who had served them cider in the taproom below had cast a leering stare their way as they started up.

"Don't worry about him," Zack said as they hurried down the dim hall toward his door. "He won't say a word to anyone. Barkeeps are used to this sort of thing."

His turn of phrase bothered Persia. "What *sort* of thing?"

"Don't be upset. I didn't mean it that way. What I meant to say was that people who run inns have a broader view of society and morals . . . Oh, forget it. Just come inside."

He realized he was getting himself in deeper and deeper. Just get her into the room. Then the need for words would cease. He hadn't decided yet how far to press her. He didn't want to scare her off, but he must make it very plain to her that there was no backing out, that he considered her *his* already. Now that Europa was spoken for, his course was set and Persia was his destination. Should he make shore and plant his standard this very afternoon? The idea was enticing.

He had to admit that the entire outcome of their walk pleased him. From the first he had been far more taken with Persia than with her haughty older sister. Although he still could not conceive of himself with a wife on a long-term basis, a temporary marriage of convenience to Persia Whiddington struck him as a most enchanting prospect. Their marriage would be followed shortly by his departure for sea once more. It would be easy enough after that to lose himself in the wide world. Perhaps he'd leave the ship in Naples and sample the charms of the hot-blooded Latin women Enrico Sorrentino raved about before signing on with another crew. At any rate, he would win his bet and get to bed this fire-haired beauty in the bargain.

"Come in. Come in," he insisted as she hesitated at the threshold.

Persia, too, was laying her plan of attack. She loved this man, and she didn't intend to let him get away. Still, she would not stoop to trickery, as Europa had told her most women did. No, she must be honest and aboveboard with Zack. But she must be firm, too. She meant to know his intentions this very day. Never mind courting; there wasn't time. Their parents would hear two proposals this evening, if she had her way.

Zack stood in the center of the tiny room and stripped off his tailed coat. His scarlet greatcoat had already been flung across the bed.

"Let me help you out of that," he offered, reaching to accept her fur-lined cape.

Persia clasped it to her for an instant, remembering that underneath she still had on the revealing gown she'd worn at dinner. It was one thing to wear it in company, but quite another to stand alone before Zack, knowing that he was the type of man who undressed women with a mere glance.

At her hesitation, he said, "You aren't cold, are you?"

"No." Reluctantly, she gave up her wrap.

Zack tossed it next to his, then came back to stand before her. Slowly his eyes traveled over her, as she had known they would, taking in every detail of her face and form. Her breath froze even as her temperature climbed when his gaze paused at her breasts, encased in the thin material that was cut shockingly low to reveal a creamy expanse of bosom. She felt her nipples hardening against the soft fabric. Could he see? Her face flamed at the thought.

"You are a beautiful woman, Persia Whiddington. Perhaps the most beautiful I've ever seen." He reached out and curled one wisp of hair around his finger, tugging her gently toward him until she could feel his breath on her lips. "You're *exotic,* that's the word I've been groping for. You're the northern lights—bright, ever-changing, vibrant, and exciting."

She made no answer. There was nothing to say, and no voice with which to say it, anyway, as his words seemed to caress her physically. She could only stand there mirrored in his dark gaze—listening to the words she longed to hear, feeling his hand stroking her hair, breathing in his spiced, masculine scent.

"I'm going to kiss you," he said in a husky voice that steeled her for the promised intimate contact.

When she closed her eyes, ready, he said, "Not this very minute. I want you to think about it, mull it over in your mind just the way I'm doing. Imagine it, feel it in the deepest parts of you. When my lips touch yours, when my tongue caresses you, I want you to want me . . . to need me . . . the way I need you. You see, this kiss will be special." His gaze had her locked in an embrace, stoking her deep-burning fires. "This kiss, my love, will be the one you'll remember on the coldest nights when your bright hair has turned silver and you are trying to conjure up in your mind what love was like when it was new and fresh and so sweet it made you ache inside."

She *was* aching! How did he know?

He let the curl drop from his fingers and clasped both

hands about her beribboned throat. His touch was cool, his hands hard and strong. With his thumbs, he kneaded the underside of her chin, forcing her lips closer still to his. He bent to her, holding his open mouth barely the breadth of a hair above hers. Her lips parted, waiting for his. The next words he spoke flowed into her mouth with a warm rush of breath.

"I want to marry you, Persia. I can't go back to sea without knowing that you'll be waiting when I return. I'm sorry there's no time to court you, to win you, to flatter you, and bring you pretty presents. But if I leave now, you'll be another man's wife before I return. I couldn't stand that. I need you too much."

"And I need you, Zack."

Her earnest, fervent whisper was the last sound in the room before flesh met flesh in a communion of physical need and emotional desperation so profound that both of them felt the impact like the sudden jolt of lightning.

Zack tore free for an instant and stared down into Persia's wide, adoring eyes, his own registering disbelief. "My God!" he breathed before taking command of her lips once more.

In that instant, he came to realize what Persia had known all along . . . that their relationship was not of the moment, but for all eternity. He would marry her, yes. But he could never go away with no intention of returning to her. He wanted more than a few days in her bed. He wanted to spend the rest of his life in her heart. This was a whole new experience for him. Never had he been conquered so suddenly, so totally. The wager meant nothing any longer. All that mattered was that he have this woman, now and to the end of time.

Persia, locked securely in Zack's strong arms, could feel his heart pounding against her breasts. The sensation added a oneness to their kiss, as if they were no longer two people, but a single pulsing entity, forever welded by love and desire.

His forceful hands cradled the small of her back with a touch that was both commanding and gentle. Then, as if they were exploring the miracle of femininity for the

very first time, his fingers searched her back, her bare
shoulders, her arms. She trembled as his touch streamed
fire over her body, and pressed herself more securely to
his chest. She could feel the pulsing heat from his loins.
This new experience frightened her for a moment. She
tried to pull away. But Zack's hold on her would not be
denied. His tongue did tantalizing, delicious things to
distract her from her momentary fear. She relaxed once
more and allowed herself to savor, to enjoy.

His lips left hers for a moment, pressing against her
ear. "I want to make love to you, Persia," he whispered. As he spoke, his hand found her breast, stroking
it with such a knowing boldness that she went weak in
his arms.

"I can't stop you," she murmured. "I can only beg
you not to allow me to give in."

He drew away and stared down into her flushed face.
"I don't want you to *give in*. I want you to be ready for
love, too."

She laughed softly. "Oh, my daring, I am! Without a
second thought, I would let you strip away my gown and
do as you please with me. But . . ."

He smiled and kissed her nose. "But *Mother would
die*?"

"Exactly, I'm afraid."

She sighed, and her peaked nipples brushed his chest.
He shuddered and moaned with desire and frustration.
Righting her, he put her at arms' length and reached for
his coat. "Home before dark was the admonition, I
believe."

"*Well* before," she added.

"I'm used to taking orders, but not from mothers. Still,
I suppose I'll have to this time. Mark my words, though,
woman, you've laid the groundwork for a long and strenuous wedding night."

Laughing aloud, Persia threw her arms around Zack's
neck and hugged him. "Oh, I hope so! I'm looking
forward to it. Truly!"

"I'm happy to hear that. But first I must ask the

captain for your hand." Zack looked worried. "What do you suppose he'll say?"

Persia tugged his cheek down to her lips and kissed him quickly. "Darling, don't fret. He'll say yes, of course. What else can he do once Seton has asked to marry Europa?"

Her bright tone did little to dispel Zack's doubts. "I hope you're right, my love." Suddenly, he looked down at her and his eyes blazed. He grasped her in an embrace so tight that she could barely breathe. "He *must* say yes!"

Both couples arrived home at the same time. Both sisters were beaming with secret happiness. The four of them entered as a group, so that no one would have guessed that they had gone their separate ways for most of the afternoon. Mrs. Whiddington gave her daughters close scrutiny, but nothing seemed amiss. And it wasn't quite dark yet.

Europa nudged Seton, prompting him to speak. "Mrs. Whiddington, could I have a word with the captain?"

"I'd like to speak with him, too," Zack added, somewhat chagrined that he had let the other man get ahead of him.

"Well, my word!" exclaimed Victoria. "I'll see. He's working in the library."

She came back a moment later and told Seton to go in.

Leaving their beaus to the task of convincing their father that he must give up his two daughters—both in the same day—the girls hurried upstairs to their separate rooms. They barely spoke, each seeking privacy for her dreams.

While Persia lay across her bed upstairs, hugging a pillow, gazing at the ceiling, and going over every detail of the afternoon with Zack, he sat below, awaiting his turn in the captain's library.

The dainty chair was far too small to hold his large frame comfortably. He perched on the very edge, rehearsing what he would say to Persia's father. She was

so young, and he ten years older and worlds apart from
her in experience. Would that be a reason for Captain
Whiddington to turn down his petition? No! It couldn't
be! The captain himself was a good deal older than Mrs.
Whiddington, anyone could see that. It made sense for a
young woman to marry an older man—one who was
mature, stable, and well able to provide for her.

The library door opened after a short time and Seton
Holloway hurried out. He looked pale and shaken. He
spoke not a word to Zack but nodded, grabbed his hat,
and left. It didn't look good.

"Please come in, Mr. Hazzard," the captain ordered,
unsmiling.

Zack didn't like it. Captain Whiddington had called
him by his first name at dinner. Now suddenly the man
was all formality again.

The captain indicated a deep leather chair for Zack
and took his place behind his massive, heavily carved
desk. The lamps in the room were turned low, and the
green glass shade on the one nearest Whiddington cast
an ominous glow over his stern face. Zack felt his throat
muscles tightening.

"Well, Mr. Hazzard, speak up. I have work to do
tonight, and young Holloway has already taken up more
of my time than I can spare with his mindless chatter."

Mindless chatter? Did that mean that Captain Whiddington had turned down Seton's plea for Europa's hand?
Zack wanted to ask, but he didn't dare. Perhaps the pot
roast at dinner had disagreed with the captain's diges-
tion. Something had happened. He certainly was not the
jovial man he had been a few short hours before.

"I'll get right to the point, sir."

"I hope you will."

"I realize that I'm practically a stranger to you, but I
hope you won't hold that against me. In all modesty, sir,
I'm a hardworking, ambitious man. I know what I want
and I will get it!"

"Your point, Hazzard?"

Zack held his breath for a moment, steeling himself to
say the words—not because he didn't mean them, but

because he suddenly knew fear for the first time in his life. Fear that Persia's father would turn him down flat.

"I want to marry your daughter, Captain Whiddington."

The wind whipped outside, rattling the tall windows at the end of the room. Other than that, there was not a sound. Zack's heart pounded, and his palms grew clammy as he waited for an answer.

"You'll be going back to sea soon, won't you?"

"Yes, sir. It's my life."

"And what about my daughter then?"

Zack almost answered that he hoped by that time Persia would be carrying his child and would have that to keep her happy and occupied while he was away. But discretion stayed his tongue. He answered simply, "Before I leave, she will have a home—our home. And I'll see that she never wants for anything."

"She'll be wanting for a man. What will she do about that for the two, four years you may be away?"

"Begging your pardon, sir, but what did *your* wife do?"

Captain Whiddington suddenly looked down at his desk and shuffled some papers about. "She suffered a great deal, I'm afraid."

"But she is a strong, faithful woman, and she survived."

"Aye, lad, well put."

"Your daughter is every bit as strong."

"And does she love you?"

"I believe so, sir. She says she does, and it's in her eyes."

"I can't say this comes as a surprise. I saw the way she looked at you at dinner today. A woman can speak volumes with her silent observation of a man. It is, however, quite sudden. I wish there were more time."

"I wish that, too, sir. But if I stayed ashore to court her properly, I'd lose valuable time working my way up the chain of command. You understand that, don't you?"

"Aye. And no doubt the result would be the same. She'd wait and pine her life away until you came back to marry her."

"Then you approve, Captain Whiddington?" The question was spoken with almost painful relief.

The man's gray head shot up and his steely eyes narrowed. "No, dammit, I don't approve! If it were up to me, I'd make old maids of both my girls, pretending to the day I die that they're too young to marry. But what would that make me? Some kind of ogre in their eyes. If this is what she wants, so be it. You have my blessing."

Zachariah rose solemnly and went to the desk, offering his hand to the captain, who shook it firmly. "You do me a great honor, Captain Whiddington."

"Mind you treat her well! As long as you do, we'll be friends. Raise a hand to her in anger or drunkenness, and your death is a foregone conclusion."

"You have no need to fear for her. I love her more deeply than I ever believed was possible."

They shared a toast to the occasion and passed a quarter hour in man talk. Then Zack was given his cue to depart. He desperately longed to see Persia to give her the good news. But that was for her father to do. He would come to supper the following evening to make it all official. At that time, he might kiss her cheek to seal the engagement. They would be married in two weeks at the church on Main Street. Zack had asked for a shorter wait, but the captain told him that would be impossible.

Zack walked out the front door never feeling his boots touch solid earth. Light, powdery snowflakes were beginning to fall. They swirled in pretty patterns in the lamplight streaming from the windows. Moving on without even realizing he was walking, Zack shuffled through the fine covering of snow until he stood in the exact spot where he had first seen Persia. He glanced up. She was there at the window, and his heart gave a sudden, soul-wrenching lurch. He ached to have her in his arms, to kiss her, to touch her, to tell her all the wonders of love that they would share.

"Soon," he whispered. "Soon, my darling."

*   *   *

Persia stared down at the darkness. She couldn't see Zack below on the street, but somehow she knew he was standing there, watching her window. She had heard the front door close moments before. And the gooseflesh prickling her skin told her that someone was staring up at her unshaded window. It had to be Zack . . . *dear Zack*.

If only she could see his face. She would know then what had happened with her father. How could she wait any longer? This was a slow kind of death—waiting and not knowing. She had half a mind to storm downstairs and demand to know what had been said between them. After all, it was *her* life that was being decided! But no. She could not disrupt the accepted way of things. She would simply have to try to sleep tonight and wake up in the morning to find out the news—good or bad.

It *had* to be good! She wouldn't allow herself to think of any other possibility.

Persia had changed out of her blue-and-yellow dress and now wore a long flannel gown that covered her from ankles to chin. The soft material caressed her bare flesh as she moved, causing her nipples to respond each time she thought of Zack.

Tucking the hem under her feet, she curled up in the window seat and stared out at the swirling flakes dancing past. She let her mind flow, imagining what it would be like to snuggle close to Zack's warm body on such a night. In his arms, she would have no need of long gowns to keep her from the cold. She would be wrapped in his love and filled with the heat of their newfound passion. Even now, she could imagine how it felt to have his full lips taking possession of hers, demanding with his silken tongue that she obey his fierce will. A weakness of willing surrender washed over her. She could remember the intense sensations aroused deep within her when his fingers fondled her breasts. What would it be like when no fabric stood as a barrier keeping flesh from aching flesh? She shivered at the mere thought, and a gnawing ache took possession of her deepest, most private parts.

"Zack," she sighed. 'Oh, my darling, how I need you!"

Persia had drifted off to sleep dreaming of her wedding night by the time her father finally gave up work at his desk and climbed the stairs wearily. He had planned to finish early tonight. He needed Victoria's softness beneath him, surrounding him. He had planned to make slow and satisfying love to her tonight.

But now it was late. He would probably have to wake her. And once she heard his news, she would be in no mood to lavish affection on him. He knew that the last thing she wanted for either of her daughters was marriage to a seafaring man. Victoria was adamant about it. But what could he do? They were in love. And the man had saved her life! But for Zachariah Hazzard and his daring rescue, they might be anticipating a funeral now instead of a wedding.

Asa moved down the hallway silently. Both his daughters' doors were closed and their rooms quiet and dark. He didn't want to wake them. Reaching for the brass handle to the bedroom he shared with Victoria, he turned it soundlessly. She was sleeping, her lovely dark hair spread out on the pillow like lush strands of black silk thread.

He undressed and pulled on his nightshirt before waking her. When he reached the bed, he touched her linen-covered breast, kissed her cheek, and whispered, "My darling?"

Her eyes fluttered open and a slow smile curved her elegant mouth.

"Home from the sea, my captain?"

"Aye, woman! And demanding my usual welcome," he said in a teasing voice.

"Well, you shan't have it!" She turned away from him, playfully daring him to steal a kiss from her.

Instead, he touched her arm lightly. "Victoria, we must talk."

She turned back to him, her smile gone and a worried look in her eyes. "What is it, Asa? What's wrong?"

"Nothing's wrong, darling. It's just that we may be about to lose one of our girls."

She sat up in bed, her face wild with apprehension. "What are you saying?"

"It seems love has struck, my dear."

Her worried look smoothed itself into a mask of delight. "You mean that's what Seton wanted to talk to you about? He's finally asked to marry Europa?"

Asa waved a hand in annoyance. "No. No. He only wanted to ask my advice on some tedious point of nautical law. A pure waste of my time. Persia would have known the answer to such an elemental question. It's Zachariah Hazzard. He made an honest and noble plea for Europa this evening."

"You turned him down, of course!"

Asa reached out and stroked his wife's cheek. "Dearest, how could I? They're in love."

"I won't have it!" she stormed. "She'll be no better than a widow most of her life. I have it all planned. She's to marry Seton Holloway."

"That's *your* plan, Victoria. I believe Europa has plans of her own. We can't stand in the way of her happiness. Not when we know the wonders of love."

As he spoke, Asa stripped the gown from his wife's shoulder, baring one breast. The nipple stared up at him—wide, erect, inviting. He circled it slowly with the center of his palm, and Victoria caught her breath.

"Would you deny your own daughter such pleasures with the man she loves as you and I have found together, my darling?" He whispered the words onto his wife's bare flesh and felt her breast shudder against his hand in response.

"Don't talk of such things. It's indecent to think of one's own daughter doing . . . feeling . . . ah-h-h!"

Asa kissed her nipple, letting his tongue tease its tip just before he sucked it into his mouth. Victoria fell back among the pillows, unable to offer any further protest to her daughter's marriage or to her husband's needs.

*   *   *

All the while, their daughter Persia lay wrapped in the down quilts of her bed, dreaming of the time when she could give up her body and her love to the man of her choice—Zachariah Hazzard—having no idea that he had unwittingly promised himself to her sister, Europa.

CHAPTER NINE

*E*UROPA was up early the next morning. She swept into Persia's room without knocking, her face aglow with anticipation.

"My stars, Persia! You're not dressed yet? You know, of course, that Seton asked Father for my hand last night. It seems to me you'd have a little more consideration and hurry for once in your life. It's cruel to keep me waiting like this. I was awake all night. I can hardly bear it a moment longer. Father *must* make the announcement at breakfast."

"It's only six-thirty, Europa. Father is probably still sleeping." Persia started to add that she was just as excited and eager to get to the breakfast table as her sister. But she stopped herself. What a grand surprise it would be when their father announced *two* engagements over breakfast! Yes, it would be worth the wait just to see the look on her sister's face.

While Europa paced the bedroom, her lavender-blue woolen skirt whispering over the floor, Persia did up the last of the pewter buttons at the neck of her red-and-black Scots plaid dress. She brushed her hair out and let it hang to her waist. Her fingers were trembling far too much to pin it up or even to braid it.

"I'm ready," she announced.

Europa turned to her younger sister, and suddenly her haughty composure slipped. Tears brimmed in her eyes and her lower lip quivered.

"Europa, whatever is the matter?" Persia cried. She'd never seen her sister this way.

"Oh, I'm so frightened!"

The next instant she flung herself into Persia's arms and let out a sob.

"Frightened of what? Surely not of Seton. You love him, don't you?"

Europa, fighting for control, stepped away. "Love him? Why, I haven't the vaguest idea whether I love him or not. I'm *used* to him. I know what to expect from him. But *love*? Actually, I've never put much stock in that emotion. It just comes naturally after marriage, I'd always supposed. That's not troubling me in the least."

Persia stared at her sister, unable to form an answer. How often she had felt jealous of Europa, but not this time. It must be dreadful not to know about love!

"Then why are you so upset?"

The lip commenced trembling again. "Supposing Father said no. I'm practically an old maid now. And if I had to start all over, allowing some new suitor to woo me, I'd be gray and arthritic before he proposed."

"Oh, bilge water!" Persia replied, using her favorite sailor's curse. "Is that all that's bothering you? You know Mother is all for this match. She wouldn't have allowed Father to turn down Seton's proposal."

"I certainly hope you're right." Europa laughed suddenly, and the tears dried at the same instant. "You know, for a time I thought it might be interesting to try taking Zachariah Hazzard from you. But then I saw that he was only toying with your affections anyway and I lost interest. Still, he came in handy. Seton certainly jumped right in to pop the question when he saw me making eyes at Zack. He's a fascinating man all right. But he'll never be a one-woman man. Why, I imagine he has girls in ports all over the world. No, he's not the sort for me. And you're lucky you're too young to have your head turned by his pretty talk. Because that's all he is . . . *talk*! The woman who agrees to marry him will have a *glorious* wedding night and then live in misery for the rest of her life.'' She cocked her head and gave Persia a sly smile. ''Still, it might be worth the pain to spend just one night in those great, muscled arms of his, to be the victim of his ravenous kisses from dark till dawn. He is such an *animal*!'' She finished in a husky whisper, with a shudder of delicious dread.

Persia was seething inside, but she managed to control her outward emotions. So Zack was all talk, was he? Well, Europa would soon find out the truth of the matter. As for the glory of her wedding night, she could hardly wait. But there would be no misery following it, only love . . . to the grave and beyond. And her mind was made up. She and Zack would move to Boston and make their home there once they were married. She refused to spend the rest of her life having Europa remind her daily that she, too, had been held in Zack's arms and had tasted his kisses. In Persia's eyes, such vicious, sisterly taunts would be grounds for murder.

The tinkling of a silver bell signaled the sisters that breakfast was about to be served. Persia was still furious as they started downstairs, but with every step her racing pulses calmed. Europa would soon have to eat her words with her oatmeal for breakfast. Oh, what a joy that would be!

Both girls sensed good news in the air the moment they reached the floor below. Breakfast was not set in the little blue room off the kitchen where they usually ate their morning meal, but in the formal dining room with its lovely mural. Once more, elegant lace graced the table and the best china lay gleaming in place. Persia and Europa exchanged knowing glances as they entered.

''Well, ladies, won't you be seated?'' their father invited, a merry gleam in his silver-gray eyes.

There wasn't the slightest hint of the smell of oatmeal in the air. Instead, the mouth-watering aroma of cinnamon and apples drifted in from the kitchen. Dried apples were a well-guarded commodity in the Whiddington household, kept in barrels in the root cellar. Although the Whiddingtons had a fine orchard out back, most of the fruit it produced was sent on the ice ships to India, where fresh frozen apples brought their weight in silver. The bright red beauties were too dear to be consumed in large quantities by the household.

"Apple muffins? Why, Mother, what's the special occasion?" Europa sounded as if she hadn't the faintest idea in the world of what was going on.

"Sit down, dear, and let Fletcher serve us. Then your father has a few words to say."

Fletcher eased his way into the room like a blue-clad specter, gliding soundlessly from one chair to the next, serving the prized apple muffins with fresh-churned butter, apple jelly, and thick slabs of honey-cured ham. As much as the girls would have wished it, he could not be rushed. The native servant was as methodical as the tattooed pattern dotting his face. Finally, he poured coffee, tea, and chocolate, then disappeared.

"Well, Captain?" Victoria was back to the usual formality she used in front of family, friends, and strangers alike. This might be the same dear husband who had caressed her to frenetic ecstasy in the privacy of their bedroom last night, but now the door to that room was shut, and he was no longer "darling," but "Captain Whiddington" to his wife. "I believe it is time."

He chewed the rest of his muffin with excruciating care, swallowed, then reached for his coffee cup and drank deeply. Persia and Europa both sat bolt upright in their chairs, their mouths closed to food until they heard what their father had to say.

As usual on such auspicious occasions, the captain was not one to get straight to the point. He was a firm believer in preamble at the speaker's rostrum.

He rose slowly, pushing out from the table, and stood, gripping his napkin as if it were the helm of a ship.

"Ladies . . . ahem. It is with great pleasure and, I admit, no small amount of fatherly pride that I make this announcement to you today. It has been evident for some time now that you, Europa, are the most sought-after maiden in all of York County. I have lost track over the years of how many suitors have come and gone. This doesn't surprise me. You were a cunning child, and now you are a fetching woman—as bright as you are beautiful." He paused and smiled directly at her.

"Thank you, Father." Europa's voice was as thin as a cobweb.

"No thanks to me, my dear girl. Your mother deserves all the credit." He extended a hand toward his wife as if he expected her to rise and take a bow. Victoria only smiled and nodded encouragement for him to get on with it. He did, turning to his other daughter.

"Persia, my dear, I see that you are following in your lovely sister's footsteps. In that gown you were wearing yesterday—"

"*Captain!*" Victoria interrupted, a scold in her voice.

He cleared his throat once more before he continued. "Your day will come all too soon, I fear."

Persia frowned. Something about his tone and her mother's interruption set her on edge. What was he saying? That her time had not come yet? It certainly sounded that way. Had he accepted Seton's petition for Europa's hand, but rejected Zack's offer for hers? But why? It had to be her age. Still, she was no younger than her mother had been when she had married. Suddenly she felt faint and sick. Her father's next words didn't help the feeling any.

"Europa, last night a young man came to me and asked for your hand in marriage. Although your mother had some reservations at first, she has now agreed."

Now Europa was frowning. Her mother had pushed for her engagement to Seton Holloway all along. Why would she suddenly raise objections? And *what objections*?

"We have discussed the matter thoroughly and are in

total agreement that the man is worthy of such a lovely and gracious wife. He assured me that even when he is away you will be well taken care of."

"*Away?*" Europa said the word without even being conscious that she had spoken aloud.

"Why, of course, my dear. You don't expect that he would give up his life's calling to marry? That would be demanding too much, even of a man who loves you so dearly."

"But Seton never goes anywhere. He's *always* right here. Sometimes I wish he would go down to Boston or up to Portland . . . anywhere, just to give me a few hours to myself. Where on earth is he planning to go, Father?"

Captain Whiddington's face had gone pale and blank. He looked to his wife. Her smile had vanished.

"Europa dear," Victoria said gently, "I'm afraid we aren't talking about Seton."

"But didn't he speak to you last night, Father?"

"Yes. About nautical law and some other gibberish that I never even listened to. The man is as dull as last month's news. He seemed never to get to the point of what he wanted to say. The thought struck me that he came to speak to me on one subject, then lost his nerve and fabricated questions that didn't interest him any more than they interested me."

"Then what are you talking about, Father?" Europa's voice was nearing an hysterical pitch.

"Your *engagement,* of course!"

"To whom, if not Seton?" she demanded, rising from her chair.

"To Zachariah Hazzard! He came to me last night and asked to marry you, Europa."

Persia felt the words stab through her heart as if her father had just thrown one of Fletcher's native spears and struck his target point-blank. *No!* There had been some mistake! Zack couldn't have asked for Europa's hand. He loved *her!*

Persia turned to Europa for salvation. She knew her sister cared nothing for Zack. She would laugh at the mistake their father had made and set the record straight. Tonight, when Zack came to dinner, they would *all* have a good laugh over it. But when she looked at her sister, Europa was smiling and nodding.

"So, he really did it! I actually thought he was joking when he mentioned marriage to me, Father."

"Are you telling me that Mr. Hazzard's proposal is some sort of jest? I won't have it! No one plays my daughter for a fool or me, either!"

"Calm yourself, dear. Remember your heart," Victoria cautioned.

"Damn my heart! I'll have the man keel-hauled!"

"Father, don't get so upset," Europa said pleasantly. "I'll gladly marry Zachariah Hazzard. He's quite the most fascinating man I've ever met."

Persia's intake of breath was heard all around the table.

Her mother rushed to her and patted her back. "Dear, are you all right? Don't eat your muffin so fast. You'll choke on it."

Persia was choking all right, but not on an apple muffin. Suddenly, Europa had stolen her black-and-white puppy all over again. Only this time the pain was far worse. This pain was excruciating, soul-rending, *killing*. In that awful moment, a tale Fletcher had told her came to mind. He had said that in some ancient culture the native priests sacrificed their victims to the gods by cutting out their hearts with razor-sharp ceremonial knives while the poor human creatures still lived. She had been both fascinated and horrified at the very idea. Now she knew how those victims of antiquity had felt. She knew their pain . . . their hopeless anguish.

"Persia dear, are you ill?" asked her mother.

Before Persia could answer, Europa piped up, "Don't worry about her, Mother. I'm afraid she's suffering a sudden attack of envy. She's had quite a crush on Zachariah since first they met." She turned her glowing but false smile on her sister. "Think of it, Persia darling, you'll have Zack as a big brother now. Won't that be wonderful? And your time will come, as Father said.

Perhaps Seton might be right for you. He's very nice, even if he isn't the most romantic fellow in the world. And he's always told me that he's quite fond of you."

Fond? Fond! Persia would have laughed if she hadn't felt so numb. Fond was hardly what she wanted from a husband! Zachariah Hazzard was the man she wanted, and she wanted a husband's love from him, not a brother's!

If his marriage to Europa was to take place right away, before he went back to sea, she wouldn't even have a chance to talk to him—to find out what happened—before the wheels were set into irreversible motion. Once her mother had spoken to Reverend Osgood and reserved the date for the church, there would be no calling it off. And she was sure to visit the minister this very morning with so many preparations to make in such a short time.

"Excuse me, please," Persia said, her mind set now on a course of action. "I feel like taking a walk."

"But dear, it's snowing out," her mother protested. "And besides, you haven't even eaten your apple muffin."

"Let Europa take it," she replied, wanting to add, *She takes everything else that belongs to me.*

But this time she really couldn't fault her sister. Something had gone amiss. Europa could only be blamed for accepting what was handed to her.

As Persia headed for Jefferd's Tavern, wrapped in her fur-lined cape and bent forward against the wind-whipped snow, her mind churned with uncertainty. Maybe Europa was right. Maybe Zack was all talk. Could it be that he had taken her to his room the day before hoping to seduce her? Was he the type of man who wanted to sample the charms of both sisters before he decided which one, if either, he wanted?

No! He had decided. And apparently Europa was his choice. Maybe there wasn't anything she could do about it, but she could certainly give him a piece of her mind.

The tavern was all quiet at this still early hour. She slipped in unnoticed and hurried past the front desk, where the innkeeper slumped in his chair dozing. With all the stealth she could muster, she made her way to the second floor. No one was astir in the hallway. She all but ran to Zack's door. She tried the knob and found it unlocked. In the blink of an eye she was inside his room with the door closed and latched behind her.

There he was, sleeping. Propriety forced her eyes away for a moment, but curiosity brought them back. He lay sprawled in his bed—naked, she could tell. His bare chest with its forest of golden hair rose and fell softly with each breath he took. The sheet had slipped nearly to his groin, and she saw that his belly was well-furred as well, his man-hair growing in an inverted triangle that pointed to a pulsing rise under the sheet. One long leg dangled off the side of the narrow mattress, the toes of his foot almost touching the floor. His hair was tousled, but his face calm.

She felt such a need to go to him, to kiss the slightly parted lips, to stroke the hair on his chest, to touch the white belly exposed to her eyes for the first time. Then she remembered Europa, and all tenderness fled her body and mind. How could he have hurt her so?

Suddenly, she felt as if another presence had entered the room. Gooseflesh crawled up her arms, and her face felt hot for no discernible reason. She looked from his belly to his face. His eyes were open, devouring her with an odd sort of hunger.

"Persia?" His voice was raspy with sleep. "What are you doing here?"

"I had to come. To tell you what I think of you. *You bastard!*" The words quivered from her lips, and her eyes misted with tears. "Don't try to defend what you've done. I may be young, but I'm not stupid, Zachariah Hazzard!"

He propped up on one elbow and squinted at her. "Persia, what the hell are you talking about?"

Her smile held no humor. "Oh, that's the way you plan to play it, eh? 'Persia love, there's been a terrible mistake!' "

"I'm not playing anything any particular way. I'd just

like you to tell me what's going on. It's not often that I'm awakened by a woman who looks as if she might kill me on half a dare.''

He noticed all at once that his body was nearly exposed to her and yanked up the thin sheet. It did little to disguise the full erection aroused by the sight of her in his waking vision.

"I could kill you! Don't doubt it for an instant!" She grabbed up his knife from the table near the door and started toward him. "Maybe I should just castrate you like Father has Fletcher do our little bullies. That would put an end to your fun and games!"

Zack was backing up in bed, pulling the sheet with him.

"Persia darling, tell me what I've done. Even a condemned man has a right to know what he's accused of."

"Did you speak to Father last night?"

"Yes. I did. Just as I promised I would."

"And did you ask for *my* hand?"

"Of course. And he agreed."

"Liar!" She screamed the word and plunged toward him, the knife upheld in her right hand.

Zack caught her wrist just in time. Whether she would have really driven it home through his heart neither of them would ever know. The sharp steel weapon clattered to the floor and Persia collapsed, sobbing against his chest. He held her, stroking her hair, murmuring to her, trying to console her and to find out what had happened. But she was incoherent, hysterical.

"Persia, Persia," he crooned. "My love, my darling. What can I do?"

Her hand crept over his chest. She twined her fingertips through the golden forest of hair, not noticing that when by chance she stroked his paps he stiffened, moaned, and thrust toward her.

"Love me, Zack," she whispered between sobs. "Love me as if I were the only woman in the world you cared for."

"But you *are*, Persia!"

"Make me believe it." Her warm, moist breath tingled over his chest, and one tear dropped down, stinging his flesh.

He caught her up in his arms, searching her tear-salted mouth with his tongue. She quivered against him and sighed into his open mouth.

This was the moment . . . the *woman* . . . he had been dreaming of all his life. He held her with one arm and with the other began unbuttoning her bodice. She made no protest at first, but when his hand found her bare breast, she pulled away and stared at him with anger in her flashing blue eyes.

"It doesn't matter to you, does it?"

"*What* doesn't matter to me?" he asked in a voice strangled with passion. God, how could she do this to him—lead him on and then turn away?

"The woman's body beneath yours? One's as good as another, isn't it? The more the merrier, that's what Europa says."

"Europa? What the hell does she have to do with this?"

"*Everything!* You find her appealing, don't you?"

Still holding her with the front of her gown parted so that her breasts were bared before him, he shrugged. "I won't deny it. What man would?"

"The man I'm going to marry would!"

"Be reasonable, Persia. I'm only human. I may look at Europa with appreciative eyes, but it's *you* I love. If I didn't love you, I promise you, you would be stripped and beneath me this very moment."

She stared down at him, trying to read the very depths of his eyes. Her own were filled with uncertainty.

"But Father thinks when you spoke to him last night that you were asking to marry Europa."

"*Europa?* But that's impossible!"

"Didn't you say *which* sister you were asking for?"

"Of course I did!" He frowned and clawed a hand through his wild shock of golden hair, uncertain. "I *must* have. And besides, Seton spoke to your father before I did. He asked for Europa's hand."

"So we thought, but he lost his nerve. You must not

have mentioned my name. Since Seton didn't ask for
Europa, Father would have turned you down if you'd
asked for me. She has to marry before I will be allowed
to.''

"But he gave us his blessing, Persia."

She shook her head sadly, the fight gone out of her.
"He gave you and *Europa* his blessing."

Zack closed his arms around her and Persia sank into
them, sobbing against his bare chest as the full impact of
the hopeless situation crushed her with it's weight.

Stroking her hair, he murmured softly, "Darling, it's
nothing to be so upset about. All we have to do is go to
your father and tell him there's been a mistake."

"No, it's not that simple. Europa has accepted the
engagement. She *wants* to marry you! She said you were
the most fascinating man she'd ever met."

He drew back, smiling. "Did she really?"

Until that moment, Persia thought she had no heart
left, but his words and their tone tore the rest of it from
her living flesh.

"You want her, don't you?" she accused, pulling
away.

"I want *you,* Persia love. *Only you!*"

He clasped her about the waist, bringing her lips up to
his. For the next moment, Persia gloried in his velvet
exploration of the secret depths of her mouth. How easy
it was for him to turn pain to pleasure! Did such a talent
come through broad experience?

"What are we going to do, Zack?"

He turned her, pressing her back against the mattress,
and stared down into her tear-streaked face. One hand
caught at the hem of her skirts, moving the full fabric up
her stockinged leg. "We could seal our bargain now.
They wouldn't *dare* refuse to marry us!"

It was tempting, but she shoved his urgent hand away.
"A child born prematurely? You think that's the answer? No, Zack. I won't have it that way, as much as I
want you."

She was lying there on her back, the bodice of her
dress spread wide before his eager eyes . . . and lips.

Slowly, he lowered his head and touched one strutting nipple with his tongue. She winced with pleasure and surprise. Her tender flesh crinkled at the unexpected contact. He pressed his assault, drawing the sensitive bud between his lips. Persia gasped softly.

"Shall I stop?" There was mischief in his voice as his breath tingled her tender flesh.

"Yes!" The answer was firm and strong, even if she didn't mean it.

He looked down into her eyes, his own dark and seething with desire. "Your first lesson as my wife, Persia dear. *Never* invade my bedroom first thing in the morning unless you are in the mood for love."

Holding her shoulders firmly against the pillow, Zack took his morning sup at her breasts. She tossed and twisted beneath him, dying a thousand small deaths to have him take the rest of her. Her flesh ached with desire, and she murmured his name, pleading over and over again, but Zack contented himself with what lay naked before him. The rest, he resolved, would wait for their wedding night.

When he could take no more without crumbling that resolve, he pushed himself away and closed her bodice with an air of finality. Slowly, while Persia stared up at him with pleading eyes, he refastened each and every one of her twenty pewter buttons.

"There! You're safe now, my darling."

She raised up on her elbows and gave him a half smile. "Am I?"

"What do you mean?"

"The only way I'll be safe, Zachariah Hazzard, is as your wife. Which will it be? Are you going to marry me or Europa?"

"Well-l-l . . . let's say I'll give you my answer at supper tonight."

She caught him about the neck with sharp nails and answered, "Let's say I'll do you bodily harm if you don't marry *me*!"

He fended her off. "All right! All right! Now I have a threat for you. Either you leave in the next two minutes and let me get my pants on, or you're going to find out, in the most shocking and exciting way, exactly what I put into them!"

Persia was very tempted to stay but didn't dare. Gathering herself in her cloak, she hurried out, secure in the knowledge that all misunderstandings would be righted by evening and *she*, not Europa, would be Zachariah Hazzard's betrothed.

As she hurried down the stairs, not looking where she was going, she literally ran into the innkeeper. He caught her shoulders with his beefy hands for a moment to steady her.

"I'm sorry," she mumbled.

"Quite all right, Miss Whiddington."

She stared. How did the man know her name?

"Been visiting upstairs again with your gentleman friend, Mr. Hazzard?" He gave her a broad wink and a highly suggestive grin. "You needn't worry that I know all about your little rendezvous. I'm deaf, dumb, and blind when it comes to such delicate matters."

Persia gasped in horror. She had to defend her honor and her innocence. "It so happens that Mr. Hazzard and I are about to be married."

The man bowed to her and chuckled. "Then let me be the first to congratulate you. You'll be snagging a rich man."

"Zachariah? *Rich?*"

"Indeed! He made a wager that it seems he's won."

"What kind of wager?"

The man squinted at her, considering. "Well, now that's for him to tell. But he'll be collecting a small fortune for his amorous efforts."

Persia stared at the man, and her mouth dropped open. *A wager?* What kind of games was Zack playing?

She pushed her way past the innkeeper, confused and more upset than ever. She couldn't go home yet. She was still too angry to face Europa. She hurried blindly down Main Street, letting the snow whip her face with its cleansing coolness.

After all that had happened, did she still love Zack? Did she still want to be his wife?

Yes! The answer was as clear to her as the memory of the sensations aroused by his mouth suckling gently at her breasts.

CHAPTER TEN

ZACK sat on the edge of his bed, listening to the tap-tap of Persia's footsteps fade down the hallway. He leaned forward, staring at the wide pine boards of the floor, but not really seeing anything. His body might be here, but his mind was miles away, trying to figure out where he had gone wrong. Thinking back over it, he realized that the past days had been like a dream . . . *a nightmare, perhaps?*

What was he doing here? If he'd only gone on to Boston with most of his shipmates, he'd be happily drinking in some tavern, a willing doxy at his beck and call and not a care in the world. He stared down at himself and the hopeless erection throbbing against his belly.

"Damn!" he swore.

Matters had been bad enough before Persia had presented herself this morning. Her kisses, the honeyed taste of her breasts, even her anger had aroused him. If only *honor* hadn't chosen that very moment to rear its bothersome head!

He got up and dashed his face with icy water from the ironstone pitcher on the washstand, shivering at the shock. The fire in the grate had gone out during the night and the room was cold. Distractedly, he poked at the few glowing embers. The thought came to mind that their deep-burning glow was the color of Persia's hair in bright sunlight.

"Persia, Persia," he murmured, tossing his head back to stare at the gray ceiling. "What am I going to do about us?"

He could, of course, take the coward's way out—leave the whole mess behind and leave Quoddy Cove forever. The thought was suddenly appealing. No doubts. No worries. Just take off and ship out as quickly as possible. Yes! That was what he'd do! Damned if he needed *two* women fighting over him!

So resolved, he dressed quickly and shoved the remainder of his belongings into his duffelbag. He went to the shaving stand to collect his toilet articles. That would do it. Then he could go.

But standing there in front of the mirror, he caught sight of his own accusing eyes staring at him. Something clutched in his guts. He was no coward! And Persia Whiddington . . . sweet, innocent Persia . . . didn't deserve such treatment from any man.

He shied away from the dark blaze of his eyes in the glass. Who was he trying to fool? It wasn't for Persia that he must stay. It was for himself. He loved her. He wanted her. And he meant to have her! But he couldn't wait all day to untangle this mess. He would go to the Whiddington house now and straighten out the misunderstanding. *This very minute!*

As he dashed past the front desk, the innkeeper said, "My congratulations, Mr. Hazzard! When's the wedding to be?"

He never looked at the man but called out in answer, "As soon as I settle the question of which sister I'm to marry!"

He didn't see the man's eyebrows shoot up in sur-

prise as he slammed out the door into the snowy
morning.

The distance between Tavern Hill and Gay Street
took Zack only minutes to cover. The wind caught his
coat and whipped it like a scarlet sail as he mounted the
steps to the front door of the Whiddington residence. He
had not yet pounded the knocker when the door opened
to him.

"Why, Zachariah! You're hours early. But never mind.
We'll have some time together this way."

The woman before him looked enchanting, her heart-
shaped face glowing like shell pearl inside the ebony
frame of her hair. The scent of summer's first roses
emanated from the folds of her lace-jaboted bosom, and
her hand felt like warm silk as it touched his almost
shyly.

"Europa, I'm here to see your father." His tone was
all business, never mind roses and soft, scented flesh.

"Oh!" She sounded disappointed and taken aback. "I
naturally assumed, under the circumstances, that you'd
come to see me."

"Those *circumstances* are exactly what I must speak
to your father about."

She offered him such an apologetic and alluring smile
that some of the stiffness melted from his body.

"I'm sorry, but Father is meeting with some other
investors down at the docks this morning. Some tiresome business about buying an ice ship, I believe. Mother's in quite a state over the whole matter. She can't see
and neither can I how anyone can do other than lose a
fortune by trying to transport ice to hot climates."

Europa's whole speech was accompanied by a fluttering
of eyelashes and lace ruffles. She continued stroking the
back of Zack's hand while she spoke. By the time she
finished and took a gasping little breath, she had Zack
under her spell.

"There's a fortune to be made in ice, Europa. Hasn't
your father ever explained the business to you?"

She smiled sweetly. "Oh, he's tried. But my poor
brain is filled with feathers, I'm afraid, when it comes to

business. Perhaps if you told me all about it, I would understand.''

"Of course, if you like.''

They were still standing in the open doorway. Europa glanced back down the hall to make sure no one was about before she opened the door wide for him to enter. She was safe. Her father wouldn't be back for hours. Her mother was upstairs lying down. And Fletcher was in the back of the house helping the cook get everything ready for their special dinner. As for Persia, Europa had no idea where she might be. She hadn't yet come back from her walk. But should she happen in on them, that would be perfectly all right. Persia would have to get used to seeing them together . . . for the rest of her life.

"Do come in, Zack. You must be freezing.''

Europa showed him to the parlor across the hall from her father's study. She had been in there since breakfast, poring over fashion books, trying to decide which wedding gown would best suit her. The walls were a rosy hue, enhanced by the cheery light of the fire. As the captain's study was a man's room, so the parlor was decorated to suit a lady's tastes with its pastel brocades and gilt-framed watercolors of flowers and birds in delicate tints.

"Come sit here beside me. It seems we have a lot to talk about, *darling*.'' She said the word pointedly, to let him know she knew.

Zack tried to keep his distance on the cramped love seat, but there was not that much space and Europa seemed set on intimate contact.

"We do have a lot to talk about. You're right. There has been a mistake. That's why I'm here. I hope you'll understand, Europa.''

She turned to him, her eyes fairly gleaming, and cradled his cold cheeks in her soft palms. "Darling, the only mistake was in my thinking that I could ever marry a man like Seton Holloway. You are the one I want . . . the one I'm going to marry. I knew the night at the pond that you were only playing up to Persia to get to me. Then when you risked your life to save me, why, I

would have agreed to marry you that very evening!''
She looked up at him shyly, peeking through her lashes.
''The way you held me in your arms as you carried
me . . . the way you kissed me later when we were alone.
I could tell you wanted me, Zack, just as much as I
wanted you.''

He was tempted to point out to her that she was
half-frozen and nearly drowned when he took her in his
arms and that *she* had kissed him, not the other way
around. But the gentleman somewhere deep down inside
refused to allow him to be so blunt with her.

''Well, it all paid off, my dearest,'' she continued.
''You have me now, and we're quite alone. Let's not
waste our time on needless chatter. You may kiss me.''

''Europa . . .'' he began, but her lips pressed his,
sealing off his protests.

He sat still and unresponsive for a time, willing himself not to be aroused by the pressure of her lips, the
scents of roses and female flesh filling his nostrils, or
even the warmth of her breasts against his chest. But
when her hand found his thigh and worked its way to the
throbbing crotch of his trousers, he had no will to fight
her. His arms came up, drawing her harder against him.
She parted her lips, inviting him to enter. Still maintain-
ing some willpower, he refused. It was no use. An
instant later, her velvety tongue was gliding over his
lips, parting them, seeking what she longed for.

Summoning more strength than he thought he possessed, Zack pulled back. ''No, Europa! This isn't right!''

Her eyes were veiled by half-closed lids. Her lips, still
parted, looked red, puffy, and inviting. While he watched,
one of her slender hands went to her throat, unbuttoning
the lace with slow, seductive ease. Soon Zack found
himself staring at the deep, satiny valley between her
firm breasts. She reached for his hand and pressed his
palm against her chest.

''*This* isn't right, Zack darling?'' she said in a husky
voice. ''Then you show me what is.''

He groaned deep in his throat and allowed his hand to
be guided from the valley to the soft mountain peak just

beyond. Europa murmured a sigh and leaned into him, increasing the pressure on her breast.

"My darling," she gasped, tearing at her bodice to bare more of herself to him. "Oh, I know how you've wanted me! You've been dreaming of this moment since you first saw me. And I knew even then that someday you would take me. It was there in your eyes, even as it is this very moment."

Suddenly, she was like a female animal in heat—clutching at him, begging him, offering to allow him to take unspeakable liberties with her body. Quite frankly, he was shocked. Drawing away, he caught her by the shoulders and shook her roughly.

"Europa, what's come over you? What do you think you're doing? I didn't come here for this. I came to tell you that there was a mistake made last night. I asked your father for *Persia's* hand, not yours. You're a beautiful, desirable woman, but it's your sister I love."

If she had reminded him of an animal before, the effect now was even more startling. Her eyes narrowed. Her breath escaped with a hissing sound. Her teeth were clenched in rage.

He was still clutching her shoulders, trying to keep her away from him, when the door to the parlor opened. His hands dropped away from her and he stood up abruptly. But not before Persia, her face drained of all color, saw them huddled on the love seat together with Europa's bodice gaping wide in invitation.

"Persia, wait! It's not what you're thinking!" He charged after her, but she was already out of the house and racing down the icy walk.

"Please darling!" he shouted. "Let me explain."

She didn't answer, only ran faster and faster, finally darting off the road into a stand of evergreens. Therein lay the undoing of her flight. The deeper snow in the woods slowed her pace. And instead of losing Zack in the maze of trees, she left a deep trail for him to follow.

When he caught up with her and grabbed her from behind, she screamed. The piercing sound dislodged a wet clump of snow from a branch overhead, showering them both with its white coldness. Persia fought him with every ounce of strength she had—pounding his chest, kicking and biting. But Zack would not release her.

Finally, tripping over a log, Persia fell backward, toppling Zack with her. On her back, pressed deep into the soft snow, she could no longer resist him. His weight held her to the spot where she had fallen. One ironlike hand gripped her wrists so that she couldn't claw his face. She could only lie there, gasping and sobbing, wanting nothing so much as to be far, far away, hidden from his probing gaze and his lying tongue forever. But even as she tried to shrug away, his mouth came down and took hers with a force of passion she had never known. It was as if he were putting his brand on her for all time—letting her know that he would do as he damn well pleased and she could like it or go to hell.

But following close on the heels of his near brutal kiss, his words to her were surprisingly gentle. "Persia, please, don't fight me. Listen to me. I love you!"

She ceased struggling, but the hard lines of anguish in her face did not soften.

"I don't believe you." Her words were as lifeless as if they had been spoken from the grave.

"You *must*! What you saw back there at the house means nothing, I tell you."

"*Nothing?* Then I suppose what you're saying is that if someone had walked in on the two of us this morning while I lay half-naked in your embrace in your bed, that would also have meant nothing!"

"No, no, no!" He shook his head furiously. "That's not what I mean at all. There is nothing between your sister and me. I love *you* and only you. And I intend to marry you."

She still refused to be convinced. "Oh, I understand now. Zachariah Hazzard doesn't have to love a woman to undress her and take liberties with her. He is above such plebeian codes of morality. He is free to do what he will with *any* woman—his fiancée, his fiancée's sister, or any other female in any port of the world,'' she said sarcastically.

Even though he was plainly in the wrong and realized that Persia had a right to her anger, her words wounded him deeply. He was new at being in love and he'd managed it badly. But even ignorance and stupidity shouldn't be dealt with so harshly. Once, as a new seaman, he had been tied to the mast and flogged for insubordination, receiving the usual ten lashes with a cat-o'-nine-tails. On occasion in his most terrible nightmares, he still relived that burning, flesh-rending, bone-deep pain. But even that paled before the anguish of the punishment Persia was inflicting.

Still, there must be some way to make her forgive him. Zack knew his only convincing defense would be to accuse Europa of the seduction, but he had never been one to hide behind a woman's skirts. If Persia truly loved him, she would have to believe him and forgive. If she didn't, well . . .

Releasing his hold on her wrists, he rose from her and offered a hand to help her up. She eyed him suspiciously.

''You'll freeze lying there in the snow,'' he said matter-of-factly. ''Get up.''

She took his hand warily. When she was standing upright, Zack turned and started walking away.

She watched him go for a time before she cried out, ''Wait!''

He turned back toward her but didn't speak. His face looked exactly like the fierce, carved figurehead of Neptune she had seen once on a ship's prow. She waited for him to say something until it became apparent that he would waste no more words on her.

''Where are you going, Zack?''

''Boston.''

Her heart sank as she asked in a trembling voice, ''When?''

''As soon as possible. This evening, I would imagine. I'm out of money, but I have a gold watch I can sell to settle up my bill at Jefferd's and to hire a sleigh and team.''

In her present agitated state, Persia didn't remember that the innkeeper had told her Zack was a rich man.

"Zack?"

"Yes?" His voice was as stony as his face.

"Did you really mean it . . . what you said?"

"Mean what, Persia?" As much as he longed to, he couldn't allow himself to make this easy for her. If he softened now, all would be lost.

"About loving me, wanting to marry me?"

"If you have to ask, then maybe I shouldn't marry you."

He might as well have been in a high-stakes poker game. His heart was thundering. His arms were aching to hold her. Words of love were fighting to get past his tight lips. But he must hold his tongue and breast his cards. He'd tried reasoning with her; it hadn't worked. Now he must stick to his bluff, play his cards as if he couldn't care less whether he won her or lost her. Make her come to him. That was the only way.

She looked down at the toes of her boots, sunken deep into the snow. "You mean you'd still consider it?"

A long, unnerving silence followed before he answered, "I might. But there would be conditions."

His words tore at her tender heart. *Conditions!* She knew what that meant. He was about to tell her that even if he married her, there would be other women and she must resign herself to that fact or else. Could she live with that? She looked up at him suddenly, and her eyes filled with tears. She would have to live with his conditions because she certainly couldn't live *without* him.

"I understand." A tearful whisper was all she could manage. "May I ask one favor?"

His own heart was breaking as he stared at the misery in her eyes, misery that *he* had put there. "Ask."

"Just don't ever tell me about your other women. Let me imagine that I'm the only one."

He could take no more. He rushed to Persia and

swept her into his arms, kissing the tears from her cheeks, hugging the breath from her body, crooning her name over and over. When he set her on her feet once more, he cupped her cold face in his hands and kissed her lips very gently.

"Oh, Persia my love, I'll never tell you about any other women because there won't be any others. Not ever! How could I look at anyone else with you as my wife?"

"Zack darling," she sobbed. "Hold me. Please hold me. Don't ever let me go!"

Walking back to town hand in hand, they made their plans swiftly but carefully. They would have to play a painful charade until Persia's family was sleeping that night. There was no way either of them could get out of the "engagement dinner" without arousing suspicion. Afterward, when all was quiet, Persia would slip out to meet Zack. He would be waiting outside for her with the hired sleigh to speed away to Boston. Once they were far away and safe, they would be married.

It all sounded so simple. But Persia found herself cringing with pain that evening as her father toasted the happy couple—Zack and Europa. There was talk of the wedding plans. As Persia had supposed she would, her mother had already met with Reverend Osgood to set a date. Europa had sketched the gown she wanted. And, as an added surprise, Captain Whiddington had struck a deal that day with Frederick Tudor, New England's first and foremost ice merchant. He and Tudor, along with two other investors, were having a new ice ship built.

A beaming Asa Whiddington raised his glass of port to his prospective son-in-law. "I'd like to drink a toast to her new captain—Zachariah Hazzard."

A twitter went round the table.

"Oh, it won't be right away, mind you. The ship will be several years in the building with finances and supplies what they are. But someday, mark my words, Captain Zachariah Hazzard will sail her to Bombay and back!"

Persia was careful not to let Europa get Zack alone all evening. When her sister urged Zack outside to view the rising moon now that the snow had stopped falling, Persia trotted along, chattering nervously all the way. When Europa lured him into the parlor to look at sketches of her wedding ensemble, Zack's true intended scurried in to see for herself and to offer her unwanted comments.

Still, there was nothing Persia could do about the good-night kiss. She was sent off to bed, followed immediately by her mother and father, so that Europa and Zack could be left alone in the hallway for a few intimate words.

Persia crept to the landing above and hid in the shadows, peering between the carved spindles of the banister. She was forced to bite her lip to keep from protesting as she watched Europa insinuate herself into Zack's arms and raise her parted lips for his kiss. The only thing that saved her sister from a good hair pulling was the fact that Persia knew this would be the *last* kiss between the two of them.

Finally, she breathed a huge sigh of relief as Zack extracted himself from Europa's clutches and made a quick exit into the night. Persia hurried back to her room so that Europa wouldn't know she'd been spying on them.

She was all packed, and dressed in her warmest clothes. The old stagecoach route from Quoddy Cove to Boston was roughly one hundred miles. They would be riding all night and well into the next day, something over twelve hours even with the wind at their backs. They could stop off at the stage inn in Portsmouth for the night, if the weather turned foul. But from the looks of it, the snow was over. And the bright moon would be reflecting off the large, granite milestones erected by George Washington along the old Colonial Post road all the way to Boston.

Persia heard Europa's door close. There had been no other sound upstairs since her mother and father had come up. Still, she must wait a while and make sure everyone was sleeping before she ventured downstairs.

She took a seat at her writing table and drew out paper from one of its pigeonholes. Dipping her pen in the ink flask, she poised it to write a convincing explanation of her actions. But no words came. How do you tell your parents that you are running away to be married to your sister's fiancé? After several attempts at consoling them—none at all convincing, even to the author—Persia scribbled a simple, straightforward message:

> *Dear Mother, Father, and Europa,*
> *I am leaving tonight with Zack. We are in love and will be married by the time you read this. Forgive me. I never meant to hurt any of you.*
>
> > *Your loving and obedient daughter,*
> > *Persia*

On rereading her brief message, she took her pen, dipped it once more, and scratched out the word "obedient." Tears brimmed in her eyes as she folded the paper neatly three times. She would give anything if it didn't have to be this way. But she had no other choice.

As she was wiping her pen point on the chamois cloth to put it away, she heard a low whistle from outside. Every nerve in her body jumped, then tingled.

"Zack!" she murmured.

Grabbing up her portmanteau, she opened her door and peered out. Only low lights glimmered in the hallway below. Everyone was sleeping. She tiptoed out, casting one last look at her childhood bed and Lady Guinevere, staring wide-eyed at her, before she turned and started down the stairs.

Zack would be waiting out back in the leafless, frozen orchard. She turned toward the kitchen, gaining speed with every step. Only a short distance now and she would be free—free to live and love as she pleased. She gave the swinging door a sharp shove and hurried through, only to run into an immovable object. Her breath froze.

"Miss Persia?" inquired a deep, English-accented voice.

Persia clasped a hand to her heart and breathed in with relief. "Fletcher! You scared me half to death!"

The servant's hard-surfaced tattooed face, shadowed grotesquely in the dim lamplight, was enough to frighten anyone who didn't know him into heart failure. But Persia knew the man and had adored him all her life.

"You are leaving with him." This was a statement, not a question. Fletcher often exhibited an unnerving second sight.

"Yes, and you mustn't try to stop me," she commanded, then begged, *"Please!"*

"I would not. He is your man. Go to him. And take this with you." He pressed an English gold piece into the palm of her right hand. "My father gave it to me many years ago. It has guarded me all my life and brought me good fortune. But you need it more now."

A sudden rush of affection for the strange savage took possession of her. She hugged him soundly, realizing that tears were flooding her eyes once more.

"Take care of them, Fletcher. Try to make them understand. I love him so much. I can't let him go to Boston without me."

Another shrill whistle echoed in the night.

Fletcher led her to the door. "Go to your man, Miss Persia. And the gods be with you."

Zack was waiting just outside to sweep her into his arms and then into the sleigh. She felt breathless. Her whole body tingled with anticipation. She kissed his hands, his face, his lips.

"Zack, my darling Zack! We've done it!"

Already he was whipping the horses down the road as they snuggled close beneath a warm robe of bear fur.

He laughed into the cold wind—a gleeful sound in the still night. "Ah, my love, we haven't done *half* of it yet. Just you wait!"

The team of chestnut horses clattered onto a covered bridge at the edge of town. All went black suddenly as the light of the moon was obscured by the roof overhead. Zack reined in the pair and gathered Persia into his arms, his lips only a breath away from hers.

"I've heard tell around town that this is called the 'kissing bridge.' Right or wrong?"

"Right," she answered, trembling as one of his hands found her breast and squeezed gently.

"Well?"

His lips captured hers and she melted against him. She had worried that she might be cold on this midnight ride. But Zack dispelled that fear. How could the chill of the night air bother her when his lips were boiling the blood in her veins?

After caressing her mouth and her breasts thoroughly, Zack whipped up the team. They sped off down the icy, moon-silvered road.

But there were many kissing bridges along the way, and just as many kisses, each one more fervent and stirring than the one before it.

By the tenth milestone, any apprehension Persia might have felt about her hasty decision to run away and marry Zack had melted like a snowbank in bright May sunshine.

They rode on into the night, her head upon his chest, his arm around her, his hand fondling her breast. At each of the granite markers along the way, Zack proclaimed his love for her anew. Persia snuggled against him, sublimely happy and certain that there was not a luckier woman on the face of the earth. Or a woman who was more in love.

CHAPTER ELEVEN

BEFORE they arrived the next day, the early winter twilight had crept over Boston, shrouding church steeples and ships' masts alike in its pearly gloom. Persia and Zack were both happy, but cold, weary, and ready for a hot meal and a soft bed.

"We'll find a preacher first thing," Zack said, slowing the horses as they neared the Boston wharves.

In spite of herself, Persia yawned. "Can't we wait until tomorrow, Zack? I'd like to remember my wedding. If we're married this evening, I'm afraid I might sleep through the whole ceremony."

He stared down at her, his eyes narrowing with uncertainty. He didn't want to wait. All these long, cold miles, he had imagined taking his bride and had relished the inviting fantasies that tripped through his mind.

Persia smiled up at him sleepily and touched one downturned corner of his mouth with a fingertip. "Don't look so gloomy, darling. It's not as if I were trying to put you off forever. We'll be together."

Misinterpreting her words, Zack stopped worrying and

smiled. "You're right. Tomorrow is soon enough for the vows. There's no need to rush our wedding now. The bed comes first."

The sleigh moved slowly now that they were in the city. Other vehicles crowded the way, while boys on crude sleds and makeshift skates frolicked about, presenting a traffic hazard.

Persia watched all this, but only with a passing interest. Her mind was as weary as her body, and sleep remained uppermost in her thoughts. "Where will we stay, Zack? Father prefers the United States Hotel. He says it has dignity and is the perfect hostelry for East India captains."

Zack laughed. "You forget, my darling, that I'm not a captain yet. And I may never be—not on your father's ship, at least, since I'm marrying the wrong daughter. I always stop at the Tail of the Devil Tavern when I'm ashore. See, there it is, just ahead." He pointed toward a dingy, two-story building that seemed as worn out as Persia herself. The filth-smeared windows gave the impression of tired eyes, and a weathered red sign groaning in the wind dangled askew. The painted board depicted Lucifer's head, tail, and pitchfork. "It's a favorite among my shipmates."

"A *tavern*?" Persia, with a growing sense of unease, watched as a sailor, none too steady on his feet, ushered a painted strumpet through the front entrance. "Oh, I couldn't!"

The dismay in Persia's tone surprised him. But seeing the seaman and his woman entering, he realized she was absolutely right. One of the small rooms over his favorite drinking establishment was hardly the place to take the woman he loved. Still, they couldn't go trooping into the United States Hotel. Common seamen simply didn't rub elbows with Boston's captains. It wasn't done.

He placed a hand on her arm understandingly. "I know of a small boarding house on Charter Street. It's nothing fancy, but it's clean and quiet. Would that suit you better, darling?"

Relief flooded through her. "That sounds delightful.

Actually, any respectable place will do as long as it has a bed,'' she said with a sigh.

Once again, Zack was thinking one thing while Persia was saying another. His heart gave a loud thump at her words, and he felt a hot surge in his groin. So, she was as anxious as he!

Unbeknownst to Persia, Zack wrote their names in the registry as ''Mr. and Mrs. Z. Hazzard.'' It wasn't until the landlady showed them upstairs and unlocked the door that Persia realized they would be sharing one room with one bed in it. But she could hardly protest when the prim, white-haired woman said, ''I'm sure you and your mister will find this comfortable, Mrs. Hazzard. The supper he's asked for will be brought to your room in half an hour or so. Let me know if I can be of any other assistance.''

''Thank you, Mrs. Wilkes.'' Persia closed the door firmly behind her and turned toward Zack, arching a brow. ''Where are *you* going to sleep?''

He grinned and flopped down on the bed, his weight making the ropes groan in complaint. ''Right here, unless you would prefer this side. It makes no difference to me. Starboard or port. Either one will suit me fine.''

''Zack, we're *not* married yet!'' Persia's face was flaming and her stomach churning. Her head and heart told her that a few words spoken over them and a few hours made no difference. But her stern New England upbringing rebelled against the idea of sharing a bed with a man—even the man she loved and wanted desperately—while she was still unmarried.

''You're the one who wanted to wait till tomorrow, Persia. Don't blame me.''

''But I thought you were getting *two* rooms for tonight.''

Suddenly she stopped. Back in Maine, Zack had said he was out of money. Maybe there wasn't enough left to take a second room. She decided instantly not to offer any more objections. The last thing she wanted to do was embarrass him. She could handle the situation and Zack. He would simply have to understand that she intended to remain a virgin until she was a bride. He was probably only testing her, anyway.

She smiled at the thought of sharing an intimate dinner with him in front of the cozy fireplace. And she decided she definitely would not fight him off if he tried to steal a kiss or two. In fact, their embraces along the old Colonial Post Road had only whetted her appetite for more. She was shameless! Even now, she found herself thinking back to their time alone in his room at Jefferd's. The thoughts filled her with a languid warmth that flowed from her heart into her breasts, then down to the center of her longing and on to her legs, making them nearly too weak to support her. There was something almost reverent about the way Zack's hands caressed her body, the way he kissed her. She supposed that was as it should be when a man and a woman loved each other.

"This will do nicely," she said, offering him a warm smile.

"I'm glad it suits you, darling. I think it's perfect."

She glanced about to see what provisions for modesty the tiny room offered and was relieved to spy a Chinese folding screen in one corner. She would have to change clothes, and she wasn't sure she could pry Zack from the comfortable bed. It would still be a trial to undress with him in the same room, but she could do it with the screen to shield her from his prying eyes.

She noted that the hard glare of ironstone flashed at her from under the edge of the bed—a chamber pot. Although it was standard fare in any bedroom, using it would prove most embarrassing. After she was changed, she would find some excuse to go down and speak to Mrs. Wilkes. Surely the boarding house was equipped with an indoor privy. If not, she would simply be forced to follow the path out back.

"Our supper will be here soon, Persia."

"I know," she answered, trying to work up the nerve to go behind the screen and begin removing her rumpled clothes in order to wash up.

"I'm hungry, aren't you?"

He had been lying on the bed, his hands clasped

behind his head. Slowly, he rose and came toward her. She noted that certain gleam in his dark eyes. It was always there just before he kissed her.

He stopped at the foot of the bed, about six feet away from her. He stood there, hands on hips and his boots planted wide apart. Although she tried to keep her eyes on his face, her gaze strayed maddeningly down, taking full measure of the bulge in his tight trousers. Quickly, she forced her eyes away.

"Come here," he commanded.

"Zack, I really need to freshen up. I'm a mess."

"Persia, I said *come here*!"

Slowly, as if drawn by the steel glare of his gaze, she moved toward him. She stood directly before him, feeling her flesh tingle as his eyes roved over her. He was fondling her without ever laying a hand on her. How could he make her feel this way with only his eyes?

His hands came up to her neck and began unfastening her cloak. He drew it from her shoulders and tossed it aside.

"There! Isn't that better?"

"Yes," she murmured. "It is warm in here." It was warm all right, but the heat wasn't coming from the meager blaze in the hearth.

Suddenly, his eyes caught the firelight and seemed to flare with light. Or *was* it a reflection? Persia couldn't be sure. Perhaps the brilliance came from within. He gripped her shoulders and massaged them gently.

"Persia, do you realize what's happening to us?"

His question confused her. She wasn't even sure what was happening inside her, much less what he was thinking and feeling. She answered him with a shake of her head.

"The two of us are about to become one living, breathing entity. If birth is a miracle, a man and woman finding each other is even more of one. Deep, deep down, I know that you and I have been meant for each other since the day we were born. But what if I had decided not to stay over in Maine? What if you caught a cold and hadn't come to the skating pond? What if your family had caught you slipping out last night and forced you to remain at home instead of leaving with me?''

"No . . . n-no!'' she gasped. "None of those things could have happened.'' She didn't want to think of such horrors.

He looked solemn now as he stared into her eyes and said, "Oh, yes, they could have. Fate is the trickiest thing in the world. I've known a lot of people who never found the ones they were meant for. That includes my own mother. I never thought I would. Hell, I never thought there was a woman for me! Then . . . *boom!* . . . you dropped right out of the heavens, riding the northern lights down to where I was standing.'' He shook his head and grinned from ear to ear. "Don't you see what I'm saying? I'm so stunned and so happy and so much in love I don't even know how to act. We're something really special. We have to keep it that way . . . *always.*''

He cupped her face in his hands and brought her lips toward his. Persia felt tears welling up in her eyes. He was right! Whatever force or configuration of the stars had brought them together had been powered by a fragile form of energy. The miracle had happened. Now it was up to the two of them to make it succeed.

"Oh, Zack,'' she whispered. But he silenced anything else she might have said.

His lips held hers prisoner for only a moment, then he drew away. The next instant, she felt the velvet of his tongue tracing her mouth. His whiskers grazed her, like raw Chinese silk abrading her skin, but she loved the feeling. She clung to him, forgetting all else except that she wanted this man with a fierce longing that turned her blood to fire and her will to water.

"God in heaven, Persia, I love you!'' His words sounded like a prayer.

"Zack, oh, Zack . . .'' It was all she could manage.

His hands were at the bodice of her dress, fumbling with its closing, when a knock at the door wrenched them apart. Zack muttered a curse under his breath before he turned and strode stiffly to open it to Mrs. Wilkes.

"I do hope I'm not disturbing you and the missus, Mr. Hazzard. But supper will be a bit longer than I expected," she said apologetically. "Abigail, the cook, burned the bread. There's another batch in the oven this very minute. It won't be long now. I am sorry."

"That's quite all right, Mrs. Wilkes. My wife wants to freshen up before we eat, anyway."

Zack closed the door and turned back to Persia, his mouth quirked in a smile of amused anticipation. "Well?"

"Well what?"

"I thought you meant to bathe and change."

"Oh, that." Her face took on a rosy hue. "I don't suppose you'd want to wait outside?"

He shook his head, the same smile curving the gold of his mustache. "Not a chance, my love. I've been waiting anxiously for this moment. I know how you feel, but not how you look."

"Very well, then." She began undoing her bodice, a mischievous gleam dancing in her blue eyes, and Zack's smile broadened.

"You just lie there on the bed, darling, and enjoy. I won't take long."

He lounged down, all attention. "You take as long as you like. Supper will keep."

When Persia stretched out the screen with its brightly painted birds and flowers, she saw Zack's grin die a sudden death and almost chuckled aloud. So, he wanted to see his bride, did he? Well, he would just have to wait a bit.

Scurrying behind her shield and putting Zack from her mind, Persia began striping off her soiled clothes. One by one, she tossed her wrinkled garments over the top edge of the screen until she stood naked and shivering slightly. She poured warm water from the pitcher into the washbowl and began bathing.

"How are you doing back there?"

Zack's voice, coming to her from so near while she stood without a stitch on, caused her to cover herself with her hands in an automatic response. Then she smiled at the ludicrous action.

"I'm doing quite well, thank you. And how about you?"

Zack's voice held a husky tone that sent a tremor through her whole body as he answered, "Oh, I couldn't be better . . . not unless you were over here beside me."

"Zack!" she cried, shocked.

But she would have been even more shocked had she known why he was doing well on the bed. The screen might protect every inch of her from his direct view, but a mirror on the side wall offered him a perfect reflection of her rose-tipped breasts, shapely buttocks, well-turned thighs, and now and again a glimpse of the flaming triangle of hair between them. She was a marvel from head to toe. He'd never viewed any woman but Mahianna in light without clothes. He longed to tear the screen away, scoop her into his arms, and throw her to the bed—unprotected by the wall of clothes she normally wore. But he knew he could do no such thing. For the time being, he would have to enjoy from a distance, in silence. If she knew he was watching her, she would be furious and ashamed, as silly as that seemed to him.

When, at last, Persia came out from behind the screen, she was wearing a high-collared dress, much the same as the one she had worn when she'd left home.

"I thought you were going to get ready for bed," Zack said.

She offered him a nervous smile. "I am ready. I'll sleep in my clothes tonight."

With a sharp twinge of disappointment, he suddenly realized her plan. He would not be able to lay a finger on her until after they were married. Had he guessed as much, he would have dragged her off to a preacher the moment they hit Boston.

Another knock sounded—Mrs. Wilkes delivering their supper. She set it on a small table before the fire.

"There now. Is there anything else I can bring you?"

Zack noted that she had not forgotten the jug of wine he'd ordered with their meal. "No, thank you. This will do us just fine."

"Have a good night, then," she answered.

"Oh, we will," Zack assured her with more certainty in his voice than Persia enjoyed hearing.

Persia found she was ravenous. The boiled beef and cabbage warmed her and filled her. And the musky, smoke-flavored wine wasn't bad, either. At first, she refused to drink it. She'd never tasted spirits before in her life. But when Zack insisted that they toast their coming marriage, she had little choice in the matter. The wine burned on the first taste, but she soon grew accustomed to it, and the liquid caressed her tongue and throat like warm velvet.

When they had finished their supper, some wine remained. Zack, toying with her fingers, poured her another glass.

Her eyes, misted with a film of exhaustion and drink, gazed down at his hands on hers. She watched his strong, thick fingers walk up her hand to her wrist and then climb back down again. The sight gave her a strange feeling. She knew exactly where he was touching her, she was watching it happen. However, the sensations he aroused did not manifest themselves in her fingers, but deep down inside her, tugging at some inner cord that seemed attached to her nipples, stomach, and womb. It was all very disconcerting, but she could not deny that she loved the feeling. She smiled.

"Persia?" He squeezed the fingers he had been fondling.

"Yes, Zack."

Slowly, she tilted her face up to his. She had no idea the urgent message the blaze in her blue eyes was transmitting. *She* knew what she was feeling . . . wanting. But she was sure the secret was her own. Never would she have dreamed of coming right out and saying to Zack: "I want you to make love to me." That would have been unthinkable!

Silence reigned between them for some time. Their locked gazes and the impact of their hands touching were far too weighty to leave enough breath for speech. The small clock on the mantel chimed twelve times in the stillness.

"Time to come to bed now, Persia," Zack said softly. "This is our wedding day."

They rose as one and went to the opposite sides of the bed. Together, without a word, they turned down the red-and-blue quilt. Zack moved about the room, blowing out the lamps, until only the soft glow of the fire repelled the darkness of midnight.

Persia sat on the side of the bed and removed her shoes. Then she stretched out, tucking her skirts close in under her, and pulled the quilt up to her chin. She lay tense, waiting, too nervous to turn her head to see what Zack was doing. She heard one boot drop, then another. Her heart gave a rapid flutter. When his weight sagged down the mattress next to her, she had to bite her lip to keep from crying out. He stretched out beside her but didn't touch her. She felt as if she were stranded in some unsettling suspension of time and space—needing him, wanting him, but terrified that she might betray herself.

"Persia? You aren't asleep, are you?" His hand touched hers, and she jumped.

"N-no!" she cried. "I'm awake."

"Good."

Good? Why good? she wondered. What was he thinking? What was this *stranger* going to do to her?

His finger traced along the line of her lower lip with no more pressure than a feather. She trembled and a burning sensation throbbed in her lower body.

"Do you want to go to sleep, Persia?"

"Zack!" She turned toward him abruptly, and the finger that had been tormenting her lip tangled in her hair. "You know I'm exhausted. We both are. We need sleep."

"Persia, darling." His lips were so close to her face now that his warm breath bathed her flesh. "I need something else more than I need sleep. *I need you!*"

When his mouth met hers, there was a pleading urgency in his kiss. It fired her own need, as hard as she tried to fight it. Still holding her prisoner with his lips, Zack let his hands move to her bodice. Her breasts

strained to meet his touch. With dexterous fingers, he
freed her from her gown, lifting her in his arms to pull it
away.

"Oh, Zack, please . . ."

The "no" that would have completed her sentence
lodged in her throat as his moist lips searched down her
neck to her breasts and found the nipple they sought,
peaked and ready to be taken.

White fire flashed through her body, and she arched
to meet him, thrusting with her hips. She hardly noticed
when he dragged her camisole and petticoats down,
finally shoving them away with one foot. All she knew
was that explosions of desire were igniting deep inside
her. Shaking her. Pounding her. Turning her from a
woman of flesh and blood into a trembling mass of
molten longing.

She moaned his name and twisted beneath him, thrusting once more with such force that the sharp edge of his
teeth grazed her tender nipple. Then Zack's hands were
on her hips, pressing her down, holding her in place.
The fact that she could no longer move only aroused her
more. Her head tossed from side to side. Her fists
clenched and unclenched in his thick hair.

He gave up his hold on the aching tip of her breast for
a moment. The cessation of feeling gave her a sudden
sense of having been cut loose from a mooring. She
drifted, breathless, glad that he had released her, but
yearning to be taken in tow once more.

She reached out to him. Sometime, she wasn't sure
when, he had shed his clothes. Her hands touched his
bare chest. Her fingers curled through his tight man-
hair. She felt him shudder against her open palms.

"Oh, Persia," he moaned. "Oh, dear God!"

He found her parted lips in the darkness and suckled
her mouth in much the same tantalizing fashion that he
had tortured her nipple moments before. It was almost
more than she could endure. She wanted to scream and
cry and beg. But she could do nothing. He held her
voice prisoner in the same manner that he was captor of
her body and her senses.

Without even knowing it, Persia's hands were doing things to Zack that seemed calculated to drive him mad with need. Her nervous fingertips seemed unable to rest—roaming over his chest before moving up his neck to entwine themselves in his hair once more. Tiring of that, they strayed over his ears and down once more to his shoulders, where they paused, nails digging into his flesh. As her body strained against his and her breasts kissed his chest, her silken, nomadic hands discovered the small of his back, drawing tight little circles on his skin. His buttocks tightened, awaiting the next assault. When it came, her hands cupping and releasing in a torturous rhythm, he rose from her, throwing his head back with a primeval cry of need.

When Zack leaped off the bed, Persia's shock and disappointment were total. He had brought her to this fiery threshold. How could he leave her there, with the very quick of her longing exposed to the painful night?

"Zack," she whispered in a trembling voice. "Come back to me. *Please.*"

But in the next moment she realized that he hadn't left her. He was kneeling beside the bed. His warm hands cradled her foot, massaging the arch, stroking her toes. She relaxed once more under his tender ministrations. But she let her guard down too soon. A moment later, she felt his tongue glide up her sole. She gasped and struggled, but his hold on her ankle was like iron. As he sucked at her toes, stroking the soft flesh between them with his tongue, Persia felt the heat of his touch shoot up her legs, making them weak. And such a burning ache scourged her body that she could hardly stand the pain, although it was not pain at all.

When he had done with both feet, he climbed onto the bed, kneeling between her legs. With his palms flat on the inside of her thighs, he moved up to her slowly, parting a way for what was to come. At the moment his hands met at the V where her limbs joined her body, his fingers touched the fiery tip of her womanhood and she cried out. He ignored her pleas and let his fingers dip into the warm fountain he had discovered, exploring the

cavern at his leisure. He touched and stroked, teased
and soothed, until Persia was beyond speech, beyond
hearing, almost beyond breathing. All she could do was
feel. And the feelings were beyond her powers of
description.

"Persia . . . my love . . . my bride."

Zack's words seemed to come from far away. She was
conscious only of an emptiness gnawing at the very
heart and soul of her. An emptiness that demanded to be
filled lest it consume her totally.

Then he was there once more—his lips on hers, his
hands on her shoulders, his weight bearing her down.
But she became aware of a new pressure, hot and throbbing, between her thighs. She knew somehow that their
moment had come. Instinctively, her muscles tightened,
refusing him entry. One hand moved from her shoulder
down and down. He raised his hips. He stroked the
aching juncture where all her yearning seemed to come
together and intensify. Her muscles relaxed. She parted
a way for him.

He filled her. A single thrust and it was done. Pain
and shock gave way to a sense of wholeness, oneness.
Her body seemed to expand to accommodate his size
and strength. Flesh and fire mingled. She thought she
heard music from far away—or was it coming from
inside her body as it sang out its delight, its ecstasy?

He stroked slowly at first, allowing her to catch his
rhythm and match it with her own. But as they rode the
dark sea of love together, the tempest within them both
grew and accelerated until they were whirling, flying,
speeding through uncharted waters to a fragrant, distant
shore. But would they ever arrive? Was the blissful
peace her mind and body sought only a shimmering
mirage on some far horizon?

"Darling, I love you," Zack whispered.

The words beckoned her toward that calm port. But
first they had to cross the reef, the tumultuous white
water that called its siren song to them even as it menaced.

Suddenly, Persia knew she was there. Warm foam
broke over her while cold spray stung her body. The sun

blazed down, searing her through and through. She clung to Zack, begging him not to let go until they were safely on the shore. He offered a deeper, surer thrust to let her know he was with her. They rode it out together until finally they burst through, onto shimmering white sands—exhausted, sated, euphoric.

Persia fell back among the pillows, her whole body tingling. Her breath came in short bursts. Zack eased himself out of her and rested his damp head on her breasts, sucking gently and whispering quiet endearments to the woman he loved . . . the woman who was his wife now, even if no vows had been exchanged.

"Zack," she murmured at last. "I do love you. You'll never doubt that, will you?"

"Not if you're always the way you've been tonight, darling."

"I didn't quite believe what you said earlier about being born for each other, but now I'm sure it's true."

He laughed softly and pressed his palm to her belly, feeling it quiver at his touch. "It's true all right! Thank heavens I didn't decide to marry Europa to collect my bet. All the gold in the world couldn't have paid me well enough if I'd lost you in the bargain."

Persia was frowning. Marry Europa? Had he ever really considered it? And what bet was he talking about?

"What do you mean, Zack?"

He kissed her breast and then her lips before he answered, "Nothing, my love. Nothing at all. Come here." He gathered her into his arms. "I want you close in case I wake up and need your love."

Zack fell asleep soon after that with his lips close to hers and his body pressed so tightly against her own that she could feel his every heartbeat. But Persia couldn't sleep.

His mention of Europa had been ill-timed, and it had brought with it a rush of guilt and pain and doubt. What would her selfish actions mean to the members of her family? Would they ever forgive her for running away . . . for creating such a scandal?

The wondrous world she had discovered in Zack's

arms drifted to the background of her mind, replaced by black doubts and fears. And when she slept at last, her dreams were peopled with grotesques and monsters from the deep.

Even when Zack awoke near dawn and drew her beneath him to take her once more, her troubled mind denied her the ecstasy she had experienced earlier. Chilly from the heart outward, she climbed from the bed to put on the nightgown she'd packed for her wedding night.

Afterward she slept, worn out by Zack's loving thrusts and the jabbing of a thousand devils' pitchforks.

CHAPTER TWELVE

PERSIA stayed in bed most of the next day. Sometime near noon, Zack woke her with a loving caress. But when she glanced at the window, she wasn't sure of the hour. The sky looked brown as the sun's faint rays tried to pierce the driving, wet snow. Frost fogged the panes. The wind howled at the eaves like demons searching for lost souls.

"I'm going out for a while, darling."

She accepted Zack's kiss on her cheek, then pulled the quilt up to her ears once more. It wasn't until she heard the door slam behind him that she came fully to her senses. She sat up and called his name, but it was too late. She was left alone to face the full impact of what had happened the night before. It weighed heavily on her conscience.

This wasn't the way she had planned or imagined it would be. She and Zack were meant for each other. Their love was perfect and right and perhaps even holy. So why should she be feeling this nagging guilt about

Europa? Why had he even mentioned her sister's name the night before?

She sat up in bed and stared out the window without even seeing the snowstorm raging in silence. Her body felt heavy. Her limbs ached. Her brain burned around the edges as if what she and Zack had done last night had somehow tainted her mind and soiled her soul. She shivered at the thought.

"No!" she said in quiet desperation. "No, it wasn't wrong. It couldn't have been."

The longer Zack was gone, the blacker the mood that took hold of her. She watched the hands of the little china clock on the mantel creep slowly around its enameled face. Once, twice, a third time. The storm inside her raged as furiously as the one outside the window. She bathed, she dressed, she nibbled absently at the light lunch the landlady brought up to her. Slowly, what little light there had been to the day began to fade. And with the coming of darkness, her fears grew larger and more ominous.

When, at last, she heard Zack's footsteps approaching the door, she leaped up from her chair and ran to meet him.

"Oh, Zack!" Even to her own ears, her voice sounded almost hysterical.

"Darling, what's wrong?" He held her away from him and smoothed back a lock of hair from her forehead.

She looked up at him, taking in the warm concern in his brown eyes and the crease of worry marring his brow. He was there. He was real. She was touching him at this very moment—gripping his damp sleeves with tense fingers. What did she have to be anxious about? Suddenly, all her hours of apprehension seemed a silly waste of time and energy.

She forced a laugh, but it was thin, with an edge of nervousness still clinging to it. "Nothing's wrong. It's just . . . I'm just . . . I'm glad you're back. The storm . . . it's getting dark, " she stammered.

"My little Persia." He pulled her to his chest and cradled her there, rocking gently as if she were a terrified child. "I've heard of women being afraid of the sound and fury of a thunderstorm, but never a snowstorm."

"I know. I'm just being silly. And now I feel horribly foolish. Forget it, darling." She buried her face against his chest and hugged him tightly.

But Zack refused to let the matter drop. Slipping his hand under her chin, he raised her face to his and kissed her lips gently. There was no mistaking the deep shadow of worry in her usually clear eyes.

"*Something* is wrong. Out with it! There'll be no secrets between us, Persia Whiddington!"

She shuddered slightly at the mention of secrets. Without realizing it, Zack had hit upon the exact nature of the problem. She didn't want there to be secrets between them, either. And although her guilt at running away troubled her deeply, she understood in that moment that Zack had been keeping something from her. *That* was what bothered her most.

"I agree, Zack. We should tell each other everything."

Silence followed her quiet statement. Zack thought she was working up the nerve to tell him what was troubling her, while in truth she was waiting for him to speak.

Finally she said, "Well?"

"Well what?"

She didn't want to have to pry it out of him. She wanted him to give to her freely, as she had given to him the night before. "Please, Zack, tell me what you meant . . . about the bet."

Persia watched a tense nerve throb at his temple. His eyes narrowed for the briefest moment just before his smile broadened to almost unnatural brightness.

"Oh, that's nothing. I shouldn't even have mentioned it."

She kept her voice steady and quiet. "But you *did* mention it. Now, please explain."

"Darling, there really isn't time for that," he replied. "I've spoken to a minister who's willing to marry us within the hour. But we have to hurry. He's several blocks away, and the storm is getting worse. If we don't leave now, he'll be gone by the time we get to the church."

Zack's words only served to bring out Persia's stubborn streak. She dug in almost visibly, shaking her head slowly as she continued to stare at him.

"If we miss him today, he can marry us tomorrow. After last night, a few hours or a few days will make little difference."

Zack felt the smile melt from his face. He knew he was frowning, but he couldn't help his sour expression. What was she saying? Had she changed her mind?

He cursed himself silently for having mentioned the bet at all. If he tried to explain at this point, he could only make matters worse. Still, he refused to begin their relationship with a lie. The wager had been the foolish act of a sailor ashore with too much rum in his belly after a long, dry voyage. Surely Persia would understand that. After all, her own father was a man of the sea.

Zack took her hands in his and led her to a chair by the fire.

"I'll tell you what you want to know, but first you have to promise me something."

"What?"

"Promise me that you will try to understand and forgive me. Promise?"

A new kind of terror gripped her. Could it be that more had gone on between Zack and Europa than she had been led to believe? No! She couldn't allow herself to imagine such thoughts. Still, if that was what Zack was about to tell her, she wasn't sure she could live with the knowledge. She almost told him to forget her demands.

Don't explain anything. Don't even talk. Just take me to the church. Marry me! Love me! The words were screaming in her brain and trembling on the tip of her tongue, begging to be spoken aloud, but she couldn't bring herself to say them.

"How can I promise I'll understand when I have no

idea what you're about to tell me?" She reached out and touched his hand. "I promise I'll try, though."

Her answer was not what Zack had hoped for, but there was no turning back now.

He cleared his throat and began. "Persia, that first night I met you, I did something utterly stupid. Instead of going straight up and getting the rest I needed when I got to the tavern, I stopped off in the taproom. One of my shipmates was there and called me to join him. Mind you, I'm not blaming Enrico in any way. He tried to keep me in line. But there was a lot of backslapping and drink buying. They were all calling me a hero for saving Europa."

Seeing Persia wince at the mere mention of her sister's name, Zack realized his task was going to be more difficult than he had imagined. But he plunged on.

"To make a long story short, one of the other men in the bar bet me a fortune that I couldn't get either you or Europa to agree to marry me within the week."

Persia felt a stab at her heart and caught her breath audibly. Tears of anger and disappointment pressed just behind her eyes. She wanted to scream at him, claw his face, tear out his eyes. But most of all, *she wanted to die*.

How could any man have played such a cruel trick? To convince her to leave her family and run away with him. To tell her he loved her. To make love to her, using as his carrot on a stick his promise to marry her. And she, like the little fool she was, had gone right along with his plan. *What* was she supposed to do now?

Her voice came in a cold rush of fury. "So you tried to convince Europa to go along with your scheme, and when that failed you turned to her silly little sister."

"Persia, no!" Zack cried. He dropped to his knees before her, gripping her arms. "No, that's not the way it was! I never wanted Europa. I was trapped into the wager, in over my head before I even realized what the other fellow was proposing. By then, it was too late. The tavernkeeper had my purse—every cent I had in the world. I knew I loved you. Granted, it might have taken me longer to get around to asking you to marry me had it not been for the bet. But you have to believe me when I tell you that I would have. I love you!''

Tears blurred her vision and she was aware of his face only as a dark form, silhouetted against the bright orange of the flames in the fireplace.

"Do you love me more than you love Europa?''

"Yes! I mean, *no*! I don't love Europa. I never even thought I could love her.''

"But you wagered that you could marry *either* of us. Why was that? If I hadn't agreed, would you then have tried to convince my sister to be your wife? What kind of man are you? I don't know you at all!''

Her hysterics unnerved him. He rose and tried to take her in his arms to kiss her, but she turned her face away.

Feeling defeated, he said hesitantly, "Persia, I'm the man who loves you . . . who loves *only* you.'' He tried once more to capture her lips.

"Please don't!''

He moved away. "Then you refuse to understand?''

"It's not that I refuse. I simply *can't* understand such manipulation in the name of love.''

"But it wasn't manipulation. I did love you. I *do love you*! The bet was simply something that happened, but had nothing really to do with the feelings I had for you already. Please, Persia, you have to believe me. Don't do this to us.''

"*Me*? What have *I* done? I've allowed myself to fall right into your trap. You should be grateful that you haven't yet married me. You're a rich man because of me. And since we aren't married, you won't have to support a wife.''

"But I *want* to marry you!''

"But maybe I don't want to marry you any longer, Zachariah Hazzard!'' She had been screaming, wanting to hurt him as he had hurt her. But now her voice went quiet and cold.

"All right!'' His tone echoed hers. He was not a man to beg. He had asked Persia and she had refused him. It hurt. "I'm going to leave you for a time and let you

think all this through. But I want you to remember how
it was last night . . . how our bodies sang in tune and
our hearts beat against one another . . . how I fit into
you as if you were the mold and I had been cast from it.
It was good, Persia. You can't deny that. I don't want to
lose you. But I won't make a further fool of myself by
staying here and groveling. If you decide you still want
to be my wife, I'll be at the Tail of the Devil Tavern.
Remember, we have only an hour before the preacher
leaves. If you haven't come by then, I'll go. And I won't
bother you again.''

Persia stared up at him, her mouth open and her eyes
wide. She knew Zack was everything she wanted. But
how could she give in to such an ultimatum?

He hesitated at the door, waiting for her to speak. But
her lips drew tightly together to close off any further
communication. She refused even to look at him.

He shrugged and turned the doorknob. ''There's money
in my satchel if you decide you want to take the stage
back to Maine.''

''Take your satchel with you. I don't want your ill-
won money!'' she raged. Then, remembering Fletcher's
gold piece, she added, ''I can pay my own way home.''

''Whatever you say.'' His voice sounded dull and
hopeless as he picked up his bag to leave. ''Just remember this before you decide: I love you and I always
will.''

The click of the latch as he left was like a shot fired
point-blank at her heart. Persia wanted to slump to the
floor and sob the ache away. But there wasn't time. She
glanced at the clock: four twenty-five. Her whole destiny would be decided in the next hour.

''So little time,'' she murmured. But still, she could
not make herself move. She sat where Zack had left
her—stock still in the chair, staring into the fire.

The only sound in the room was the ticking of the
clock.

Zack jammed his fists deep into his pockets and bent
his bare head into the windblown snow. His boots

crunched loudly, caving in the ice-crusted drifts in great, angry bites. He was too angry and hurt and frustrated to feel the chill bite of the blizzard against his face. But the sensation he was most aware of was an aching emptiness.

"Dammit," he growled down into the collar of his coat. "You stupid, arrogant bastard!"

Already he sensed that his show of stubbornness would get him nowhere with Persia. He should have handled everything differently. He should have explained about the bet before he ever brought her to Boston . . . before he ever made love to her. Then, if she'd turned him away, at least it wouldn't have hurt so. He'd never have known what he was missing. He would have shipped out, and the memory of her engraved on his heart would have blurred with time. But after last night his very soul bore her mark. If she did not come to him, he would no doubt have other women in the coming years. But he knew he would never enjoy them as he had before. Not after last night. Not after Persia.

He shouldered his way through the door of the tavern. The small room was thick with smoke from pipes and cigars and a faulty flue in the chimney. His eyes smarted, and the tears he was too much a man to shed over Persia now oozed from the corners of his eyes. He swiped at them angrily and shouted at the barkeep, "Goddammit, Clancey! I thought you were going to get that fireplace fixed before I made port again."

"Zachariah Hazzard?" bellowed the big-bellied man presiding behind the rough bar. "Can it be you, man? In the flesh? I was sure by now you'd been swallowed up by one of them monsters of the deep—or at the very least caught the pox and been put ashore to fester and die. Welcome home! Will you have an ale?"

"Aye! In the biggest tankard you've got."

Their conversation was soon interrupted as two lean and leathery drifters in dark clothes came in and sidled up to the far end of the bar, speaking between themselves in whispers. After a quick glance in their direction, Zack went back to sipping his ale. He noticed that the same doxy he and Persia had seen entering the Tail of the Devil the day before was here again, but with a different sailor. He watched as she rose and took the man's arm. She nodded to Zack as she came toward the bar to get a key for one of the rooms upstairs.

"I'll be down within the hour, mate, if you're in need of anything."

The woman looked worn and well used. No doubt she was far younger than her lined and painted face made her seem. She had probably been pretty not many years back. And her cultured accent told Zack that she came from a higher class than most of the women of her profession. The thought flickered through his mind that perhaps she had once lived in a big white house similar to the one on Gay Street, and that perhaps it was some sailor's misdeeds that had brought her down to this level. He felt a pang of guilt. He should go back to the boarding house and try to reason with Persia. If she still refused to marry him, it was his duty to see her safely home again before they parted.

"Well, love?" the woman prompted. "Shall I meet you in an hour?"

"Thank you, but no. I already have an engagement."

She arched a painted brow and drew her bright lips into a pout. "I'm the best on this side of Boston. Are you sure?"

"I'm sure," Zack answered. "I'm getting married this afternoon. But thanks anyway."

A strange look of envy crossed the woman's face for the briefest instant before her forced smile returned. "Well, here's a kiss for luck, mate. And should your bride be a bit tender a few days from now, you know where to find me."

After a quick peck at his cheek, the woman escorted her customer up the stairs and out of sight.

Zack glanced at his pocketwatch. Four forty-seven and still no Persia. He would give her until five-fifteen. If she hadn't come by then, he would go back to their room and offer to see her home. He placed the watch on the bar, inside one of the damp circles left by his tankard. He sipped his ale and watched, mesmerized, as the hands crept slowly toward five.

So fascinated did Zack become with the physical passing of time, he never noticed when the barkeep spoke quietly to the disreputable-looking pair down the bar and then pointed in his direction before accepting their gold. He didn't see the two men, their unshaven faces shadowed by brimmed hats, as they sidled ever closer to where he stood. It was not until he felt a hard hand on his arm that he looked up. But by then it was too late.

His last vision contained an odd collection of impressions: half the grinning face of the barkeep hidden behind a thick, hairy arm raised over him, and fingers with dirty nails clenched around a length of black pipe. These things in his line of sight meant nothing; they had no connection in his mind. By the time he heard the crack of his own skull, felt the trickle of blood down his face, and then the pain, all vision had faded.

One final word escaped with his breath as he sank to the floor: "Persia."

When the little clock chimed five, bringing Persia out of her daze of misery, she realized it was almost too late. Whatever demons had plagued her, allowing her to let Zack leave, had also used up precious time with their tormenting folly.

Of course she wanted to marry Zack! She couldn't just let him walk out of her life. She loved him! He was her man!

Like a slender birch tree suddenly whipped by a brisk wind, Persia whirled out of her chair and into action, her heart light and her mind made up. Zack was absolutely right—they were meant for each other. And their love was strong enough to weather any storm. She would not allow a ridiculous wager, jealousy of her sister, family ties, or even her own stubbornness to stand in the way of her happiness.

Quickly she changed into warmer clothes, brushed her hair, and pulled on her coat, aware that only minutes remained before Zack would leave the Tail of the Devil and she might never see him again. She refused to let herself feel anxious. She would make it in time, and they would go directly to the minister. An hour from now, they would be Mr. and Mrs. Zachariah Hazzard. And before the night was through, she would once again know his love and his body and the ecstasy that both brought her.

The landlady tried to stop her for a chat—asking if they would be in for supper and if there was anything else they needed—but Persia was uncharacteristically brusque with the woman, sweeping past her with hardly a word. Outside, the storm still raged, but she made haste as best she could. The ache of the cold cut through her body, making every step painful, every breath labored.

How far was the Tail of the Devil Tavern? She couldn't remember exactly. It had seemed no distance at all the day before, but then they had been in the sleigh. Afoot in a blizzard was an entirely different matter. She trudged on, praying she would be in time.

Her heart pounded faster when she glanced up and saw the swinging sign ahead. No one seemed to be about. Perhaps in this awful weather, Zack would be the tavern's only customer. She hoped so. She would find it most unsettling to run into a woman like the one they had seen yesterday.

Persia hurried on but stopped three buildings away when she saw the door of the tavern open and a thin shaft of light creep across the snow. The sound of boisterous voices made her shrink back into the shadows of a warehouse entrance. She peered cautiously around the doorframe.

Three men—two of them supporting their drunken friend—came out into the twilight gloom. The man in the middle, who was really only a dark shape to her from where she stood, seemed unconscious from drink. His arms were draped over the shoulders of the other men and his boots dragged along in the snow, making deep ruts. She shuddered. How could she enter such a place? What if Zack had left already and she came upon more men such as these?

She stayed secluded in her doorway until the three men disappeared in the direction of the wharves. Then, taking a deep breath to bolster her courage, she headed for the tavern door at the fastest clip she could manage.

Shoving the door open with no small amount of effort, she was assaulted by the stale, smoky air and an acrid odor that stung her eyes. For a few moments, she could see nothing at all except the fire roaring on the hearth.

"See here, ma'am, this ain't no place for a lady." The gruff voice boomed at her from somewhere deep inside the reeking cavern.

"I realize that," she answered, speaking only to the gloom. "But I'm to meet someone here."

"Begging your pardon, ma'am, but you must be mistaken. There's not a soul in the place but me." The unseen man laughed in a disconcerting tone. "If it's me you're looking for, the saints be praised! But it's been a few years since anyone as fetching as you gave me the time of day."

Time of day. The familiar phrase leapt out at her as if she had never heard it before in her life.

"What time is it, please?" Persia asked.

Her eyes were adjusting. She saw a large, swarthy figure behind the bar peer down at a gold watch exactly like Zack's.

"It's nigh onto five-thirty, ma'am. What time was you to meet your gentleman friend?"

"He should have been here almost an hour ago. And he promised he'd wait exactly one hour in case I came. Perhaps you know him. Zachariah Hazzard? He told me he's stayed here often when he's ashore."

The big man made a clucking sound with his tongue. "A sailor, eh? The whole lot of them should be keel-hauled for tampering with ladies such as yourself. Begging your pardon, ma'am, but you ain't the first to be taken in by one of those satin-tongued sea dogs."

"No! It wasn't that way." Persia's panic was rising. "We're to be married this afternoon. Please, he *must* have been here. Didn't he say where he was going?"

"I'm sorry, miss." The barkeep shook his head in

seeming sympathy. "I know no Zachariah Hazzard. And it's been a slow afternoon on account of the storm. If a stranger'd come in, I would have noticed. There is one man upstairs with a woman named Chastity. Could that be *your* man?"

"No!" Persia cried, fighting hard to hold back the tears.

"You're sure?"

She hung her head, not wanting the man to see her face. No, she wasn't sure. But how could she admit that? Her silence spoke for her.

"If you'd care to take a peek, miss, the room next door's empty and there's a knothole in the wall behind a picture. I'll let you have the key. It wouldn't take no more than a moment to be certain sure."

Persia's eyes were still downcast. She couldn't see the lewd grin of enjoyment splitting the barkeep's face even as his voice dripped sympathy and understanding. Zachariah Hazzard was not the man upstairs with Chastity and Clancey knew it. But the feel of the ill-gotten gold in his pockets and the fine new watch hanging at his belt made him bold. There was a certain pleasure, too, in knowing that this beauty had belonged to Hazzard, but that he would see her no more. By dawn the *Alissa May* would have sailed from Boston harbor, and she alone would be the shanghaied sailor's mistress from now on. As for this fiery-haired beauty old Zack had meant to marry, perhaps a peep through the hole at Chastity and her man would put the lass in an amorous mood. And Chancey was ever ready to accommodate a pretty woman.

"I'll show you the way," he offered.

Persia could not find her voice to answer. But when the man took a key off the wall and started toward the stairs, she followed.

The upstairs hall was dark and cold and smelled of unchanged linens and unscrubbed floors. A rat scurried across the boards, and Persia bit her lip to keep from shrieking. How could Zack have stayed in a place like this?

"Well, here you be," the man announced, holding the door for her. "Just climb up on the bed and move the picture of George Washington aside a bit. You'll be able to see if he's your man."

Persia hesitated. She wanted to ask the man to leave her, but she couldn't bring herself to do it. He stood in the doorway after she entered, blocking the whole frame with his bulk.

Carefully, she climbed up and shifted the country's noble hero.

"Go ahead, miss. Put your eye right to the hole."

She did as he ordered and immediately had to stifle a cry of shock. There on the bare mattress in the adjoining room lay a man and woman, their naked bodies tangled in much the same manner she and Zack had been entwined the night before. She could see clearly the woman's painted face as she lay beneath her partner's sweating, heaving body. But the man atop her was unidentifiable. It could be Zack. He was big of frame and his tousled hair was the same sun-streaked brown. Persia forced the rising bile to remain in her throat even as she commanded herself to continue gazing at the pair.

The man's white buttocks jerked as if in spasm as he thrust at the woman beneath him. Their moans and sighs mingled, making Persia burn all over. This couldn't be Zack! She would die of shame if it were.

Finally the man rolled away from the woman, and Persia saw them both clearly. She was sure they must have heard her gasp of relief and the scrape of the picture as she quickly covered the hole in the wall.

"Well?" Clancey asked expectantly.

"No!"

"I'm sorry," he said.

Sorry! Persia's heart was rejoicing. How could he express sorrow? Then she realized what he meant. Now she had no idea where Zack might be.

"Miss, I'd like to help." The man was clutching her arm too tightly as he assisted her down from the bed. "If he's left you stranded, I've been needing a girl in the bar to help out. The job's yours for the asking."

The very idea horrified Persia. She had a difficult time keeping her voice civil as she declined his offer.

"Boston can be a cold place for a woman alone," he warned.

"I won't be staying here. I'm going home."

"And you think they'll welcome you back?" He chuckled in that ugly way of his. "Ask Chastity about that. She tried to go home after her man left her. Wealthy people, her folks are. Real society. You see how she ended up. It could happen to you. I'm offering you a way out. A *respectable* way."

"Thank you very much." They were downstairs now and Persia could hardly wait to escape the Tail of the Devil. "I'll come back, if my plans don't work out."

"You do that," he said, breathing foul breath into her face.

She broke away and ran for the door. Not until she was once more plodding through the snow all alone did the desperate weight of her situation strike her. Tears burned cold tracks down her cheeks and a hopelessness settled over her like none she had ever known.

She wandered aimlessly for hours in the snow. She was freezing, but she no longer felt the cold. Finally, she found herself at the waterfront, standing before a ship that was readying to sail. The carved figurehead was that of a beautiful woman with flowing red hair and full, peaked breasts. Her eyes were painted blue and she seemed to be gazing down on Persia with contempt. Persia read the name on the ship's scroll . . . the *Alissa May*. The name meant nothing to her, although she knew many of the vessels that sailed out of Boston and their owners' and captains' names as well.

She moved away, wandering aimlessly into the night. But the water kept drawing her back. If Zack was gone, she might just as well be dead. She stared down at the dark, lapping sea. She'd always heard that drowning was a fast and painless way to die. A quick plunge into the icy depths and all the pain would flow out of her. She inched closer to the edge, then closer still.

She could almost feel the cold black water closing

over her . . . the release . . . the welcome nothingness. She closed her eyes. She took a deep breath and held it. She leaned forward, ready to meet death.

But suddenly some unseen force pulled her back. She stood shivering, crying, and staring down at the very place that had almost been her grave.

She couldn't do it! Zack was alive somewhere. He hadn't left her forever. She would find him again if it took the rest of her life.

PART TWO

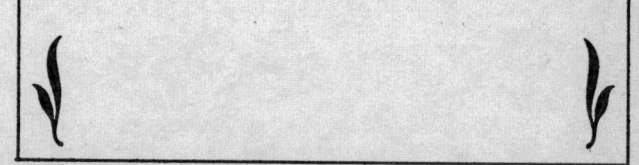

1846

CHAPTER THIRTEEN

O_LD_ Captain Whiddington, his face lined and his silver-gray eyes dulled to pewter by the events of the past ten years, leaned heavily on his daughter Persia's arm. They were waiting in the crisp October sunshine for the brigade of cars to pull into the station not far from the United States Hotel, where they had been staying for the past two weeks.

Two weeks? Had it only been fourteen days since they had taken the cars down from Maine? the captain pondered. Too often nowadays each hour seemed to drag its feet. Still, so much had happened. So much had changed. Sometimes, in the dark of night, he longed to pull the years back, to bring Victoria out of the grave, to hear Persia's bright laughter trilling through the old house on Gay Street once more, even to have Europa back with them. He couldn't help but feel a certain sadness at the relentless march of time and the havoc the advance of years had wreaked upon his family.

"Father, it won't be long now. I heard the whistle.

Are you warm enough? You should sit down until the train comes."

He glanced up at her. His "little girl" was taller than he was now. The years had bent his back and stooped his shoulders, while Persia still, in spite of everything, stood bowsprit straight with a proud, unyielding set to her head and a cold blue gaze that dared the world to scorn her for what she had done.

"My dear, you fret over me too much. I'm neither tired nor cold." He was both, but he had never been one to complain.

"Well, I still say these long trips are getting to be too much for you, Father. There isn't a reason in the world that I couldn't have come to Boston and taken care of the auction of our cargo at Central Wharf while you stayed at home and nursed your gout."

"*Blast* my gout!" He whacked his boot with his scrimshandered cane to show his contempt for the ailment and the anger he felt at having to rely on his daughter for almost everything these days. It wasn't right. Old men should take to their graves, not to their beds!

Persia ignored his reaction, knowing that any further comment would only make him feel worse. Her father's outbursts at his many infirmities had become routine to her over the past years. Once—long ago, it seemed—he had been a man who never raised his voice except in laughter. But time had dealt him one blow after another, beginning that night she had run off with Zachariah Hazzard, continuing with her mother's sudden death— some said from heartbreak over her daughter's elopement—and culminating in Persia's long years of disgrace. There was not a soul in Quoddy Cove who didn't know that Persia had run off with Europa's man, only to be deserted by him before they reached the altar and brought home by her father a *shamed* woman. She had paid a great price for her one night of folly. And in her heart Persia knew she would continue to pay for the rest of her life. It hardly seemed fair. But then who ever promised that life would be fair?

Persia assured herself at least once a day that she never thought about Zack any longer. What was the use? Why should she care what had happened to a man who had taken her innocence one snowy night, then walked out of her life never to be heard from again? She didn't feel a thing for him after all these lonely years. But, whether she realized it or not, the very act of denying her love was her way of holding on to it.

Just being in Boston brought back so many memories—their night of love, the awful moment in the tavern when she'd realized that Zack had not waited for her as he'd said he would, her desperation at the dock when she had almost ended her life, and the days that followed when she had had to decide what she was going to do. For a time, she had considered taking the offered job at the Tail of the Devil, not so much because she was desperate for money, but because she thought Zack might return there. But in the end, after holing up in the boarding house for several days, unable to make a decision, her fate was decided for her.

She had been careful in her note to her parents not to mention where she was going. But when Fletcher surprised her in the kitchen that night, she had slipped, perhaps subconsciously on purpose. In any case, Fletcher had told her father, and he had come in search of her. Not to drag her home, he'd said, but to make sure she was safe and happy. She had been neither when Captain Whiddington found her. And home had sounded like heaven.

But it was not, she had discovered on her return.

Her mother, by that time, had taken to her bed, physically ill with worry and heartbreak. Although her spirits rallied upon Persia's return, Victoria Whiddington was never strong again. She made it through Europa's wedding to Seton Holloway, a hastily arranged affair that took place on the date originally scheduled for Europa's marriage to Zachariah Hazzard. But after the couple left to honeymoon in the White Mountains and then make their home in Portland, Victoria seemed to let go, growing thinner and weaker by the day. Her smile, which had

once been as quick as her temper, showed itself seldom
and then was only a wan reflection of its former brilliance.

When Birdie Blackwell stood before the congregation
on a bright Sunday morning and pointed one arthritic
finger at the "scarlet woman," as she styled Persia,
demanding that the church censure her actions, it was
the beginning of the end for Victoria. Collapsing, she
had to be lifted from the pew and carried home. Nine
days later, the family gathered in a soft spring rain at the
town burying ground and bid their farewells to Victoria
Forsyth Whiddington, "aged 42 yrs. 3 mos. and 12 days,"
as the inscription below the weeping marble angel read.

The death certificate accused pneumonia of dealing
the killing blow. But the people of Quoddy Cove accused Persia.

"That poor, dear soul, I warned her," Birdie Blackwell
moaned over tea and cakes to the members of the Ladies' Missionary Society, her black eyes snapping with
malice. "I told Victoria time and time again that no good
would come of that fire-haired vixen. *The devil's own,*
that's what my brother called her after reading my letters about her wicked deeds." To which her sanctimonious listeners nodded, clucked their venomous tongues,
and poured more tea, spicing it with their own tidbits of
gossip about Persia Whiddington.

Persia ignored their scorn as best she could. She had
no time to deal with the guilt other people were heaping
upon her since she blamed herself more than any of
them ever could. If only she hadn't fallen in love with
Zack . . . If only she hadn't run away to Boston . . . If
only she hadn't let him make love to her before their
marriage . . .

If only! What a stupid, ineffectual phrase!

She still attended church every Sunday, but only because her father needed her strong arm to lean on. She
endured the congregation's stares, their whispers, their
accusing silences. But more and more she turned within
herself, staying about the house to avoid those waiting
to jeer at her in the streets. She knew she would never
marry—not in this place, not after what she had done.

So she tried to content herself with keeping house for her father, and, bit by bit, she took over his shipping business as well. Hard work was a poor substitute for a loving husband. But at least she fell into bed every night, too exhausted to ache for very long before blissful sleep released her from her loneliness. There was no time for self-pity with the ice business booming.

The ice ship that had been only a glimmer in her father's eyes ten years before had become a prosperous reality. Each winter, after the ice was harvested from the Kennebec and Penobscot rivers and the ponds of Maine and Massachusetts, his ship's hold was loaded with two-hundred-pound blocks packed tightly in sawdust to be shipped to the markets in Bombay and Calcutta.

Captain Whiddington himself had gone along as supercargo on one of the trips a little over a year after he lost his wife. Persia had insisted upon it, hoping the voyage would relieve some of his grief. Although he had sold the ice at a fantastic profit, he refused to make a second trip, saying, "I'm too old, Persia. My sea legs are gone and my heart's back here. It's time I left the sea to younger men."

"And *women*?" she'd replied, trying to draw him into a rousing debate and also to remind him that she, too, would make a respectable supercargo.

But he'd offered her only a shake of his head as he'd replied, "Aye, everything's changing and passing me by these days. Steam stacks smoking up the seaways and blacking the sails. It's an abomination! I wouldn't be at all surprised to see women in command of ships one of these days."

Persia had never considered captaining one of the ice ships, although it was something to think about now that he'd mentioned it. But she did long to see India. At least that childhood fire had not left her soul. She dealt often with the Boston auctioneers and merchants. Why, then, couldn't she sail to foreign ports and barter the cargoes there as well? She didn't know of any other female supercargoes, but that certainly didn't mean there could never be one.

*   *   *

"All aboard!" The train pulled in, and a sooty-faced conductor was motioning them toward the round-topped passenger car.

Persia took her father's arm, making it appear that he was helping her instead of the other way around. Walking slowly, they mounted the steps at the end of the car. Long wooden benches lined either side of the boxlike compartment. Persia knew from experience that they felt as hard as they looked. Still, it was considered fashionable to "take the cars" nowadays. Almost no one traveled by steam packet between Boston and Maine. There was something in the souls of sailing men that refused to allow them to acknowledge those smoke-belching transports, much less travel the waterways on them.

"It's heresy, I say!" She'd heard the words from her father often. "No God-fearing sailor would dare smut up his sails or go against the wind!"

The four pairs of wheels under the car ground forward, slowly at first. But soon, as the train picked up speed, Persia and her father were both gripping the edge of the bench and steeling themselves against the bucking and jerking that pulled at their backs and wrenched their necks. Once they were clipping along at an awesome seventeen miles per hour, the ride would become smoother, but hardly more pleasant. Soon cinders and smoke would drift back from the funnel-shaped smokestack to pollute their breathing space. Persia took two linen handkerchiefs out of her valise and handed one to her father.

"Don't need it," he shouted over the deep rumble of the wheels and the clanking and grating of couplings.

"Just in case," she answered, forcing the linen into his hand and tying hers outlaw fashion across her nose and mouth.

"Persia . . ." The captain had to yell to be heard over the din. "I've been thinking about what you said a good while back."

She stared at him, trying to figure out what he might be talking about. "Yes, Father?"

"Surely you remember. About women and the shipping business. I've been giving it a good deal of thought, as I said." A smile—his old smile, filled with mischief—crept over his face. "I have a new duty I want you to take over for me."

Persia's mind spun with possibilities. Her father and his partner, Frederick Tudor, were about to launch a new ship, the *Madagascar*, from the Quoddy Cove yards. For a moment, her blue eyes grew wide atop her bandana cinder guard. Could it be that they were actually considering her for the post of supercargo?

She looked down at her hands then, embarrassed by her own folly. Of course they weren't thinking any such thing! This might be 1846, but her father and Mr. Tudor were the same old sea dogs who refused to set foot on one of the newfangled steam-powered sailing ships. She almost laughed aloud at her own wild imaginings. She didn't have an icicle's chance on the Fourth of July of being hired on as their supercargo! More likely her father was about to bestow upon her the honor of christening the *Madagascar* when she slipped down the ways to become seaborne for the first time.

She removed the linen from her face and offered him a sweet smile. Laying her hand on his, she said, "Father, I do appreciate your offer, but do you think it's wise? If I christen your new ship, not a person in Quoddy Cove—port, landing, or village—will come down to bid her well. You know how they feel about me."

"The whole lot of them be damned!" he yelled. "You'll send the *Madagascar* off in style. Aye! But that's not the duty I had a mind to speak to you about."

"What, then?"

"It's the ice harvest. October's near gone. In no time now, the Irishmen from down Boston way will be showing up to set to work. I'd like to pretend that I'm up to the task again this year, but the fact is I'm not. I want *you* to oversee the harvest for me, daughter."

Persia could only stare at her father. Never had she

dreamed of suggesting to him that she might take on
such a job. She could do it, of course. She had observed
the process for years. She knew the men who came up
from Boston to cut the ice, and they knew and respected
her. But to supervise such a rough crew was something
no woman would dream of trying to do.

No woman but Persia Whiddington!

"Thank you, Father, for your confidence in me." The
words sounded calm and assured, but inside, Persia's
heart was turning somersaults. She could and would do
it! Tongues would wag, but didn't they stay busy at their
gossip about her anyway? It was just too bad that old
Miss Birdie Blackwell had fallen down her well three
autumns back. She most of all would have gloried in this
shocking news.

Persia smiled as a thought struck her. She vowed
silently to tell her tidings to the well. That way Miss
Birdie wouldn't be left out since she was still down
there. By the time folks had discovered she was in the
well, she'd been there too long for them to try to haul up
the remains. The smell had been something powerful. So
the Reverend Osgood had come and preached her funeral service at well-side, then they'd filled it in. Her
brother, the missionary, had sent money for a tomb-
stone to be erected at the site. Persia thought, as did the
rest of Quoddy Cove's residents, that it was just as well
Cyrus Blackwell was far off ministering to the heathens
in India and hadn't had a chance to see the stone image
of his dead sister. It looked regrettably like her, and
that, coupled with the eerie fact that her remains were
still down below, had marked the old Blackwell place as
a haunted spot.

"It's good to see you smile like that, Persia," her
father said. "You're pleased about your new job, then?"

"Oh, yes, Father. More pleased than you'll ever
know!"

Asa Whiddington continued to watch Persia out of the
corner of his eye. He half hated what he was doing.
There wasn't an Irish ice-cutter alive who was worthy of
her. But, dammit all, she needed a husband, and it was

for sure she'd never find one from York County or the
vicinity. There might be some single men somewhere in
the county who hadn't heard of her disgrace, but even
then it would be hard to find a man who wanted to
marry an old maid of twenty-six when there was younger flesh to choose from. But the Irishmen were different. They didn't care what people said about Persia;
they liked her. And she was still a pretty woman, in
spite of her advanced age. Working closely with the
men, she was sure to get at least one proposal of marriage. And her father figured she'd jump at it, if only to
get away from Quoddy Cove and its wagging, cutting
tongues.

"Are you all right, Father?" Persia touched his hand,
then felt his forehead.

"I'm fine," he blustered. "Don't fuss over me."

"I'm sorry. It's just that you went so quiet all of a
sudden."

He looked at her face as if he were seeing it for the
first time—the bright hair like a burnished frame surrounding a portrait of a sad-eyed woman. Her eyes still
danced with sapphire lights. But if you bothered to look
below the surface, you could see the pain. And her full
mouth, which used to curve up all the time in a smile
that showered the whole world with love, now had a
downward pull to it. Still, it seemed that the past painful
years had only made her more beautiful.

"Persia, do you ever give any thought to marrying
these days?"

She laughed softly, but there was no humor in the
sound. "Marriage? At my age? Oh, Father, you are such
a romantic!"

"I'm not talking about romance, child," he said gently.
"I'm talking about a family, a home of your own, and
comfort in your old age."

She didn't laugh, and the small smile faded from her
lips. "Yes, Father. I think of it all the time. But what's
the use?"

He patted her hand but said no more. They sat in
silence and listened to the melancholy song of the iron

wheels and the moan of the whistle echoing off the
frozen land.

Persia's excitement at the prospect of overseeing the
ice harvest had faded at her father's mention of marriage. She ached for a man to love, to give her a home
and his children to bear and raise. But maybe it wasn't
meant to be. Maybe some women were put on earth to
do other things. And maybe Persia Whiddington was
one of them. Any other possibility seemed highly un-
likely at this stage of her life.

She sighed and stared out the cinder-frosted side windows of the train, searching the forbidding, snow-
blanketed landscape for some answer to the uncertain
scheme of her life. But the cold, bleak land only intensi-
fied her loneliness. She closed her eyes and tried not to
think, not to need, not to long for things beyond her
reach.

It was on a Saturday that Persia and her father returned from Boston to the house on Gay Street. Because
of their tiring trip the day before, she almost talked her
father into staying home from church the following morning. Had she been able to persuade him, her whole
future would have been altered, for better or worse.

As it was, the captain, dyspeptic and disgruntled after
the trip, was in no mood for a preacher's ramblings that
morning, either. He might have suggested staying home
himself, if Persia hadn't first. But he was in a temper to
argue with the gatepost. Cook made pancakes—his
favorite—for breakfast; he wanted oatmeal. Fletcher laid
out his black suit to wear; he ordered it away and chose
the dark blue. And when Persia said, "Father, I really
am quite worn out this morning. And the weather looks
so threatening. I think we might be better off staying in
today," he blew up.

"Not go to church? Have you lost your wits, woman?
We'll have every tongue in town slicing us to bits. They
all know we returned last night."

"Do you really care what they say? We've heard it all
before. Besides, if we're not in church, maybe they'll be

able to concentrate on the sermon for a change instead of staring at me.''

"Persia, I won't let you take the coward's way out. We are going to church and that's that!''

She started to argue and tell him that it was *his* welfare she was thinking of, not her own. But what good would that do? She had seen him like this before on infrequent occasions. She might as well go up to the rooftop and try to win a debate with a howling nor'easter.

She shrugged her acceptance and went upstairs to get her cloak and gloves. While pulling on her fur-lined boots against the freezing cold and the wet snow they would have to slosh through on their walk to church, an idea formed in her mind and a smile tugged at one corner of her mouth. It was madness to walk on a day like this, especially with her father's gout acting up. But she would never be able to convince him to travel to church any other way than they had always done. However, given his sour temper this morning, there might be a possibility.

He was waiting in the hallway for her when she came down the stairs.

"What took you so long, Persia? We'll be late now because of your fussing before the mirror.''

"Then we will just have to be late,'' she replied haughtily. "If you're about to suggest that Fletcher drive us in the sleigh, I won't hear of it. We *always* walk!''

For a moment, the old captain looked uncertain. His gray eyes narrowed and a nervous twitch set his jaw muscle working.

"See here, now! You know my foot's paining me. If I want to ride to church, I'll ride! Fletcher, hitch up the team!''

Fletcher shot Persia an amused glance and said, "As you wish, Captain Whiddington, sir.'' He hurried out to bring the sleigh around before Persia's father could change his mind or figure out what his daughter had been up to.

So, on that cold, snowy morning, instead of having to slosh along on foot, Persia Whiddington rode in style to meet her destiny.

CHAPTER FOURTEEN

*P*ERSIA was relieved when Fletcher stopped the sleigh in front of the church. Unaccountably, her father had brought up the subject of marriage again as they rode along. He seemed obsessed suddenly with the topic. And he was making her exceedingly uncomfortable.

"Please, Father, you needn't worry about me. I have other things I want to do before I settle down. Besides, I'm perfectly content making a home for you."

The captain continued his harangue as they climbed out of the sleigh. "What other things could you possibly be thinking of? Every woman wants a husband, a family, and a home of her own. As for your caring for me, I'm thinking about going back to sea. Not as captain, mind you, but I make a *damn* fine supercargo!"

"*Father!*" Persia scolded in a whisper. They were practically on the steps of the church, and even if the other arriving worshipers hadn't heard his curse, God certainly had.

She noted a group of sailors huddled in a nervous little knot in the lee of the church. They would be shipping out within the week and were expected by their captains and their ships' owners to make peace with God before setting out to sea. She knew from having observed such reluctant churchgoers in the past that they would wait until the very last minute before slipping in to settle themselves uncomfortably on the back pews.

On her father's arm, with her black taffeta skirts rustling softly, Persia made her way down the center aisle toward their usual seats on the second pew. It still seemed strange that the two places beside them—those once occupied by her mother and Europa—were empty now. But Persia had little time to ponder over that before Reverend Osgood mounted to his pulpit and commanded, "Let us pray!"

After his booming "Amen," Persia settled back to endure the sermon. But the white-haired clergyman surprised her by veering from his usual Sunday routine. Holding up a long sheet of foolscap for all to see, he announced, "I have in my hands a plea from one of our brethren in a far-off pagan land. You are all acquainted, I feel sure, with the name of Cyrus Blackwell, our missionary to Bombay, India. Not many of you will remember him, since he left us as a mere lad to follow his holy calling. But we all knew and loved his dear sister, Birdie, a saint of a woman."

The congregation muttered their agreement, making Persia twist in her seat and bite her lower lip for control. A *saint* indeed! she thought angrily, remembering the pain the woman had caused her and her mother.

The minister continued, "Only this week I received a letter from the good Reverend Blackwell with a most unusual request. I will read his words to you."

Persia focused her full attention on the bespectacled cleric as he held the rough sheet under his long nose, squinting hard at it. A letter all the way from India! She had no idea what the missionary might be writing back to Maine about, but that didn't matter. Her imagination was fired by the fact that his words had crossed the oceans of the world. She leaned slightly forward, anxious to hear all.

The minister cleared his throat loudly, then began reading.

> Bombay, India
> May 23, 1846

My Dear Brother Osgood and Fellow Christians,
It is with great sadness and humility that I write to you with a special request. Were it for myself alone, I would never consider making so bold a plea as this. But it is in behalf of the poor brown heathens of this land that I beseech you thusly. Their spiritual needs come first above all others. This is my mission and my zeal.

One month ago this very night, my dear partner in life, Hannah, was called to serve the Master.

Reverend Osgood paused, clearing his throat again. He decided to omit the next few sentences of the missionary's letter, which relayed all the details of Hannah Blackwell's demise after she'd wasted away for weeks in the throes of a mysterious tropical malady.

And so it is that I find myself at the mercy of the good Christians of Quoddy Cove. You have supported me faithfully with your contributions, your supplies, and your prayers in the years that I have been here. Now I must ask for the ultimate sacrifice on your part. I need a wife to help me minister to my flock. Is there a good Christian woman, robust of body and spirit, among you who will take up this cross and bear it faithfully and without complaint? If so, I call that woman blessed, for so she will seem to these poor, suffering natives and to the lone soul who now tends them.

My letter, I know, will take four months to reach you. And my bride four more in arriving. I can only hope that within the year my prayers will be answered.

The letter went on, with Reverend Blackwell explaining that life in India would be neither easy nor overly comfortable. But Persia heard none of this. Her face felt hot and her hands were sweating and trembling in her lap. *Bombay!* The exotic name whispered through her mind like a hot, fragrant wind, exciting her senses, making her feel light-headed and giddy. The time, the place, and the man himself were right. What poetic justice that the brother of the woman who had branded her a wanton would now return her dignity by bestowing his respected name upon her!

The missionary, Cyrus Blackwell, had just handed her her longed for place in society along with her long-awaited ticket to India.

"Whither thou goest, I will go," Reverend Osgood boomed, taking for the text of his sermon from the Book of Ruth, first chapter, sixteenth verse. "And where thou lodgest, I will lodge: thy people shall be my people, and thy God my God."

Immediately following the benediction, Persia was out of the pew and hurrying up the aisle. Her father watched her brush past the other women of the church, who were huddled in excited knots, discussing Reverend Blackwell's bizarre request.

Persia heard the exclamations from the church ladies as she passed them:

"India! Can you imagine? Why, I'd sooner see my daughter headed for hell than that dark, heathen land!"

"It mightn't be so bad to go there as Cyrus Blackwell's wife. I remember him from long ago. A handsome scamp—nothing like poor Birdie in looks or temperament. I always thought, had he stayed here, that he and I might have married. In fact, if it weren't for my husband, I'd be packing my bags the minute I get home."

"You can't mean it, Clarinda! Why, the very idea! And said aloud right here under God's own roof!"

Persia half smiled as she watched the portly Mrs. Archibald Leeds blush, then reply, "God knows my heart's been Cyrus Blackwell's all these years. He won't be shocked."

But the other ladies were. Persia was, too. Clarinda Leeds was not a young woman. How old, she wondered, was Cyrus Blackwell? Then she decided it didn't matter. This was not to be a marriage of love, but one of convenience on both sides. She hurried on as the women began casting wild guesses as to who might volunteer to go on this mission of mercy to India. It was no surprise to Persia that her name was not on their list of possibilities. She smiled, thinking how shocked they would all be.

Simple shock was hardly the word for her father's reaction when she told him. By the time he made it up the steps and inside the house—slowly, since Persia, in her excitement, had dashed out of the sleigh and forgotten to lend him her arm—she was in the library already. He found her leaning over his desk, thoroughly engrossed in a navigation chart.

"Persia, what *is* going on?" he demanded.

When she glanced up at him, there was a glow about her face and a glitter to her eyes that made her look feverish. Concerned he went to her, placing a hand on her forehead.

"Are you ill, daughter?"

She laughed with the kind of joy she'd exhibited as a girl and whirled away from him, sweeping into a lively waltz about the room.

"Father, dear Father, I've never felt better in my life!"

She sang the words. He was quite astounded. Although, as a man of the sea, he was not puritanical in his notions about singing and dancing, he did not hold with such frivolities on the Sabbath. A tiny "damn" from a grown man was one thing, but a woman prancing about as Persia was doing only invited the devil.

"Enough!" he bellowed in his best tone of command, the one usually reserved for mutinous seamen. "Sit! I'll have no more of this disturbing of my Sunday peace!"

Persia whirled breathlessly into a wing chair and let her arms fall limp over the sides. She was grinning at him like a cat full of cream. He hadn't seen her indulge in such foolishness since she was thirteen years old and had tried to stow away on one of his ships dressed as a cabin boy. He had to smile at the thought in spite of himself. Damned if the cunning little imp hadn't nearly got away with it!

He forced a stern expression and a sterner voice. "Now, Miss Persia Whiddington, I'd like to know exactly what's going on."

"Oh, Father, it's just what you've been wanting. I thought you would have guessed by now."

He gazed down at her, looking perplexed. "What are you talking about, girl?"

"I'm going to be married."

"Married?"

"Yes! I'm going to India to marry Reverend Cyrus Blackwell!"

He drew away from her abruptly, and his eyes narrowed under their bushy brows. "The hell you say!"

"Don't you see? It's what I've always dreamed of . . . ever since I was a little girl. I've always wanted to cross the oceans. And to actually *live* in a foreign land . . . in *India*, of all places! Why, it's as if my prayers were heard by Reverend Blackwell and his by me. This is the perfect solution for both of us. And now my life makes sense for the first time ever. I was never meant to marry Zachariah Hazzard. That's why things didn't work out. I was being saved for grander things. I'll start packing tonight. When the *Madagascar* sails, I'll be on her!"

"I forbid it!"

She backed away from him and her smile faded. "I'm sorry you feel that way, Father. I was sure you would understand and be happy for me."

"How can I be happy that you're going around the world to marry a man you don't even know, much less love? I know you need a husband, Persia, but I simply can't allow this."

Persia went to him and brushed his grizzled cheek

with her lips. "I'm sorry, Father, truly. But I'm not a child any longer. And although I'd like your blessing, I'm going regardless."

She turned to leave, but his words stopped her. "How can you marry Birdie Blackwell's brother, after all the terrible things she said about you? Doesn't it mean anything that her vicious gossip broke your mother's heart?"

Persia shook her head. "He can't be anything like Miss Birdie was. Didn't he leave her when he was very young? Probably he went away because he recognized her as evil and wanted to be out from under her influence. He's a man of God, Father. He *must* be a good man!"

Before he could say another word, Persia hurried off to her room. She spent the rest of the short winter afternoon there, sorting her thoughts and her clothes. The heavy woolens that wouldn't be practical in India she folded into a neat pile. Those would go to Europa in Portland. She cast aside her scarlet cape—hardly a fitting color for a minister's wife!

The supper hour came and passed, but Persia did not go downstairs to eat. She wasn't hungry. She had too much to think about, too much to do. Besides, she had said what she had to say to her father. If she faced him across the table this soon, he would only start in on her again. He would come around, but she had to give him the time he needed.

She undressed, donned a warm nightgown, and climbed into bed. But far into the night, she tossed and turned on her mattress. A feverish excitement gripped her, and sleep refused to come. Finally, she lit her whale-oil lamp and reached for her Bible. If she was going to be the wife of a missionary, she would have to take her religion more seriously. She concentrated hard on the tiny print, but her eyes soon closed and the book slipped to her breast.

Asa Whiddington had spent a long, lonely evening in the library. He loved these wintry nights when Persia was with him. Unlike most fathers and daughters, the two of them could talk. And they did talk—endlessly—about foreign lands, ships, the sea, the winds, the stars. Suddenly he sat up in his chair, realization coming to him like a blow. Yes, they had talked, but always of the things *he* loved and knew. When had they ever discussed Persia's dreams and hopes?

"Never!" he told himself unhappily. He had spent all these years filling her head with the very things that were now about to take her from him forever. "You selfish old bastard," he muttered. "Serves you right."

Heaving a weary sigh, he shoved himself up from his chair. It was time he made peace with her. She was right: he wanted her to marry, and he wanted her to be happy. She could probably do neither by staying here in Maine with him. He didn't like what she was about to do, but did he really have any right to object? He had lived a full life. Now it was his daughter's turn to choose her own path, even if it took her far away from him. At least he could talk to her, calmly and rationally, instead of hurling abuses as he had done earlier. He might be able to bear having his daughter go away, but he would die if he lost her love and her respect.

He climbed the stairs slowly, trying to frame the proper words of reconciliation. He decided that he would simply apologize for his abominable behavior earlier, then let her do the talking for a change. Maybe during a civilized discussion, it would dawn on Persia that this was not what she really wanted at all. It wasn't much of a plan, but it was the best he could come up with.

Not a sound issued from her room. Her father knocked softly but received no answer. Lamplight gleamed into the hallway from underneath the door. Sudden fear gripped him. What if he had driven her away? What if she'd packed her things and fled into the night, unwilling to hear more of his tirades?

He grabbed the brass knob and wrenched the door open. His heart thudded with sudden relief. She was sleeping, a soft smile curving her lips. He stood just inside the door for several moments staring at her, his heart brimming with tenderness for his most precious daughter. She looked far younger than her years with the lace-edged collar of her nightgown tied demurely under her chin and her long, shining hair flowing over the pillow. The patchwork quilt that covered her rose and fell evenly as she breathed. One hand, fingers curled delicately, rested on a book, while the other was thrown back over her head. He tiptoed across the room and took the volume from her grasp.

"Her Bible," he said, nodding. He looked to see what she'd been reading. It was opened to the Book of Ruth. "No doubt where your thoughts were when you fell asleep, my child."

He leaned down and kissed her cheek, then blew out the lamp. She never woke as he tiptoed out and closed the door.

Her father slept soundly that night, but Persia's quiet slumber gave way to troubled dreams. She was on a ship upon a storm-tossed sea. In the distance, she could barely make out a lush green shoreline. Two dark figures stalked her night passage, so that neither sea nor shore offered calm repose. She couldn't make out the visage of the man waiting on the beach, but suddenly the sun came out in her dream and she recognized the long-loved face of Zachariah Hazzard. She awoke with a start and a sudden cry.

In the darkest hour of that dark night she resolved not to wait. She would seek out Reverend Osgood at first light and offer herself as Cyrus Blackwell's bride. As she had told her father, when the *Madagascar* sailed at the end of November, she planned to be on board.

Her true fate had found her at last. She would not delay but would rush into its waiting arms.

Persia had hoped to be out of the house before her father woke up. But when she hurried down to the kitchen to have a quick cup of tea to guard against the cold before starting out for the church, she found the captain already there. So absorbed was he in his paper that he seemed not to notice her when she sat down.

Their breakfast passed in silence, but it was of the

companionable sort. Not a word needed to pass between them for Persia to know that the storm had blown over.

She watched as he folded his paper and laid it aside. His eyes held a merry glitter as he smiled and said, "Are your sea chests packed?"

Relief flooded her. "Not yet, Father, but almost."

"Well, you'll be needing some new things anyway. Some traveling suits, fashionable riding costumes, and a ball gown or two."

Persia stared at him, stunned. *"Ball gowns?* Father, I'm to wed a missionary, not an ambassador!"

He reached across the table and took her hand. "That may be, my dear, but before you become a missionary's little church mouse, I have another role for you. You know I've talked of sailing on the *Madagascar* myself. But we both know such a plan is sheer folly. I'm too old, too ill. So I've come to a decision. The captain we've signed is a fair merchant as well. But there's not a man alive who could barter my cargo of ice as well as you can. Those Parsee merchants in Bombay will fall in love with you at first sight. They'll wine and dine you and treat you to fancy balls in their palaces, and then they'll empty their silk purses to buy our ice. Mark my words, it's a solid business move!"

Persia was struck nearly dumb. Why had her father decided this now? Maybe he thought that this last fling, this taste of Oriental luxuries, would dissuade her from marrying Cyrus Blackwell. If that was what he had in mind, he would soon find out it was no use.

"Father, I'm flattered and pleased that you want me to act as your supercargo. I'll do a fine job for you, I promise."

"That's exactly what I plan to explain to Tudor. He'll have no qualms, I'm sure. But why are you frowning, daughter?"

She waved a hand in the air to dismiss her passing expression. "Oh, it had nothing to do with that. It's just that I decided last night I have to go first thing this morning to speak with Reverend Osgood." Her face suddenly became a mask of worry. "Father, what if he turns me down?"

"Turn *you* down?" the captain blustered. "Never! Why, the man would be an idiot not to send you as Blackwell's wife, if you choose to go!"

"But the gossips . . . Birdie Blackwell in particular. What if Reverend Osgood feels as they all do—that I'm a scarlet woman because of one foolish, impetuous act in my youth?"

"Don't you worry your pretty head over that, Persia my girl! I'll go with you to speak to Osgood. He'll accept your offer, or else."

Persia smiled, knowing that her father was going against all his own wishes to help her realize hers. He was a wonderful man. She would miss him desperately.

Persia had dressed carefully for her audience with Reverend Osgood. She wore a simple dress of stark black jersey and a bonnet with a black veil that hid every inch of creamy skin and every strand of fiery hair. She had seen ministers' wives before in just such drab attire and had felt sorry for them. But now her one goal was to create the impression that she, too, could be unassuming in appearance and especially in attitude.

They found the minister hidden away in his tiny office at the church, counting the collection from the morning before while he sipped a steaming cup of tea. He seemed quite annoyed by their intrusion. Persia noted that his whiskers twitched and his small green eyes narrowed when they walked in on him.

"Sorry to disturb you so early on a Monday morning, Brother Osgood," the captain said cheerily, ignoring the man's cold stare, "but my daughter and I have important business to discuss. I'm afraid it won't wait."

The reverend glanced from Asa to Persia and back again. "Well, I suppose I can give you a few minutes, if it's *church* business, that is."

"Oh, indeed it is! I'd never dream of bothering you otherwise. I know you've been wanting to add a new iron fence around the burying ground. And I thought, since my business is going so well, I might be able to see myself clear to donating the materials and labor.''

Osgood's face lost its sour expression, but Persia's countenance captured exactly what he had cast off. She'd certainly had no idea that her father meant to come here and *buy* her a husband. But a moment later she realized with a sinking heart that even the much needed cemetery fence would not be enough to purchase a mate for a ruined woman.

"That's most Christian of you, Brother Whiddington. Bless you!" Reverend Osgood said.

"You'll bless us both when you hear what my daughter is offering.'' The captain turned to her with an encouraging smile. "Persia, tell him.''

"I've come to accept Reverend Blackwell's proposal,'' she said with quiet dignity.

For several moments, silence reigned in the room. Persia watched the minister's face turn pale, then as scarlet as the cape she had cast aside the night before. His whiskers set to twitching again, and he leaned toward them across his desk.

"No! By all that is holy, I will not send Brother Blackwell a *used* woman!''

Persia was quaking with fury inside her black gown, but her father remained calm. "And whom will you send, Brother Osgood? I didn't notice a line of applicants waiting outside to be interviewed.''

"Better no bride than a tainted one.''

"You seem to speak with great authority about my daughter's sins. Perhaps you would like to number them for us so that she might offer some defense before she is condemned,'' Captain Whiddington said.

Osgood shrank back, unable to find the words for a moment. When they came, his voice quivered with outrage. "There's no need for me to list her transgressions. Everyone knows. *You* are the one she disgraced, Whiddington. How can you speak so calmly about all this?''

Persia watched a benign smile light her father's face. "I never felt I was disgraced. My daughter was a mere child, who was enticed away by a man she thought she loved. She's a woman now. She knows what she's doing.''

Osgood jumped up, pointing a finger at Persia excitedly. ''There! There! You've admitted it yourself, Whiddington! *She went away with a man!* What more terrible crime could an unmarried woman commit?''

Persia half rose from her chair. Her voice was muted by the heavy veil as she said, ''Please, Father. Let's go now.''

Asa Whiddington touched her hand, indicating that she should remain seated. Then he turned his attention back to Reverend Osgood.

''Perhaps the greatest sin of all is for us to judge and refuse to forgive. Surely the Lord has forgiven my daughter's one transgression. Are you telling me that neither you nor Cyrus Blackwell can possibly do the same?'' He paused, but Osgood offered no answer. The captain's voice rose to an angry pitch for the first time. ''And you call yourself a man of God?''

''See here, now, Brother Whiddington, there's no need to shout. I suppose you're right. We should make allowances for her youth when she strayed from the fold. And, too, if she goes off to India, she won't be a blight on the village any longer.''

Persia was wavering between tears of shame and anger. This was far more difficult than she had anticipated. Reverend Osgood made her feel as if she really were a bad person. She was glad she could hide behind her veil.

''By damn, I won't have you making statements like that about my daughter, Osgood! The only *blight* on this village are the tongues of the busybodies, and yours is one of them! Come along, Persia. We've taken up too much of the *good* brother's time.''

They were at the door when Osgood called, ''Wait a moment! About the fence . . .''

The captain was about to tell the man where he could put his fence when Persia pressed his arm urgently. ''Please, Father,'' she whispered.

Whiddington calmed himself forcibly. ''You'll get your

fence and a share of profits from the ship that takes my daughter to India to wed Cyrus Blackwell.''

The hint of a smile twitched at the corner of Osgood's mouth. It was by far the best offer he was likely to receive. And it would make life easier for him if Persia Whiddington was half a world away. The women of his congregation plagued him constantly about her. They feared for their husbands, their sons. As for Cyrus Blackwell, that godly man, he would probably never lower himself to bed a woman anyway. This would be a spiritual mating alone. The missionary would never find out that he had been sent damaged goods.

''Well?'' said the captain.

''Done!'' Osgood replied.

The word sent a strange shiver through Persia. Her fate was sealed, for better or for worse.

CHAPTER FIFTEEN

A mixture of sleet and heavy, wet snow sliced almost horizontally across the pitching deck of the *Mazeppa*. Periodic flashes of lightning hurled from the Stygian sky revealed a tall, ghostlike figure on the ship's quarterdeck. The man's thick arms hugged his massive chest, and his stanchionlike legs anchored him where he stood. His oilskins flapped like sails in the gale winds, and torrents of water poured off his bristling white beard. A livid scar snaking up the right side of his face through his whiskers stood out like an arrow, pointing to the cold glitter in his dark eyes.

"Haul in more sail!"

The master of the *Mazeppa* shouted the order to his first mate. Immediately sailors gripped the lifeline and hurried without question to do the man's bidding. Each one had learned during this two-year voyage that under this captain's command there could be no hesitation, no argument, or else. They feared the man, some even hated him. But they respected him, too. And if ever there was a night when they needed to feel they could depend on someone's judgment, it was upon them now. After going to hell and back across three oceans, it seemed doom might catch up with them here, almost in sight of the Boston Light.

Because of the dirty weather, they had dared approach Boston only by the long way round, through Vineyard Sound, Nantucket Sound, and the backside of Cape Cod. Now they had rounded the cape, but Massachusetts Bay could be the death of a ship in heavy seas. With the Boston Light not yet in view, a mistake of a quarter of a point in the compass heading could send them crashing into Cohasset rocks or The Graves. The captain knew this full well, and his jaw was rigid with tension and concentration.

"Signal the pilot," he commanded, ordering a blue light to be flashed in the direction where pilot boats usually anchored, awaiting ships to be guided in. When this failed to arouse any attention, he had rockets set off. But they sputtered and died on the cold, wet air.

"Damn these New England winters!" he spat.

"But sir, didn't you say this was your home?" asked the first mate.

"I've got no home," he growled in reply, and lightning struck across the sky again, seeming to make his eyes flash with bitter hate.

The first mate said no more. The long night passed slowly, painfully.

Only with first light did help come. The little boat dashed out from behind the Boston Light, where she had lain protected in its lee all through the stormy night. With the pilot safely on board and in control, and the weather settling, the captain went below to change out of the clothes that were nearly frozen to his skin.

A monkey of a cabin boy met him at the door, a heated tankard of grog at the ready.

"The storm, she's over?" asked the brown boy, wide-eyed.

Before he answered, the captain put the cup to his mouth and downed the fiery drink. He swabbed his lips with the back of his big square hand and thrust the container toward the boy. "Another, Jocko!"

"Aye, sir."

"In answer to your question, lad, the storm's over. And I hope not to see another night like this one in my lifetime. Cold as a witch's tit it was on deck, I can tell you. And the wind howling and spitting like the souls of the damned! All of them out for *my* blood!"

The boy, who had been grinning at his master, sobered suddenly. "You're having the dreams again," he said. "You're thinking that them Africans from the slave ship are after you? It wasn't your fault, sir.'"

"Shut up!" The words boomed from his twisted lips, and he brought back a hand as if he meant to strike the boy. But Jocko stood his ground, knowing his captain was not given to violence without cause.

Anxious to be out of the man's way all the same, the boy said, "I'll fetch water for your bath, sir."

The big man slumped into a chair and ran nervous fingers through his wild shock of silver-streaked hair. "Aye, do that, lad."

When the boy left him, he leaned heavily on the chart table and grimaced as if he were in pain. He was, but not of body. It was a hurting of the soul. These past ten years had been a torment. But it was almost over now. No more would he sail the slavers, making his gold by selling other human beings. That last cargo of black ivory had been his undoing.

He had carried other guilts like festering sores on his heart for years and years. But none so painful as this. Would he ever be able to forget that dark night he'd guided his final shipload of slaves from the Ebo tribe up the marshy waterways of the Georgia coast? He had planned that one to be his last contraband cargo. It was time to give it up when dreams became nightmares . . . when the stench refused to leave his nostrils . . . when the slaves anguished cries would not be banished from his brain.

"Too bad you were such a greedy bastard," he snorted

in self-derision. "Had to have one more pouch of ill-got gold, didn't you?"

But in the long run, it was he who had paid.

He could still see it all when he closed his eyes. The ship had anchored in a deep cove where the slave traders had awaited their precious goods with dogs and whips. He'd ordered the plank laid down. Then he'd watched as, chained together, the Ebos had marched out of the hold, chanting mournfully: "Water brought us here. Water take us away."

Before anyone had realized their intent, his entire cargo—three hundred prime Africans, three hundred *human beings*—had marched themselves not to shore, but into the deep muddy water of the river.

They had drowned. Every last man, woman, and child of them had died—choosing mass suicide over the white man's bondage. He had seen his share, but this was a horror like none he had ever before witnessed.

No more would he ply the southern climes. Yes, he hated the New England winters, but there cargoes were clean and honest. He would sell the goods in his hold—tobacco, molasses, and rum—on the Boston market. And then he would seek out a post on an ice ship.

Long ago, that had been his plan. Long ago, he had had many plans. But fate had seemed determined to have her way with him. Now, after all these painful years, he was determined to reshape his destiny and make it of his own choosing.

He took out his ship's log and dipped a quill into the inkpot. In a bold black scrawl he wrote: "Arrived Boston harbor in foul weather, but with crew and cargo intact, on morning of November 1, 1846."

Too weary to write more, he simply signed his name: "Captain Zachariah Hazzard."

It was a stupid thing to do! Zack knew it, but he couldn't stop himself. Almost ten years had passed since the day they should have been married. And not one of those days passed on which he hadn't thought of Persia Whiddington. She was like a fever in his blood.

Ten long years!

Why, they should have children belt buckle high by now! Instead, all he had were memories of their one, long-ago night together. That seemed little enough to keep romance alive.

Still, he'd been dreaming all this time of seeing her again . . . imagining how it would be. But now that he was nearing Quoddy Cove again, he felt nervous and foolish somehow. What would he say to her?

"Pardon me, madam. You may not remember me, but you and I ran away to be married once. We didn't quite make it, however. You see, I got shanghaied . . . was on the Alissa May *for five years, unable to escape . . . almost drowned when the ship was wrecked off Java . . . washed up on that island more dead than alive, but this lovely golden-skinned native girl nursed me back to health, you'll be happy to know . . . and when I came out of it and tired of life in paradise, I signed on as first mate of a slaver plying the southern seas . . . stayed on as captain out of sheer greed until I couldn't stomach the job any longer. But I always thought of you . . . I* always *meant to come back. And now here I am if you'd still like to marry me!"*

"Balderdash!" His breath exploded in the cold air.

He had his nerve going back to Persia with such a tale! Even if she had loved him before, she'd certainly never be able to find it in her heart to love the bounder he had become. He should have moved heaven and earth to get back to her before now. But then, maybe she'd been happier without him. He was no prize catch, after all. Persia deserved better!

Yes, he had been right to stay away all these years. Surely by now she had a passel of children, fathered by some worthy and loving man. And the last thing he wanted to do was intrude on her life.

He revised his plan. He would make no attempt to see her, he told himself. He only needed to go back to where it had all started between them. Maybe then he'd be able to purge her from his senses and lay the past to rest.

Still, he couldn't deny it, going back to Quoddy Cove *was* a stupid thing to do!

Zack Hazzard's reason dueled with his emotions all the way from Boston to Quoddy Cave. He was so absorbed in his own thoughts that he had trouble keeping his hired team on the snow-covered road.

He was nearing the village. For one mad instant, he thought about driving right up Gay Street, halting the sleigh in front of her house, and pounding on the front door. What would she do? Would she melt into his arms as if the past years never existed? More than likely, if she was even there, she would order him away with angry words and ice in her blue eyes.

He controlled his urge to drive by her house and headed instead for the pond. At least he could sit there for a time, remembering how it had felt to hold her in his arms as they skated . . . how that first kiss from her innocent but willing lips had tasted so very long ago. Perhaps that would be enough to satisfy him.

"Perhaps," he murmured. "But I doubt it."

On the morning she was to be married, Persia felt she had to get away by herself for a time. She felt nervous, uncertain, and ready to back out of the whole thing. Never mind going to India! She would stay safe in her snug Maine harbor town for the rest of her life.

She dressed quickly in the simple taffeta gown she'd made for her wedding and slipped out before her father was awake. Without even thinking where she was going, she headed for the ice pond.

By the time she reached it, she had her emotions in hand. The heavy sound of the Irish ice-cutters' booming voices and the jingle and slap of the horses' harnesses as they worked came as a comfort to her. This was here; this was now. She needn't worry over Cyrus Blackwell, the reality of her future, or Zachariah Hazzard, the fantasy from her past.

Lifting her dark skirts and brushing aside the heavy veil she had adopted as part of her missionary's wife's costume, she quickened her pace. Soon she was standing at the edge of the pond, which was alive with men, horses, and ice-cutting tools. It was going well, she could see.

Every phase of the operation was in progress at once—clearing, scoring, grooving, and sawing. Closest to her, thick-muscled men were hard at work with shovels, clearing the packed snow from the ice. One man was using a horse-drawn scraper. He spied her watching and waved. She waved back.

On the far side of the pond, she saw one of the workmen seated on the scoring sled—a chairlike contraption pulled by a single horse. The apparatus had iron runners with saw teeth about eighteen inches apart. As the scoring sled was pulled by the horse, the man's weight upon it dug even lines across the ice.

Next would come the grooving operation. Long lines would be cut by a plowlike machine at ninety-degree angles in the other direction, marking the ice off into blocks roughly three feet square. Men with hand saws would then cut it free.

"A good mornin' to you, boss lady. Would you be wantin' me to clear a patch for you to skate?"

"Thanks, no, Mike," she called back. "I've only come down to see how the work is progressing."

"Oh, ma'am, we'll have that new ship of your daddy's packed tight with these crystal cubes of Yankee coldness before Paddy's pig can blink his eye at a serpent."

Suddenly, Persia's gaze traveled beyond the copper-whiskered workman to the far side of the pond. A strange sleigh was drawn up under a stand of elms. One lone figure sat behind the team, staring across the ice field at her.

"Mike, who's the man over there watching us?"

He glanced in the direction she indicated and shrugged his wide shoulders. "Beats me, ma'am. He's been there a while, though. I was over to that side of the ice about a half hour ago and got a close look at him." He squinched up his jowls and whispered, "Evil-looking cuss, he is! Scar down his face that would frighten Old Nick himself. But he's not in the way and doin' no harm, so I didn't chase him off. I will, though, if you want, ma'am."

"No, Mike. He's probably just curious to see the ice harvest. It does seem odd, though, that a stranger would be out here this time of morning."

"Takes all kinds, ma'am."

"Yes, of course, you're right."

Sensing that the "boss lady," as all the men called Persia, had drifted off into her own thoughts, the ice-cutter went back to work.

She was indeed in her own world, thinking of Zack and their first night together at the pond. She could still see him as he had been that night—strong, tall, and ruggedly handsome, his face smiling down into hers. Warmth crept through her veins as memories tumbled from some secret, long-locked part of her heart. She realized suddenly that she was smiling, but at the same time tears swam in her eyes.

It hurt to think of Zack. It hurt like the very devil, even after all this time!

She found her gaze straying across the pond once more to the lone man pacing beside his sleigh. He had a slight limp, but he carried himself with a certain re-strained, arrogant power that touched a spot somewhere deep inside her. No, she decided suddenly, it wasn't the stranger who had touched the chords of her heartstrings, but an old love—gone forever.

She turned from the pond, unable any longer to en-dure the pain brought on by the memories this place held. She had no right to feel this way. Before noon, she would be another man's wife.

Without further ado, she hurried up through the woods and out of sight of the man whose dark eyes followed her.

She had no way of knowing that the stranger across the pond was sharing similar disturbing feelings or that he had been wondering who she was and why the sight of the woman dressed in black with her face hidden by a heavy veil should cause a painfully pleasant surge in his loins.

When the woman across the pond disappeared, Captain Zachariah Hazzard climbed up into his sleigh and urged the horses toward the Old Post Road, headed back to Boston.

No need to linger here, he thought. The memories were far too disturbing to endure. And Persia was gone—as good as dead to him.

It wasn't much of a wedding. In fact, it almost wasn't one at all. But to this very day, those interested in York County history can find it recorded in the old church ledger: "Married this tenth day of November in the year of our Lord, Eighteen Hundred & Forty-six, Miss Persia Whiddington of this village, by proxy, to the Reverend Cyrus Blackwell, Bombay, India."

Still, at the time, Reverend Osgood took great exception to having a tattooed heathen stand in for his bridegroom and almost refused to perform the ceremony.

"It simply isn't fitting! The man is more cannibal than Christian!"

"See here, Osgood, that's no way to talk about my man," thundered Captain Widdington. "Fletcher will be traveling with my daughter to see her safely to her husband in India, so I find it more than fitting that he should take Brother Blackwell's place. I demand that you proceed!"

They were gathered in the tiny church office, not the sanctuary where most nuptials were celebrated. The Reverend Mr. Osgood had stood firm in his conviction that Persia's checkered past precluded any thoughts of allowing her to marry in the usual sight of God. Captain Whiddington tried to kick up a fuss about it, but Persia persuaded him to be still. There was more than ample space in the church office, the bride pointed out, to accommodate the wedding party—herself, the preacher, Fletcher, and her father. Europa had been notified, but purposely not in time for her to arrive for the ceremony. She would be coming in on tomorrow's stage from Portland. Besides, holding the wedding in the church would have only pointed up the fact that no guests were in attendance.

The whole town was in a furor over Persia's marriage to Cyrus Blackwell. If Persia thought she had been gossiped about before, that was nothing compared to the wagging of tongues now. Still, it would have been worse had she planned to journey all the way to India unwed. That would have been a scandal to end all. But at this point she could endure whatever was whispered about her. It wouldn't last much longer. Soon she would be on her way, leaving her old life, her old name, and her old enemies far behind.

Right now, she just wanted to be done with it. Ever since the meeting with Reverend Osgood a few days before, her mind had been straying in odd directions. Years ago she'd given up all hope of ever seeing Zachariah Hazzard again, or so she'd thought. But these past few nights she'd lain awake, dreading sleep and the dreams it brought. He came to her in these dreams—bold, naked, and ready to bed her—forcing her to relive every intimate detail of the time they had shared so long ago. The visions of him gave her an eerie, unsettled feeling. It almost seemed as if Zack had been far, far away for a long time, but was on his way back even now. She could almost sense him drawing nearer. That was ridiculous, of course. Why, after all these years, would he suddenly decide to drop back into her life?

It was probably just the idea of marrying a man she didn't know that had her emotions in such a turmoil. After all, this was a big step. And her only other brush with wedlock had been with Zack. She was sure that was all it amounted to. Still . . .

Reverend Osgood was clearing his throat, bringing Persia's thoughts back to the business at hand.

"Dearly beloved, we are gathered here today, in the sight of God, to join this man and this woman . . ."

Persia barely heard the words. She was conscious of the stiffness of her horsehair petticoats against the dark taffeta of her skirt, the creaking of whalebone as she breathed, the spreading coldness in her heart. It was almost as if she were closing a door on something . . . or someone.

"In the name of His Most Holy Lordship, the Reverend Mr. Cyrus Blackwell," Fletcher intoned importantly, "I do."

In spite of her agitation, Persia made the required responses to the proper questions. She had spoken these same phrases in her mind a thousand times. But somehow they now sounded odd to her ears. She didn't feel like a bride. She felt strangely removed from the whole scene, as if she were floating somewhere overhead, watching and listening to strangers.

"I now pronounce you man and wife. You may kiss the—" Reverend Osgood looked stricken suddenly as he gazed up into the blue patterns of Fletcher's face. He cleared his throat, trying to cover his slip. "No, I don't suppose you'd better."

Out of pure spite, and appreciation, too, Persia reached up and gave her father's servant a peck on the cheek. Fletcher smiled. The minister bristled.

"Well, I suppose that takes care of it," Asa Whiddington said.

Persia stared down at her left hand and the gold band encircling her finger. It had been her mother's wedding ring. It felt tight and heavy, as if it didn't belong there. She was tempted to remove it, but that would only create more gossip. She let her hand drop.

"Can we go home now, Father?"

"By all means, Mrs. Blackwell." The captain grinned at her, but his eyes looked pained when he spoke her new name.

Persia Whiddington Blackwell's wedding night was not as she had imagined it would be. Following a light, silent supper shared with her father, she excused herself and went to bed. She had eaten little, but the emptiness she felt deep inside had nothing to do with her slight appetite. She longed for something else far more than she craved food.

Slowly, she undid the buttons on her black wedding

dress. The somber fabric reflected her mood, and threatening tears stung the insides of her eyelids.

She tried to imagine what her wedding night would be like if her husband were here with her. Would he be gentle and patient, taking her mistakenly for a virgin? Would he find her disgusting and hate her once he discovered she was not pure? Or would the holy missionary simply spend their first night together praying over her, asking God to make her worthy of their mission?

"No!" she gasped. "Please, God, not that!" The tears she had been holding back flooded her eyes as she realized for the first time that it wasn't merely a husband she needed, but a husband's love.

On sudden impulse, she went to her bureau and rummaged through the bottom drawer. Buried deep down beneath a pile of shawls and blouses that needed mending, she found what she was looking for. She caressed the fine white fabric lovingly. This was the first time she had set eyes on it since she'd hurriedly packed it away on another tearful night almost ten years before.

Dare I? she wondered.

She drew out the gown and placed it to her cheek. The feel of the soft linen against her skin brought back a rush of memories. Her heart swelled with emotion. Her hands trembled.

Quickly, she shed her underthings and slipped into the gown—the same one she had worn that night in Boston with Zack. She could still remember the thrill that had coursed through her as his fingers had fumbled at the ties in their urgent haste to find her breasts only moments before he'd left her that long-ago morning. But, oh, how precious those few moments had been!

This was the purest kind of folly. She was only inviting unhappiness. But she couldn't help herself. This was her wedding night! She would wear the gown her mother had made for the occasion.

Slipping between the cool sheets, Persia felt almost wicked. Zack's hands had touched this gown, and then they had touched her. She closed her eyes, remembering. All the need and love and passion came flooding back to drown her senses. Her tears flowed freely.

In her mind, she saw his face, his body—throbbing its need for her. She remembered how she'd caught her breath in that wonderful, terrifying moment when his weight had sagged the bed. She could still feel the shock of his first touch, the urgency of his kisses. She twisted in her bed now, moaning softly, aching through and through.

She tried to recapture the memory of his first thrust. But all she could remember was that following the sharp stab of pain, she'd felt filled and whole and infinitely loved. After that had come such sheer ecstasy that there was no way for her mind to recreate it. She would recognize the feeling, if ever she was lucky enough to experience it again. But for now the memory of that magic moment eluded her.

She hugged herself, trying to imagine that Zack was there with her—holding her, kissing her, possessing her totally. But it was no use.

Suddenly, a great sadness swept over her. She realized in that instant that this was the end of it. All these years, she had waited and hoped. She had always believed deep down that she would find Zack again. But now, she had killed whatever glimmer of hope still existed. She had severed the final bond between them by sealing her marriage to Cyrus Blackwell.

In a moment of perfect anguish, she tore the linen gown from her body and tossed it furiously across the room, then collapsed on the bed, sobbing in utter torment. She cried most of the night away. And before sleep from exhaustion finally overtook her, she experienced a hopelessness, and emptiness, a bitterness toward life like none she had ever known before.

"Honestly, Father! I simply don't know what to say! *Married?* How could you have condoned such an impetuous action?"

Europa Whiddington Holloway—still pretty, but plumped out considerably by having borne six sons in nine years—stood in the entranceway of her childhood home, hands on her hips and her cheeks bright red from more than the cold wind outside. She had just arrived; Seton and Fletcher were still hauling bags inside from the pung, but already her tirade was under way.

"I've begged you and begged you to send her to Portland," Europa continued. "I could have found *someone* for her there. No one in Cumberland County knows about her indiscretions. But to permit her to marry a stranger!" Europa gave a little snort of indignation. "Mother would never have allowed this to happen!"

"It's not Father who got married yesterday, Europa. If you have something on your mind, please address me directly," Persia said, coming down the stairs.

Europa huffed in exasperation. "I don't see any use in talking to *you*! Obviously you've misplaced whatever wits you once had. *Married*!" she repeated.

"Yes, married, sister, the same as you." Persia was determined not to be bullied by Europa. She'd had enough bullying from her own memories the night before.

"Well, I'd hardly say that your marriage to this . . . this *missionary* is the same as mine to dear Seton."

"Perhaps not at the moment, but give me a few months. I'm sure I'll soon be carrying my first son, just as you were immediately following your wedding."

"Persia Whiddington!"

"The name is *Blackwell* now, Europa." It still felt queer on her tongue, but Persia didn't let that show. "Please try to remember it."

"Girls, girls!" interrupted their father. "Must you lock horns the moment you set eyes on each other? Really, Europa, your sister's marriage is quite legal and official. And she will be sailing for Bombay on the *Madagascar* in a few days to join her new husband."

Europa's hand flew to her trembling lips. She looked as if she might faint at any moment. "You can't mean it! She'll be traveling *alone*? This so-called *husband* of hers is allowing her to journey halfway around the world all by herself? Why, Father, that's the most indecent thing I've ever heard in my life! What will people say?"

"I won't be traveling alone. Fletcher is escorting me."

Europa cut her eyes in a quick glance at the manservant, and the rest of the blood drained from her face.
"Fletcher is *hardly* a suitable companion for a lady!"

Persia smiled smugly in spite of herself. She knew that
her next statement would silence her sister one way or
another. "I don't really need any companion, actually,
since I'll be sailing as a part of the ship's company. You
see, Father's offered me the position of supercargo and
I've accepted the job."

Seton Holloway came through the front door with the
last of the baggage just in time to catch his wife as she
fainted.

"My word!" he exclaimed. "Did I miss something?"

Europa's husband might have missed the first scene in
the drama, but he got to see and hear it replayed almost
hourly. His wife refused to let the matter rest, even
though she knew there was nothing she could do to
change things.

Finally, on a fine snowy morning after a particularly
heated contest over breakfast, Persia stormed out of the
house. Seton, always the peacemaker, ran after her.

"Wait, Persia," he called.

She slowed her angry strides, kicking at clumps of
snow on the path while giving him time to catch up.

"Will it help any if I apologize?" he offered.

Immediately, some of the anger left her. "Oh, Seton,
you have nothing to apologize for. She just gets me so
riled up that I have to get away from her or I'm afraid
I'll start pulling her hair like I used to do when we were
children."

"Maybe she could use some hair pulling from time to
time. I'm afraid I'm too easygoing to keep her in hand."
He offered his sister-in-law a sheepish grin. "I can't
help it. I love her."

Persia patted his arm. "Of course you do, Seton. I do,
too. I have to admit, though, that I'm awfully glad you
moved her off to another county and tied her down with

CHAPTER SIXTEEN

T_{HE} Tail of the Devil was gone, "burnt to a cinder of a cold January night back in forty-two," Zachariah was told when he inquired of an ancient sailmaker at India Wharf in Boston.

So, his former "home" and the scene of his downfall was no more. Too bad, he thought. He'd planned to pay one last visit to beat the living be-Jesus out of the tavernkeeper, if he was still around. The two men who had cold-cocked him and hauled him off to the *Alissa May* that long-ago night had laughingly confided in him later that his "good friend," Clancey the barkeep, had set the whole thing up.

"Pay him two dollars a head, we do, to tip us off to likely prospects. Fine man to do business with, the bloke is. No muss, no fuss, no law on our tails."

The grungy pair had laughed and spat and pounded each other on the back in congratulation when they told him the details of their excellent shanghai operation. Then, without ceremony, they had kicked him down the ladder into the *Alissa May*'s reeking hold, where he was

given a few hours in the lonely darkness to recover his
senses before he was set to work. He'd been more slave
than seaman for the next four years, until the ship had
wrecked off Java and he'd washed ashore.

Before taking his leave, however, he'd settled his
score with those two. One disappeared over the stern
without a trace on a hot, stormy night into the shark-
infested South Pacific waters. The other *poor fellow*
"lost his footing" in the rigging and plummeted to his
death on the filthy, steaming deck of the *Alissa May*. All
through the years since, Zack had been intent on planning how the third conspirator would meet his Maker.
He had whiled away more hours than he could count,
when he was chained belowdecks awaiting his watch,
plotting the barkeep's destruction. He felt almost cheated,
hearing from the sailmaker that Clancey had "sizzled
like pork fat" as his inn burned down around him.

Zack gave the sailmaker a silver dollar for his time,
then he sauntered off down the quay. He was at loose
ends now. There was no reason for him to stay on in
Boston. And certainly his trip to Maine had been a
mistake, opening old wounds that tore at his heart.

Better, he thought, to ship out at once than sit about
counting his woes and feeling sorry for himself.

For some unknown reason, his mind wouldn't let go
of the woman in black he'd seen across the pond several
days before. He'd been half tempted to go to her and
ask her name. Maybe she knew Persia. Maybe she could
have told him whether Persia had ever married. But, in a
way, he was glad he hadn't asked. He'd lost Persia; that
was all that mattered. His sins were too many to go
crawling back to her, begging her to see him again.
Finding out that she was happily wed to some other man
could hardly have helped him. Still, it was damned unfair!

Heading up the street, he turned toward the United
States Hotel. There agents could always be found who
were looking for captains ready to sign on. But he spotted a sign in the dirty window of a low brick building
that stopped him.

"Ship's crew needed—IMMEDIATELY!" it read.

Immediately was exactly the time he wanted to ship out. He shoved the creaking door open and stepped inside. The room was small and cluttered.

"Help you, mate?" The pale, shriveled man behind the desk never looked up but answered the bell over the door when it jingled.

"The name's Hazzard—Captain Zachariah Hazzard, late in command of the *Mazeppa*. I'm looking for a new berth, an ice ship, if there's one leaving right away."

"A cap'n, eh?" The tired-eyed clerk looked up, squinting hard at the tall man before him. "A bit odd, ain't it, for a ship's commander to be out trying to hire on like a common seaman? You pile your last one up on the rocks, maybe?"

Zack realized that his method of finding employment was unusual for one of his experience and position, but the man's tone annoyed him nonetheless. "I've lost but one ship in my entire career, and that was some years ago off the Irish Coast in heavy seas with a *woman* on board."

The clerk's pinched face twitched in a grin. "Ain't partial to women much, are you, Cap'n?"

"Not on board my ships."

"Too bad. I might of helped you out otherwise."

"What do you mean?" Zack leaned over the desk, all attention.

"Well, it ain't a for-sure, just a maybe, you understand. But the ship's due to sail in no more than a week. She's got a ship's master signed on, but he come down with a broken leg. Ice being a meltable cargo, the owners don't want to wait for their captain to mend up. He swears he's still going, but one of the two owners whispered it to me not an hour ago that I'm to be on the lookout for a suitable replacement."

"What about this woman? Who is she?"

"Oh, some missionary's wife on her way to Bombay. A Miz Blackwell."

The clerk didn't bother to add that she was also the daughter of one of the owners and part of the ship's company.

Zack's mind raced ahead. A missionary's wife would be the least difficult type of woman passenger to take along, if any female was less than impossible. And if she'd spent time in India already, she'd have made the passage before. She would know the discomforts and dangers facing her. Also, the sailors weren't likely to give a preacherman's wife a second look. There'd be no grumbling in the ranks over her because even rough seamen dared not cast lustful glances at such a woman. Yes, it might work out all right.

"By God, I'll take it!" Hazzard boomed, giving the desk a sharp smack with his fist.

"Here now, you just hold on! It ain't been offered right yet. Give me a list of the ships you've commanded and such. I'll pass that along to the owners and we'll see what we see. Stop by again in a couple of days."

Zack's spirits sagged. He was ready to go *now*. "You've got nothing else? Perhaps leaving sooner?"

The man cast a suspicious eye at the tough-looking, scar-faced captain. "It appears to me you're a mite eager. You sure you ain't in no trouble?"

"Of course not! I just need to feel the sea under me again."

Even as he spoke the words, Zack realized the sea wasn't all he needed under him. The trip back to Maine and his constant thoughts of Persia had put a giant-sized ache in his groin.

When he left the office, after assuring the clerk he would be back, the first person he saw was one of the dockside ladies who plied their trade among seafaring men.

"Buy me a drink, mate?" she asked, putting a long-nailed hand to his chest and bringing her painted face close to his.

Zack started to brush past her, but something in the faded prettiness of her features and the shabby elegance of her attire stopped him. She was young, perhaps twenty, but as well used as the cast-off gown clothing her supple body. He saw that she was shivering. Reaching out, he pulled her threadbare cape more closely around her shoulders. Her feet, he noticed, were clad not in boots against the ice and snow, but in worn-out dancing slippers. No wonder she was freezing!

"You've got a room?" he asked gently.

"A cold one."

Her big eyes, he realized suddenly, were almost the same blue as Persia's, and her hair was a tawny reddish gold. He felt a new flow of warm blood at the thought.

"Well, it won't be cold tonight. Lead the way, girl."

He stopped off to buy brown bread, cheese, and wine. The bright-eyed, warm-bosomed girl—whose name he never got around to asking—took him to her dingy room and into her well-used bed. And all the snowy night through, they kept each other from the cold.

In the deepest dark of the hours past midnight, her full breasts felt good against his bare chest . . . but not as good as Persia's. Her kisses were urgent and hot and sweet . . . but not as sweet as Persia's. And when he mounted her and entered quickly with a sudden hunger so devastating that it would not be denied, her body opened to him and seemed to welcome his thrusts. But there was none of the depth of love and longing and tenderness that he had known with Persia.

At dawn's first light, Zack rose and dressed. He left more money than was due and went away, not waking her to say good-bye. He felt empty somehow and used up. The ache was gone from his body, but not from his heart or his soul. It never would be, he realized. Not with Persia gone.

The trip wasn't starting out well. All the omens were bad, Persia thought. First, there had been the trouble with the *Madagascar's* launching; the new ice ship had nearly foundered as she'd slipped down the ways. Then, a dreadful storm had blown up as they'd set out on the bark's maiden voyage from Quoddy Cove to Boston, with snow thicker than New England clam chowder and the temperature so low that the new masts were sheathed in thick ice. And, finally, Captain Gideon's dreadful accident. He had been tossed out of his bunk during the height of the storm and, smashing into the bulkhead, had broken his leg in two places.

"Poor man," she said to herself. "Such an inglorious way to get dry-docked."

Persia was glad her father had stayed at home rather than making the journey up to Boston to see her and his new ice ship off to India. This way, since he knew nothing of Captain Gideon's misfortune, he wouldn't worry himself sick over it. First Mate Barry had assured Persia that Frederick Tudor would take care of hiring on another ship's master before the rest of the ice was loaded at Gray's Wharf in Charlestown.

Now things seemed to be going more smoothly. The weather was clearing—still cold enough to make an Eskimo shiver, but the snow had let up and the seas were smoothing out before them. Within the hour, they would make port and begin taking on the balance of the ice, cut from Fresh Pond.

Persia glanced about her. The captain's cabin on board the *Madagascar* was a fine compartment with its firm oversized bunk, chart table, desk, chairs, and bookshelves. She had made it a point before sailing to stock the shelves with books on medicine, religion, botany, and astronomy. Only a few of her favorite romantic novels were among the leatherbound volumes, and she had taken care to hide those behind her prized copy of Dr. Bowditch's book on navigation. It would never do for a supercargo—*or* a minister's wife—to be discovered reading Sir Walter Scott's *Ivanhoe*.

She had protested at first when Captain Gideon had insisted she take the master's stateroom. After all, she wanted no special provisions made simply because she was the only woman aboard. But, having let him convince her, she was now used to her surroundings and quite happy with them. She only hoped that the new captain would be as understanding as his predecessor and not order her out of his bed the moment he set sea boot on board.

She sat in the small rocker she'd brought from her bedroom at home. From now on it would be her only

anchor to her old life. Even its irritating little creak
seemed good and familiar to her. Staring down at her
pale hands folded against the dull black of her skirt, she
wondered what lay ahead for her. She touched the wide
gold band on her left hand. It felt cold and alien to her
still.

"Married," she whispered. "Wife of the Reverend
Cyrus Blackwell. Persia Blackwell."

She sighed. Neither the name nor the thought of having a husband seemed right to her yet. She had assumed
she would adjust to her new status in a short time.
Goodness knows she had reminded herself who she was
often enough these past days. But ever since that morning at the pond, she had felt like a craft set adrift with no
direction, no snug harbor waiting. And, too often for
comfort these days, when she should be looking forward
to the future, her thoughts instead lingered on the past
. . . on Zachariah Hazzard.

A knock at the door came as a welcome interruption.

"Yes?" she called.

"Miss Persia, we have made port. Should it please
you to come on deck, I shall willingly act as your escort."

"Thank you, Fletcher. Give me just a moment."

Persia went to the spirits chest, which she was using
as a *bonnetière*, and drew out her veiled hat. Carefully,
she adjusted it on her head so that not a wisp of her
bright hair showed. Then with a flip of her wrist, she
tossed the thick black netting down to cover her face.
Only her gold wedding band and a scrimshandered cross
of whale ivory relieved the stark black of her costume.
She looked every inch the proper missionary's wife.

She went out into the passageway to find Fletcher
waiting. She smiled beneath her veil as she took his arm,
thinking to herself what an odd appearance the two of
them presented. Fletcher, too, had taken to wearing
austere black costumes. With his long, oiled black hair
and the tattooing on his copper-colored face, he looked
like the devil himself. She had noticed the crew's reaction to her servant from the very first. The sailors all
feared Fletcher. It was just as well, she thought. She

wanted to keep the men at a distance at all times. Having "the devil" always hovering nearby would ensure that.

By the time they reached the upper deck, the ship had docked and the loading of the ice was already in progress. Under gray morning skies, a long line of pungs filled with blocks of ice waited alongside the *Madagascar*. A hand-operated hoist was set up on deck, consisting of a horizontal windlass and two gigs—platforms to hold the huge blocks. The cable wound around the drum of the windlass made a creaking, complaining sound as it strained under the weight. While one of the gigs was below on the platform, being loaded with ice, the other was on deck being unloaded so that the great blocks could be sent below to the hold by way of a large chute. Persia could hear the men in the hold singing as they packed the precious cargo in sawdust. She knew that by nightfall, three hundred tons of the "Yankee coldness" would be stowed below.

"Mr. Tudor was here when we docked," Fletcher told her.

"Oh, I should have come up to give him Father's regards. Why didn't you come down for me, Fletcher?"

"He begged your pardon, but he had an urgent errand. He will return soon. There is much worry over finding a suitable captain. He said, however, that you should not concern yourself, Miss Persia. He has received one promising application and is going to interview the gentleman."

"Fine! It will be a relief to have a full crew again."

Persia felt a sudden chill and pulled her cape closely about her. "Perhaps I'll go below now. The wind seems to have shifted. I feel a storm in the brewing."

Fletcher glanced at the sky with a keen eye. If anything, the clouds were lifting. A stray sunbeam was peeking through here and there. But he was not one to dispute his mistress. He offered his arm to see her safely to her cabin.

*   *   *

The storm that was brewing was in Frederick Tudor's office. The keen-eyed merchant had no liking for the man who had come to interview for the position of captain of his ship. There was a wildness in his dark eyes and a brashness to his speech. Granted, the master of a ship had to be self-assured, but this Hazzard fellow went beyond the limits.

"See here, Captain Hazzard, as owner of the *Madagascar* I say what goes. She sets sail the day after tomorrow and not a minute sooner. If that doesn't suit you, then I'll bid you good day and offer you my best wishes in your attempt to find a berth elsewhere."

The tall, grizzled seaman standing before his desk was strangling the hat in his big hands.

"I don't mean to tell you your business, sir, but if some extra men were put on to help pack the ice, the loading could be speeded up and we could be on our way hours ahead of schedule."

Tudor bristled. "I don't remember telling you yet that you would be master of the *Madagascar's* crew. Your *we* seems a bit premature, sir!"

Zachariah Hazzard felt his temper rising. What did the man want him to do, *beg*?

"Excuse me. I was under the impression that you needed a captain."

"But I'm not desperate. I don't mean to sign on just anyone."

"Begging your pardon, but I'm not *just anyone*. I've been at sea since I was twelve years old. I worked my way up through the ranks. And I've worked harder than most. I was shanghaied ten years ago and spent four long years doing the dirtiest work to be had on the high seas. Since my escape, I've come up to second mate, first mate, and finally ship's master. I've commanded barks out of Havana, New Orleans, the Indies."

"But never an ice ship," Tudor put in.

"Maybe not, but I know the ice business. And I'm a New Englander, born and bred. That should count for something."

Tudor eyed the man up and down. Aye, by God, it did

count! And this seafaring man had spunk and a drive
that would make him a fine master.

"All right, Hazzard, you've got the job. But mind
you, you'll follow my orders."

Zack nodded. He didn't like the owner's attitude, but
it seemed the *Madagascar* was the only ship to be had
right now. Still, there were some things that needed to
be settled before he put his name to paper.

"I understand there's a woman on board."

Tudor frowned. The subject of his female supercargo
was a sore spot with him. He'd been dead set against the
arrangement, but her father—his partner—had insisted.
Tudor decided it was best not to mention Persia's official status to Captain Hazzard. Let him find out for
himself once he was on board.

"There is—a missionary's wife, going to join her husband in Bombaby."

"I'm not fond of the idea," Zack added.

Tudor offered him a sly smile. "That she's on the
ship, or that she's married? You needn't worry about
Mrs. Blackwell, Captain. She comes of a seafaring family and she knows the ropes. Besides, she has a manservant with her to see to her needs."

Zack's brows shot up in surprise. He'd never heard of
a woman traveling with a manservant before. But perhaps he was one of her husband's Indian retainers. Zack
had been told that they were the most trustworthy servants to be found.

"A woman is bad luck aboard a ship," he persisted.

"Then you don't want the post?"

Zack backed off. He got Tudor's meaning—the woman
went, whether the captain liked it or not.

Tudor read the resolve in Hazzard's face and shoved
the papers toward him across the desk. Zack signed
quickly.

"That's fine, Captain Hazzard. The *Madagascar* is
berthed at Gray's Wharf. You may go aboard as soon as
you like."

Zack shook the man's hand. It was odd, but suddenly
he felt a strange elation, an almost boyish glee. He

hadn't experienced this kind of sensation since he'd boarded his first vessel as a cabin boy.

"I'll be going on board within the hour, sir."

He turned quickly and strode out of the office.

Later that afternoon, Persia decided to avail herself of one last homeport luxury before they sailed. During the long months ahead at sea, all fresh water would be reserved for drinking. There would be only brine from the sea for bathing. Thus she had asked Fletcher to heat water for the copper tub and bring extra buckets to the compartment so that she might wash her hair thoroughly one last time.

When the door flew open unexpectedly, she was swathed in a length of toweling with another wrapped turban fashion around her wet hair. She gave a startled cry and turned her back before the intruder stepped into the cabin.

"If you *please*!" she shrieked.

A low laugh greeted her embarrassment.

"Whoever you are, leave my cabin this minute!"

"*Your* cabin?" The man's deep voice held a mixture of anger and amusement. "I beg your pardon, madam, but I'm the new captain of the *Madagascar*, and unless I'm very much mistaken, this is the *captain's cabin*."

Persia was shivering with cold and embarrassment. "Can't we discuss this later?"

"No," replied the husky voice behind her. "I think we should settle it now. I was told there was a woman on board, but Mr. Tudor also stated that you were a *married* woman. He mentioned nothing to the effect that I would be sharing my quarters with you. Still, I don't mind, if your husband doesn't."

"*Really!*" Persia was furious, outraged. "If you don't leave this minute, sir, I shall be forced to call my servant and have him throw you out!"

Zack stood his ground. He didn't really understand why he was giving the woman such a hard time. It was hardly the gentlemanly thing to do. There she stood with her nicely rounded buttocks plainly molded inside the damp towel, her creamy shoulders quaking invitingly, and her shapely ankles and feet bare for the admiring. The thought struck him suddenly that her missionary husband probably had never seen her so enticingly garbed, with her skin glowing a warm, pearly hue and droplets of water clinging to her slender neck and arms. He should be ashamed of himself for staring . . . but he wasn't. All he felt was a peculiar heat flowing through his blood and a pulsing in his groin.

"Damn," he muttered harshly. He'd expected the woman to be a matronly crone. He'd hoped so, anyway. But even without seeing her face, he could tell she was a beauty.

"I don't see what you expect to accomplish by this humiliation, Captain," she said, interrupting his thoughts. "I can hardly move out of your quarters until I'm dressed, and I certainly can't get into my clothes with you standing there gawking."

He knew he had to leave. Any other man would probably be long gone already. But something in the tone of her voice—its challenge, its boldness—made him offer one last thrust.

"Shall I summon your manservant to help you dress, Mrs. Blackwell?"

The question shocked Persia so thoroughly that she almost turned to face the man but stopped herself in the nick of time. It certainly wouldn't do to offer him a view of her breasts straining over the top of the towel. That would please him far too much, she could tell.

"Thank you, no. Just *leave*!"

Zack smiled at the frustration in her voice. "Then I'll bid you adieu for now, Mrs. Blackwell. The pleasure, believe me, has been all mine."

At the sound of the door closing, Persia turned. He was gone. She stood for a long time, staring after him. For the life of her, she couldn't understand what was happening. She felt warmed through and through. Her heartbeat was rapid, her head light. It almost seemed as if the captain's rough, strangely familiar voice had fondled her physically. Her breasts were suddenly peaked with desire, and an almost forgotten ache throbbed deep inside her. She sank down into the green velvet rocker, feeling the soft fabric caress the bare calves of her legs. She forced herself to breathe deeply, calmly.

"Get hold of yourself, Persia," she commanded. "The man is a cad, a bounder."

Then she smiled. Hadn't she said those same things about Zack at one time?

Thoughts of Zack brought a new flush to her skin. And she realized suddenly that the strange effect the captain had on her was caused by the fact that his voice reminded her of Zack's. Oh, the captain's was deeper and huskier, but certain inflections in his tone were very similar. Zack, dear Zack!

She forced his name and his well-remembered face from her mind. She was a married woman! It was downright sinful to keep dwelling on the past.

Suddenly, a real worry took possession of her. How would she ever face the captain after he had seen her unclothed in his own cabin?

She glanced about the room, frantic. Her eyes lit on the spirits cabinet and relief flooded through her. The veil! She would hide her face all the way to India, if need be. That would keep the brash captain from seeing the flame he brought to her cheeks.

She rocked slowly, thinking to herself that it was going to be a long, unnerving voyage.

Suddenly, she sat up straight and her towel dropped to her waist.

"Why, the man never even bothered to introduce himself! How rude!"

CHAPTER SEVENTEEN

H*AD* it not been for Fletcher's memorable tattooed face, Captain Hazzard might have sailed the entire fifteen thousand miles from Boston to Bombay without ever realizing that Mrs. Blackwell and his Persia were one and the same.

He had not made any mental connection between the towel-swathed missionary's wife and the woman he loved. As for recognizing her voice, the woman whose bath he'd interrupted had alternately shrieked at him and whispered nervously. He certainly had no intention of becoming friendly with her in any case. He was already angry with her for being young and a beauty. That much he'd been able to tell even from the back, with the towel leaving just enough of her uncovered to arouse.

He grew angrier still when First Mate Barry informed him that she was also part of the ship's company. The two men were standing on the quarterdeck, passing the final hours before time to cast off. Barry commented that it would be interesting to see if a lady could fetch a higher price for the cargo than the male supercargoes before her.

Zack stared at the man, stunned, then ranted, "A *missionary's* wife, acting as supercargo on *my* ship?"

"Aye, sir," answered the tall, wiry mate. "But she's not just that. She's the daughter of one of the owners. Didn't Mr. Tudor tell you? She supervised the ice harvest and all, too. She's as good as any man aboard." When Barry saw his captain's eyes flash angrily, he quickly added, "Present company excepted, of course, sir."

"Well, I don't give a damn whose daughter she is! Just see she stays out of my way!" Zack bellowed. Then he turned and stormed off across the deck, cursing Tudor under his breath for keeping all this a secret from him—on purpose, he was sure.

First she had taken over the cabin and now she had usurped his duties. He had known that having a woman on board would be a bad idea, but this was almost too much to abide.

She'd better stay clear of him, he thought, or he just might tell her so!

Persia was delighted to stay out of the captain's way. On the day he'd barged into her room without even knocking, she had packed up her belongings to move to another compartment at his orders. The next moment he'd had her unpacking again. He'd changed his mind, the steward told her. She was to remain in the master's stateroom. It was the least he could do to make such a delicate lady less miserable in the long months ahead at sea, Steward Dawkin repeated.

Persia imagined that she could hear the very words from the captain's sarcastic lips. She bristled. *A delicate lady* indeed!

"Well, that's just fine, Dawkin," she answered in an annoyed tone to the innocent steward. "But you tell your captain for me that, if I'm to remain here, this will no longer be referred to as the 'master's stateroom.' And I want no further intrusions upon my privacy. If he would like to have a word with me, he may speak to my man Fletcher and arrange an appointment, as he would if he were a *gentleman*."

"Yes, ma'am," Dawkin replied, bowing his way out of her compartment. He wasn't sure how Captain Hazzard would react when he delivered her stinging message, but he didn't relish the thought. He decided to tone it down a bit before passing it along.

During the remaining time that the ship was at Gray's Wharf loading its cargo, Mrs. Blackwell and Captain Hazzard had no trouble keeping their distance. Zack spent most of the time making final arrangements in town for the loading of the ice and provisions. As for Fletcher, he had yet to meet the captain. Persia had sent him ashore to enjoy his final days of freedom before they sailed. The weather was foul, so for the time being she kept to her cabin. She saw no one except for the steward who brought her meals, and he made no mention of the ship's master, knowing the animosity that already existed between the pair. She still didn't know the captain's name, but she refused to ask Dawkin, knowing that he would report her curiosity to the man himself. She wouldn't give him that satisfaction.

Persia read, she slept, she wrote final letters to family and friends. Until—if luck were with them—they happened to speak a homebound ship at sea, there would be no further opportunities for posting mail until they reached Bombay in four months' time.

When Fletcher came on board at dawn the morning they were to sail, Captain Hazzard was far too busy to notice the man. More dirty weather was blowing in, and there wasn't a moment to lose if they wanted to get under way on the appointed day.

Fletcher spied the captain at a distance. The ship's master was shouting orders to First Mate Barry, trying to be heard above the rising wind. Persia's servant noted the scar running through his wild beard and the tangled mass of silver hair whipping about his grizzled face in the wind. The man looked evil. Fletcher shivered with a premonition of disaster, then hurried below.

Although Persia had kept to her cabin, awaiting their sailing, she'd followed, by the sounds, all that was taking place above to ready the ship for sea. Now, on the very morning of their departure, she could go down the list as if she'd had an active part in the loading operation. The day before, provisions for the journey had been brought on board. She had heard the clucking and squawking of chickens, geese, and ducks. Even now she could hear a dozen or so pigs grunting in their sty on deck. The sheep and the vegetables—winter squash, turnips, carrots, potatoes, and pumpkins—would be safely stowed belowdecks until their time to grace the table. Barrels of flour and molasses, hogsheads of water, jugs of wine, demijohns of rum—all were in their places. The last item to be loaded would be the hundred barrels of Baldwin apples, literally worth their weight in silver on the market in India.

As she sat in her little velvet rocking chair, she could hear the tramp of boots coming up the gangway. That would be the crew, returning from their final shore leave. Fletcher would be among them. She wondered if the captain had stayed on board last night, or if he was the sort to seek out a woman in these final hours before land and its intimate comforts slipped away. If he had stayed on the ship, where had he slept? Were those his boots she'd heard pacing the smaller compartment next to hers late into the night?

Persia rose and flung the book she hadn't been reading onto the bunk. She was annoyed with herself for even thinking about the man. Why did she let him upset her so?

Besides, she had much more important things to concentrate on. Finally, after dreaming about it all her life, she was about to set sail for *India*! She refused to allow anything—even an arrogant captain—to spoil the excitement of this moment for her. And, too, she was about to embark on a whole new life—as a wife, and eventually, she hoped, a mother.

She decided not to wait for Fletcher to come for her. If he was back, he was probably busy stowing his own gear in his assigned compartment. There could be nothing wrong with her going on deck alone. She pulled on her veiled bonnet, flung a warm cape around her shoulders, and left the cabin.

The harbor pilot, who would see them safely down the Charles River, was on the quarterdeck, talking to the captain, whose back was to her. The gangway was hauled aboard. The lines were cast off.

Persia stood back, out of the way. This was a precarious time, she knew. Everything had to be done with split-second precision in order to get the *Madagascar* under way without a hitch. Orders flew back and forth faster than seagulls on the wing. Persia leaned against the rail, eyes closed, savoring the song of the sea.

"Heave short!" She heard the groan of the hand-operated capstan and the creak of the anchor cable as the slack was taken out of it.

"Set the tops'ls!" This order was followed by the flap-flap of canvas in the wind as the six topsails unfurled. She knew without opening her eyes that the sailors aloft in the rigging were overhauling the running gear while the sails were set.

Then came the most exciting call of all: "Break her out!"

The anchor was up. They were under full sail. And Persia's heart was singing.

The motion of the ship and the sound of the wind zinging through the rigging, pushing the canvas before it, worked together to fire her blood and spark her imagination. She didn't even notice when the ship slowed to allow the pilot to climb down into the smaller craft that would take him back to the Boston Light.

Not until Mr. Barry and Second Mate Stoner began choosing the starboard and port watches did Persia's attention return to the ship's crew. The sailors—dressed smartly in black tarpaulin hats, red-and-white shirts,

blue bell-bottomed pants, and pea coats—queued up at
the vessel's waist for this routine procedure. The two
mates took their places near the poop deck. Persia viewed
the whole scene with interest, knowing that these few
moments would decide with whom each man ate, slept,
and worked for the next four months. As the sixteen
sailors were called, name by name, each man moved to
the starboard or to port, to work either with Barry or
Stoner.

The captain was nowhere in evidence. Persia knew he
would be in the charthouse, recording the bearing taken
shortly after the pilot's departure, noting the weather in
his log, and plotting the ship's exact position on the
charts.

"Starboard and port watches chosen, Captain, sir!"
the first mate boomed out suddenly.

Through the black veil, Persia saw the tall figure as he
came out on deck as if through a haze. He stopped just
outside the charthouse door, and his gaze seemed to
lock on her. A strange chill ran through her veins, only
to be followed a moment later by a curious, caressing
warmth. The man was magnetic, if nothing else, she had
to give him that.

Releasing her now from his imprisoning gaze, he stood
before his crew, raising his big hands for silence, even
though there was no need for such a command. He was
tall, craggy, whipped by the wind and the seas like a tree
trunk turned to driftwood. Persia thought she had never
seen a man who looked so cruelly used by life—his hair
and beard white before their time, his face scarred and
lined. She couldn't imagine why she felt attracted to
him. Maybe it was those eyes, so dark and burning, or
the powerful stance that made him seem a part of the
ship he commanded.

Suddenly, his voice boomed in the quiet. "Hear me,
men of the *Madagascar*! I am a hard taskmaster, but
just. You will heed my orders. You will do your duty.
You will put this ship and its cargo first at all times. *Or*
you will pay the price for your shiftlessness and insubordination."

Persia stood frozen, mesmerized, listening to his voice.
There was something so familiar about it—not from their
first encounter aboard ship a short time ago, but from
the distant past. The inflections, the huskiness, the very
tone of it, sent a delicious shiver through and through
her.

He continued, "We have a lady on board . . . a missionary's wife." He inclined his head toward Persia, and
several of the crew members turned to stare. Some eyed
her coolly; some smiled at her. "You will belay the
rough talk whenever she is about. I will not have a lady
insulted in any fashion while she's on my ship. Am I
understood?"

"Aye-aye! Yes, Cap'n!" the crew chorused.

"Very well, then. We understand each other." He
waved a hand at the men as if dismissing them, then
added, "By the way, for those of you who don't know it
already, my name is Hazzard. Captain Zachariah Hazzard."

Persia felt her knees go weak beneath her. She gripped
the railing to keep from sinking to the deck. A red haze
filmed her eyes.

Zachariah Hazzard? It couldn't be!

Her gaze was frozen to the man. *Her* Zack? The only
man she'd ever loved . . . the man who should have
been her husband and the father of her children? Her
heart pounded a frantic tattoo. A kind of joy filled her
that had been absent since that snowy night in Boston
long, long ago. She started toward him. She had to tell
him.

"Zack, darling . . ." The words trembled, inaudible,
on her lips.

Her tears were brimming. She mustn't cry—not now!
Slipping her left hand under the veil, she brushed at the
dampness on her cheeks. When she did, she felt cold
metal chill her flesh. The freezing sensation went straight
to her heart.

Withdrawing her hand, she stared down at her wedding ring as if it had suddenly appeared there out of
magic. *Evil magic!*

Now her tears came in earnest. She had no right to Zack any longer. She was another man's wife. How could fate have played such a cruel trick?

She turned and started back to her cabin, but his voice stopped her. "Mrs. Blackwell, please, might I have a word with you?"

She faced him, fighting for control behind the veil. "Yes, Captain?" Her voice was a muted whisper. Her whole body was trembling.

"I want to apologize for the other day. I shouldn't have burst into the cabin, even though I did think it was mine. And I certainly should not have lingered there, embarrassing you so. I hope you'll forgive me. I don't think we should begin this voyage with bad blood between us."

His full lips quirked in a smile, and she felt herself melting before him. Zack! Yes, it was truly her Zack!

He went on, "This ship isn't large enough to contain petty quarrels. I thought we might put an end to our differences over dinner tonight."

She waited so long to give him an answer that he finally asked, "Mrs. Blackwell, are you all right?"

"Yes, Captain. Quite," she replied at last. "I accept your apology, but I must decline your offer this evening."

"Oh, really. I'm disappointed. Perhaps some other time?"

"Yes, Captain, thank you."

She didn't wait for him to say anything else. She couldn't stand another moment of gazing into those warm brown eyes, of hearing that voice, of knowing he was back but that she couldn't have him. Turning quickly, she hurried below to the cabin.

Barring the door, she tossed her hat and cape aside and fell to the bunk, sobbing her heart out.

"Zack, Zack," she cried. "Why now? Why here? Why after all this time, my love?"

Zack stared after the woman. What an odd way to act. He could almost swear from the quiver of her voice that beneath that black veil she had been crying. But surely a

simple apology couldn't have moved her to tears. Still,
who could ever figure out women? He certainly never
expected to be able to. For instance, why had she declined his invitation to dinner? Didn't she know that it
was customary for the ship's master and the supercargo
to take their meals together? Didn't she understand that
there was a certain ship's etiquette to be observed? *He*
was trying to be civil, but if that didn't work . . .

By God, he could *demand* her presence at his table!
And maybe he would!

"Captain, we're passing the Cape Cod Light," Mr.
Barry called.

Zack turned, his attention shifting from the woman to
the last sight he would see of American soil for a year or
more. He leaned against the rail, staring out over the sea
as the light flashed dimmer and dimmer. There was a
fresh wind. They were moving well. Soon even the faint
echo of the light on the clouds would be lost to him. It
was time to face the other direction—to look ahead, not
back.

Suddenly, a strange melancholy stole over him. It
always came at this point in a voyage. Perhaps it always
would. Leaving behind his native shore meant that he
was also leaving Persia behind. It didn't seem to matter
that he hadn't seen her in ten years or that he probably
never would again. His heart remembered and ached for
her still.

As Persia lay in the roomy cabin, exhausted emotionally and physically, the walls seemed to be closing in on
her. What was she going to do? She couldn't stay cooped
up here for four months in order to avoid him. Her black
veil would serve for a time, but only until they passed
out of the cold climate. She certainly couldn't continue
to smother herself in netting once they crossed the equator and passed into the tropics. Sooner or later, she
knew from hearing her father tell of those dreadful times,
they would be caught in the doldrums. Not a breath of
wind. Only the blazing eye of the sun scorching everything in its view. During those long, stifling days, every-

one lived on deck in order to survive. She would die of the heat if she stayed belowdecks.

But all that was weeks away. The here and now were what worried her most. She had to become accustomed to the idea of having him close to her again before she let him know who she really was. She decided to tell the steward, Dawkin, that she was indisposed and would be forced to remain in her cabin for the time being. No one would think it odd that the only woman on board was feeling a bit queasy the first days out. She might even stretch her isolation into a full week. They would probably assume that it was her time of the month. Yes, it might work! And she would have time to adjust to Zack's presence and figure out what to do next.

Satisfied with her plan, she forced the matter out of her thoughts. She undressed and climbed back into bed, taking her Bible down from the shelf. Surely reading it would calm her. After a short time, she dropped off to sleep.

Fletcher's knock woke her early in the evening. She donned a dressing robe and unlocked the door.

"Miss Persia, excuse me, please. I did not know you were napping."

"It's all right, Fletcher. Come in."

The man stood very erect beside the door, nervous at being in his mistress's bedchamber.

"Is there anything I can get for you or do for you, Miss Persia?" he offered.

"No, thank you, Fletcher. I can't think of a thing."

"Well, then I will be in the galley with the cook, if you don't mind. The fellow is from Pitcairn Island, the same as I. We have much to talk over, Rolf and me. We may even be cousins!"

"That's fine. I shouldn't be needing anything this evening. See to it that Dawkin brings my supper. I plan to turn in early. And I won't be about tomorrow at all. I'm not feeling very well."

Concern distorted the tattooing on the man's face. "Miss Persia, should I ask the captain to bring the medicine chest?"

Horror struck at Persia's heart. She had forgotten for the moment that the ship's captain also served as physician to the crew. The last thing she needed was for Zack to come to her bedside and learn the truth there!

"No, don't do that. I'll be fine. I've just had too much excitement these past few days. You go along now and enjoy your visit with the cook."

Persia was trembling when she closed the door behind Fletcher. She didn't know how much more of this she could take. It was one thing to plan one's life carefully and know exactly where it would lead. It was quite another to have fate tangle and twist it until nothing made sense any longer.

She sank to the bed, staring at the calm sea out the stern windows. It was sunset. Patterns of apricot, plum, and scarlet quilted themselves across the face of the waves. The sight was beautiful beyond anything she had ever seen in her life. Tears filled her eyes again, but this time she wept with pure joy.

The thud of boots in the compartment next to hers brought her out of her tranquil mood. It was *him*! She was sure of it.

How had he happened to sign on to the *Madagascar*? Her conversation with Seton Holloway suddenly came to mind. If it was Zack's name on the other ship's cargo manifest, it meant that he hadn't been long in port. He must have applied to Mr. Tudor's office when word spread about Captain Gideon's accident. And he'd signed on without ever knowing she would be aboard. That must be it. If he'd known, certainly he would have said something immediately.

Then another thought entered her mind. What if he had simply forgotten all about her? Ten years had separated them. And how many sea miles . . . how many other women?

She was glad when Dawkin arrived with her supper. She didn't want to think about it any longer.

"The cap'n sent this with his regards, ma'am." Dawkin placed a bottle of chilled wine on the table. "He said to tell you he hopes you'll be dining with him soon."

"Thank him for me, won't you, Dawkin?" She managed a smile for the steward. "But tell him that I'm a bit weary. I plan to stay in my cabin for a few days, until I'm rested up and have my sea legs under me."

"I'll pass the word right along to him. Eat hearty now, ma'am. There's nothing makes sea travel harder to take than an empty stomach."

Hours later, Persia was still tossing in her bed. She had only nibbled at the breast of chicken and baked winter squash and sipped at the wine. She had no appetite. And sleep refused to come. The cabin felt stuffy and too warm. Outside the windows, the moon was playing silver tricks with the sea, while a million stars cast down their gleaming reflections. Suddenly she remembered the night of the aurora borealis. The air had been so cold and clean that long-ago evening, just as it must be up on deck this very minute.

She dressed quickly, not forgetting her veil, then opened her door very carefully. The passageway was empty. She hurried out and up the ladder to the quiet deck. Never had she seen such a sight. Miles and miles of serene ocean in every direction. The sound of the wind pushing the sails and the lap of the waves seemed to have lulled the whole world into a calm euphoria.

She moved to the railing and gripped it gently. She stared out over the water, thinking back to the many hours she had spent atop the house on Gay Street, dreaming of this moment, pretending that the widow's walk was her own private quarterdeck.

She never heard a sound until he was standing beside her and said quietly, almost reverently, "A beautiful night, isn't it, Mrs. Blackwell?"

Every nerve in her body came alive. She was burning, freezing, tingling, aching . . . for *him*.

"Magnificent, Captain," she whispered back.

"I hope, for your sake, that the whole trip will be this way."

Unsure if he was serious or only testing her, she

turned toward him and said, "You needn't worry about me, sir. I'm quite seaworthy!"

He laughed—that deep, rumbling, caressing laugh she remembered so well.

"I'm sure you are, madam. Heaven help the storm that crosses your path."

She looked down, stroking her trembling fingers across the smooth oak of the rail. "Forgive me, Captain. I didn't mean to sound testy or harsh."

"I thought neither of you. I approve, Mrs. Blackwell. The voyage to India isn't easy. I'm glad to hear a certain amount of grit in your voice. You'll need it." He paused, and Persia thought he must be gazing intently at her, trying to measure her through her veil. "Is this your first voyage to Bombay?"

"Yes. I'm to meet my husband there."

Zack's voice sounded slightly disapproving when he asked, "Why didn't he take you with him? I certainly wouldn't let my wife travel so far all alone."

Persia wanted desperately *not* to discuss her husband. She cast about for another topic of conversation. "You're married, then, Captain?"

"I should be, but no. I'm not."

"You should be? I don't understand." Was he saying that he'd left behind a woman carrying his child? Her heart raged at the thought.

"What I mean is that I had my chance, long ago. I was in love with a very beautiful woman, but I let her get away from me. As I'm sure you know, Mrs. Blackwell, once you've loved totally, you never fall again. At least, I never have."

Persia was dying to ask his lover's name—her own, she was sure. It would be so wonderful to hear it spoken from his lips once more. But she dared not go too far.

Then his next statement took away her joy. "I don't think I was ever meant to marry, though. It probably turned out for the best this way."

So he had left her, thinking it *for the best*. Her pain grew until she thought it would consume her, right there before his eyes.

Suddenly his hand gripped her elbow. He might as well have taken her naked heart in his grasp.

"Why don't I see you back to your cabin, Mrs. Blackwell? It's getting cold up here. Perhaps we could share a glass of wine."

She pulled her arm away. "No, please, Captain. I don't want to take you from your duties. And I am very tired. I only needed a breath of air."

She hurried below so quickly that he never had a chance to bid her a good evening. But she still couldn't sleep. She lay in bed until dawn, listening to the steady pacing of boots in the next cabin.

Captain Zachariah Hazzard wasn't sleeping either.

CHAPTER EIGHTEEN

*T*HE *Madagascar* took the course charted by her captain—southeast into the mid-Atlantic until she was halfway between Cape Hatteras, North Carolina, and the Canary Islands. At that point, she hove sharply southward to pick up favorable trade winds. For a time, she would parallel the Brazilian coast before heading southeasterly again to pass the Cape of Good Hope at the tip of Africa. Turning north and east on reaching the Indian Ocean, she would then pass the island whose name she bore and sail on to her first port, Bombay.

Once the ship was at sea and the course plotted, time weighed heavily on Zachariah Hazzard's hands. The captain, above all men, was the least useful on board his own ship as long as everything was going smoothly. His first and second mates kept the rest of the crew in hand and busy at all times. Meanwhile, the cook cooked; the sailmaker mended sail; the steward served; and the captain waited.

And during these long, quiet hours, while he trod the deck or holed up in his cabin—glad that all was well, but alert to any impending disaster—Zack thought and thought. He turned over in his mind every word the woman on board his ship had said. He summoned up the image of her bare white shoulders. He tried to imagine her face without the veil. He recalled to mind the warmth of her flesh through the sleeve of her dress when he had touched her. And that remembered warmth brought a searing to his blood. Even now, as he lay on his bunk in his darkened cabin, he was conscious of his growing arousal.

"Goddammit, man! Have you lost your wits?" He launched himself off the bed and swept the charts from his table in a moment of frustration and anger. "She's *married*!"

He sank down into a chair and ran his fingers through his hair, pulling at it as if that might yank the craziness out of his brain. He'd never let a woman get to him like this before. No woman except Persia, but of course that was a far different case.

Here they were only three days out of port and he was driving himself to distraction over another man's wife—a woman whose face he had yet to lay eyes on. In fact, since the night of their sailing, he hadn't seen her at all. It was almost as if she were some ghost who had haunted him for a while and then deserted him just as abruptly.

And that manservant of hers was definitely some kind of spirit. Zack had heard the others talking about the odd fellow, but he had yet to see even his shadow. Seemed he was spending most of his time in the galley. There was some talk among the crew, so Mr. Barry had told Zack, that Mrs. Blackwell's servant and the cook were related.

It was late—far into the dog watch—past midnight. But he knew she wasn't sleeping. He had heard her moving about the stateroom next to his a while earlier. Now another sound from the far side of the bulkhead drew his attention and provoked his discomfort.

"She's crying again, dammit!" He spoke the words softly as if fearing he might disturb her misery.

He'd heard her sobbing in the night before, and it tore

at his heart. Why was she so unhappy? Maybe that's
why she stayed to herself and always wore her heavy
veil. She must be in mourning for someone. But who? A
child? A parent? A lover?

"Idiot," he told himself. She didn't have a lover; she
had a husband.

Still, if she had lost someone recently, that could be
why she was traveling all alone, why she always hid
behind her veil. And why she had trouble sleeping at
night.

He glanced up at the scarred leather medicine bag that
had made many voyages with him. It contained nothing
that could take away her sorrow, but there was something inside that could help her rest. He reached for the
satchel, then changed his mind. Perhaps he shouldn't
intrude on her grief. He would just wait. She would send
for him if she needed his aid.

He grabbed his coat and shrugged into it. A brisk turn
on deck. That's what he needed to clear his head and his
senses. He lurched out his door, running full tilt into a
strange man in the passageway.

"Begging your pardon, sir," said the stranger. "I
should learn to look where I am going."

Zack squinted hard at the dark face before him. The
man was dressed in black. His hair was black. His eyes
were black. But the tattooing on his face was bright
blue. From one of the cannibal tribes of the South Pacific, he would guess.

"Who are you?" Zack demanded.

"I am nobody, sir," Fletcher answered.

"A stowaway, you mean?"

"No, no! I am but a servant to Mrs. Blackwell."

Zack backed away to get a better look at the man.
"So you really do exist."

"Beg pardon, sir?"

"If you're the lady's servant, why haven't you been
looking after her needs? Do you know that she's in her
cabin crying at this very moment? She could be ill—
dying! And where have you been all this time?"

"Oh, please, sir! I had no idea. I must go to her at once!"

Zack let the man pass and went up the ladder. Not until the cold wind on deck blew over him, wiping the cobwebs from his brain, did he realize he had seen the blue-faced servant before. He turned, his jaw dropping open, as he rememebered suddenly *where* he had seen the man before. This tattooed savage was part of his own past—his past with Persia Whiddington!

At that very moment, Persia was learning from Fletcher that he and the captain had had their first confrontation on board.

Fletcher had pounded on her door a moment earlier, crying, "Open up! Please, let me in, Miss Persia!"

She ran to the door to find her servant wild-eyed and anxious.

"Are you dying, Miss Persia?" were the first words out of his mouth.

"Dying? Of course not! Whatever gave you such a notion, Fletcher?"

"The captain, he reprimanded me outside. He said you were crying, that you could be very ill and I was neglecting my duty."

"You talked to the captain?" Persia's tears of self-pity and unrequited love dried in the startled blink of an eye. She had known this moment would come. And she had dreaded it. There was no way to hide Fletcher from Zack. And certainly there could not be two such blue-patterned faces on earth. Zack was sure to recognize him and start adding things up.

"What did he say to you, Fletcher?" she asked, sounding almost desperate.

"Only that I should be more mindful of my mistress, and he is correct!"

"He didn't recognize you?"

Fletcher stared hard at her, wondering if the sea voyage really had made her ill. "Of course not, Miss Persia. We have never met before."

A nervous little laugh escaped her. She turned to her

sewing box and drew out a gold coin. "Remember this, Fletcher? You gave it to me a long time ago. The night I ran away with the captain of this ship."

Fletcher's eyes grew wide. He mouthed the word "no" but uttered not a sound. The silence stretched on for some minutes until he found his voice once more. "You mean, *this* Captain Hazzard is the same as . . ."

"Not in appearance, but he is the same man."

"What are you going to do, Miss Persia?"

She shook her head slowly. "I don't know, Fletcher. I just don't know."

"That is why you have been staying in your cabin . . . why you were crying?"

"I'm afraid so. I simply haven't been able to face the truth yet, or should I say, to face *him* with the truth."

The captain made his usual rounds on deck. But his mind was hardly on this routine task. Instead, his brain was whirling, trying to puzzle out the mystery of the woman below in her cabin.

How could it be Persia? Surely she would have told him right away, if that were the case. But perhaps not. After all, she hadn't come to the Tail of the Devil that long-ago night. Maybe she thought she could keep up her veiled charade all the way to Bombay so that he'd never know who she was, other than "the missionary's wife." But that was another odd thing. Of all the women he'd ever met, Persia Whiddington seemed the least likely to sail half the world around to join a man of the cloth. She had too much spunk . . . too much adventure in her soul . . . too much earthy love to give, and too much need in her.

But who else could it be? He knew the servant's history. The man . . . Fletcher, his name was . . . had been like a member of the Whiddington family since he was a little more than a suckling. He wouldn't have left their service. So whoever was under that veil had to be a Whiddington.

"Europa?" he asked himself aloud. Then he added

quickly, "No!" She was far too vain to hide that lovely face of hers.

Perhaps Mrs. Whiddington, he thought, widowed and now remarried. He shook his head. That couldn't be right, either. The woman he had seen—fresh from her bath—was vibrant, supple, glowing with youth.

"Persia!" He whispered the name as reverently as if it were a prayer. Then, turning on his heel, he made a dash for the ladder.

As soon as he reached the passageway, he could hear low voices coming from her cabin. It didn't matter; there was no stopping him now.

He paused outside and brought his fist up to knock. But he quickly changed his mind. He didn't intend to give her the time she was sure to request so that she might cover the face he loved with that damned veil.

Persia was still trying to explain the situation to Fletcher when her door flew open, banging back against the wall. Zack filled the opening, his broad shoulders touching the frame on either side. His hands were clenched into fists on his hips. And his face was a mask of unreadable, dueling emotions.

"You may go now, Fletcher." His voice held stony command in that husky timbre that seemed to vibrate to Persia's very core. His eyes imprisoned her, devouring the first sight of her naked face and making her feel as if her dressing gown had suddenly been stripped away. "Your mistress won't be calling on you the rest of the night. I plan to see to her needs . . . *personally!*"

A small gasp escaped Persia. She backed away from him, until her legs hit the edge of the bed, almost causing her to lose her balance.

"Miss Persia?" Fletcher said, begging with his tone to be told what he should do.

"Do as the captain says," she answered, but only after waiting so long that Zack started toward her with a menacing gleam in his dark eyes.

"If you're sure . . ."

"She's sure!" Zack snapped, never taking his eyes from hers.

Silence hung like a heavy fog in the room until the door closed softly after Fletcher. Even then, for long minutes, she and Zack held their places, saying things to each other with their eyes that no spoken words could have conveyed.

He was coming toward her, and she had no place to go. She could only stand, and wait, and . . . and *what*?

Suddenly he was there before her, his changed but well-loved face filling the whole of her vision—her *world*. His lips were parting. His breath was caressing her blush-warmed flesh. His hands were sliding about her waist—drawing her closer, closer, closer . . .

"No, Zack!" Did she say the words aloud or only think them? She had no idea. It didn't matter, anyway. He never heard.

She felt the loving, needing, bruising grip of his strong fingers about her waist. Before their lips ever met, he drew her hard against his heat and held here there, letting the sparks, the fire, the ache of longing arc from his loins to hers. This slow, sweet torture forced a moan from her lips. Her arms hung limp at her sides, her head lolled back, her breasts lifted toward his chest— not quite touching him, but close enough so that her nipples distended from his nearness, his heat. And all the while, from the waist down, they kissed—bellies, thighs, and knees.

"Persia, my dearest, my love." His words touched her lips the moment before his mouth covered hers. Now their kiss was total.

His tongue found no barrier to impede its passionate progress. She welcomed his hard, velvet assault. She languished in his search for the hidden places that sent liquid rainbows flowing through her blood. She matched his need with her own, doubling and redoubling it.

Gone was the present, the past, and the future. Only at this very instant in eternity was she real and alive and in love—while his lips possessed her, his hands claimed her, and his body melded itself to hers.

His hands moved with urgency now—caressing their way up her sides. He drew her closer still, cradling her throbbing, peaked breasts against his hard chest. He gave up his pleasure with her mouth to kiss her cheeks, her eyelids, her forehead, her chin.

She stood, trembling, in his embrace—wanting it all, wanting it never to end. She felt like crying, screaming, laughing, dying. He was her *here,* her *now,* her *forevermore.* All the years, gone! All the hurt, suffered! All the pain, past!

"Zack, Zack," she murmured over and over. "Oh, please, my darling . . ."

"There's no hurry," he whispered back between kisses. "We'll love our way across three oceans. I'll show you pleasures and joys you've never dared dream of. Oh, Persia, it's been so long . . . so cold without you."

His hungry hands found her breasts and kneaded gently through her gown and robe. His lips trailed down her neck, then lingered there to taste her flesh. Each place his mouth touched burned with a portion of the need that was threatening to consume her totally—body, mind, and heart.

"Persia, Persia darling," he moaned. "I can't wait any longer!"

Suddenly, he was stripping the robe from her shoulders, the gown from her body. He pressed her down, onto the captain's bunk, and feverishly began removing his own clothes.

Through eyes half-closed in longing, she gazed at his strong chest and torso. His face might have changed, but that wonderful, powerful body was the same as she remembered it from so long ago—from before he went away, from before she married.

Suddenly, a hateful trick of her mind and conscience brought reality rushing back. She gripped her robe tightly over her breasts as if it were some antique coat of mail that would protect her against her foe. Her body still ached for him. Her heart still cried out for his love. But she belonged to another man.

"Zack, no! We can't. I'm married now." Her words

in their force came like a cold wave from the sea, breaking over both of them, dousing the fire of passion to a stuttering flicker in the dark night.

He turned on her, his eyes almost black with rage. "What do you mean, *no*?"

"This isn't right," she said in a tiny, unconvincing voice.

"*Not right?* By God, woman, you intend to turn me away *now*?" His voice boomed, echoing off the bulkheads and hammering at her heart.

"I'm not turning you away, Zack. I love you. I always have. But it's different now. I'm not the same person, neither are you. Can't we just be friends?"

He stared at her, his face as blank as the surface of the sea on a calm day. Then his nostrils flared and his eyes narrowed. "*Friends, Persia?*" His voice was so quiet and controlled that it frightened her. "You can lie there with your own body— *admit it, damn you!*—quivering to have me take you, and suggest that we be *friends*?" He threw back his head and laughed long and hard, laughed until his humorless mirth turned into a wail of pain. "Oh, Persia! Oh, my dearest, you have so much to learn. But don't worry. I'm here now, and I intend to teach you well!"

Before she could reply, Zack lunged for the bunk. He straddled her legs and pinned her arms above her head. "Now, my darling, your time has come!"

"Zack, no," she begged, but there was nothing she could do to stop him—nor did she really want to.

He ripped away the layers of clothing he found until her pale, bare flesh gleamed before him. His eyes drank her in. His lips murmured of her wonders and spoke his desires.

She lay helpless—quivering, begging, sobbing. But he was deaf to her pleas.

Still, belying the anger in his voice, his hand was gentle on her flesh. He stroked her breasts, fondled her aching nipples, massaged her neck, kissed her tenderly. When he bent low to suckle her, she went almost faint with desire. He couldn't have planned her punishment better. She writhed beneath him—longing, burning, dying for his body. But he made no move to enter her and take away her pain.

Instead, his knowing hand stripped her of her last defenses. It killed her conscience with desire. It made a wanton of her, twisting and begging beneath his touch. That wicked, loving, tormenting hand—five fingers bent on her destruction—scaled down her naked body. They teased her ribs, taunted her belly, and finally found their destination. When she felt the pull of her hair, she gasped. Her lips rose to meet . . . *nothing*. Empty air filled her. Then, his fingers were on her once more. Searching, testing, torturing. When they found that which they sought, she cried out. He laughed.

"Please, Zack!" Her thrusting hips begged him even more than her words.

He gave her no answer, either verbally or physically. Instead, he leaned down and took her lips, kissing her with a slow, maddening thoroughness that left her breathless.

She was on the very brink of ecstasy. Another stroke of his skilled fingers, a single plunge, and she would be there. But neither came. He drew away. She lay before his eyes, her pale skin sweaty with lust, her blue eyes glazed with passion.

He rose and offered his hand. "*Friends*, Mrs. Blackwell?" he said with a sardonic smile.

"You go to the devil!" she spat at him.

He threw back his head and laughed before he began pulling on his clothes. When he was fully dressed and she still naked, he turned back to her. He reached out with the same hand that had taunted her so mercilessly and drew a line with one finger from the hollow at the base of her neck to the apex of her womanhood. She quivered convulsively, but clamped her lips together, refusing to utter the moan that fought to escape her throat.

"All well and good, isn't it, for a woman to lead a man on? But the reverse isn't so pleasurable, is it, Mrs. Blackwell? I'll leave you now."

And he will, too, the *bastard!* Persia thought, very aware that her body was still burning for him.

At the door he turned, smiled, and bowed. "By the way, Mrs. Blackwell, I assume you're aware that it is ship's etiquette for the captain and the supercargo to dine in company. You may expect me here tomorrow evening promptly at eight bells. Until then . . ." He swept her a deep, courtly bow and blew her a kiss, then frowned. "Oh, and one more thing, Mrs. Blackwell. Put some clothes on, won't you, before you catch your death!"

When the door closed behind him, Persia grabbed up a shoe and aimed it squarely before she let it fly.

"Bastard!" she yelled. Then she fell into her pillow sobbing.

CHAPTER NINETEEN

"*I* trust you slept well last night, Mrs. Blackwell."

Zachariah Hazzard—his beard trimmed, his wild thatch of silvery hair tamed, and his best suit on—sat across a well-laid table from the most bewitching woman he had ever laid eyes on.

"And why should you think otherwise, Captain?" Persia replied, her voice as smooth and exotic as watered silk, one flame-tinged eyebrow arching provocatively.

He never bothered to answer. They both knew. She hadn't slept at all. Neither had he.

But the captain was far too busy drinking her in to waste time on words. Since last night, there had been an amazing transformation in Persia Whiddington . . . *Blackwell,* he corrected in his mind, though he still refused to accept the idea of her marriage. She had discarded her drab garments and heavy veil for the most tantalizing costume he had ever seen draped over female flesh.

Her tissue silk gown was not quite the color of a

sapphire, nor was it exactly the shade of the sea on a
clear day, nor even the brilliant china blue of Persia's
eyes. It was almost the startling hue of Saint Elmo's
fire—alive, electric, *shocking*. It made a man hesitate to
touch for fear of being stunned senseless.

Perhaps, he mused, that was its purpose, but never
mind.

Gone, too, was the demure buttoned neckline. Even
as he sat across from her—not leaning forward at all—he
could savor the rise of creamy flesh that immediately
surmounted the darker rosettes he knew lay just hidden
from his line of vision. Her arms were bare, and her skin
held the luster of deepwater pearls from cold, clear
Oriental waters. And only in a sunset at sea had he ever
before beheld such a riot of bronzed golds as he saw in
her gleaming tresses—piled high on her head and adorned
with a blue-pearl tiara.

Her voice was as soft as her skin. Her eyes invited—
promised. What was she up to?

Persia felt cold, in spite of the fact that they were
nearing the equator and would soon be sailing into the
Tropic of Capricorn. Her chill was heart deep. Last
night with Zack had done something to her. Maybe it
was no longer possible for the two of them even to be
friends. He was at this very moment dining in her compartment, not by invitation, but by virtue of the fact that
he was captain and had *commanded* it so.

Still, she refused to cower behind her veils and black
bombazine any longer. If she must deal with his wrath,
she would do it on her own ground—gowned in the
costumes of her supercargo's office. Let him stare and
ogle and sweat. He deserved no less after what he had
done to her last night. Or *hadn't* done, she added
morosely.

"Some wine?" he offered, poising the thin-necked
bottle over her glass.

"Please."

The ruby-red liquid caressed the crystal sides of her
goblet almost erotically as he filled it three-quarters full.

He watched, mesmerized, as her elegantly tapered fingers wrapped the stem. She raised the glass slowly, peering at him over its rim. She let him see her mouth open to receive the sweet red liquid—teeth of pearl to match her tiara, tongue as smooth and cool as the silk of her gown, throat deep and dark and inviting, swallowing the wine he offered into her body in such a way that his blood would rush, longing to be welcomed into her in a like manner.

"Excellent wine," she offered.

"Only the most desirable for the most desirable."

"I'm married." The statement was blunt, to the point, as cold as the ice below in the hold.

He nodded once toward her, saying with his expression that he knew, but it didn't matter.

She translated his unspoken reply and added, "I went to the Tail of the Devil. You were gone."

Her words sent an unexpected jolt through him. All these years, he had never known. He had assumed their argument in the room had finished it for her. But he couldn't let her see the pleasure her accusing statement brought him. "You shouldn't have taken so long making up your mind," he answered.

He could almost see a chill passing over her flesh before his very eyes.

"Marriage is a lifelong proposition," she replied. "An hour isn't long to decide in."

Zack couldn't help himself. His gaze traveled to the gold band encircling her finger, and the words tumbled pell-mell out of his mouth. "How long did it take you to decide to marry the Reverend Blackwell?"

"From the time you left me?" He could hear the hurt and the anger in her voice. "Almost ten years!"

One shaggy eyebrow shot upward. "Then you're newly married. But how can that be? Did your husband go out on a ship just ahead of ours?"

"No." She looked down at her untouched plate and whispered the words. "He's been in India for many years."

"Then how . . . ?"

"He sent back for a wife. It was a proxy marriage."

He was on his feet now, towering over her. "You mean you don't even know this man you married? Persia, have you gone mad?"

She glared up at him, her eyes a hard, determined blue. "If I have, it's your fault!"

"*My* fault?"

"Yes! I loved you, Zack Hazzard, as I will never love another man! I wanted to marry you. Oh, you could never begin to understand how much I wanted that!"

She was out of her chair now, pacing about the room. "But you were a man of the world. An experienced man. An impatient man. 'An hour is too long to wait!' " she mocked. " 'She was a fine diversion for one night, but who wants to spend a lifetime with a woman who can't make up her mind?' "

"Persia," he began, meaning to tell her the whole truth of what happened that night. But she refused to allow the interruption. She hurried on, releasing all the pent-up frustration and rage of ten long, lonely winters and as many sad springs, dreary falls, and fruitless summers.

"Well, I waited, Captain Zachariah Hazzard! I watched the marine news—the ships arriving and those spoke at sea. Always searching for your name. Always hoping and praying that you were safe. You'll never know how terrified I was every time I sat down to scan the black-bordered column of disasters in the *Marine Journal*. I have never been a bride, yet I know how a grieving widow feels."

Her words struck home. He hung his head and said softly, "You might have married anytime you liked. I was sure you would."

The shock of her bitter laughter brought his head up sharply. "The *scarlet woman* of York County, marry? Surely you jest! My one night with you in Boston cost me my reputation and all hopes for a normal, happy life. I couldn't go to the village market without having to endure the whispers of the other townspeople, the jeers of naughty little boys. Why, even the mongrel dogs about town seemed to know of my evildoing! They yapped at my heels, trying to bite me.''

"Persia, you're dramatizing all this just a bit, aren't you?''

She tossed her head and gave him a haughty look. "Perhaps I am. But then, perhaps I have a right to.''

"I won't argue that.'' He moved closer, trying to take her in his arms, but she turned from him. "All I can say is that I never meant for it to turn out that way.''

His words and his gesture did soften her slightly. When she spoke again, her voice was quieter. "Zack, for years I've thought about how things would be between us if we ever met again. I swore to myself that if you were alive, I would never say one harsh word to you. I would just be happy. I would ask no questions; I would only love you.''

"Then why did you refuse me last night?'' He was totally mystified by the sudden change in her. "Surely you know how much I needed you . . . how much I *still* need you!''

Persia thrust her hand out so that the candlelight gleamed in the gold on her finger. "Do I have to say it again? I'm *married*!''

He caught her hand and tugged the ring from her finger. "There! Now you're not! This is all you have of a marriage. You don't have love. You don't even have a husband yet. The only things standing between us are this sentimental token and your own stubborn pride. I'm about to dispose of one. It's up to you, Persia, to put an end to the other.''

He started toward the porthole as if he meant to toss the ring into the sea.

"Zack, don't!''

"Why not? This means nothing. You can't tell me that you care for the man. You've never even met him.''

"No,'' she whispered. "But the ring, Zack . . . *No!*'' She ran to him and caught his arm as he drew back to throw it through the opening. "It was my mother's! Please!'' she sobbed.

"Persia, Persia, I'm sorry. I didn't know.'' He cradled her in his arms, trying to soothe her, sorry that he had almost done such a stupid thing and had upset her so. "Here, take it."

He seized her hand tenderly in his, and when she realized what he was about to do her breath caught, choking off a sob. She stared at his strong brown fingers gently slipping the gold band onto her hand. She could feel the slight pressure even in her heart. How many years had she dreamed of this moment? Now it was happening. He was placing a wedding band on her hand. But it meant nothing! It was another man's ring . . . she was another man's wife.

She was limp against him, wrung out from all the warring emotions within her. He placed one finger under her chin and raised her face to his.

"Usually this solemn act is followed by another."

Through her tear-starred lashes, Persia watched his lips coming down to hers as if it were all happening in slow motion. Her heart was racing. Her face was flaming hot. Somewhere deep inside her, the word "no" was fighting to get out. But it seemed she had lost all control over her mind and body. She could only cling to his arm and wait for the wine-sweet taste of his mouth. She closed her eyes, parted her lips—waiting, longing, aching for his passion to overthrow her reason.

But the hungry assault she had expected never came. For the briefest moment, his warm mouth covered hers. And then he released her.

When she opened her eyes, he was staring at her. His face wore an expression of pain like none she had ever seen before.

"Zack?" she said softly.

"I won't try to force you again, Persia. I was wrong last night. I'm sorry for what I did to you."

The disappointment she felt stunned her. He was agreeing to play by her rules. So why should his words leave her feeling so empty?

"Let me make one last statement and we'll leave it at that. I loved you ten years ago, Persia. I love you even more now. When we ran away together, I was little more than a brash youth. You were a mere child. We're both adults now, with the awareness of life that it takes to love deeply and forever.''

She felt her panic rising, and tears flooded into her eyes once more. He need not lay a finger on her to make her tremble. He was standing there, five feet away, ravaging her with his eyes, his words.

"Zack, please don't!"

"Don't what, darling? I'm only telling you the truth—perhaps the only truth in this whole insane world. You and I were meant to be together. We've put in our years of heartache. Now is the time for love."

She sank onto her chair and put her face down in her upraised palms. "Oh, if only I'd waited a little longer."

He came to her and stroked her arm. "Don't blame yourself, darling. Fate seems to be playing especially cruel tricks on us. I was in Quoddy Cove earlier this month. Had I gone to your house or spoken to the woman at the pond, I might have found you before you went through with this arranged marriage."

She faced him, her eyes wide suddenly. "The woman at the pond?"

"Yes, something drew me back to the place we met. I stopped awhile to watch the ice harvest while I was thinking. And across the pond there was a lady in a black veil, and she . . ." His words trailed off as realization struck. "*You*, Persia?"

She nodded. "I was married an hour later."

"In black?"

"White hardly seemed appropriate."

"Oh, God!" he groaned. "I came so close to speaking to you. I was going to ask you if you knew Persia Whiddington."

"Zack," she whispered, "I almost did the same. I even asked one of the workmen who you were. He didn't know."

"Damn!" He struck the table with his fist. "How could we have let this happen?"

She touched his cheek. "How could *life* have let this happen?"

The thought of what might have been left them both subdued. They ate their cold meal almost in silence. Since the previous sleepless night had taken its toll on both of them, Zack said good night early.

At the door, he paused and asked, "Persia, will you at least think about it?"

"I don't know what you mean."

"About us, about what life could be if we were together. You aren't bound to this proxy husband. There's been nothing between the two of you. Nothing like what we've shared."

"Zack, I gave him my promise."

His eyes went almost black suddenly, and the scar down his face twitched with anger. "You gave *me* your promise, too. Long before you spoke any vows to him!"

Then he left her cabin and closed the door behind him.

Normally at this time of night, the captain went on deck to make his rounds. But at the moment, Zack didn't want to see or speak to anyone. He needed a drink—a stiff one.

He went to his cabin and jerked open the door to his spirits chest, grabbing a bottle of one-hundred-fifty-proof rum by the neck as if he might strangle it. Slamming it down on the table, he flopped into a chair.

"It's just you and me now, mate," he said to the brown bottle. "I'll be the end of you or you the end of me. We'll just see which comes first."

He grasped the bottle, flipped the cork out with his thumb, and turned it up to his lips. For long minutes, he let the fiery liquor scorch its way down his throat. It lit a fire in his gut and sent hot clouds to his head. Then he put the bottle back down, recorked it, and sat there staring at nothing. He shook his head slowly.

"Sorry, my old friend, but you're not the answer this time." He rose and stowed the rum bottle, then slumped back down in his chair, running a hand through his hair.

"Persia, Persia," he sighed.

How could he make her understand how much he

loved her and needed her? Theirs hadn't been merely a one time fling on a snowy night—a lark for a sailor ashore. Maybe if he told her about how he'd been shanghaied . . . But that seemed the coward's way out. A lame excuse to cover a deeper problem. He should never have left her and gone to the tavern, demanding that she meet him "within the hour!"

He rose slowly and left the cabin. Stopping outside Persia's door, he raised a hand to knock but changed his mind. All was quiet within. Perhaps she was sleeping. He had no right to disturb her again.

The air on deck was warm and moist. Before long, they would be crossing the equator. There were several men on board who had never crossed the line before. That crossing would bring wholescale tomfoolery as the initiates were ushered into the fraternity of seamen. He smiled to himself, thinking that perhaps the event would lighten Persia's mood.

He glanced up. The night sky was like a glittering dome with a million stars blinking down at him. Somehow they always looked closer and brighter at sea. He watched the fiery trail through the sky as one fell from the heavens. He almost made a wish but stopped himself, thinking that it would take more than idle wishing to get what he wanted.

Zack sighed and moved on across the deck.

"Evening, Captain," the first mate hailed.

"Mr. Barry." Zack nodded. "How goes it tonight?"

"All's well, sir. We've a fine, fresh breeze out of the western quadrant. I've had the men add extra canvas as you ordered. And the sea's so calm the helmsman's handling our girl with one well-placed finger."

"Carry on, then."

"Aye-aye, sir."

One well-placed finger, Zack mused, conjuring up in his mind a vision of Persia stretched naked on her bed.

"Damn!" he said quietly. There were no two ways about it. He meant to have Persia Whiddington! She might think he was lying back, letting her go right ahead with her plans to be another man's wife. But it would be in spite of all his cunning and, in the end, *over his dead body!*

His final decision made, he went below, more than ready for sleep.

Persia felt drugged. She lay in her bed after Zack left her, going over everything in her mind. Yes, she still loved him. No, she did not love Cyrus Blackwell, and she probably never would. It would be so simple to arrive in Bombay, discharge her duties as supercargo, and then sail on to Calcutta with Zack. Reverend Osgood had told her that Blackwell probably would not be there to meet the ship when she arrived. The reverend had instructed her to send a message to the island of Elephanta, six miles off the coast, where Blackwell lived. So there would be no dockside recriminations. Not if she simply failed to send word of her arrival.

Then, after they returned home, she could get an annulment of her proxy marriage and wed the man she had wanted for so long. She smiled in the darkness, feeling the rightness of her plan. But after only an instant her pleasure faded.

Once before she had gone against society and brought disgrace upon herself and her family. Had heartbreak really caused her mother's death? Certainly it had contributed. There was still her father to consider. He had weathered all storms so far, but he was old and weak now. What would it do to him if she stirred up more scandal?

A tear squeezed out of the corner of her eye and dribbled down her cheek. She was not a child any longer, and she knew right from wrong. Right was accepting her place as Cyrus Blackwell's wife. Wrong was bringing more sorrow to everyone by forsaking her holy vows to be with Zack.

She turned her face into her pillow to muffle her sobs. But they never came. She lay there, feeling empty, used up, all alone in the dark night . . . in the dark world.

CHAPTER TWENTY

THE days at sea progressed in a calm, bright blue procession. The only storms raged within. Persia battled blizzards of loneliness and uncertainty, while Zack faced the driving onslaught of thwarted hopes and dreams. They were overly cordial to each other, but Persia was always careful to keep her distance, and Zack felt reluctant to press her just yet. And all the while, looming ever present in both their minds, like the black clouds of a typhoon on the distant horizon, was the featureless visage of a man named Cyrus Blackwell.

Still, life aboard ship went on as usual. Their cargo of "Yankee blocks" lay secure in its own cold below. Their course unfolded before them in a calm stretch of aquamarine, as the trade winds sped them ever closer to the invisible line at the waist of the world.

"We're in for a treat tomorrow," Zack told Persia as they shared their nightly dinner in her cabin. "We'll be crossing the equator."

Persia, who had been feeling sad all day and was only picking at her dinner, looked up. Her eyes glittered with excitement at his words. Since she'd been old enough to dream, she had longed for the day she would sail into the Southern Hemisphere.

"Just wait till you see what goes on tomorrow," Zack continued. "We've at least three greenhorns on board. They'll be in for it!"

"*All* of them?" There was mischief in her tone.

"Yes, all!" he answered. Then he laughed. "Not you, of course. It would be beneath the dignity of a *married woman* to be dunked upside down in the flour barrel or hauled aloft by her pretty ankles." A wide grin spread across his face. "On second thought, it would make an interesting sight!"

"Zack Hazzard, don't you even think such things," she threatened. "Or I'll . . ."

"You'll what?" The challenge was there; she heard it plainly.

"I'll lock myself in this cabin and refuse to come out—*ever!*"

He laughed and reached across the table, casually squeezing her hand. She looked so lovely with her cheeks flushed that way, mirroring the rose tint of her beribboned India-cotton gown. She was so wonderful to look at . . . so wonderful to be with. And they had grown comfortable with each other in the past weeks. It almost seemed to Zack that because he had been denied her physical love, he had learned to love her in other, deeper ways.

"Please don't lock yourself away, Persia. Then you'd miss all the fun."

Just as casually as he had taken her hand, he brought her fingers to his lips, but she snatched them away. She looked down, concentrating all of her attention on the cold slice of pork that had not interested her at all earlier.

"I'm sorry," he said softly. "I forgot myself."

She made no reply, nor did she raise her eyes to acknowledge his simple apology. She couldn't let him see how much she wanted him.

*   *   *

Persia awoke the next morning to a raucous racket coming from the deck. A drum was pounding out a solemn rhythm while tin pipes tooted and whistles shrilled. She sat bolt upright in bed, trying to think what could be happening.

Just then someone pounded on her door. "Rise 'n' shine, Persia! The initiation is about to begin." She recognized Zack's voice and grinned.

The *equator*!

Scurrying out of bed, she pawed through her gowns until she found exactly the right thing—a bleached muslin with a wide neck and full skirt. In this heat—it must be eighty degrees already—she would need something cool. She slipped quickly into the dress, whipped a brush through her hair, and tied it back with a sunshine-yellow scarf. Then she hurried out to see what was happening.

"Ah, there you are," Zack called. "We couldn't start until you got here."

She noted that even the captain was dressed casually for today's fun and games. He wore a full-sleeved shirt, open at the neck. No stock, vest, or jacket. In spite of herself, her eyes lingered on the V of dark-tanned flesh and the silvery thatch frosting his chest. She felt a little shiver run through her and forced her gaze away. But his trim waist and tightly encased hips and thighs gave her little ease of mind or conscience. Dressed as he was, anyone could tell that his silver hair was premature, for never had a man of advanced age possessed such a powerful and perfect body. Persia found herself blushing shamefully as her eyes strayed time and again to the bulging outline of his crotch. But when had she ever been timid with Zack Hazzard?

"Ahoy, mates!" Second Mate Stoner called out. "With the captain's permission, I mean to call this little shindig to order now."

Stoner, his wide, flat-featured face grinning broadly, turned toward Zack, who nodded. "Permission granted, mister."

"Very well, then. Spratt, Callisio, you boys bring out the prisoners!"

Persia couldn't help it. She squealed with delight when she saw the three unfortunate fellows who were crossing the equator for the first time. She had wondered how they would handle the initiation with a woman on board, since usually—she knew from tales her father had told—the men were stripped naked for the event. These sailors looked far more embarrassed by what they were wearing—canvas diapers, fashioned for them by the sailmaker. They stood before her—all hairy legs and knobby knees—looking everywhere but at her.

Following a roll of the turtle-shell drum, First Mate Barry paraded onto the deck, gesturing regally to his mates and offering Persia a deep, majestic bow. She curtsied, bringing a delighted whoop from the other men. He was costumed as Neptune, Lord of the Deep, in a robe of canvas sheeting, a crown made from a broken rum jug, and a belaying pin as his scepter. Sticking out of his back pocket was a large ripe fish. The men had caught the wahoo several days before especially for Neptune's use today.

"Hear me, you sorry sons of landlubbers!" boomed His Lord High Majesty of All the Ocean Seas. "You dare to cross my oceans without asking my permission or paying homage to me?"

He threatened the three victims with the belaying pin until they chorused, "Aye, sir!"

Neptune turned to the other sailors. "What say ye, mates? Shall I take what's rightfully mine out of their tough, horny hides?"

Stoner, bowing and scraping, came toward the first mate. "Begging your pardon, Your Most Holy and Briny Lordship, but the boys and me've been talking." He leaned over to whisper into Neptune's ear.

By the time the second mate was through, Neptune was grinning maniacally and nodding so that his crown slipped down over one eye.

"You're an evil, cruel lot, lads," he said to Stoner

and his cohorts. "My blessings upon you all! We'll do it your way. Cook! Front and center!"

Suddenly, an unearthly yell split the air. Heads jerked to starboard, and all eyes fastened on a dark, evil-looking figure standing on the quarterdeck—bare feet planted wide apart and hands stretched toward the heavens. In his right fist, he clutched a wicked blade. The wind whipped his long hair wildly about his face, and his lips were curled back in a vicious snarl.

"Why, it's Fletcher," Persia said to Zack.

"Aye," he said with a chuckle. "Your manservant insisted upon taking a part in the festivities. Seems he and the cook have been plotting this below in the galley for days."

"The seven seas save us," Neptune gasped dramatically. "It's himself, the devilfish man from the cannibal isle of Goonie-Goonie, come to carve up you hapless mates for his big black pot."

One of the diapered men laughed, and Fletcher sprang toward him, brandishing his sharp knife.

The cook, a rotund man with a perfectly bald head, hurried toward Fletcher, who had the man by the hair while the blade of his knife rested on the quaking fellow's throat.

"See here, my good man," the cook said to his kinsman; "you can't just dice these sailors up for stew. Who'll tend the sails and the rigging? Who'll swab the decks? Who'll grumble about my cooking?" The cook looked thoughtful, then sour. "Go ahead! Slice 'em up! Make stew of them. An ungrateful lot they are, anyway!"

"Don't want stew, want make pictures," Fletcher answered in pseudocannibalese, pointing with the tip of his knife to the tattooing on his own face.

The unfortunate chap whose hair Fletcher was pulling gasped and clutched at his chest in horror.

"Oh, well, if that's all . . ." the cook began, immediately producing a pot of indigo dye. "Here, this should do nicely."

"Cap'n, *please!*" wailed the terrified seaman.

Zack stepped forward, frowning. "We'll have no dis-figuring, Cook!"

The fat man gave him a twisted little smile. "Then how about dis*membering*, Captain?"

"Maybe later." Zack walked back to where Persia stood.

"Officers just take all the fun out of these things," the cook complained in an aside to the pale, frightened initiates. "Well, since we can't tattoo you, I suppose we'll just have to do the next best thing. Bring out the barrel, Fletcher."

Persia expected the flour barrel, since Zack had mentioned it earlier. She did not expect to see the initiates' heads dipped into the molasses barrel to come out dripping sticky goo—each man coughing, snorting, and trying to dig the sweet muck out of his eyes, ears, and nostrils. When the lot of them had been doused, their mates brought out bags of feathers, saved from the many fowl that had gone to the butcher block to provide meals for the crew.

Soon the air looked like a New England snowstorm. And the three poor fellows on deck looked like creatures from a nightmare. Persia felt for them and was glad she was a woman, not forced to endure such discomfort and ridicule. But they did present the funniest sight she had ever seen. She struggled to catch her breath through gales of laughter.

"Think it's funny, do you?" Zack whispered to her. "Well, your time is coming, madam!"

She sobered immediately and turned to flee to her cabin, but he caught her arm. "Stay," he commanded, and she had little choice.

Neptune was storming about the deck now, waving his belaying pin in all directions. "Look at this bloody mess you've made! And I suppose you plan to dump them into *my* ocean to clean them up. Well, that's just fine—sticky goo and feathers all over my mermaids, my pearls, my coral reef. Now you three are *really* in for it! You'll pay for this!" He reached out and flicked some goose down from the end of one sailor's nose, making him sneeze. "Bring out the cat-o'-nines!"

Stoner rushed forward, his hands flung up in protest. "That's fine. We'll get the whips for the floggings. They'll pay for their sins, Your Brinyship, but all in good time. What say we have a little entertainment first?" The second mate motioned to his musicians. "Play us a bit of a tune, lads. Let's see if these savages can dance."

Not one of the three was listening. They hadn't heard a word past "cat-o'-nines." Now Stoner held the evil-looking whip with its twisted, knotted leather thongs in his right hand, impatiently flipping it this way and that. When they failed to respond to the music and the first mate's request for a dance, he touched them up about the bare legs with the whip. They were doing a jig soon enough.

Zack noticed that Persia, surely unconscious of her own actions, was swaying gently to the music. He caught Lord Neptune's eye and nodded toward her. "His Brinyship" sauntered over and stood before them.

"This must be the other one," First Mate Barry boomed. "I heard there were four in all." He bowed again to Persia and smiled. "Which shall it be, my lady, the molasses and feathers, or will you give us a dance?"

"Oh, no . . ." Persia tried to protest.

But Zack wouldn't let her. Pushing her gently toward Barry, he looked into her eyes, laughing, and said, "Oh, *yes*!"

The Lord of the Deep held Persia's hand lightly and went into a lively cavort. At first, she was too embarrassed to join in, but soon she grew used to all eyes being on her. She executed a few simple dance steps, and Barry passed her on to Stoner. Soon the men were whirling her from one to the other. Her head was spinning, her skirts flying, her hair—loose from its scarf—was streaming in her eyes. And in the background—over the lap of the sea and the flap of the sails, the hands clapping and the music playing—she could hear Zack, laughing and shouting encouragement to her.

Suddenly, another man took her. But this one didn't

clasp her hand gently as the others had. Instead, he
pulled her hard against his chest as he whirled her round
and round. Her pulses were racing. She felt perspiration
running down her sides and making a river between her
breasts. She would faint from exhaustion if he didn't
release her soon.

"Please," she cried. "Let me go! I can't dance any
longer!"

He stopped, but he didn't let go. When her head
stopped whirling and her vision cleared, she looked up
at him. Zack! She should have known. But he wasn't
smiling now. He was gazing down at her with an intensity that made her shiver deep inside. She went weak all
over. She couldn't summon the strength to push herself
out of his arms.

Still holding her prisoner with his gaze, he called, "Be
on with it, men!"

"Aye, Captain!" they called back.

Zack led Persia back to the shaded area where they
had been standing earlier. But he kept a possessive grip
on her waist and an even stronger hold on her soul with
his eyes.

"Grog, ho!" went up the call, and all hands answered
with a cheer.

Each man, including the three unfortunates, was served
his portion of one part rum to two parts water.

"If you want long sweetening in it," the cook said,
"just ask one of these sorry clods to let you scoop some
of that blackstrap off his noggin."

When Fletcher brought a mug to Persia, she said,
"No, thank you."

"Drink it," Zack ordered. "You'll need the fortifica-
tion for what's coming."

His voice was so ominous and his face so deadly
serious that she turned the tankard up and drained it,
feeling a lightness in her head as the rum hit her empty
stomach.

"You men there," Stoner boomed when all had drunk
their grog, "fetch His Lordship a throne so he can plant
his scaly behind during the upcoming proceedings."

Two sailors scurried forward, setting an empty chicken coop in place for Neptune. He sat heavily, making the wood groan beneath him.

"Now," he said to the three feathered sailors, "which of you wants to go first?"

They looked at each other, then all shook their heads.

"So be it!" boomed the throned figure. "I'll choose. You there on the port end of the line. Step forward!"

The largest of the three sailors took a hesitant step away from the others.

"Blindfold him!" Neptune roared. "Blindfold them all. This will be too ugly to have them watch. It's time we turned the cat loose."

Persia felt her skin crawl. She watched in fascinated horror as the sailors tied rough sacking over their mates' eyes. Two men were hustling the first initiate toward the mast. He was trying to fight them, screaming, "No! Please! Cap'n, you can't let them do this to me! I ain't done nothing to be flogged for."

Persia gripped Zack's arm. "Aren't you going to stop them?"

"No," he replied, his face stony.

"Then I'm going below!"

He grabbed her arm. "No, you're not. You're going to stay and watch this."

Her stomach felt queasy. Her head was spinning. It would serve him right if she threw up or fainted. What kind of captain allowed innocent men to have their backs laid open for sport?

The poor fellow was tied to the mast now—begging, crying, praying. The other two were cowering together, wondering which of them would be next. They could see nothing, but they could hear everything.

"Shut up, you scruvy coward!" Neptune yelled, waving his foul-smelling fish for emphasis.

Persia watched, unable to look away, as Stoner stepped forward with the cat-o'-nines. He twitched it back and forth on the deck a time or two, getting the feel of it. She noted that close to the knots at the end, the leather was almost black. Perhaps stained by the blood of other sailors? she wondered. The thought made her cringe.

Something odd was going on, she couldn't quite figure out what. Stoner still hesitated. And meanwhile, two sailors had moved the molasses barrel close to the man with the whip, and Neptune himself, ripe fish still in hand, had climbed down from his throne. He was now standing next to the man who was about to be flogged. On the other side of the unfortunate creature, the cook had taken his place.

"Ready?" Stoner called.

"No, please!" sobbed the victim.

The whip whistled in the air, bringing moans of dread from the other two who awaited their turns to be lashed to the mast.

Persia's eyes widened. She felt a giggle tickling her throat. But it didn't seem right to laugh when the two men were truly enduring mental torture. Still, when Stoner let the lash of the whip strike the barrel, the cook yelped in very real-sounding pain, and Lord Neptune whacked the bound sailor across the buttocks with nothing more hurtful than his dead fish, she couldn't help but laugh. They all laughed, even the man receiving the smelly punishment. Only the screaming cook and the other two sailors were not crying with tears of mirth.

When Neptune untied the "flogged" man from the mast, he called out, "Might as well deep-six this one. He's a goner!"

Several sailors rushed forward and tossed the man over the side so that he might wash off the molasses and feathers and join his laughing mates on deck as the other two received their punishment.

By the time the three men had been fish-paddled, released, tossed overboard, and helped back on deck, Persia was weak with hysterical exhaustion.

"Zack, how awful," she said. "To scare those poor men that way."

"I didn't notice you trying to stop it. Seems to me you enjoyed the whole spectacle as much as any man on board. Come on now. There's one more thing you must do.''

''Oh, no! You're not tying me to any mast, Captain!''

He cupped her sunburned cheek with his palm and brought his lips down to hover over hers. She could feel his breath on her mouth as he said, ''I'd like to tie you, Persia, but to myself, not the mast.''

''Time to cross the line,'' Neptune announced.

Stoner had all three initiates lined up on the north side of a piece of rope stretched across the deck. Zack took Persia to her place beside the men.

Mugs of grog were being passed out again, and an expectant hush fell over the ship as everyone waited for the three sailors and Persia to ''cross the line.''

''Ready, mates?'' Neptune boomed. ''Go!''

All four jumped over the piece of rope, and a great cheer went up.

Persia turned her glowing face to Zack. ''Now there are no more greenhorns on board,'' she said.

''But there's still one woman,'' he answered, slipping his arm about her waist.

Zack requested that their supper be served on deck that evening. After the long, hot day, the night air felt gentle and cool, scented with spices and flowery perfumes from islands far away across the sea. The stars glittered above, reflecting in Persia's bright eyes. Everything seemed so good, so warm, so right between them now.

They sat at a little table, sipping iced white wine and listening to some of the sailors play flute, pipes, and fiddle. Gone was the raucous atmosphere of earlier in the day. Everything was quiet, subdued, magical. Soon voices joined the instruments—singing songs of home and love.

''I'll be sailing my dreams tonight, back to a shore so bright, back to my own sweet love, with her lips of wine and her hair so fine. Wait for me, love! Wait for me-e-e . . .'' One young sailor's tenor voice, as sweet as the love he was singing about, filled the clear air.

"Wait for me," Persia murmured, listening to the words and feeling a hard ache in her chest.

"That's what every sailor hopes . . . that his lover will wait for him," Zack said quietly.

"Is that what you hoped, Zack?" She tilted her head in such a way that a long wave of hair fell forward, hiding one side of her face.

He shook his head slightly and reached out to stroke her cool fingertips. She didn't pull away from him this time. "I never dared hope at all." His eyes were on her—caressing, fondling.

"Then why are you hoping now?" she asked.

"Maybe I'm not. Maybe I've given up all hope."

She looked away from him suddenly. "That's what I did. I gave up all hope."

"Don't, Persia," he said softly, hearing the hint of tears in her voice. "It's too lovely a night for that."

"Yes." She sighed. "It's so lovely it makes me ache inside."

"For home?"

She turned back to him, her gaze level, her lips firm, unsmiling. "For *you*," she said simply.

He tried to laugh off her reply, but his mirth died a quick death in his throat. What was she saying to him? Had she decided to ignore her conscience and give in to her desires—desires he read plainly in her eyes every time he looked at her?

A long silence followed her statement. Only the background surge of the sea and the sailors' soft singing disturbed the stillness.

"Rolling home, rolling home, rolling home across the sea. Rolling home to dear New England, rolling home, dear love, to thee."

"Persia?" Zack clasped her hand, drawing it toward his lips.

She only smiled faintly and nodded.

Her hand, when it touched his mouth, felt as soft as cool velvet. It was scented with roses and lilac. Emboldened, he touched its back with his tongue, bringing a shiver from Persia. She tasted of honey with a faint, pleasing trace of salt.

"Where are we right this minute, Zack?"

He frowned slightly, unable to guess what sort of answer she desired. They were at a small table—on the quarterdeck of the *Madagascar* . . . in the South Atlantic . . . just below the equator.

"I don't want our longitude and latitude. I mean, exactly where are we in time and space in relation to every other living being?" She paused, then hurried on. "Remember the tales of the explorers in ancient times, who thought the world was flat and who feared they might sail over the edge and be gobbled up by dragons? Well, maybe they were right. Maybe all that has passed and all that will come is only an illusion. Maybe right now, right here, this very minute, is the only time and place that really exists. Maybe we've sailed right over the edge already and this ocean is all we'll ever see again."

"Persia, you're either talking foolishness or poetry. Which is it?"

"Neither! I'm discussing reality. And you and I are the only reality I believe in right now, this instant."

"And?" He was intrigued.

She leaned close and brought his hand—still holding hers—to her lips. She kissed the coarse hair on his knuckles. "And, I can't make any promises for the future. It makes no sense to live for anything except the present instant. And right now, my long-lost darling, I want you to make slow, careful, very thorough love to me."

Zack's eyes met and held the unblinking blue of hers. There were no more doubts or dark shadows lurking in their depths. Without a word, he rose and drew her to his side. He started to kiss her, then remembered the sailors on deck.

"Come with me," he ordered huskily.

She went—willingly, lovingly, without hesitation.

CHAPTER TWENTY-ONE

S*LOW, careful, very thorough*—that was the way Persia had requested that he make love to her, and Zachariah Hazzard meant to follow her every instruction.

The candle lamps bracketed to the wall cast a golden glow over the captain's cabin. And the gentle rocking of the ship upon the waves seemed to imitate the motion of lovers' bodies entwined as they entered the compartment hand in hand. Zack closed the door softly and stood staring at Persia.

She returned his gaze—nervous now, wondering how she could have been so bold. She wanted him—yes! But was she really a woman who could live for the moment alone? Still, there was no backing out now. Even if she wanted to, which she didn't, she could tell by the hot gleam in Zack's eyes that he wouldn't allow her to thrust him away again. Not now. Not when they had come this far.

He moved toward her slowly, shortening his usually bold stride as if he meant to prolong the moment and keep her waiting as she had kept him. When he took her into his arms, it felt right. His hands were around her waist, drawing her closer and closer. His eyes held her a moment before his mouth came down to meet her.

In that instant, it seemed to Persia that nothing had ever been so right, so perfect. Her lips parted for him, but he seemed in no hurry to glide into her waiting mouth. His tongue smoothed over her lips, flicked at the corners, and finally—when she was aching for the taste of him—found its way through the opening to begin its thorough search.

Persia shuddered in his arms. How long had she waited and dreamed of this moment? Of feeling his heart beating against her breasts, his hands caressing her, his tongue stroking her?

After a long, long time, he pulled away slightly and looked at her, a tender smile on his face. "Ah, this is good," he murmured.

"So good," she echoed.

"Persia, remember the night in Boston?"

His question was purely rhetorical, she knew. How could he think she would ever forget it?

"Remember how you went behind the screen to undress? I wanted so to watch you, but you wouldn't allow it. I want to undress you tonight—to see the woman I'm about to make love to."

"Zack . . " She started to object, but his hands playing over her bare neck and shoulders took away her last defenses. She nodded her assent.

Guiding her with his hands now on her waist, he sat down on the bunk and drew her onto his lap. She could feel his heat radiating up through her skirt and petticoat.

Slowly, as if she were made of some fragile china and might break at his slightest touch, Zack began untying the laces at the front of her white lawn gown. Soon his fingers spanned her chest, forcing the opening wide. He eased the gown off her shoulders and down to her waist, leaving only the thin camisole she wore beneath. His hands brushed lightly over her breasts.

"Look at your nipples strut for me, darling," he whispered in her ear. She gazed down, slightly embarrassed, to see the dark, jutting circles that strained against the sheer fabric.

His moist lips trailed down her shoulders and over to her breasts. Her head fell back and she gasped as his mouth covered one nipple and sucked at it through the fabric. He released her, only to catch the strap of the camisole in his teeth and slide it down her arm. With one hand, he pulled the other down. And soon her proud, white breasts were free.

"Ah, so lovely," he said with a deep sigh.

Persia could feel the long-remembered weakness creeping into her legs, as if she were walking into warm, gently stirring waters. His hands were holding her now—kneading her flesh, fondling her nipples, making her want to cry out for him.

He pressed her down on the bed and stood over her, hands on hips, staring at her with an appreciative smile.

"Do you love me, Persia?" he demanded.

Her eyes, which had been half-closed in ecstasy, flew wide. A tremor ran through her. His question was not what she had expected.

"Yes, Zack, I love you." It was the truth! Why not admit it?

"Good! Love is all that matters."

He knelt beside the bunk then and drew off her slippers. His strong fingers slid up her legs, under her petticoat, seeking the tops of her stockings. Finding her garters, he released one and then the other. Then slowly, with great deliberation, he rolled each stocking down and drew it off. By the time he pressed his warm palms to the naked soles of her feet, fingering her toes gently, Persia was aching with exquisite need.

Slowly, patiently, he divested her of the rest of her garments, kissing her bare flesh as he explored each part of her with his eyes, his hands, his tongue. She thrashed and moaned, sighed and begged. But he would not be rushed.

"You said *thoroughly*, my love," he whispered. "I will give you nothing less. This is what you've been waiting for all these years. And you shall have your full measure. That I promise you!''

The candles were still burning. He was still fully clothed. To Persia's mind, there seemed something utterly pagan about the scene. It was as if she were about to be sacrificed on some heathen altar. Suddenly she remembered stories Fletcher had told her about virgins on far-off isles being thrown into volcanoes to appease angry gods. Yes, this was like that! She might not be a virgin, but Zack looked every inch the angry god!

Giving up the nipple he had been torturing so tenderly with his tongue and teeth, he rose from the bed and strode across the floor. Persia thought he meant to get out of his clothes, but instead he opened one of the cabinets and peered in.

''Yes, this should do nicely,'' he commented, holding up a green-glass bottle as he started back toward her.

She raised up on one elbow, unaware of how tantalizing a picture she presented in that pose with her breasts thrust toward him.

''For what?'' she asked.

''Never mind. Just turn over,'' he ordered. ''On your belly.''

Persia lay there, tense, unable to see him for the hair tangled over her eyes. She had no idea what he was about to do to her.

''I got this idea today when I saw the men dipped in molasses,'' he said matter-of-factly. ''I thought what a pleasure it would be for me to lick away all that sticky sweetness if it were on my Persia.''

''No, Zack!'' she cried.

She tried to rise, but he put one arm across her waist, holding her down. And just then, she felt the first drops of liquid dribble across her shoulders. It felt cool and soothing, not sticky at all.

Zack laughed softly as he massaged the creamy ointment into her skin. ''Had you going there, didn't I, darling? No, I'm not going to drown you in molasses. You're sunburned, that's all. You'll be in a great deal of pain by tomorrow, if it's not tended to. And after all, I am the ship's doctor. I'd be remiss in my duties if I didn't see to this.''

She relaxed and smiled. His hard fingertips were working magic on her neck, shoulders, and back. She didn't even protest when he moved lower, pouring the cool ointment onto her buttocks and down the backs of her legs—where she couldn't possibly have gotten the least trace of sun.

He rubbed, he kneaded, and finally his hard fingertips did some exploring as well. She might have tensed with shock at this unexpected touch, but he had worked his magic on her mind as well as her body. She was completely, totally his—to do with as he would.

''Not sleeping, are you, love?'' He leaned close to her ear and nibbled as he asked.

''Hardly,'' came her breathy answer.

''Then turn over.''

She did as he ordered and was rewarded for her compliance by more magical liquid from his green bottle. He trailed it drop by drop across her chest and shoulders, onto her breasts, down over her belly, and into the silky triangle at her thighs.

She lay perfectly still, waiting and watching him, as he straddled her and pulled off his shirt. His palms came toward her and rested lightly on her erect nipples, making lazy circles and sending incendiary sparks through her blood. His hands flattened then, and his fingers gripped her breasts. At the same moment, her own hands shot up, grasping the top of his britches in a near desperate hold.

''Go ahead, darling!'' he encouraged. ''Unbutton them.''

He was sitting astride the very top of her legs. She could feel his heat and the pulse of him against her own quickened flesh. Slowly, she drew the bone buttons through their fabric notches. As each was released, the coarse man-hair of his belly sprang free to tingle her fingertips. The hair was dark, not frosted like that on his chest.

While she worked at his remaining clothing, his hands

were busy, too, stroking the quivering plane of her stomach, circling into her navel, gripping her hips. When he reached a particularly sensitive area just below her hipbone, she fell back and uttered a deep sigh. Taking advantage of the moment, his palms slid down over her and his fingers dug into the tight little curls, which were an even brighter flame color than the hair spread out on her pillow. His fingers tangled themselves in the curls as he tugged gently.

"Zack!" Persia gasped, half rising.

Using no great force, he pushed her back to the pillows. Once more his inquisitive fingers set about their exploration. In no time, he had discovered the secret place he sought beneath that flaming forest.

Persia heard herself panting, but she couldn't stop. Her eyes were tightly shut. And in her mind, she could see the circles his fingertips were tracing. They glowed against the blackness in hot, vivid colors. Her legs went numb now in her need. Her breasts ached with a delicious sort of pain. And the heat—the terrible, wonderful heat—was rising to temperatures hot enough to melt her insides. Any moment now, she would lose her grip on reality and float off to some distant, unknown realm.

But a moment before that happened, he stopped. He took his hands from her body and sat back.

"I think you'd better finish what you started, darling." His voice was low, husky, almost pleading.

She went back to his buttons, her fingers trembling so now that she could hardly manage them. Then, suddenly, she freed him. He burst out like a great tree trunk that had suddenly fallen into her own forest. Tentatively, she touched him. He groaned and gripped her waist. She curled her fingers around the velvety flesh. He sounded as if he were choking. She released him.

"*No!*" he gasped. "Don't stop!"

As she lay there, holding the hot, throbbing shaft in her palm—squeezing gently, moving her fingers this way and that—a new kind of need filled her. She had been right. There was no other time or place. There was only here, now, the two of them . . . and this wonderful, miraculous tool of pleasure she now held in her sure, all-powerful hands.

She fondled the smooth tip; he moaned. She let her fingers slide to the base; he shuddered. She tightened her grip; he collapsed forward, seeking her breasts, sucking hard and battering her nipple with his rough tongue.

And then tree and forest met—one dry and insistent, the other warmly moist and accepting.

She cried out when he entered her, but the sound had nothing to do with pain. He had loved her slowly and carefully. Now he would fulfill the rest of his promise by loving her thoroughly.

Deeper and deeper he plunged. She felt as if his hard core were stroking at her very heart. His mouth possessed hers, allowing his twin thrusts to join forces, taking her to new and unreal heights of pleasure. She felt as if her body were glowing inside and out. And then it happened . . . the whole world exploded, sending their joined bodies flying off into space to take their shining places among the stars.

A new kind of bond had been forged between Persia and Zack. In the dark night, upon the dark sea, somewhere south of the equator, these two had seen the meaning of life in a great, draining, cleansing, restoring, blinding flash of light. Nothing would ever be the same for either of them. They knew that, and they accepted it gratefully. As Zack had said shortly before their miraculous transformation took place: "Love is all that matters!"

The *Madagascar* sailed on. At times, gale winds whipped the mighty sails and giant waves slammed into her, sending spindrift over her decks. At other times, the sea was as brilliant and calm and smooth as the new-found love between her captain and his sweetheart. But day in and day out, one thing never changed—Zack and Persia were together now and, they hoped, forevermore.

"I don't think you should even see him when we reach Bombay, darling," Zack said to Persia. They were strolling the deck together on a particularly fine morning after a night of exceptional lovemaking.

"Well, certainly, I'd just as soon not, Zack. But I do owe the man an explanation. After all, he's expecting his bride any time. Surely he's received Reverend Osgood's letter by overland mail by now. Undoubtedly he's been making all sorts of preparations."

Persia was dreamily preoccupied this morning. At the moment, she was staring up at a flock of seagulls playing in the airstreams overhead. It had been a while since they'd been close enough to land to see a bird. But now they had rounded the Cape of Good Hope and were sailing through warm seas off the island of Madagascar.

"Persia, are you listening to me? If all goes well, we'll reach Bombay within the month. You have some important decisions to make."

"I know, Zack. I know," she said, smiling up at him. "But I've made the most important one already. I'm going to be *your* wife. Still, I don't like even thinking about Cyrus Blackwell. It makes me feel so guilty."

"Guilty? Why, that's the most ridiculous thing I've ever heard in all my life!" He took her hand in his, and his voice softened. "Darling, you don't even know the man. And he's been married before. Surely he'll understand that love is involved here and give us his blessing. But I still say a well-worded letter to him would suffice. I see no need for you to have to meet with him."

"Oh, darling, look at that cloud!" Persia cried excitedly, pointing off to starboard at a looming, purple-tinged formation. "It looks just like a fairy dancing in the top of a lilac bush!"

Zack laughed softly and shook his head. "My dear, impossible Persia! Only you could see such a vision in a storm cloud over the Indian Ocean. Time you went below. I'm afraid we're in for some dirty weather before long."

And they were—the worst they'd seen. For a time, it seemed to Persia that she would never see the sun, dry land, or Zack again. She remained below in her cabin in eternal darkness, not daring to light a lamp for fear of starting a fire. And Zack had insisted that the deadlights be fastened in place over her windows for the duration of the storm. These heavy, wooden, shutter-type affairs blocked out every ray of light but kept the glass from shattering and possibly causing serious injury.

However, she hardly saw what further injuries she could suffer. The ship alternately wallowed in the deep troughs between waves and was then tossed skyward by the violent, crashing seas. One moment Persia was up and the next moment she was down. She had bruises all over her body, a lump on her forehead where she'd been thrown against a wildly swinging cupboard door, and a fresh gash in her arm from a broken lamp that was paining her considerably.

She lay on her back in the very center of the bunk, gripping the mattress with both hands. But still she was tossed and buffeted. Through it all came the scream of the howling wind, the groan of the ship's straining timbers, and the constant roar of the sea. And from below, she could hear the grinding sound of the ice shifting.

She was so tired. If only she could sleep. Then she could dream herself out of this nightmare. Still holding on tightly, she closed her eyes.

"Man overboard!"

She sat up in bed, fear turning her blood to ice. At first she thought she'd dreamed it. But the thudding of boots racing topside told her it was a terrible reality. No call was more dreaded at sea, and in a storm like this there would be little hope of saving him. Still, every man in both watches would turn out to lend a hand.

Forgetting Zack's orders to stay in her cabin, Persia slipped into the oilskin foul-weather coat the sailmaker had fashioned for her and fought her way to the door. It was a matter of one step forward and two steps back as the ship lurched and shuddered. Finally, she made her way into the passage and up the ladder.

Rain and seawater poured down the hatch to soak her through. The whole world seemed a dirty, wet shade of purplish gray. And the ship was as dark as a cave. Was it day or night? She couldn't remember, and she certainly couldn't tell from looking.

She watched hazy figures moving about deck, clinging

to lifelines that had been rigged from forecastle head to the break of the poop, along both sides of the ship. Shredded sails flapped above, looking like grave shrouds of the damned. She swiped at the water clouding her vision. She wanted desperately to catch sight of Zack, to know that he was all right. But she could make out no faces, only dark shadows moving about the deck. Her heart sank.

What if Zack was the man who had been swept over the side? How could she live without him? Then darker thoughts began to crowd into her mind and weigh heavily on her heart. What if this was her punishment for having loved him when, by rights, she belonged to another?

She stumbled back down the ladder, slipping twice and falling to her knees in the passageway that was now awash with saltwater. Crawling on all fours, she made it to her cabin door. She was exhausted, crying, hurting all over. Summoning more strength than she thought she had left, she shouldered the door open. Just then a mighty wave hit the ship broadside. The deck tilted beneath her, rolling her as if she were an empty barrel until she slammed painfully into the side of her bunk. She lay there, stunned, for a few moments, waiting for the ship to right itself. Then slowly, she climbed back into bed and gave herself up to racking sobs.

Minutes, hours, it could even have been *days* later to Persia's mind, a hand gripped her bruised shoulder.

"Are you all right?" demanded a familiar, husky voice.

"Zack?" she cried. "Oh, Zack, I thought you were dead!"

She threw herself into his arms, but his touch was cold. His arms seemed frozen at his sides.

"I saw you when you came up the ladder, Persia. That was a damn fool thing to do. I told you to stay put and I meant it!"

She drew back from him, feeling like a chastised child. "I heard the cry and all the men running. I only wanted to make sure you were safe."

"Well, I'm fine, as you can see. But I certainly won't

be if you get yourself swept overboard and I have to go in after you."

Suddenly, she returned to her senses. "Zack, who was it?"

"Mister Barry," he answered in an icy voice. "He went up in the rigging to batten down some sail. A monster wave hit, and . . ."

"And?" Her voice was small. She already knew the answer.

"He's gone."

"Oh, Zack, I'm sorry."

"Not nearly as sorry as you'll be the next time I see you coming on deck. In fact, I won't risk it. Lie down!"

Grabbing up a length of rope that had slithered in from the sea outside her door, Zack quickly lashed her to the bunk.

"There! That should hold you," he said. "It's not over yet, and it's going to get worse before it gets better."

Furious, she screamed his name and a few foul epithets after him, but he paid her no heed. She lay, trussed like a fish in a net, seething and straining to escape. But Zack knew his craft well. She would not be free until he came back to release her.

Totally exhausted, she closed her eyes. Although the ship was still rolling, she was no longer being tossed about from pillar to post. She relaxed within her bonds and let sleep carry her away.

Sometime later, deep in the night, near the end of the second dog watch, she awoke to find the lamps lit and Zack standing over her. The storm seemed to have passed. He fingered the rope and grinned.

"Oh, could I amuse myself with you in this position!"

He tugged at one of her bare feet, then let his hand slide up her leg. Leaning down to kiss her, he brought his hand to her breast to play there a bit.

She squirmed against her bonds, but they held her tight. She was totally at his mercy. The thought both repelled and thrilled her.

Ever so slowly, his hand drifted down her body—

pinching here, teasing there. Then his fingers moved lower, to a more tender region, to concentrate on more serious fondling.

Persia, inflamed, pulled her mouth from his and demanded, "Zack, untie me! This minute!"

She was oddly disappointed when he did as ordered.

The *Madagascar* had literally been thrown back across the equator by the fury of the storm. Luckily, their cargo had not thawed enough to shift dangerously. Still, there was a great deal of damage and, of course, one man lost. But miraculously, the ship was still seaworthy and still on course. With the right winds, they would see Bombay in only weeks.

But their luck did not hold. After the storm came the calm. The *Madagascar* lolled, motionless, in the region about the equator called the doldrums, caught in the void between the two trade winds. They were one hundred and fourteen days out. They had made good time. But now it looked as if they might be trapped in this same airless spot of ocean for days or even weeks.

The ice now became their main concern. The warm seas caused rapid melting. All day and all night, the rasp and cough of the hand-operated pumps on deck disturbed the hot, airless silence. The ship's hold had to be kept as dry as possible. Otherwise, the melting process would only speed itself up. A fortune could be lost in a span of days.

Zack had been busier than usual since his first mate was taken from him by the sea. Stoner was a fair second mate, but the man would never be officer material. So it was up to the master of the ship to fill both positions. Most difficult of all was keeping the sailors of the starboard watch busy at all times. He had them polish all the brass from ship's bell to binnacle and then start over again. They swabbed, they varnished, they painted, they scraped. Down on their hands and knees in the baking, tropical sun, they holystoned the decks until they gleamed.

But as temperatures soared, drinking water ran short, and still there was not a breath of air, tempers erupted.

The sound of the never-ceasing pumps, sending useless water into the sea, only made matters worse. By the end of four days, two of the sailors were below, sweating it out in chains for having come to blows over a coconut one of them had fished out of the sea. Everyone else, including Persia, lay up on deck, sweltering and blistering through the long, hot days.

The sailmaker had rigged a tentlike affair to protect Persia from the sun's fiery rays. She appreciated the thought and it was a help, but the covering kept any breath of air from reaching her. There was nothing for it but to come out every hour or so and stroll the deck to breathe.

During one of these interludes, Zack spotted her. His eyes narrowed. He had seen the way the sailors were looking at her. Normally they wouldn't have posed a threat. But these circumstances were anything but normal. He had seen women attacked on board other ships when the sun had baked the senses from a man's brain. He came up behind her and took her elbow, steering her back toward her shelter.

"Do you want to get sunstroke?" he demanded.

"No. I just came out for a moment. I thought there might be a breeze."

"There's no breeze, my darling. Just a dozen or so womenstarved sailors, half-crazed from thirst and boredom. Do us all a favor; stay out of sight."

"But Zack . . ."

"No buts! That is an order, madam!"

Sulkily, she crept back into her shelter. He might at least have joined her for a time. What was wrong with him these days? He was grumpy, harsh, even impatient with her. And they hadn't made love . . . since when? Not for a week, at least. Surely he couldn't have tired of her already! The thought nagged at her. She dismissed it. It was too hot to worry over things she could do nothing about.

She gazed out across the deck. It shimmered in the heat. She could see a group of about ten sailors huddled together a few yards away. They seemed to be in deep discussion. And they kept glancing toward her. She was curious, but the heat did not lend itself to long concentration on any one thing.

Using a seagull-feather fan one of the men had made for her, she stirred her own breeze. But it was a hot one. She opened the neck of her gown and fanned determinedly, shading her eyes with her other hand to scan the skies though the tent opening for any sign of a cloud. Rain would be such a blessing!

"Ma'am?" The voice just outside her little shelter made her jump. "Miz Blackwell, ma'am, could I speak to you a minute?"

She gave the young man a smile. He wasn't bad-looking—tall, tough, sandy-bearded. She'd seen him many times but couldn't recall his name just now.

"Yes?" she answered. "What is it?"

He edged closer under the awning with her. He was grinning and seemed a bit nervous.

"Well, ma'am, you see, me and the boys've been talking it over. It bein' so fearful hot an' all, we figured you could do with somethin' to drink."

"That's kind of you, but the water's rationed. I wouldn't want to take any more than my share. We don't want to have to melt down our precious cargo in order to survive."

He laughed. "Aw, we wouldn't steal no water, ma'am. The cap'n would skin our tails. Now, I got something better. A little present from the boys." He pulled a flask out of his pocket and shoved it toward her. "Here!"

A bit of the amber liquid sloshed from the neck of the bottle, staining Persia's white cotton skirt. She stared at the sailor, unsmiling.

"Where did you get this? You know spirits aren't allowed among the crew! Why, the captain will—"

"The captain will *what*?" Zack's voice boomed.

The sailor turned pale and might have scurried away if Zack's well-placed boot hadn't sent him sprawling first.

"Stoner, arrest this man," the captain ordered. "Take him below and chain him. He'll be brought before the mast at noon tomorrow."

A stricken wail followed the sailor down the ladder.

"Zack, you can't do that. He didn't mean any harm. He only offered me something to drink."

"Yes, I can tell. You *reek* of it! And what did you offer him in exchange?"

"Nothing! Not a thing! How dare you?"

"I'm the captain of this ship, and it's up to me to keep order. I won't have you or anyone else disrupting things, Persia."

"I never!" she protested.

"Oh? And just what do you call those little prome-nades on deck you've been indulging in? The men's scorched eyeballs nearly pop out of their sockets when you go prancing around out there with your dress open to your navel! Persia, I don't know what's gotten into you!"

"Nor I you!" she replied angrily. Then she hurried below to the oven that was her cabin. She would stay there until Zack apologized.

But she had sweated it out only about ten minutes when she heard the familiar sound of wind filling sail and felt the ship shudder to life around her. She laughed out loud with pure relief and hurried up on deck.

The ship was alive again, and so was the crew.

"Stoner, release the prisoners," she heard the captain order. "We need all hands to get under way. And pass out an extra ration of water. We'll make Bombay with plenty to spare!"

That night, when Zack came off watch, he was a changed man. Persia didn't need an apology—he gave her so much more! He made her wish that this voyage could go on forever. She never wanted to be any farther away from Zack than she was right now. They were everything to each other. The rest of the world had ceased to exist. She loved and was loved in return. That was her total, eternal reality.

CHAPTER TWENTY-TWO

*P*ERSIA leaned over the railing, thinking that she had never seen as lovely a sight as Bombay harbor. Even the caws and shrieks of the black clouds of crows circling over the distant city added their own exotic touch to the scene.

"March 28, 1847," she said, smiling. "A new day, a new world!"

Her eyes swept over the lush green outline of Malabar Hill, along the western shore of Bombay Island. Directly ahead of them lay Prongs Reef and the floating marker and light at the harbor's entrance.

Suddenly, the boom of a cannon marred the quiet of the early, golden morning. She jumped, then relaxed as she realized the *Madagascar* had been spotted from the lighthouse and its arrival duly noted. She spied the harbor pilot's boat, already on its way to guide them safely into port. The jaunty little craft was painted bright red with a number in black on the bow to identify the pilot. Its lateen-rigged sails flapped prettily in the morning breeze.

"That'll be for us." Zack's voice came from behind her.

She turned, stared, and did a double take. "Zack! You look different!"

He rubbed a big hand over his smooth chin. "The whiskers had to go in this heat. What do you think?"

She smiled. "I think you are indeed a handsome devil."

He reached out to stroke her cheek with his fingertips. "And you, my love, are a cunning liar."

"Look over there!" she cried excitedly, pointing to port. "It's the ancient city. I recognize it from Father's descriptions and the sketches he made when he was here." Her eyes swept to starboard, over the palm-fringed shoreline of the island. "Oh, Zack, I can just make out the peaks of the Western Ghat Mountains. The whole scene looks like a painting. It's too beautiful to be real!"

He twined one of her curls around his finger, tugging gently to bring her back to face him. "So are you, Persia. So are you."

She did look particularly lovely this morning in a white-on-white embroidered frock of Indian cotton. The collar was high and the sleeves full and long, but the tight-fitting bodice displayed her charms to their very best advantage. She had swept her hair up into a red-gold pile of waves, with side curls framing her face and feathery wisps at the back of her neck. Tiny river pearls glowed at her ears, reflecting the iridescence of her delicate skin.

She offered him a flirtatious smile, knowing he was admiring her costume. "I like your white linen, too. And the sun hat is a nice touch."

He tipped his pith helmet to her, then opened his jacket and strutted about in a circle, allowing her to admire every linen-clad inch. "The very height of fashion in *Injia*, my dear girl!" he teased, successfully imitating the accent of the Britishers who ruled the land.

"Cap'n Hazzard, sir, the pilot's ready to board," Stoner called.

"Permission to board granted," Zack answered back.

Then to Persia he said, "Duty calls. We'll be anchoring in the harbor within the hour. Then you and I will go ashore to pay our first calls on the ice merchants."

"I'll be ready," she promised.

With the pilot safely on board, as law dictated, they began their slow progress into the crowded harbor. Entering the congested waters was something like threading a needle, Persia thought as they wove their way among ships from every nation, dows, lighters, and houseboats where naked babies crawled about the decks amidst chickens and dogs while wrinkled old grannies watched with alert black eyes.

They anchored in a choice spot near the waterfront. Ice ships, she knew, were given preferred berths so that their precious cargoes could be unloaded with as much haste as possible. They could expect to have lost about one-third of their merchandise to melting already during the journey. But even at that, ice was so dear in India that it was a profitable cargo at three halfpence a pound.

Hating to leave her vantage point for an instant, but knowing that Zack would be impatient to get ashore, she hurried below to retrieve her wide-brimmed straw hat, parasol, and white gloves. When Zack saw her come back on deck, he was quite convinced that she would be the prettiest supercargo the ice merchants of Bombay had ever laid eyes on.

The pilot received his pay of one hundred and ten rupees, then left them. But before Zack and Persia could climb down into their own launch, visitors arrived. The customs house officer, who would be required to live aboard for the duration of the *Madagascar's* stay, came up the ladder. He was a short, stocky, jovial sort, who waxed eloquent on Persia's charms and bowed over her gloved hand longer than Zack considered proper.

Hardly had the captain and his lovely supercargo finished talking with the customs officer before two Parsees— members of a religious sect who were also Bombay merchants—pulled up in their small boat, bringing mail that had arrived for Persia. There was a letter from her father and one from Europa. Both had been sent by overland mail after her departure, traveling by way of a Cunard steamer to England, then on another boat by way of the Strait of Gibraltar through the Mediterranean to Alexandria, and from there by camel caravan to Suez before sailing on across the Arabian and Red Seas to reach her in Bombay. There was also a third envelope with only her name scrawled across it in unfamiliar handwriting.

Persia longed to read her letters, but she understood the necessity of first paying her respects to the white-turbaned Parsees. Undoubtedly, the success of her ice-selling mission would depend to no small degree upon this pair of swarthy, softspoken Indians. They introduced themselves as Allbless and Jeejeebhoy.

"You and the captain will take tea with us later, Madam Blackwell?" invited Jeejeebhoy, the taller of the twosome, bowing subserviently all the while.

Persia was shocked. Not by his invitation, but because of the way he addressed her. Zack had introduced her to these men as "Miss Whiddington." How could they know of her proxy marriage?

"We'll be happy to." Zack, frowning, answered when he saw that Persia could not.

"Then we will expect you around four." The pair bowed themselves off the ship and departed back to the city.

"Persia, what's got into you?" Zack demanded.

Her face was pale, her hands trembling. "Didn't you hear what he called me, Zack? How could he know?"

Zack dismissed her worries with a wave of his hand and a broad smile. "Forget it, darling! As you said, Blackwell has probably received the letter announcing your arrival. News has a way of spreading, even in the far corners of the world. Besides, isn't your mail addressed that way?"

"Oh, yes. How silly of me! Hearing him call me that . . . I don't know, it just sent a chill through me."

"The boat's ready, Cap'n," Stoner called.

As was the nautical custom, Zack waited until Persia,

Stoner, and the steward, Dawkin, were in the longboat
before he hopped aboard. The other two men would buy
fresh supplies ashore while he and Persia saw to their
business. The rest of the crew, even those rowing them
in, would not set foot on dry land until all the ice was
unloaded.

Even as the longboat made its way to Buna Bandar,
the docking place, half a dozen red-sailed bumboats
were on their way out to the ship to try to sell all
manner of exotic gewgaws to the *Madagascar*'s crew.
Persia spied some of their merchandise—sandalwood
boxes, ivory carvings, fresh dates, even live monkeys.

The dock was a mob scene. No sooner had Zack
leaped to the quay and offered a helping hand to Persia
than they were besieged by vendors of all sorts. One
shrunken old man with a wispy goatee pressed them to
buy his fresh produce—strange, bright-colored fruits like
none Persia had ever seen back home in New England.
Another offered colorful fabrics by the bolt. And still
another, silk and ostrich-feather fans decorated with glistening pearls.

Zack must have noticed Persia's eyes sparkling when
they lit on these. "Would you like one, darling!" he
asked.

"Oh, Zack, they must be very expensive!"

He laughed. "There's hardly a thing around here that
could be less dear than feathers, silk, or pearls." He
beckoned to the young merchant. "You there, girl! Let
us see your fans."

The dark-faced beauty pushed through the crowd and
spread her wares before them on a reed mat. Persia
couldn't decide. There were fans of silk and lace, and
feathers tinted every color of the rainbow. The attached
pearls—from black to gray to pinkish white—all cast a
soft glow. Suddenly she noticed an exquisite fan of the
palest gray silk. It looked almost silver in the bright
sunlight. It was edged with blue-gray pearls and trimmed
with delicate lace medallions shot through with silver.

"That one, girl." Zack pointed to the very fan Persia

had been eyeing. *"Kitna?"* he demanded, asking how much in the native tongue.

"One *Yanqui* dolla', John!"

"Oh, Zack, it's lovely!" Persia enthused. "Thank you!"

Persia spread her fan and gave it a good wave under her chin. Then she brought it up to cover all but her eyes and offered Zack a slow, seductive wink.

He chuckled at her. "Now, don't you go flirting with these hot-blooded Indians, darling. I bought you that to keep you cool. Remember it!"

Suddenly, Persia's eyes went beyond Zack's laughing face to a figure lurking at the edge of a group of men. The others were sailors on shore leave; she could tell by the way they were dressed. They seemed not even to notice the man, so intent were they on puffing at their hubble-bubble pipes.

The stranger resembled no one else she had seen so far in Bombay. He was robed in white cotton drapes that covered him from head to toe, leaving only his swarthy face showing. She felt a tremor pass through her. She tried to look away but found she couldn't. His bold gaze held her hypnotized.

Slowly, the strange man raised one hand toward her as if beckoning her to him. She had taken several steps in his direction—totally against her will—when Zack caught her arm.

"Persia, where are you going? The customs house is this way. Darling, you must stay close to me. I can't have you getting lost in this mob. It's not safe."

"Zack, look at that man over there." She pointed to where he had been, but he was gone. Perplexed, she scanned the crowd. He seemed to have vanished into air.

"What man?" Zack asked.

"I know he was there. I *saw* him!"

"You'll see a lot of odd beings before we leave this place. Look at that fellow over there, charming his snake, and that one with the wire-walking rat." He felt Persia shudder at the sights. "Come along now. Cunningham will be waiting for us."

As they inched their way among the throng, Persia kept

glancing back over her shoulder. She had the feeling that the man was still there somewhere, staring after her.

Finally, they turned into the main street that would take them to the customs house. There they would meet with the Tudor Ice Company's Bombay representative to make arrangements to have the cargo unloaded and taken to the elaborate stone ice house in the heart of town. Packed in rice chaff there, it would be safe from further loss until it was sold.

The street was jammed with humanity—natives who ranged in color from ebony to coffee, foreign sailors, staid officials of the East India Company, and ever-present sacred cows, plopped down wherever they pleased. The foot traffic flowed like waves parted by a seawall around these unconcerned beasts.

"We'd make better time if we hired a palanquin," Zack said, already motioning toward four coolies carrying one of the boxlike conveyances on their shoulders.

Persia wanted to object. She had finally shaken off the unsettling effect of the strange man's gaze and was now enjoying the exotic sights all about her. But they were here for a purpose, and in their particular business every moment counted.

The four thin but muscular men, who wore what appeared to be handkerchiefs about their waists and tablecloths about their heads, stopped before the pair to let down their shouldered carriage. Zack handed Persia inside and then stepped in himself. Curtains on all four sides flapped loosely but kept out some of the dust and noise. When the men took up their heavy burden again, the motion sent Persia sprawling across Zack's lap. He righted her, laughing. A moment later, they were on their way at a quick, steady trot.

"There, that's better," Zack said with a sigh. "The place is dizzying—all that humanity. It's like being trapped inside a beehive." He reached out and fingered the coarse gunny material surrounding them. "I like these curtains, too."

Persia was about to comment on his poor taste in yard goods when all of a sudden she understood his true meaning. Before she could open her mouth to say a word, he was kissing her—very deeply, very thoroughly. His kisses always thrilled her, but this one especially so. There was something more exciting than usual about being paid such lavish and intimate attention in the broad light of day, in the middle of a busy city street, even if no one could see them. It made her feel quite wicked, in fact!

"Hm-m-m," he sighed. "I wish it was farther to the customs house and this bower of ours was a bit larger."

She stroked her folded fan across his smooth cheek seductively. "Sorry, my love. You'll have to wait for the rest."

He cupped her breast and squeezed playfully. "Why, darling? I could pay our four good fellows a few extra rupees to carry us off to some secluded spot under a banyan tree and leave us there for a time."

She sniffed haughtily at his suggestion. "And meanwhile, in this heat, we would be losing hard cash to severe meltage!"

He groaned. "Spoken like a true supercargo."

The customs house was very British in character, as were most of the newer buildings of the island city, all cool stone and tall windows. While Zack went to file the required papers of entry, Persia waited in an antechamber for Tudor's agent, Mr. Cunningham, to receive them. She was glad for the time alone to read her mail.

Her father's letter was all excitement over her trip and good wishes on her new venture. He meant, of course, her sale of the ice, not her marriage to Cyrus Blackwell. It was plain to Persia that he was receiving a vicarious thrill from her adventures. She was glad. She made a mental note to write him immediately after dinner tonight with full details of everything she had seen and done so far in Bombay.

Europa's letter reflected her usual state—complaining about the cold, the children, Seton's job, and yet another pregnancy. Persia smiled at the thought of being presented with one more nephew. It certainly looked as if her brother-in-law had set about the task of populating the vast reaches of the state of Maine!

The third letter chased the first two from her mind, leaving her numb and frightened. The note was brief—to the point.

> *Elephanta Island*
> *March 21, 1847*

> *My dutiful wife,*

> *I have been made aware of your impending arrival. Brother Osgood has written, explaining to me that you are not the perfect bride he hoped to send. But we will not study on evil, you and I. Whatever sins are on your soul shall be purged. I will see to it, personally.*

> *I plan to collect you within the week. See that all your affairs are in order promptly.*

> *Your Husband and Savior,*
> *Brother Cyrus*

Persia was still staring at the letter in her trembling hands when Zack came into the chamber. He hurried to her, sure that she had received terrible news from home by the pallor of her cheeks and the look of horror on her face.

"Darling, what is it?" he asked.

"Oh, Zack, he knows!"

"*Who* knows *what*, Persia?"

"Cyrus Blackwell," she whispered. "He knows I'm here."

"Well, of course, you expected that he would, didn't you? You told me yourself that Reverend Osgood intended to write to him."

She looked at Zack, and her eyes were wild with fear. "But he knows about *us*!"

"All the better. We'll make fast work of explaining to him that you plan to seek an annulment and marry me."

He was trying to treat the matter lightly, to reassure her, but it wasn't working.

"No, I mean he knows that I'm not a virgin. He says he will *purge* the sins from my soul! What does he mean?" She was nearly hysterical now, trembling all over.

"Darling, darling," Zack soothed. "You mustn't be frightened. It doesn't mean anything because I won't allow you to see him. Let me read that."

Zack took the note from her and scanned the page quickly. "Damn the man! What kind of pompous, unfeeling creature can he be to write such tripe to his wife?"

"You may come into Mr. Cunningham's office now," the agent's male clerk announced to them.

Zack crushed Blackwell's note in his fist and crammed it into his pocket. "Come along, Persia. And don't worry about a thing, I'll take care of this matter."

Their meeting with Mr. Cunningham went smoothly. He would arrange for the ice to be unloaded the day after tomorrow—"Sorry, but that's the very soonest possible," he said when Zack objected to the delay. On the brighter side, the British governor was giving a fancy ball at the Bombay Club the next evening. The two of them were most cordially invited. "It's dress, of course," the man added.

Persia hardly heard a word of the conversation. Cyrus Blackwell's words kept flashing before her eyes in the painfully precise handwriting that had seemed to taint the very page it was written on.

There were other distractions, too. A bevy of Indian servants hovered about—one stroking an ostrich-feather fan through the hot air, one at the humidor should either of the gentlemen desire a cigar, another at the water pitcher, others holding various wine decanters, and two or three who seemed to have no set task to perform other than being there and at the ready. Persia eyed them curiously. Each man bowed to her, grinning broadly.

How could one overfed ice agent require so many servants? she wondered.

It seemed Zack had just asked Cunningham a similar but more politely phrased question. "Oh, labor's dirt cheap here. And the poor devils have to eat. The British chaps will tell you that it's beneath them to have only one man to remove their stockings at night. Any decent, self-respecting Englishman will hire two—one for each foot!" Cunningham followed his story with a belly laugh that shook him like a volcano preparing for major eruption.

"What about lodgings, Mr. Cunningham?" Zack asked. "I think Miss Whiddington would be much more comfortable ashore."

The agent quirked a brow. "Superior suggestion!" He snapped his fingers, and one of the idle servants ran to him, bowing and grinning. "Run over to the India House, boy, and tell them to expect Captain Hazzard and *Mrs. Blackwell* shortly. Two of their best rooms, mind you. And don't dawdle. No stopping off to chew any bang with your friends along the way!"

Persia tensed. Did everyone in Bombay know about her marriage?

Zack rose. "Well, thank you, Mr. Cunningham. I suppose we'll see you at the Club tomorrow evening?"

"Oh, the wife and I wouldn't miss it. Big do! Everyone who's anyone will be there, even some Indian royalty.'" He smiled at Persia. "But you'll be the belle of the ball, Mrs. Blackwell, mark my words. Not many young ladies come out here. Those that do . . . well, they just don't last. The heat and all, you know. But as a missionary's wife, you'll probably stay too busy to notice the heat." He offered Persia a sympathetic smile even as he offered his hand to Zack. "Looking forward to it, yes, I am! And we're all happy to have you here, Mrs. Blackwell. You'll be a great comfort to Brother Cyrus. I know he regretted being out of town when you arrived. He's gone up-country. But he'll be back in a few days to give you a proper welcome. He's a fine man, but he needs a good wife."

Persia decided to set the agent straight. "Mr. Cunningham, I won't be—'' She broke off when Zack put a warning hand on her arm.

When they reached the door, he said, "Persia, wait for me outside. I have one more thing I meant to ask Cunningham. I'll only be a minute."

The door closed behind her and Zack turned back to the red-faced agent. "What can you tell me about Cyrus Blackwell?"

"As I said to Mrs. Blackwell, her husband is a fine man—a pillar of the community. He's built a commune over on Elephanta Island. Takes in orphans and gives them food and shelter. They'd starve without his aid. A number of familes live over there now. There's a regular village. Cyrus is a bit of an odd duck, but the man's not had an easy life. And his wife's death last year was tragic, truly tragic." He shook his head sadly.

"What's Elephanta like?"

"Oh, a lovely place—lush and green, and teeming with fascinating caves that were used as temples in ancient times."

"What about Blackwell's wife? How did she die?"

"Nobody really knows, Captain Hazzard. She was a good woman. A Christian woman. Tended the sick, took food to the hungry, saw to Cyrus's every need. She was a hard worker, full of energy. Then she just took ill all of a sudden. Maybe she caught some exotic disease from one of the children. All I know is, one day Hannah Blackwell was in the pink of health and a few weeks later she had simply withered away. Brother Cyrus thought it might have been poison from a snakebite. But who knows?" He leaned across the desk and whispered, "I've even heard from some superstitious souls that it was a death wish put on her because she was interfering with someone's business. But, of course, I don't believe in that sort of nonsense."

"What kind of *business* are you talking about?" Zack asked.

Cunningham rolled his eyes. "You must understand, Captain, that all this is strictly off the record. But the opium traffic in the city has picked up in the last couple of years. And people have been reporting children missing—not just an isolated case here and there. *Dozens* in the past year. All little girls. The white slave market is practically headquartered here in Bombay. Of course, we don't advertise the fact.''

"My God! I don't suppose you would! Drug trafficking and white slavery!'' Then he added under his breath, "This is no place for Persia.''

"See here, if you're concerned about Mrs. Blackwell, you needn't be. Cyrus's first wife was British. They never get on very well in this climate. But Mrs. Blackwell is American, and a strong young woman, from the looks of her. She'll do just fine in India.''

Zack started to tell the man that he wasn't worried because Persia wouldn't be staying. But he thought better of it. Until he had her safely away from Bombay, he felt it wise to keep their plans to himself. He had an uneasy feeling about this whole situation.

He hurried out of the agent's office, vowing to keep Persia within sight for the duration of their stay here.

CHAPTER TWENTY-THREE

*B*Y the time Persia and Zack finally reached their
rooms at the India House early that evening, she was
exhausted. Still, the *Madagascar*'s supercargo had every right to be proud of her weariness. She had earned
it, haggling politely over the price of ice with the Parsee
merchants for several hours until they finally saw things
her way. She would make more than the usual profit on
the ice *and* the Baldwin apples, but the Indians were not
being cheated in the least.

"Your father will be proud of you," Zack had told her
as they headed toward the hotel afterward. The thought
pleased Persia immensely.

Now she stood on the little balcony of her room that
overlooked a jungle garden below. A hot breeze stirred
the great fan palms, and bright lime-colored parakeets
darted among the widespread limbs of a massive banyan
tree. Two wild peacocks strutted their fans, one trying
to outshine the other. She watched other hotel guests,
dressed for the dinner hour, strolling the shell-paved

paths among the flowering shrubs and towering palms. It was a lovely, relaxing sight.

The sun was just sinking into the Arabian Sea, turning the bowl of the sky into a great fiery opal that reflected its glowing colors in the water below and touching everything within her line of vision with its intoxicating flame. She could understand why the Parsees, followers of Zoroaster, worshiped a god of fire. Who would not be convinced, at a moment like this, that all power lived in the sun?

She turned back to her sparsely furnished room. It was large and airy, with a high ceiling and wide windows, covered with slat-vented doors. Her trunks from the ship had been delivered before her arrival. And some phantom hand had unpacked the contents, hanging her gowns to shed their wrinkles and assigning her other belongings to the vanity top, bureau, and drawers. Already, the room smelled like home with her own lilac-scented powder and rose water and lemon bath salts adding their individual perfumes to the spicy aromas indigenous to the Indian air.

She smiled when she saw that even her little green velvet rocker had been brought from the *Madagascar*. No doubt at Zack's orders. He was doing everything in his power to make her feel comfortable and at home in this foreign place. That was more than kind of him. She had a feeling that the native bed was going to feel anything but homey. It was very low—nothing more than a thin mattress laid on a wooden platform that stood on four legs.

While she was examining the fanlike contraption over the bed that she had heard called a *punkah,* there was a knock at her door. She opened it to find half a dozen servants, who swarmed into her room like bright, chattering birds. One woman went to the water closet and poured tepid water into the copper tub. Another hurried Persia over to the vanity chair and began extracting the pins from her hair. Two others squabbled like a pair of pea hens over which gown the mistress would wear to dinner. One small girl with big black eyes took up her

place at the braided cord attached to the *punkah* and
began lazily stirring the hot air.

"Please," Persia begged. "I didn't send for any
servants."

The largest of the women, whose costume as well as
her demeanor identified her as the one in charge, said,
"The sahib send us to ready you for dinner. We
do—*quick*!"

When Persia had been thoroughly bathed, toweled,
brushed, perfumed, and patted, the women stood back
smiling and nodding.

"Is fine, beautiful lady," announced the head woman.

"Thank you all," Persia answered, smiling at them.
She started to reach for her purse to give them each a
silver coin as a tip, then remembered Zack's earlier
warning: "It is as bad in India to overtip as it is to
undertip. I've been told that if you pay these people
more than they think their services have been worth,
you lose respect in their eyes." Sure that Zack had paid
them well already, she overrode her first generous impulse with cool logic.

A moment later Zack knocked, ready to take her
down to dinner. The servants scurried out, giggling.

He came to her and, without a word, kissed her softly,
slowly—savoring the deep wine of her mouth as if he
were sipping some fine vintage champagne. When he
stepped away, she was breathless and slightly faint. He
could see a blush creeping up her breasts, out of the
deep ruff of antique lace that adorned the top of her
saffron-colored silk gown.

"My word, you are a dazzler tonight! Maybe I'll hire
twice as many Indian maids to tend your needs from
now on. But no. It's impossible that you could be twice
as lovely as you are this minute."

"Zack, you're embarrassing me." But the pleasure in
her voice belied the complaint in her words.

Dinner was a quiet affair. Most of the other diners had
finished before Persia and Zack made their way down to
the hotel's dining room, and the massive hall was as

silent as a tomb. They chose a table by a window that overlooked the great banyan tree in the gardan.

While the two of them sipped iced pomegranate juice and ate the spicy Indian *pulao*—a rice and seafood dish garnished with green ginger, bananas, mangoes, and cinnamon—they made plans, for now and for the future.

"When this trip is over," Zack told her, "I think we should be married immediately. I've bought some land in Maine. We'll build our dream house and settle right in. The sea is fine, but not for a man with a wife like you, darling. I could never leave you again. I'll buy my own fleet of ice ships and hire on some other poor bastards to captain them while I sit home with my boots propped up to the fire and you beside me. I want a *big* house!" He grasped her hand and brought it to his lips. "And I mean to fill it—from widow's walk to root cellar— with the patter of little feet. Starting *immediately*!"

"*Zack!*" Persia protested, glancing about to see if anyone had heard. When she saw they were virtually alone, she smiled at him and pursed her lips to kiss the air between them. "Sounds wonderful, darling!"

"Now that we have the next fifty or sixty years settled, what about tomorrow, love? Since you've finished your business, what would you like to do?" he asked.

Persia thought for a minute. There were so many sights to see, so many things they could do. "Zack, you're going to think I'm crazy or morbid, or both."

"Out with it! I'm game for anything you're up to."

"Could we go to the Towers of Silence?" Before he could object, she rushed on, trying to justify her choice. "Malabar Hill is such a landmark of Bombay, and I've heard that the garden of the Parsees is magnificent. I know you probably hate the thought of visiting a cemetery, but I'd *really* like to see it." She finished on a pleading note.

He pushed back from the table and gave her a frown. "A cemetery is one thing, but my God, Persia! Still . . ." He smiled and took her hand. "I did say *anything*, didn't I?"

Persia had heard about this unique burying ground

from her father. The Parsees believed in one all-encom-
passing God, embodied in the sun. They worshiped the
Supreme Being, never as an idol, but in the elements of
fire, water, earth, and air. Therefore, all conventional
forms of burial were forbidden to their creed. Cremation
of their dead would have defiled the holy fire as well as
the air. Likewise, interment or burial at sea would have
been a desecration. The only alternative was the one
practiced on Malabar Hill near the Sacred Flame at the
Towers of Silence.

"Jeejeebhoy told me there's to be a funeral tomorrow," Persia added cautiously.

"*Wonderful!*" Zack answered, his voice dripping with
sarcasm.

After dinner, Zack insisted upon going into Persia's
dark room with her. She made no objection to his coming in. She had hoped he would.

"You can't be too careful," he said. "The place is
alive with snakes, poisonous spiders, all manner of
vermin."

She smiled. Why was he making excuses? They both
knew why he was there. She wanted it as much as he
did.

He lit one of the coconut-oil lamps, and Persia stared
up at the ceiling. The *punkah* was moving back and forth
in slow, steady rhythm. Her gaze slid down the silken
cord to where it now disappeared through the wooden
slats of the door onto the balcony. Peering out, she
spied the tiny black-eyed girl who had been there earlier. She had the cord tied around her ankle and was
drowsing as her foot kept up its patient work.

"Zack, come look at this. The poor dear! Give her a
few rupees and send her off to bed."

He tried. But the little servant would have no part of
his deal. Her job as *punkah wallah* was a sacred duty as
far as she was concerned. She would not disturb them.
They would not know that she was there behind the
door. But she *must* stay! Otherwise, she would be in
disgrace.

Finally, they gave up arguing with the doe-eyed girl. Besides, the night was still and scorching hot. The faint breeze from the fan would be welcome.

Zack took great care unbuttoning Persia's gown in back. When, finally, it slipped from her shoulders, he took her lightly clad breasts in his hands, nuzzled the nape of her neck, and sighed. "Ah, my love, why do we waste time doing other things? Why don't we just spend the rest of our lives in bed together?"

"Sh-h-h!" Persia cautioned. She felt nervous knowing that the child was just outside the door. "We mustn't wake her."

Zack laughed softly. "You don't need to worry. The Indians understand love . . . and *sex*. I hear they have temples in the north carved with all the different positions and possibilities. Some of them even worship the erect male phallus. Not a bad place to live, eh?"

Persia tried to sound outraged, but Zack—his hard body pressed close to her back—was doing things to her breasts with his fingers that drove all thoughts of propriety from her mind.

"They even have a book here," he whispered into her ear, "that shows all the positions and gives explicit instructions on the art of lovemaking. It's called the *Kamasutra*. Maybe I should buy us a copy. It's not written in English, of course, but the illustrations should be sufficient to guide us along the proper pathways." His hand sought its own pathways, making her quiver and ache.

"Zack!" She was trying hard to sound disapproving, but the very thought of such a book made her temperature rise. And after all, they should learn everything they could about different cultures, she reasoned.

But this was no time to reason or do anything else that required mental concentration. All her energies were needed for physical, sensual enjoyment. Zack was easing her gown down over her hips, leaving her the scantest amount of covering. But her modesty was no longer a problem. He knew her intimately—had kissed every inch of her flesh. One well-placed touch could send her spiraling off into space. Still, as familiar as they were with each other's bodies, it got better every time.

"Stand right there," Zack ordered. "Just as you are."

He had stripped Persia down to nothing more than her camisole and stockings. He guided her closer to one of the lamps, stepping into the glow of another one himself.

"You may watch, if you like," he said, grinning boyishly.

Persia did watch, her eyes caressing him boldly and without the least shred of modesty.

With great care, he stripped off his coat, his shirt, his boots, and finally his linen britches. The lamplight flickered over his full erection, casting a shadow on the wall that was as large as any pagan idol she could imagine. She felt a flutter inside. What was he doing now?

He whipped a flask out of his britches and held it up for her to see. "The Indians use coconut oil for all occasions—to light their lamps, to cook their meals, and to lubricate their bodies," he said matter-of-factly. "Shall I do it, or do you want to?"

Persia didn't answer. She only stared.

He shrugged at her hesitation and began applying the oil to his shoulders and chest. "They say it keeps drafts off the body. Though Lord knows, who would feel a draft in this inferno?"

Persia stared, wide-eyed, as his hand worked the oil into his flesh—down over his belly, onto his thighs. Then, without even thinking—only burning for him—she moved forward and took the flask.

"Let me," she said in a husky voice.

With trembling, burning palms, she oiled the part of him that throbbed at her touch. Slowly, sensually, she worked the sweet-smelling oil into his flesh. He moaned when her fingertips caressed him, swaying against her while she massaged him gently.

"Oh, God, Persia, this is too much!"

Quickly, he stripped her of her undergarments. For silent moments, they stood before each other, gazing at the wonders they were about to partake of. Then Zack poured more of the oil into his palms and smoothed it down over her breasts and belly. His fingers, as if sliding on the slick oil, slithered down and down until they covered her, then entered her. With a moan of need, Persia leaned into him.

He tilted his head down and licked her ear. "Want to know a secret?" he asked. Then, without waiting for her to answer, he said, "I already have a copy of the book!"

Leading her by the hand, he went to the little velvet rocker. He sat down and motioned for her to come to him.

Persia hesitated, shocked by what he seemed to expect of her. But when he drew her down to his lap, and she felt his oil-smoothed penetration, she cast all hesitation to the wind. The motion of the rocker and their joined bodies was like nothing she had ever before experienced.

CHAPTER TWENTY-FOUR

P_{ERSIA} awoke the next morning, alone in bed and feeling dazed. Though she'd fallen asleep blissfully happy, the strong spices she'd eaten for dinner, the heat, the strangeness of the place, and most of all, her nagging fear that Cyrus Blackwell might appear to claim her at any moment had all combined to work against her. Her sleep had been troubled by hideous dreams. The nightmares had left her nervous and drained.

Today was the day Zack had promised to take her to see the Towers of Silence. She should have been excited, but instead she almost dreaded going.

Zack noticed the moment he saw her at breakfast that morning that something was wrong. Her clear blue eyes looked clouded, and there was a definite pallor to her cheeks. He questioned her, but she was vague and evasive, saying only that her thick New England blood was having difficulty thinning to accommodate the sticky heat of India.

He let it pass but kept a watchful eye on her. Maybe the climate was the problem. But he had a feeling something was very wrong. He sensed a typhoon brewing, and it wasn't coming from over the sea.

As their palanquin bearers sped them toward Malabar Hill, Zack tried to draw Persia out of her mood by making conversation. But he received only monosyllabic replies. Finally he gave up and lapsed into silence himself. Only the frown on his face bespoke the growing concern he felt. During the night—sometime after he'd left her—Persia had gone through a total change of personality. The woman sitting beside him now might be some stranger rather than his lover. What could have come over her? He had no idea.

As they neared the summit of the hill, the coolies slowed. Carefully, they set down their burden and lifted the curtains for their passengers to climb out. Zack paid them, and they trotted off to find another fare.

Uncertain about this "sightseeing tour," especially with Persia in such a sullen frame of mind, Zack glanced about. But he saw nothing to offend the senses. Their surroundings were delightful. This place where the Parsees left their dead seemed no more than a carefully tended garden with flowering shrubs perfuming the air.

"The path leads this way, Persia." He took her arm and guided her forward. She moved along slowly, silently.

Soon they came upon a small, neat building. Zack halted their progress for a moment and peered in. "The Sacred Fire," he said. "According to a fellow I talked with at the hotel, the flame came all the way from Persia. Refugees who fled the Moslem persecutions to settle here in the seventh century brought their holy fire with them. The Parsees still worship it."

Persia, who bore the name of the Parsees' ancient homeland, made no comment. They moved on, deeper into the lush garden. Zack was aware that her flesh felt cold beneath his hand. She looked paler than ever, and her eyes seemed glazed.

"Persia, are you sure you're all right? We don't have to go on. We can leave now. Maybe this wasn't such a good idea."

"I *have* to see it!" Her tone was so desperate that it sent a chill through him.

"Very well, darling. Whatever you say."

She was having trouble breathing. Her chest felt tight and her whole body ached. But still she felt drawn to the place, as if her destiny lay here in this silent garden of the dead.

Suddenly, Zack halted on the path, and she felt his hand grip her arm. She looked up. Just ahead, on the crest of the hill, she could see the Towers of Silence—five circular structures with tall white walls that gleamed like smooth porcelain in the morning sun. Their only adornment was the row of dark statuettelike birds crowning the rounded parapets. Persia cringed inside even as she stared, unable to shift her gaze away.

"Filthy vultures," Zack muttered, turning from the sight of the ugly birds. "Seen enough?"

"No!" she cried. "Let's go closer."

Persia was as repulsed by the scavengers awaiting their grim feast as Zack was. Still, the very aura of the place drew her on. As they moved closer, she felt the baldly grotesque birds staring at her with their keen red eyes. She stared back, unable to look away.

"Persia, no!" Zack commanded. "This is close enough."

Just then they saw the funeral party wending its way up the hill. The white-robed Parsees moved silently, the shrouded body conveyed by venerable priests. Solemnly, slowly, they bore their burden along the flower-bordered pathway up to the waiting Towers of Silence and the sharp-eyed vultures perched there to receive the offering. The Parsees made no display of burial. All prayers had been said, all other rituals observed. The silent mourners acompanied the remains of their loved one to the hilltop, then turned and started back down.

Persia stood perfectly still, holding her breath. Her heart was pounding, but her blood ran cold. When the last of the mourners was gone from sight, two priests removed the white shroud. The black sentries about the walls stirred to life.

Now the priests would carry the naked corpse the

final way—to the waiting grate at the top of the nearest tower, above the open pit that would receive the cleaned bones and return them to dust in time.

Suddenly, the air throbbed with the sound of great wings. The sun was blacked out as the vultures circled overhead—anxious, hungry, ready to do their duty by disposing of the dead.

Persia felt the pounding of the black wings in her chest. And it seemed that razorlike talons were tearing into *her* flesh, stripping it from *her* bones. She covered her face with her arms and screamed. Just before she fainted, she felt as though she were experiencing her own death.

When Persia awoke sometime later, she almost cried out with joy. In her mind, she had died! And in that moment before all went black—when only numbness had filled her whole consciousness—she had felt everything she held dear slipping away from her.

"Zack?" She reached out in the gloom for him.

The warmth of his hand closed around hers, and she felt him kiss her fingertips. "I'm here, darling. Right here."

"What on earth happened to me?"

The room was dark. She couldn't see the deep frown etched across his brow. He was terribly worried about her. She was usually so healthy and strong.

The British doctor he had called in had said simply, "Well, Captain Hazzard, these odd upsets can be expected out here. You newcomers—*griffins,* as we call you—always have a bad time of it. And ladies especially seem susceptible to the strange maladies of the Orient. Often they are as much of the mind as of the body. Or possibly it's just Mrs. Blackwell's time of the month."

"No, it's not," Zack answered so quickly and authoritatively that the Englishman arched a brow in shocked surprise.

"Perhaps the heat . . . the spicy food, then. Or she might have been bitten by one of these damnable pests the natives hold so sacred. Do you know they refuse even to kill the body lice that infest them! They say it might be some ancestor or such, reincarnated. Did you ever hear such bloody rot in your life?''

"She looked pale and acted strangely this morning," Zack said.

"Hm-m. Sounds almost as if she might have been drugged. The stuff's handy enough. The opium ships out of China make regular stops at some of the islands hereabouts. Seems you've been rather close to her right along. Has she taken anything?''

"Of course not!'' Zack snapped.

"Personally, Captain, I think the heat simply got to her. Londoners and New Englanders in particular are susceptible to it. Broils the brain, so to speak. Give her this quinine in water several times a day. I can't promise it will solve all her problems, but then it can't hurt, can it? And open those windows on the west side of the room. But cover them with grass mats and get some servants up here to keep them wet. That should cool her off considerably.''

Zack had accepted the brown jar of powder from the doctor, had paid him, and seen him out. It was shortly afterward that Persia came out of her deep faint.

Persia sat up and smiled at him. She looked perfectly normal—as if she'd just awakened from a good night's sleep.

"What time is it, darling?'' she asked. "It's so dark in here.''

"Only a little past noon. The shutters were closed when I brought you in. I haven't had time to open them. The doctor's been here. He says you'll be fine, but he left this medicine for you. You'd better take some right now.''

Zack crossed the room to bring the water jug. Persia watched him pour water into the glass and then sift white powder into it.

"No, I don't want any of that.''

"Persia?'' He turned to her, frowning once more.

"It's only quinine. And you must take it. Doctor's orders."

She seemed to relax, but there was still a nervous edge in her voice. "Oh, very well! I suppose there's no way around it."

When she had drained the glass, Zack put the cork back in to stopper the jar and set it on her night table. "There. It will be handy when you need it."

"I don't *need* it," she protested. "I feel fine now. When are the serving women coming up to help me get ready for the party?"

Zack stood up and glared down at her. "You are *not* going to any party tonight! And that's final!"

"Oh, Zack darling, we have to go! Besides"—she offered him a coy smile—"I want to. I've been looking forward to dancing with you for so long."

He was dead set against it, but Persia's smile and a few well-placed strokes and kisses convinced him to see things her way. She was herself again, no doubt about that—his loving, bewitching Persia.

Persia was glad she had persuaded Zack that they should attend the ball at the Club. The Maharajah Khande Rao of Gwalior, in whose honor the ball was being given, had heard of the Americans in the city and had arranged a special treat for them. At the appointed hour that she and Zack were to leave for the ball, their surprise arrived in front of the India House. They would be conveyed through the streets of Bombay, seated in a gilt *howdah* on the back of an elephant.

She stood on the portico of the hotel, gazing up at the gray mountain of a beast before her. The animal was splendidly turned out. He had been dusted with gold and painted with vermilion, his huge head looking like some fantastic tapestry similar to the real one that draped his sides. Hammered silver bells jangled about his neck. His great ivory tusks were plugged with gold. Tassels, trinkets, and large glass jewels dangled from the ancient pachyderm. At least, Persia *assumed* the jewels were only glass, but since this prized beast belonged to a maharajah, she couldn't really be sure.

At any rate, the animal's mahout was just as elegantly costumed as were the pair of "footmen" who walked on either side of the elephant, swatting flies away with their yak-tail whisks.

A crowd gathered in the street, no doubt curious to see how the lady would manage her wide skirts of silver silk as she climbed up into the *howdah*. Persia was wondering the same thing. She saw that one of the attendants had a ladder, but it wouldn't reach nearly to the summit of the elephant's broad back.

The mahout shouted an order to his charge. Slowly, as if some command from the gods had brought a mountain peak crashing down, the beast knelt, his forelegs outstretched and his hind legs folded under him. One of the men put the ladder in place, and Zack began to climb. When he was in the thronelike seat, he leaned out to assist Persia.

"Careful, darling," he said. "that last step is a big one."

"Believe me, my love, I will be *very* careful!"

When Persia sank down beside Zack, she breathed a sigh of relief and waved to the crowd below, who were cheering her accomplishment. But in the next instant, she gasped in terror and gripped his arm.

"Oh, no!" she cried. The mountain was moving beneath them.

"Don't worry, darling. Just hold on tight to me." Zack was smiling broadly, enjoying every minute.

When the elephant rose to his full height, Persia imagined that she could see the whole city in a single glance. It was like being on the widow's walk back home or high in the crow's nest of a ship. The ride, too, reminded her of nothing so much as being on the deck of the *Madagascar* in a storm-tossed sea. Until this moment, she had never given much thought to the peculiar gait of an elephant. But now she realized that the animal beneath her was raising both right feet at the same time and then both left to make his uneven progress through the streets.

The result was a swaying motion so violent that she thought she might be catapulted through the air at any moment.

"This will certainly be something to write home to your father and sister about, Persia."

She clutched Zack's arm tighter as she stared down from the dizzying height. "If I survive it!"

And if she had thought the rise of their beast of burden had been a trial, it was child's play compared to his settling back to earth. As the great animal collapsed to its knees, Persia was thrown forward, only to be slammed back into her seat as his rear end carved in under them. Once more, she felt dazed and near fainting. But this time it had nothing to do with attacking vultures or visions of death.

"Oh, Zack!" she cried, laughing, as they climbed down from the *howdah*. "We're alive!"

"Certainly we are, darling! That was a fine ride!" He leaned down quickly to kiss her blushing cheek. "Perhaps tomorrow you'd like to hire a pair of these gray fellows to take us out into the country?"

She laughed again but firmly shook her head.

"The Club," as everyone called it, was more like a palace. Persia and Zack were ushered inside by scarlet-uniformed Indian guards, through a hall of veined green marble, into a golden antechamber, and finally into the great ballroom. Persia stared about her, almost unable to believe her eyes. It was like standing at sunset inside a frozen waterfall. The walls were of mirrored, apricot-tinted glass. A dozen or more crystal chandeliers reflected the light, and their thousands of faceted prisms sparkled with dancing rainbows. Crystal columns stood at intervals about the room. The floor was pale, gold-veined pink marble, polished to a mirror finish and overlaid at one end of the massive hall with a thick Oriental carpet.

"Oh, Zack," she breathed, needing to hear her own voice to know that this wasn't a dream.

"Not exactly the Tail of the Devil, is it, darling?" he whispered back.

The array of guests proved as dazzling as their surroundings. Mr. Cunningham and his plump, gray-haired wife, Grace, immediately took Persia and Zack to greet the acting governor-general, Sir Charles Metcalf. He in turn escorted them across the floor to introduce them to their benefactor, the Maharajah of Gwalior.

The handsome ruler bowed over Persia's hand for some time, murmuring lavish compliments. When he raised his elegantly turbaned head once more and stared a direct and very bold invitation into her eyes, Persia felt herself blushing all over. She was also very aware of Zack, bristling at her side. But she could hardly create an international incident by slapping the maharajah's face, albeit he was fully deserving. All she could do was stand there with a smile frozen on her face, allowing him to stare and murmur his intriguingly accented and indecently intoned phrases to her.

Trying not to hear the man's suggestions, she concentrated on his face. He was golden; there was no other description for the color of his skin. His features were so fine and delicate that he might have looked effeminate had it not been for the thin mustache following the line of his sensuous lips. Persia found him exotic, outrageous, but hardly appealing.

Appealing was exactly what the maharajah found Persia, however. Khande Rao had admired and partaken of many women in his twenty-seven years. At present, four wives and eleven concubines kept him fairly occupied. But not one of them could compare with this fire-haired American beauty. The way her eyes shone, glittering blue like precious sapphires . . . the way her lips parted ever so slightly, as if in invitation . . . the proud column of her neck . . . those cool, pale breasts thrusting up out of their silvery silk prison, begging him to touch them, to fondle them, to suckle them until the nipples turned hard and peaked against his tongue.

"Your Majesty," Sir Charles Metcalf broke in. "The

orchestra has begun playing. Won't you and the maharani lead out?''

Persia glanced in the direction toward which the
governor-general inclined his head. She saw a lovely
russet-skinned woman, swathed in a sari of silver and
gold. A veil covered all of her beautiful face except for
her flashing black eyes and bejeweled forehead.

"I think not, sir," answered the brash young ruler. "I
would have this one as my partner."

Persia was not given an option. The maharajah swept
her into his arms and out onto the sparkling floor. The
two of them glowed in the mirrored walls—she in silver
and pearls, he in gold and rubies. She could feel the hard
gems that studded his coat stabbing into her breasts.

"Ah, you dance well for a foreigner, Mrs. Blackwell."

Odd, she hadn't thought of herself as the foreigner
here. But, of course, she was one.

"And you do not talk much," he said. "I like that in
my women."

His women! What was he saying?

"I cannot, of course, take you as a wife since you are
American. But I am sure my number-one concubine will
relinquish her position to you." He gave a low, amused
laugh. "She will have no choice, actually. No more than
you will. As for your husband, he is a reasonable man
and I will pay him well for you."

Persia found herself gasping for breath, searching for
words. The man was deranged!

"We shall return to my palace this very night. I will
order the other women to bathe you and perfume and oil
your naked body. But I myself will claim the pleasure of
draping you in priceless treasures befitting your beauty.
Rubies for your flaming hair." He reached up to stroke
her temple. "Pearls for your white throat." His slender
fingers grazed the side of her neck. "And diamonds for
your pale, succulent breasts." He pressed his hand to
one silk-encased mound.

Persia tried to pull out of his embrace, but he held her
fast and danced on. Finally, bringing his lips very close
to her ear, he said, "And when I have adorned and

adored every other part of you, then and only then shall
the jewel enter the lotus!"

Persia gasped aloud. Catching Zack's eye—not a difficult task—she pleaded silently for rescue.

A general shocked murmur went up around the ballroom when Zack tapped the maharajah on the shoulder
and swept Persia out of the startled ruler's arms and
across the shining floor.

"Breathe deeply, darling. You'll soon be all right," he
said.

"I'm fine now, Zack. I'm not sick. I just had to get
away from that horrid man."

"The maharajah?"

"Yes. He said some shocking things to me while we
were dancing. I think he planned to take me off to his
harem."

Zack laughed. "Persia, you're exaggerating. The man
already has more women than he can handle. What
could he possibly have said to get you so upset?"

His casual treatment of what had happened infuriated
her.

"You want to know what he said?" she cried. "I'll
tell you, then. He said he was going to take me to his
palace and put *his* jewel in *my* lotus!"

Zack's laughter ended abruptly. "He didn't!"

"He did!"

"The sneaking, insulting little bastard!"

Zack wasn't the only one scowling in the Bombay
Club at that moment. At the far entrance to the ballroom
a stranger had entered. He was dressed in black except
for his white cleric's collar. Dark hair framed his long,
stern face—a face that seemed to condemn the folly of
the world and of the woman he was watching. His pale,
almost colorless eyes narrowed, and his mouth tightened
into a thin, angry line.

Suddenly, his voice boomed through the chamber,
"Persia Blackwell! We'll be going now!"

CHAPTER TWENTY-FIVE

STUNNED by the sound of her name echoing through the great hall, Persia froze in midstep. Cyrus Blackwell—she knew it could be none other—stood between two crystal pillars like a vengeful Samson, ready to pull the temple down on the heads of the sinners.

"It can't be! He wasn't supposed to return this soon," she gasped, gripping Zack's arm. "What am I going to do?"

"Steady, darling," he whispered back. "Let me handle this."

Zack left Persia and strode toward the other man. "Reverend Blackwell, I presume?"

"Correct, Captain Hazzard. But you presume far too much, it seems, when it comes to my wife. If idleness tempts the devil, then dancing invites him to move right in. It's no proper pastime for a minister's wife. For any Christian woman, in fact. I've been remiss in not coming to collect her sooner. But I'll have her away from here and repenting her sins soon enough." The missionary raised one thin hand to summon Persia.

"She's not going with you, Blackwell," Zack declared.

"I don't believe that's your decision to make. The woman is *my* wife!"

The two men stood toe to toe, glaring at each other. Persia remained where Zack had left her. She wanted to flee, but where could she go?

"She's only your wife by virtue of a piece of paper. And that's as much a wife as she'll ever be to you. She wants an annulment." Zack tried to keep his voice civil, but it was difficult as he stared into the missionary's haughty and sanctimonious countenance. "She made a mistake. But we can all thank God she's realized it in time."

"You're right enough about the mistakes she's made. But I doubt God is involved in this. The devil is, more likely. He's brought you back to steal her soul. Her holy vows, however, were spoken in God's sight, as were mine. We are already one according to His law."

"But according to the laws of man, she is still her own woman. She's no slave who can be purchased, then ordered to obey."

As if summoned by Zack's words, the maharajah approached the pair and caught Cyrus Blackwell by the arm. "I would have a word with you, holy one."

Blackwell stared at the Indian ruler for a moment before he offered him an insincere smile. "In a moment, Khande Rao."

"It is most urgent. Now, if you please."

Cyrus Blackwell shot a stern glance toward Persia before he turned from Zack to hear the maharajah out.

"This woman of yours," began the Indian. "I would have her for my own. How much?"

"You do my wife a great honor with your offer, Khande Rao, but she has no price."

"Ten thousand rupees, Blackwell." The maharajah's dark eyes gleamed with excitement. He loved to barter almost as much as he loved women. "And I will give you my prize elephant also."

Blackwell hesitated, glanced toward Persia, then shook

his head. "She is my *wife*! I cannot sell her any more than you could sell the maharani."

Khande Rao looked to his own wife, as if he thought he might barter one for the other. When he turned back to Blackwell, his face was lit with the excitement of a new idea.

"Then another bargain. I will pay you the full amount that I have offered for only one night with the pale-breasted American. Let me deflower her, then I will return her to you."

Blackwell's sarcastic laughter rumbled low in his throat, making heads turn. But when he spoke, only the maharajah heard his words.

"My dear Khande Rao, whatever led you to believe my wife could still be deflowered? I'm afraid you're mistaken. Ask her *friend*, Captain Hazzard, if you don't believe me."

Zack had moved back to Persia's side. He could feel her trembling, but there seemed nothing he could do to reassure her.

"Zack, please, just get me out of here," she begged.

"That isn't the solution, darling. We have to reason with the man and finish it once and for all tonight. Then we won't have to worry about Cyrus Blackwell any longer. We'll be free."

"What do you suppose is going on between him and the maharajah?"

"I have no idea, but at least they're giving me time to think. Persia, I want you to talk to Blackwell. Explain to him that you were under a great deal of strain back home. You might even point out that his own sister created a lot of the unpleasantness you were trying to escape. Maybe a dose of family guilt will make him see the light."

Persia was about to protest his idea when Blackwell's laughter drew her attention. She stared, wondering what had been said to destroy the missionary's stern façade.

Suddenly she realized that everyone was staring at

her, waiting to see what she would do—which man she would choose. The other women in the room twittered to each other behind their fans. The men shuffled nervously, alternately stealing curious glances at her and looking directly away, coughing into tightly clenched fists. She wanted to dig a hole in the marble floor and hide herself. But all she could do was stand her ground and endure. It was Maine and Birdie Blackwell and the curious stares of the congregation all over again.

"Please, Zack! Take me out of here!"

"All right, darling. You wait in the next room. I'll deal with Blackwell."

"No! Let's just go back to the ship and set sail. Now! I have this terrible feeling. . . ."

But as the two of them headed for the door, Cyrus Blackwell barred their path.

"I think we have something to discuss, Sister Persia," he said quietly, ignoring Zack Hazzard's fierce look. "If you'll come along with me, I'd like to speak with you in private."

Persia tried to draw away. "Please, I don't want to go with you. There's nothing to discuss."

"Be that as it may, if I'm to consent to this annulment, you owe me an explanation of some sort." He smiled almost warmly.

Persia looked from Blackwell to Zack, and her eyes brimmed with happy tears. The man was willing to let her go. She'd never have believed it would be so easy.

She squeezed Zack's arm and gave him a confident look. "I won't be long," she told him. Then she let Cyrus Blackwell lead her to a private chamber just off the ballroom.

The room was a small library, its walls lined with rare old first editions. Had her mind been free of more pressing matters, she could have spent happy hours here browsing. But she forgot the books as soon as Blackwell closed the door behind him.

"Have a seat, my dear. I don't want you to be nervous. I only want you to explain to me why you've changed your mind."

Persia sat and stared up at him. His new tone and demeanor bolstered her courage. He was smiling again, and his expression softened the harsh lines of his face. She realized that he must have been quite handsome in his younger days. She wondered suddenly how old he was. She had no idea. His sister had seemed ancient, but he was many years her junior. Perhaps in his fifties.

"Take your time, Persia. I know this is difficult for you. But you must understand my feelings. I've been waiting almost a year for your arrival. I've spared neither labor nor expense to furnish my new bungalow so that you would be as comfortable as possible here. But more than that, I have great work to do, and I can't do it all alone. I *need* a wife. And I was praying that you would fill that need."

Persia felt a stab of guilt. This wasn't going to be as simple as she'd thought. Suddenly, she wondered if the time on board ship with Zack had been her reward for having married Cyrus Blackwell. No, that was silly! How could she even think that God would not only allow her to commit adultery, but would send her the man she longed for—all because she'd been a "good girl" to volunteer to marry a missionary? Her cheeks flamed at her own hypocrisy.

"Well, Persia? What about this *annulment*?"

She couldn't look him in the eye. Instead, she stared down at her trembling hands as she said, "I'm sorry if I've disappointed you. I thought I could make up for the wrongs I've done in my life by marrying you and coming here to serve your flock."

"Then you admit to having done wrong? That's a step in the right direction. We must confess our sins before they can be forgiven."

His words annoyed her. She gave him a hard look, then dropped her gaze once more. "Do you consider love a sin?"

"The wrong kind of love, yes. With the wrong person."

"How does one know the right person from the wrong one?" Again she looked at him, anxious to see his face when he gave her an answer.

He was smiling slightly, but his pale gray eyes looked hard. "It is a Christian's duty to know right from wrong, my child. The fact that you were very young when this man first tempted you is a point in your favor and a mark against him. I learned from my sister's letters that you paid dearly for that first mistake with your own mother's life. Now the devil himself has sent his henchman, Captain Hazzard, back to finish the dastardly work he began ten long years ago. You should be wiser now—more cautious of your soul." He shook his head and his face hardened. "But it seems that you were only too eager to fling yourself back into his arms when he stepped into your life again. You are no child now. You know better. You have piled sin upon sin. Your burden is heavy."

Persia felt pain twist her heart when he mentioned her mother. She lashed out, "My heaviest burden at the moment is the name *Blackwell*, sir!" She was on her feet again, angry and ready to do battle. "I would like to have done with it at the soonest possible instant!"

"I'm sorry you feel that way. Blackwell is an old and noble name. It has been respected down through generation upon generation." He stared hard at Persia, branding her with the blaze of indignation in his eyes. "And now you would refuse it? *You*, Persia Whiddington, who are no more than a common—"

He broke off, lowering his gaze and his voice. "But no. Forgive me. It is not my place to judge. That in itself would be a grave sin."

Then, before Persia could protest, he took her hand in his. "Let me just say this, my dear. God loves you, and I will, too. We are all put here on this earth for a purpose. Mine is to serve Him. But I know that there are others who serve different masters—greed, lust, personal fulfillment. Your Captain Hazzard is one of that breed, sent only to tempt you and lure you to evil. I had thought that you were different, that you had heard the calling. But if it is not in your heart to repent of your sins by tending the sick, feeding the hungry, and converting the savage, then you are better off with him. But go to him knowing that neither of you can sink without dragging down the other. Even as he stole your precious virginity so long ago, you will take from him his very soul. Sin begets sin even as love begets love."

Persia was wavering—not that his arguments had swayed her, but she refused to be branded a misfit or outcast. As for Zack, Blackwell spoke the truth. Her own position and actions had made an adulterer of him!

"If things had turned out otherwise," she began, "I'm sure that I could have served your people well. But one's heart must be in it. My heart belongs elsewhere."

He shook his head, slowly and pityingly. "I hear your words, my child. But your eyes speak other phrases. Hazzard has tricked you into thinking he cares for you. But he went away before. How can you be certain that he'll stay with you now?" The missionary sighed. "I only wish it were within my power to help you."

"I don't understand." Persia felt numb. "Help me how?"

"Think about this carefully, Persia. Is it truly your *heart* that you're speaking of, or is this great passion of yours merely a craving of the body?"

Persia gasped at his words. How dare he suggest such a thing?

"Hear me out, my child. Lust is a powerful master, especially to a woman. My own dead wife, God keep her, fought the demon bravely and conquered him at last. She was not so different from you when we first met. I took her out of white slavery. I cleansed her. I helped her to see the light. She was ever grateful . . . ever blessed."

"Your wife was a . . . ?"

"A *good woman* forced into bad ways. The same as you, Persia. But she's in heaven now. Where do *you* want to go?"

Persia hesitated in her answer. She felt confused, upset, defeated. She wanted to do the right thing, but what about Zack? She'd spent years yearning for him. Or had she been, as Cyrus Blackwell suggested, only *lusting* for him? Still, how could she turn away from him now?

Guilt riddled her conscience. She had made a commitment to this man. Not only to Cyrus Blackwell, but to the people he served. Even to God! Could she go back on *that*?

"Pray with me, Persia. Let Him cast out all your fears and doubts. Let Him show you the way."

The missionary took Persia's hands in his, and the two of them knelt together. His pleas to God to save her boomed through the air and pounded within her breast. On and on he went, filling her with his holy fire of salvation or damnation; there was no middle ground. She was a fallen woman whose shame had killed her own mother. She was a sinner in need of a savior. He was her husband, ready and willing to take on the task. If she refused him, both she and her lover would be eternally doomed. The past could be forgiven. But the future now lay in her hands and God's. She was weak. She needed to be shown the way.

Persia was trembling, quaking inside, fighting against tears of shame and doubt and hopelessness. She was five years old again, shuddering beneath the onslaught of the fiery-tongued minister in the big white church on Main Street. She was an unhappy young woman again, standing beside her mother's grave and suffering the guilt of Victoria Whiddington's death. She was floundering, searching, ever reaching for the light. Suddenly, she felt the white-hot spark of redemption, warming her through and through. She gasped.

Blackwell grasped her tightly to his chest, whispering fiercely to her, "Sister of sin, do you repent? Do you denounce your old ways—the devil's ways—to walk hand in hand with your husband and your God? Answer now or forevermore be consumed by the eternal fires of damnation!"

"Yes, yes!" she cried hysterically. "I repent! Save me!" she sobbed. "Oh, save me, my husband!"

She collapsed in his arms, weak and drained. Still holding her close with one arm, he placed the splayed fingers of his other hand over her chest.

"Out, devil!" he commanded, pressing harder. "Out, I say!"

Persia whimpered softly, her eyes closed, her mind spinning. When his mouth came down on hers, she was beyond protesting. He parted her lips with one skillful thrust and sucked at her breath.

Cyrus Blackwell was still presumably drawing out the devil in this fashion when the library door flew open.

"Persia!" Zack's shocked cry filled the room.

She tried to fight her way out of the missionary's embrace, but he held her fast.

Zack, his face contorted with rage, grabbed Blackwell by one shoulder and yanked him away from Persia. The man sprang to his feet in the very nick of time to avoid the enraged sea captain's right cross, but he did nothing to defend himself. Zack rained blows on his head, his chest, his midsection.

"Fight, damn you!" Zack yelled.

"I am a man of peace. I will not!"

The missionary turned his head, offering his adversary the other check. Zack obliged the man, sending him sprawling.

"No! Stop it!" Persia was on her feet, shaky still, but determined not to allow the one-sided contest to go on. "Zack, don't!" she cried. "Leave him alone!"

She flung herself at Zack, trying to stop the slaughter. But he shoved her away with an angry curse. Suddenly, with his eyes wild and his face a mask of hate, he looked to Persia like the devil incarnate. She shrank away from him, afraid.

"Don't you dare hit him again!" she cried.

Hearing her desperate words, Zack let his fists drop. He swung around to stare at Persia.

"What is this?" he demanded. "You're defending the man?"

"He won't defend himself. And fighting won't solve anything," she replied, going to help Cyrus Blackwell up from the floor.

Zack's unbelieving eyes followed her every move. "And I suppose the two of you solved everything grappling there on the floor like a sailor and a dockside whore! Persia, what's gotten into you? I don't understand any of this.''

"No, and you probably never will," Blackwell answered for her. "I'm afraid, sir, that you are beyond redemption. God be praised that I reached Persia in time to save her!"

"Persia, what's he babbling about?" Zack demanded, taking a threatening step toward Blackwell.

She couldn't meet his fierce gaze. She was too near the brink of hysteria. She longed to suspend time once more and live only for the moment, as she and Zack had for the past months on the ship. But no! That time had not even been real. Because of Zack, she had been living an evil lie. The hour of judgment had come. She knew what she must do.

"I'm staying here, Zack. I know you won't understand, but I have to. I have a duty. I promised. I belong here."

"You belong with me, dammit!" He started toward her, but Blackwell blocked his way.

"My wife has said all she has to say to you. Now, you will please leave us. There's nothing more to discuss."

Zack turned to her, frantic now and heartsick. "Persia?" he pleaded.

"I'm sorry, Zack, for *everything*."

"Go!" Blackwell ordered.

Zachariah Hazzard went. He stumbled to the door, ran through the ballroom, and roamed the streets of Bombay until dawn, stopping frequently to sample the native intoxicants. He was like the walking dead—empty, wounded, and cast adrift without the woman he loved. She was right. He didn't understand. He never would.

The moment Zack left them, Persia turned to her husband, seeking a sympathetic shoulder for her tears. She found instead his harsh disapproval and scathing accusation.

"Only a wanton would shed precious tears over the man who led her astray. Be quiet! Dry your eyes! Hannah would never have carried on so. As my wife, you must be a woman of dignity.''

She tried, but her tears refused to stop. The awful scene with Zack had thrown her emotions into turmoil.

"Do you hear me, Persia?"

"I'm s-sorry. I can't help it."

The next instant, she was jolted out of her hysterics when Cyrus Blackwell's hand lashed across her right cheek and then her left. She stumbled backward, horrified. Her crying stopped.

"That's better. I don't enjoy striking women, but sometimes it's for their own good. Now come along. I have a palanquin waiting."

They did not leave by the main entrance to the Club but exited through a side door. Persia, sure that the imprint of her husband's hand still blazed on her cheeks, was glad she didn't have to face the others. Quickly, he helped her into the waiting conveyance, and they sped away down the dark, fragrant street.

"Where are we going?" she demanded.

"Don't ask questions. I'll tell you everything you need to know from now on. The rest doesn't concern you."

The palanquin snaked through the streets and back alleys until Persia became quite dizzy. She was tired, too; exhausted emotionally as well as physically. Blackwell sat next to her, silent as a statue. After a time she nodded off. All through the night, she was aware of reeking alleys, squalid slums, and evil-faced men peering in at her. Sometimes when she awoke, Cyrus was beside her and they were moving. At other times, she would be alone and the palanquin still.

The sun was high in the sky by the time they reached the landing and she awakened. She came around slowly, feeling the dull ache of her body and the throbbing of her head before she could move or see. When she opened her eyes and found herself alone, her first thought was that Zack had left already to oversee the unloading of the ice.

But when Cyrus Blackwell pulled a curtain aside and

looked in, the full realization hit her. Zack had left all right . . . *for good*!

"Cap'n, the pilot's on board." Second Mate Stoner, attuned to his commander's somber mood, almost whispered the words.

Zack glanced back over the city of Bombay one last time as if he might see Persia there. But that was silly, of course. He'd been ashore already, combing every street. He heaved a heavy sigh. He'd been a prize fool to storm off the night before, leaving her with Blackwell. But Persia was a big girl. And she was as headstrong as they came. She'd see what a mistake she'd made in a few days, and probably come running after him to Calcutta.

He smacked the railing angrily with his hand. But what if she doesn't? he asked himself. What will you do then?

He didn't know. He couldn't think. Maybe this was right for her. He'd certainly caused her enough misery in the past. Still, he felt he could have made her happy, if only . . .

"Weigh anchor, Mister Stoner!"

Persia had said she intended to do her duty. Well, he had a duty, too! The ice meant for sale in Calcutta would be nothing more than water sloshing in the hold if he didn't get the ship underway immediately.

But as Bombay faded from view, the *Madagascar*'s captain felt his heart being torn as if all the vultures from Malabar Hill had descended upon him at once. He almost envied the real dead. For without Persia he was the living dead.

"Where are we going?" Persia asked Cyrus as he hurried her into a long boat with a red sail.

"Home," he replied. "To Elephanta."

"Oh!" With the daylight, she'd begun to feel very uncertain again. How could she be a wife to a man who was a stranger? The thought was terrifying.

Remembering the night before, she turned away from

him so that he couldn't see the tears forming in her eyes. She felt so helpless and empty suddenly. She must pull herself together. This was the life she had chosen. This was the only way she could atone for her mother's death and save her own soul. She would make the best of it.

On the horizon, she spotted a ship's silhouette. The sight stirred a deep yearning in her heart. She watched as it sailed farther and farther away. Suddenly, she knew with a terrible, final certainty that it was the *Madagascar*.

"Zack," she whispered, then added silently, *Zack, I did love you!*

A cool hand covered hers, and Blackwell said softly, "Your Captain Hazzard turned out to be an honorable man after all. I am not at all surprised that you should have fallen under his spell, as ruinous as the association proved. But that's all in the past now. As I was saying about the captain, he sent a message to me that I received this morning. He said he was glad you had made the proper decision so that you would be in good hands when he sailed away. He also wished us happiness."

Persia gasped softly. It hurt to know that Zack had taken their parting so casually. Granted, the decision had been hers. But she had expected him to grieve for her a little. She certainly hadn't expected his good wishes this soon. But then maybe this was Boston all over again. Maybe Zachariah Hazzard was not a man to be tied down to a wife. She had freed him. He was happy. She only wished she could be.

Cyrus Blackwell put his arms around her quaking body and patted her gently. "There, there, my dear. Everything will be fine. You'll see. A new land and a new husband always take a bit of adjusting to. But you're a strong girl. You'll manage with God's help and with mine."

Persia kept her eyes trained on the ship until it passed out of her sight. When the sea lay empty before her, she felt as if her heart had sailed away with it. There was only a great, aching void within her breast.

How could she have sent him away? Or was it her doing? Perhaps fate had played another of her cruel tricks, taking him from her again . . . this time forever.

Persia was unaware of the fact that the boat ride out to Elephanta Island took an hour and a half. She was too confused, too distraught, too far removed from the world of reality to be aware of her surroundings at all after she saw the *Madagascar* sail over the horizon. Was even the salvation of her soul worth this much pain?

But even her shattered heart beat with a fierce will to survive. This was not the first time in her life that Persia had drunk the dregs of despair. She had learned, too, that after the bitter came the sweet, if only one dared sip from life's brimming cup again. Suddenly, she felt a new surge of hope.

"Here we are, my dear." Blackwell's voice near her ear made her start.

The boat's bow bumped against the dock and he jumped out to the wet stones, turning to offer her a hand.

It was hot and steamy on the island when they arrived. The silk gown Persia had worn to the ball the night before hung limply on her. The tall missionary helped her lift her tangled skirts from the boat, then led her up a winding path at the bottom of a hill.

As they made their way upward through the lush vegetation, a new strength and fire sprang to life to fill the emptiness within her. Rainbow-colored birds darted overhead, adding their brilliance to the vivid green of the jungle setting. Exotic flowers perfumed the clear air. The whole island seemed alive and vibrant, a true paradise on earth. The thought of living the rest of her life on such a peaceful, beautiful island was like a balm to Persia's spirit. She longed, suddenly, to plunge ahead to the future, forgetting past pain.

If fate demanded that she live this life, she would live it with a vengeance. A new page had turned. A new chapter had begun. And Persia Whiddington Blackwell would see that it was written in a firm, bold hand.

Yes, she would feed the starving. Of course she would

tend the sick. And, if she had it in her, she would save the sinner and convert the savage. The only thing she feared she could never do was learn to love her husband. But with God's help, she would try!

PART THREE

1847

CHAPTER TWENTY-SIX

*T*HE narrow path wound up and up to the crest of the hill visible against the brassy afternoon sky. Persia thought they would never reach the top. She was tired, hungry, and near fainting with the heat. Her silver silk gown—the part she hadn't lost to the thorn bushes along the way—was soaked through with perspiration and clung to her like a second skin.

After the long, steep climb, she felt little inclination to survey her surroundings further. But an odd sound all about her, a shrill "churring" noise, made her glance about to find its source. After a time, she saw that the trees were alive with white-faced monkeys, signaling to one another in their peculiar, piercing voices.

"It's not far now," Cyrus called back to her.

She took heart and forced upward with renewed energy.

Just as they reached the crest of the hill, Persia heard the sound of bells, seeming to come from everywhere. The silvery tinkling grew loud enough even to drown out the chattering of the monkeys. She looked about, trying to find the source of the airborne music. A bit farther up the path she spied the burnt-out shell of a small cottage. The dried-mud chimney remained and half of one wall. Before the charred ruin, a strange sort of shrine had been erected. It consisted of a white wooden cross hung with silver bell-toned windchimes. An altar with flower offerings upon it stood before the cross.

"Cyrus, what's that?" she called to her husband.

He paused on the path and looked back at her, his face a mixture of anger and pain. "I'd like it if you would address me as *Brother Cyrus*. It's what my dear Hannah always called me. She loved the sound of windchimes. She always said the tinkling reminded her of a cool mountain stream rushing over smooth pebbles. She said it made her forget the hot winds from Bombay. That's where she died, poor woman," he said, gesturing at the ruined cottage. "Consumed in the flames before anyone could rescue her. If only I'd been here, I might have saved her." His voice took on an odd tone, and Persia could have sworn she saw a smile touch his lips for an instant as he added, "It must have been a *horrible, painful* death. I'd told her often enough about the hellfires of damnation. She hated the thought of burning."

Persia's gaze shifted from her husband back to the cross and chimes. How odd! No one had said anything about a fire. Cunningham had told Zack that Hannah Blackwell died of some strange malady that had wasted her body within weeks of the time it struck her down. She started to ask Cyrus about it, then decided against it. She didn't want to open old wounds.

Finally, her new home came into view. The "bunga-low," as Brother Cyrus called the house, looked like no more than a crude shack from the outside. The roof was thatched with palm fronds above the dried-mud walls. A rough board veranda ran across the front at ground level. An irregular fence of palm trunks guarded the perimeter of the tiny yard.

"I hope you don't mind if we forgo the ritual of the groom carrying the bride across the threshold. I'm rather too tired to be lifting hefty loads right now."

Persia didn't know whether to laugh or be angry. She

was a large woman, and because of her size she'd been called a lot of things in her day, but never a *hefty load*. Still, she was quite happy to walk into the house under her own power. The idea of Cyrus Blackwell carrying her in seemed ludicrous. And the last thing she felt like at the moment was a bride.

Inside the house, the floors, though covered with grass mats, were nothing more than hard-packed earth. But the furniture was quite another matter. Lovely pieces of French and English design were liberally interspersed with crudely made native stuff. Persia guessed that the expensive, elegant pieces must have been gifts. Surely a missionary could ill afford such luxuries.

"I hope you'll find this a comfortable honeymoon cottage, my dear."

While Persia was surveying her new surroundings, Cyrus moved to her side. He now stood very near, smiling down at her with a look she found most disquieting. Surely he wouldn't demand a husband's rights this very night. She needed time to get used to the whole idea of being married . . . to get used to *him*! Most of all, she needed time to put Zack from her mind and her heart, if that were possible.

"Brother Cyrus—"

"You'll want to bathe and change, I'm sure. Then you'll feel better. Your bedroom is the first down the hall. The water closet is attached. I'll send one of the women to see to your needs. After you've rested for a bit, we'll have supper."

"Thank you." She meant it with all her heart. Never before had she been in such need of soap and water, privacy, and a place to lie down for a time.

She was on her way down the hall—nearly to the bedroom door—when it suddenly struck her that she had nothing to change into after her bath. Certainly she couldn't put on her silk gown again. It was filthy and in tatters. She turned. "Brother Cyrus, my trunks. They're still at the India House in Bombay."

He looked unconcerned. "You won't need them. Everything has been provided for you."

Persia nodded her thanks and entered the room. Again she heard the tinkling sound of unseen windchimes. The grass matting over the window was drawn down. The bedroom was dark and stuffy. She could make out only shapes in the dimness—a brass bed, a vanity and mirror, an armoire, and a washstand. She went to the window and pulled up the mat far enough to let in just enough light to see, but as little heat as possible. Reflected sparkles danced about the room from the sun's rays glancing off the silver chimes that hung just outside the window. She knew in that moment that this room had been meant for Hannah Blackwell.

Brother Cyrus had spoken the truth. Everything had been provided, right down to a silver brush on the vanity that still contained strands of its previous owner's black hair. Persia frowned. She went to the armoire and opened the doors. The chest was filled with simple cotton dresses in white, black, and gray. They were clean. The odor of strong soap and starch permeated the air. But they were not new by the look of their faded seams and worn cuffs and collars. Like the brush, they were hand-me-downs.

She answered a knock at the door to find a lovely young Indian woman waiting with an enormous clay water jug balanced on her head.

"Brother Cyrus send me to serve you. I am Indira."

"Come in," Persia said, then reached for the jug. "Let me help you with that."

"No, no!" protested the girl. "Sister Hannah, she always allow me to do for her. Now, I am yours, Sister Persia. I will serve you."

Indira's words struck home. This girl was not the only thing Persia had inherited from Hannah Blackwell. The silver brush, the clothes, the bed, even the husband. Her flesh crawled at the thought. She determined to have Cyrus send to Bombay for her own things.

During the time that Indira was in the room helping Persia with her toilette, the pattern became ever clearer. No matter what she suggested, Indira would respond, "But no, Sister Persia. Sister Hannah likes this soap

. . . this powder . . . this gown . . .'' Always in the present, as if Hannah Blackwell were still among the living.

When Persia objected to having a dirty brush used on her hair and insisted that Indira wash it thoroughly first, the girl almost dissolved into tears. ''No, no! Brother Cyrus would be very angry with me. This is Sister Hannah's brush!''

''I realize that,'' Persia answered, near fury by now from the frustration of trying to deal with the stubborn girl. ''I also know that Sister Hannah died of what may have been a contagious illness.''

Indira's black eyes grew wide. ''No, it was the fire! God burned her for her sins!''

''Who told you such rubbish?'' Persia demanded. ''God doesn't go around punishing people by burning them up when they've done wrong. Besides, I thought Sister Hannah was a good woman. You seem to have cared a great deal for her, Indira.''

The pretty Indian nodded vigorously, but the look of fear remained frozen on her face. ''She is always good to me. I love her. But he said—''

Her words stopped abruptly when Cyrus called from outside the door, ''Indira, when you are through, I'd like a word with you.''

She looked doubly frightened as she scurried from the room.

Persia took the silver brush and, without the slightest hesitation, removed Hannah's hair and dropped the soft ball into the waste basket. Then she washed the boar bristles thoroughly with strong soap. Satisfied that she would inherit nothing deadly from her predecessor, she proceeded to brush her hair with long, even strokes.

Supper, an hour and a half later, proved a lavish affair. Indira, aided by three other women, spread an Indian feast before Reverend and Mrs. Blackwell—seafood curry, fruits, jams, and rich breads sprinkled with sesame and poppy seeds. To Persia's complete astonishment, they ate off English bone china with coin-silver forks while they sipped their iced tea from frosted crystal goblets. She had expected no better than wooden troughs, tin cups, and bone spoons. The tea, seasoned with jasmine and cooled with some of the very ice the *Madagascar* had brought from New England, completed the meal. When Indira brought in a silver bowl of ruby-red Baldwin apples—apples from Persia's own backyard—she nearly lost her grip. Her eyes filled with tears of homesickness. Cyrus put one on her plate. She forced herself to smile.

"You live well, Brother Cyrus," she commented wryly. "The Missionary Society of Quoddy Cove must have been most generous of late."

He smiled back. "Brother Osgood felt badly that he hadn't been able to provide me with a virgin bride. He urged his congregation to do what they could to make up for your lack of purity."

Persia's cheeks flamed. It seemed the man delighted in bringing up her less-than-innocent state at every opportunity. Even though he spoke the truth, she would have appreciated a bit more sensitivity from her husband.

"Generous of them," she said. "Although I hate to speak ill of my old neighbors, they generally keep a rather firm grip on their purse strings. And it hardly seems that the purchase of china, crystal, and silver would go very far toward converting the heathen or feeding the starving natives."

He laughed aloud at her sarcastic words. "You're right, of course, my dear. And actually, the Missionary Society's money bought none of this finery. It belonged to my sister. When Birdie passed away, I had it shipped out here. It has been stored until recently. I thought it would make a nice wedding gift for you. Are you pleased?"

Persia looked down and toyed with her snowy Irish linen napkin. Birdie Blackwell had died years before. Why had he stored his inheritance?

"You mean Sister Hannah never used these things?"

"She *refused* to use them. I built this fine house for her, but she wouldn't live here. She insisted upon staying in that dismal little hovel where she died. She said it was *home*, and she wouldn't feel right in a place like this." He gave a grim laugh. "I can hear her now saying, 'Let your next wife enjoy your *mansion*. Home is good enough for me!' Prophetic words, eh? But Hannah was like that. She came from a completely different background from yours and mine. She had no notion of gracious living. She would have been uncomfortable amidst such luxuries."

Persia thought of the silver brush and started to ask if Hannah had been uncomfortable using it. There was something very strange about Hannah Blackwell—her life *and* her death. But Persia decided not to pursue the matter at this moment.

"I would appreciate it, Brother Cyrus, if you would send to Bombay for my things. This gown is a bit too tight, as are all of your first wife's clothes. And it would be comforting to have familiar belongings about me."

Blackwell's eyes caressed the straining gray cotton of Persia's bodice with an appreciative gaze. "I find that frock quite becoming. It never looked so well on Hannah. But then she was not nearly as well endowed as you, Persia dear."

She looked down, blushing furiously. What kind of a man was Cyrus Blackwell? One moment he was the stern and pious missionary, ranting against sin and extolling the virtues of salvation. The next he was like any other lusty man, measuring the worth of a woman only by how well she could fill out a bodice. And if his first wife had been an ill-bred prostitute, looked down upon by the very man she married, why, then, was everything she had ever touched held sacred by her husband? Even the charred ruins of the house where she had died had been turned into a shrine to her memory.

"I'm afraid it will be quite impossible to bring your things here, Persia. I had them disposed of," he answered in a flat tone.

"Disposed of?" she said, shocked and furious. "You had no right to do that! Those trunks contained every-

thing I own in the world—everything that meant anything to me!''

He nodded toward her, unsmiling. ''I know. And now you will begin your new life as you should, with no earthly possessions to shackle you to the past. Besides, I had every right. As my wife, you and everything you own are now mine. At any rate, as a missionary's wife you won't be needing *ball gowns!* And, I assure you, your belongings went to a good cause. Your gowns were sold at auction this morning.'' He laughed and slapped the table. ''You'll be amused by this, I'm sure. The Maharajah of Gwalior bought the whole lot for a king's ransom, which will go to feed the poor of India.''

Persia wasn't amused. ''Why on earth would a man who dresses in cloth of gold and precious jewels want my modest gowns?''

Blackwell chuckled at her bewilderment. ''I suppose he bought the gowns because he couldn't buy you. He'll dress his concubines in your frills and, with the spiritual aid of his opium pipe, convince himself that he's taking you when he beds one of them.'' He gave her a sly smile. ''So if the maharajah appears in your dreams some night, you'll understand what is happening. I'm sure that when next he thrusts his great golden jewel, he'll be imagining, happily, that it is penetrating *your* pale and trembling lotus, my dear!''

Persia gasped, shocked by her husband's outspokenness and at the thought of her gowns being put to such a use.

''That fiery-blooded young nobleman was quite smitten with you, Persia. He wanted you all right—offered me more money than I'll ever see in a lifetime *and* his best elephant! Don't look so shocked. Wife-selling, after all, is a perfectly acceptable practice in his region. Aren't you impressed with my devotion, that I turned down his more than generous offer?''

''Not particularly,'' she said under her breath.

''I suppose you're afraid that I'm going to demand you repay me in a different tender for what I gave up to keep you out of the maharajah's harem. Well, I am!''

Persia stared at him, aghast. She had known his demands would come, and she fully intended to fulfill her wifely duties. But she had prayed he would give her more time. If she could put him off for only a day or so, she would be granted an extra week's grace when her monthly flow began. But tonight there was no reasonable argument she could use to stop him.

He reached across the table and grasped her hand, pulling her toward him, as he said in a fierce tone, "You will repay me for rejecting his offer by showing me that you can be the kind of wife I need. You will be faithful to our marriage vows in thought and deed, obedient to me at all times, and you will work hard to make our task of salvation a success, for God's sake. *And for your own!*"

The edge of the table was cutting across her breasts, and her fingers were going numb in his hard grip. She struggled but could not pull away from him.

"Cyrus, you're hurting me! Please!"

"Pain is nothing," he said in a strangely intense voice. "Physical pain is merely something of the moment. We can endure that. It is the pain of eternal damnation that cannot be endured. Pray with me, Sister Persia!"

Persia closed her eyes and bowed her head. She had little choice. Cyrus still gripped her hand, making her remain in the same intolerable position. Her breasts ached and her fingers burned as if they were caught in a vise, while on and on his voice rose and fell, pleading with heaven for her forgiveness, her salvation, her very soul.

"And let this woman's womb be cleansed and made ready for the worthy seed of her husband. For the time of planting is nigh, and the field must be pure and fertile so that a good harvest is assured. Amen!"

At the very instant of his final word to God, Cyrus released Persia's hand so suddenly that she fell back against her chair. She stared across the table at him, his ominous words about fertile fields and planting time still ringing in her ears. He looked like a man coming out of a trance. His face, although normally pale, was death white. His eyes had a glazed look. His thin lips trembled. And she noticed, too, that his hands were shaking.

"Go to bed now," he ordered. "You'll be needing your rest. Tomorrow we have to tour the island so that you can meet my flock and see the task we have ahead of us."

"Cyrus, are you all right? You look ill."

"Never mind! Hannah always went to her room after supper. Just leave me now! Do as I say!" He almost shouted the words at her.

Persia rose from the table and fled down the hall. She was both concerned by his erratic behavior and relieved that apparently he didn't mean to force the "planting" tonight. How could she ever find any peace with this man if she didn't know from one instant to the next what to expect from him?

It was sheer relief to close the bedroom door behind her. One of the serving girls had been in to tidy up, and the room was immaculate. She had also turned down the bed and laid out one of Hannah's linen nightgowns.

Persia shed her clothes immediately but tossed the gown over the vanity stool. The thought of wearing such a heavy garment on a night as hot as this made her shudder. There was not a breath of air outside. Even the windchimes were silent. She collapsed onto the down mattress—thankful that it wasn't an Indian-style bed—and fell asleep immediately.

Persia had no idea what woke her or how long she had slept. She only knew that the room was still pitch black and that her naked skin was covered with gooseflesh. Trying not to make the slightest sound, she lay very still, listening. She thought she heard a rustle on the other side of the room. Or was it just her imagination?

Feeling self-conscious suddenly, as if someone were staring at her through the darkness, she reached down and pulled the sheet up over her. Another hand gripped it and immediately yanked it away. Persia screamed.

"How dare you?" It was Cyrus—his voice low with fury—standing beside her bed.

"I don't understand. What's wrong, Brother Cyrus?"

Even in her confusion and fear, she was coherent enough to feel relief that he hadn't lit a lamp. In the dark he couldn't see that she was naked. She was sure that had he known, it would have been occasion for another of his long-winded prayers for her deliverance from sin.

"You know very well what's wrong! When Indira cleaned the room earlier, she found this."

Persia felt more than saw the shadow of his arm pass above her. A moment later, something soft and fuzzy fell against her breasts. Again she screamed, remembering the crawly creatures that had made her bedroom at the India House their own. She scrambled about the bed, trying to knock it way, but it clung tenaciously to her damp flesh. She was sobbing, clawing at her breasts, yelling for Cyrus to get it off her.

There was a phosphorescent flash, then the glow of the coconut-oil lamp bathed the room in soft yellow light. Persia, hunched against the cool bars of the headboard, stared down at her breasts and the dark ball clinging there. With trembling fingers, she flicked the thing away.

Cyrus had been staring at her, his eyes wide and reflecting the light. But the moment the thing fell, he immediately bent to retrieve it from the floor. When he brought it close to her face again, Persia, still thinking it was some sort of insect, shrank back, crying, "No! Keep it away from me!"

"You're asking me to put it back in the trash where you deposited it?" he hissed at her. "Indira told me what you wanted her to do. She also told me she refused. So, *you* did it! You may be my wife now, but Hannah was my wife first! I forbid you to destroy any memory of her, no mater how small it may seem to you!"

Suddenly, Persia knew what Cyrus was cradling sc gently and lovingly in his palm. It was neither scorpion nor centipede, but a ball of his dead wife's black hair. By the light of the lamp, she could see tears streaking his cheeks.

"I'm sorry, Cyrus." She could hear her own voice quivering. "I didn't know."

He turned his gaze on her. His eyes were wild and accusing. "Do not lie to me, woman! You knew what you were doing. You came here to destroy her memory . . . to destroy *me*!"

"No, Cyrus! I had to use her brush. There was no other. It hadn't been cleaned since—"

Suddenly he was upon her, pinning her shoulders to the mattress, glaring down into her face. He lashed out as he had done the night before, slapping her hard across the mouth. "Liar!" he screamed at her. "Cheat! Wanton! Slut!"

She tried to block out his voice. The chimes! She could hear the chimes now. She strained to concentrate on that sound alone, but it was no use.

Soon the intensity of his sudden attack began to diminish. With every foul name he called her, his hysteria subsided a fraction. His slaps turned to caresses. He leaned closer. By the time he whispered the epithet "whore," his mouth was nearly touching hers. She could taste the bitterness of the word on his breath. She could also smell the strong spirits he had been drinking.

His hot, trembling hands gripped her breasts while his tongue savaged her mouth. For a time, she tried to fight him. But it was no use. She knew in a sudden flash of painful clarity that this was her punishment. She must accept Cyrus Blackwell as her husband. She must endure his cruel lust along with his pious prayers. She lay very still beneath him, forcing herself to concentrate on the sound of the windchimes.

For he was her husband, and the time of planting had come.

CHAPTER TWENTY-SEVEN

*P*ERSIA awoke the next morning as if from a bad dream. For a time, she couldn't think where she was. But her aching body reminded her quickly enough of what had transpired during the night. She was now Cyrus Blackwell's wife by deed as well as by word.

She lay on the hot, sticky sheets feeling drained and used. Still, she could be thankful for small favors. After his initial attack, Cyrus had not been brutal with her. There was certainly no gentleness in the man, no tender love as she had known from Zack. But the all-out rape she had expected had not come, thank God!

Brother Cyrus had taken her as she imagined any man starved for a woman would have—forcefully, thoroughly, quickly, concerned only with his own needs. It could have been far worse, she told herself.

Afterward, he had left her immediately, taking with him his dead wife's hair, which she had so carelessly discarded. The thought made her shudder.

She frowned, remembering the other odd thing he had done. He had never called her by her name. After he

349

had run out of filthy epithets, he had murmured over
and over again, "Hannah, my darling Hannah!"

Persia turned her face into her pillow. She felt ill
suddenly. How could she ever face him this morning?

But face him she did. And she was more confounded
than embarrassed. Cyrus Blackwell was all smiles and
polite gestures. He made no mention of the night before
at all. It was as if nothing had ever happened. Could it
be that he didn't even remember coming to her room?

"Ah, there you are, my dear," he called with a sprightly
wave as she came out of the bedroom. "I've had Indira
pack us a picnic basket to take along. We've no time to
dawdle this morning. Everyone's anxious to meet you.
Come along now. You have your parasol? The sun's
beating down already."

Persia hurried toward him, trying not to meet his
eyes. Hesitantly, she took the arm he offered. He led
her to the veranda. There an armed Indian named Jammu
waited to escort them. Persia caught her breath, recognizing him as the same white-robed man she had seen in
her first hour in Bombay. Cyrus explained to her that
the man with the menacing-looking gun was there to
protect them against the island's many snakes and wild
animals. But Persia realized that the silent Jammu at
times also served as her husband's spy.

"Ah, I feel so refreshed this morning! I trust you had
a good night's sleep, too, Sister Persia." Cyrus continued to be utterly charming as they set off down the road.
"You'll need all your strength today."

It was his only reference all day long to the night
before. She really did begin to wonder if she had dreamed
the whole thing or if Cyrus, perhaps, was a lusty som-
nambulist. But no! She *knew* what had happened last
night, and the bruises on her face confirmed it.

They hiked for miles, visiting tiny huts and being
greeted by appreciative smiles. They delivered food,
tended sick babies, and saw to it that one old woman
was comfortable. There was nothing else they could do
for her. She would die soon, worn out by living over a
hundred years.

Cyrus laughed when one of the villagers presented him with a baby goat. He told Persia she could have it as a pet if she liked. From time to time, he patted her hand and asked if she was too tired to go on. She was tired, but she felt exhilarated, too. Cyrus Blackwell was, indeed, a different man this morning. He was a true man of God, the benefactor of the island's population, her own loving and solicitous husband. Perhaps last night had been a fluke, a reaction to having a new wife in Hannah's place. He had been drinking, too. That could account for his bizarre behavior.

As the sun was sinking, they started home. Persia's head was filled with the sights she had seen and the people she had met. She was beyond conversation, lost in thought, but Cyrus was still going strong.

"Have you heard about the sacred caves of Elephanta?" he asked.

"I don't believe so."

"Well, they are truly something to see! They were carved out in ancient times by some long-vanished Hindu sect. The Great Cave is the most spectacular. The *Trimurti* is there."

"The what?" Persia asked, her interest piqued in spite of her weariness.

"It's a huge carving—nineteen feet high—displaying the three faces of Siva; as Rudra the Destroyer, Brahma the Creator, and Vishnu the Preserver. Gigantic fluted columns support the overhanging cliff, and the cave itself runs back underground for over one hundred feet into the hill, with twenty-six columns supporting the roof, each twelve to twenty feet high and intricately carved. A magnificent sight!"

"Oh, I'd love to see it. When can you take me?"

Cyrus's face darkened, reminding her that he was not always such a pleasant companion. "I didn't mean you could go there. It's a very dangerous place. I only thought you'd be interested in hearing about it. Promise me you won't do anything so foolish as to try to find the cave alone, Persia. I forbid it!"

"Oh, very well. I promise. But I wish you hadn't told me about it, if I can't see it."

As they wandered up the path to the bungalow, her thoughts continued to dwell on the fantastic images his description had put in her mind. Suddenly, as she neared their compound and heard Hannah's bell chimes tinkling in the breeze, fear gripped her. It was almost dark. Supper would be ready when they arrived. After that, he would expect her to go to bed. And then what?

Then nothing! Persia Blackwell's husband left her uneasy sleep uninterrupted for the next four nights. But on the fifth he appeared again in the darkest hours before dawn—half-drunk, foul of tongue, and quick of punishing hand. He took what he came for, then left her to her unhappy tears and thoughts of nights with Zack. More and more often, she began reaching back into the past, wishing she could recapture what she and Zack had once shared. It was clear she would never find love with her husband.

Cyrus's unwanted visits formed no pattern. Sometimes he would come two nights in a row or twice in one night. At other times he would stay away as long as a week. Consequently, Persia was always on edge, never sure what might happen or when. She slept fitfully when she slept at all. Dark circles appeared under her eyes. Her appetite left her. She began to lose weight. It became all too clear that Elephanta Island was in no way paradise; that the road to salvation was not going to be an easy one.

To combat her fears, Persia forced herself to form her own daily routine. She spent her mornings and afternoons in the village, caring for a tiny sick child named Sindhu. The girl told Persia that she had been named after the river near which she'd been born. But her family were very poor. Sindhu had heard her parents talking one night when they thought she was sleeping. They needed more food for her brothers. They had two choices: drown Sindhu in the yellow water of the river or sell her into slavery. Sindhu had not waited to hear their decision. She'd run away. When Brother Cyrus had found her wandering the streets of Bombay, she had been near starvation. She was recovering now, but slowly. Persia grew to love the bright-eyed child. Their hours together were happy, carefree times.

But Persia's nights were far different. The moment she awoke to find Cyrus beside the bed, she would block out everything but the sound of Hannah's bell chimes. In this manner she learned to withstand the uncertainty and the unpleasantness of her husband's midnight visits. But her very salvation turned on her. Before long, the sound she had used to soothe her fears began to work against her. Any time the windchimes rang, a deep, soul-chilling fear would grip her, even if it were the middle of the day. She grew to hate and fear the sound of bells.

She managed to do a little exploring on her own, usually on days when Cyrus was away from the island. She discovered that his "happy natives" were a strange tribe indeed. In out-of-the-way places, she happened upon pagan altars etched with the hood of the cobra and odd hieroglyphics. She might have been fooled into thinking these were relics from ancient times, had some of the altars not held the bloody, partially charred remains of recent sacrifices.

Then there were the ships. From the highest point on the island, she could see a natural harbor at the north end of Elephanta. The first time she spied a tall mast at anchor there, her heart pounded with excitement. She was sure it was the *Madagascar* and that Zack had come back to take her away.

She worked up the courage to ask Cyrus about the ship that evening. He gave her a cold look and said, "Do not meddle in what does not concern you, Sister Persia! Tend to your prayers and your ministering to the sick. You saw no ship. And you will not go to the hill again!"

Of course she went again, and of course she saw more ships. One day she took Cyrus's spyglass along. Through its powerful lens, she could see that, under the watchful

eye of armed guards, men of the island were unloading
great barrels. Persia could think of nothing so valuable
that it would have to be guarded here on this isolated
island. Pearls, perhaps? She had heard of Oriental pearl
pirates from her father.

Suddenly she took down the spyglass and blinked
rapidly. No! It couldn't be! But, alas, she knew it was
all too possible. Her father had told her, too, about the
opium trade with China. The strong drug was now an
illegal import in India. But too many natives had become
dependent upon it. Opium was a highly profitable black
market commodity.

She scoffed at her wild imaginings. If illegal traffic in
drugs was being carried on right here on Elephanta
Island, surely Cyrus would find out about it and put an
immediate stop to it. Then a colder hand clutched her
heart. What if he already knew? If that were the case,
she was in very real danger now. She hurried down from
the hill. Cyrus must not find out she had gone back there
against his orders.

When she returned to the bungalow, visitors were
waiting: Mr. Cunningham, the ice agent, and his wife.
Cyrus had returned, too. And although he treated her
with the utmost kindness in front of their guests, she
could see the cold accusation in his eyes.

"Mr. Cunningham and I will leave you ladies to talk
now, my dear," Cyrus said shortly after she arrived. "I
want to show him some of the fine crops our people
have grown. He's promised to get us the best possible
price at harvesttime."

Persia felt flustered and uncomfortable in Grace Cunningham's presence. She had not seen the plump little
lady since the night of the ball at the Club in Bombay.
Persia was sure that there had been much gossip passed
around about her after that, thanks to the maharajah and
his unwanted advances and to the fact that she'd arrived
with one man and departed with another. But the gray-
haired lady put her at ease immediately.

"My dear Mrs. Blackwell, you have absolutely blossomed in the past weeks. Your cheeks are so rosy! Life on Elephanta must agree with you.''

Persia knew the woman was only being tactful. She replied with an equally tactful answer. ''Thank you, Mrs. Cunningham. It's kind of you to say so.''

''Do call me Grace, Persia dear.''

Indira came in then with an elegant silver tea service. Persia poured with the innate refinement of a born hostess and handed one of the china cups to her guest.

''Oh, it is such a pleasure to see this place! I know Reverend Blackwell must be much more comfortable here than in that humble cottage he and Hannah occupied for so many years. It's nice to see the dear man living so well.''

''Yes,'' Persia answered. ''He did go through a trying time when Sister Hannah died, I'm sure. The fire and all. It must have been dreadful.''

Mrs. Cunningham adjusted her wire-rimmed spectacles and peered hard at her hostess. ''Fire, my dear? What fire?''

''Why, the one in which his first wife died. Didn't you see the charred remains of the old place when you came up the path?''

''Of course. But Hannah didn't die in the fire.'' Mrs. Cunningham saw Persia's frown and added, ''Did she? I understood that Reverend Blackwell had the place burned down *after*, for fear whatever strange malady took her might spread.''

Persia sipped her tea to hide the confusion she feared the other woman might read on her face. Why would Cyrus tell her his wife had burned to death if she hadn't? And Indira had told the same tale.

''Grace, did you know Hannah well?''

''Oh, my dear, yes! Why, we were in school together. We were the best of friends even before she married. People used to say that the two ambassadors' daughters— Hannah and I—were like peas in the proverbial pod. We were inseparable until her husband decided to move her here to this island. I missed her so after that!''

Persia sat stunned. Hannah, an ambassador's daugh-

ter? A well-brought-up and educated young lady? None
of this made any sense. Cyrus had told an entirely different story. But why would he lie to her? On the other
hand, why would Grace Cunningham?

"What's wrong, Persia dear? You looked so strange
suddenly."

Persia tried to smile away her guest's concern. "Oh,
nothing! It's just that I understood Hannah came from . . ."
How could she phrase it delicately? "From *humble
beginnings.*"

Grace Cunningham laughed. "Humble? My dear, you
heard entirely wrong! Why, her parents, Lord Spencer
and Lady Elizabeth, were true nobility! They were both
mortified when Hannah announced she wanted to marry
an American—one as poor as a churchmouse, at that.
The life of a missionary's wife was certainly not what
they had planned for their only child. Why, there was
even talk of an Austrian prince in her future!" Grace
paused and nibbled at a tea cake thoughtfully. "I doubt
seriously if they would ever have given their consent for
Hannah to marry Cyrus Blackwell. In fact, on the very
eve of the accident, they were making plans to send her
back to England as quickly as possible."

"Accident?" Persia said.

Grace shook her head sadly. "It was most tragic, my
dear. Hannah's parents had been to a house party at the
old maharajah's palace in the country—a ball, a tiger
shoot, the usual. As they were being escorted home,
their little caravan was set upon by bandits. Slaugh-
tered! All of them!"

"And Hannah?" Persia asked, rubbing the gooseflesh
that had risen on her arms.

"Cyrus saved her life. She was supposed to have been
with her parents that weekend. But he'd begged her to
stay in Bombay. She pitched such a tantrum that her
parents finally allowed her to remain with the servants
at home. She was supposed to spend that weekend packing for the trip back to England. But she never went
back. It was only weeks after her parents' funeral that
she became Mrs. Blackwell. Everyone said what a god-

send the missionary was during her time of mourning. Hannah had no one.''

"How horrible! Were the murderers ever apprehended?" Persia asked.

Grace shook her head. "The bodies of Lord and Lady Spencer's chair-bearers were never found. That led the authorities to believe that they were the murderers—*Thugees,* the professional stranglers of India. For many years they have committed their heinous crimes in the name of religion."

Persia was feeling more uncomfortable by the minute, but her curiosity demanded quenching. "I've never heard of these Thugees, as you call them, Grace."

The gray-haired woman leaned closer and whispered, "Then you are fortunate, my dear. But you should be warned. These terrible men worship the goddess Kali at a Hindu temple known as Kalighat close by the great river at Calcutta. I've never been there myself, but I've heard of Kali's hideous image—human skulls about her neck and what appear to be clots of blood oozing from her wide mouth. They say the courtyard of her temple is slippery with gore from the daily sacrifices of kids and goats.''

Persia shuddered, suddenly remembering the bloodstained altars she had discovered about the island.

But Mrs. Cunningham was caught up in her tale now and rushing on. "These Thugees, as I said, worship Kali. In the old days, they roamed about the countryside in huge bands. Their ranks are smaller now, but just as deadly. They pose as pilgrims or merchants and associate themselves on the friendliest of terms with their intended victims. Then, when the opportunity presents itself, they strangle their unfortunate and unsuspecting 'friends,' rob their bodies, then bury them in graves dug hastily with pickaxes.''

"How perfectly horrible!" Persia shuddered again. "But can the authorities be certain that Hannah's parents were murdered by these Thugees?"

Grace nodded fiercely. "Oh, yes! There's not the slightest doubt. You see, these murderers consider each crime a *holy mission*. One-third of their booty is always taken to the temple of Kali and left there for the goddess. Lady Elizabeth had worn her famous parure of black diamonds to the maharajah's ball the night before. After the murders, the tiara, the earrings, and the bracelet were found in the temple of Kali, left there by the culprits. Her murderer had used the necklace to strangle her. The marks of the diamonds were imprinted on her throat when her body was found. But the necklace has never been recovered.''

Persia was suddenly gripped by terror. She tried to tell herself her fears were unreasonable. But reasonable or not, the panic refused to go away. Cyrus had told her so many things that were untrue. How could she ever trust him again? She was confused. She felt helpless. She longed for escape . . . for Zack!

She forced a smile and a bright tone. ''Grace, I wonder if you would do me a favor?''

''Why, certainly, Persia. Anything you ask.''

''I've been wanting to post some letters, to be taken back to America on the *Madagascar*. Could you, personally, see that they're sent overland to Calcutta for me?''

''Of course. Do you have them ready?''

Persia felt a wave of relief. ''If you'll excuse me a moment, I'll go to my room and get them.''

Luckily, she had written to her father and her sister the day before. She jotted a hurried note to Zack and sealed it. The gist of her message was simple and to the point: ''Help!''

When she returned with the three sealed envelopes, she felt an explanation was in order about her letter to the *Madagascar*'s captain. With only a slight blush she said, ''I'm afraid I forgot a few of my things on board ship. I'm hoping Captain Hazzard will see to having them sent to me.''

Grace Cunningham's smile held only a hint of suspicion as she curled her fingers around the envelopes and replied, ''I'm sure he'll be happy to oblige, my dear.''

*   *   *

The rest of the day went quickly and well. Cyrus seemed in high spirits after his vist with Cunningham. All during supper, he chatted amiably about crops and prices and the new infirmary he planned to build with the profits. He inquired politely about Persia's afternoon with Grace, but he did not press her for details of their discussion. She was relieved at that.

Persia longed to question him about Hannah and her death. He seemed in such a reasonable mood. What could it hurt? But something stayed her tongue. She was only too happy to excuse herself from the table as soon as they finished their evening meal. She needed to be alone so she could think everything through. She would have to be very careful with Cyrus until Zack arrived to rescue her. One slip of the tongue might give her plans away and ruin everything. She wasn't sure how she knew she was in danger, but she was. There was no doubting it!

A tremendous sense of relief overtook her the minute she closed the bedroom door behind her. But her feeling of well-being lasted only seconds. Although, at first glance, everything in the bedroom seemed exactly as she had left it, one thing was different. Propped against her vanity mirror was a familiar sheet of vellum.

She moved toward it with dread. She picked it up, read it, and her eyes widened with terror.

> *Elephanta Island*
> *May 10, 1847*

> *Dearest Zack,*
> *You must help me! Something is terribly wrong here. There's no time to explain, just please, come for me!*

> *My love to you always,*
> *Persia*

She stood staring down at her own handwriting until

the paper shook in her hand and the words blurred and
ran together as tears fell on the page.

"Cyrus knows!" she said in an icy whisper.

"Yes! I know!"

Persia whipped around to face him. She hadn't heard
the door open, and his voice nearly frightened her into a
faint. He was smiling at her, but his face was contorted
into an odd mask of warring emotions. He moved toward
her slowly.

"What I don't know, Sister Persia, is why you would
ever want to leave me. I've given you this fine house.
And you certainly can't be lacking for love. Why, even
Hannah never received my attentions so regularly. In
fact, she sometimes complained that I spent too much
time with Indira and not enough with her. But then I'd
always thought that a well-bred wife appreciated a husband who satisfied his needs elsewhere. I was wrong,
though. You're my proof. Not once have you turned
from me. Not until now. Your letter hurt me deeply."

He was directly before her now. Persia was trapped.
When his hands came up to rest on her shoulders, she
winced at his touch and bit her lip to keep from crying
out.

"You aren't like Hannah, are you? She complained
about Indira, but not because she wanted my love. Even
when I offered her gifts, she refused me. She said terrible things to me. She accused me of lusting after far
more than salvation."

His slender fingers encircled Persia's throat and he
squeezed gently, then harder, cutting off her breath. He
drew her to him and kissed her—a savage, wet, probing
kiss. When he drew away, she was shaking, gasping.

"Why did you do it?" he asked. His voice was hard
and cold.

Persia stared at him, trying to find words even as her
mind cast about wildly for escape.

"Persia, answer me! Why did you write this lettter to
him?"

"I'm afraid!" she cried out suddenly.

Cyrus clutched her to him, crooning softly, "Persia,

Persia, how silly of you! You mustn't be afraid of me. I'm your husband! I love you! Why would you think I'd ever hurt you? Look, I even brought you a gift.''

Before her tear-blurred eyes could see them, she felt the coldness of the stones about her throat. She swallowed hard, trying to control her terror.

Cyrus turned her toward the mirror. ''Look how beautiful,'' he said.

She knew what she would see even before she opened her eyes: a web of black diamonds, with a hard, dark gleam as cold and terrifying as the eyes of death.

CHAPTER TWENTY-EIGHT

PERSIA knew she must get a grip on herself. Her present terror could lead her nowhere but headlong into destruction. She touched the black diamonds with her fingertips and turned this way and that as if she were admiring them in the mirror. Cyrus stood only inches in back of her.

"They're exquisite, Brother Cyrus!" She flashed him a reflected smile. "Wherever did you find such a necklace?"

"It belonged to Hannah. She never wore it, though." He seemed terribly nervous suddenly. "She said it was evil. I'm glad you like it. Beautiful women should have beautiful things."

"Was it a family heirloom, Brother Cyrus?"

He stammered, cleared his throat, then answered, "An heirloom? No. I told you about Sister Hannah. She had no family. I saved her. Where would she have gotten such a priceless piece of jewelry? I gave it to her. I told you, it was a gift."

"Then where did *you* get it?" She turned slowly and watched him, waiting for his answer.

"I got it . . ." He was wringing his hands, licking his lips, looking everywhere but at her. "I bought it! Yes . . . I bought it from some men from Calcutta."

Inside, Persia was cringing, but she offered him a smile and stroked his cheek with her fingertips. And all the while, the murder weapon about her throat felt cold and heavy and menacing. She struggled to remain outwardly calm.

"You don't know where the men from Calcutta got it?"

"Why?" he snapped, moving away from her touch. "What difference does it make?"

"I thought perhaps it was part of a set. A tiara, earrings, and a bracelet would go with it nicely."

He kept backing away, looking more agitated by the moment. "No! There are no other pieces! I swear to you, it's not part of the set, Hannah! If you don't like the necklace, I'll take it back. Here, give it to me!"

He snatched the diamond choker away but dropped it as if it had burned his fingers. Immediately, he crouched to the floor to retrieve it. Persia heard him mutter something that sounded like "I'm sorry, Hannah, so sorry."

She stared at him, wondering. Did he really believe at times that she was Hannah? What kind of hold must the woman have had over him? And if he had given the diamond necklace to his wife, what had her reaction been? Surely she would have recognized it as her mother's. Even if Hannah had loved Cyrus better than life itself, she couldn't have condoned his taking a part in her parents' murders. An idea began to form in her brain.

"Brother Cyrus, have you seen my silver brush?" Persia asked suddenly.

He stood up so quickly that he stumbled backward. He looked terrified of her.

"I thought you might brush my hair for me tonight."

"Hannah? Is that you, Hannah?" His voice trembled between hope and fear.

Persia laughed. "Who else would it be? Certainly you didn't mistake me for Indira. If so, you may leave this instant!"

"Hannah, no! Please don't make me go!" He was begging, sobbing. "I haven't been with Indira. I promised you I never would again. I only want *you*. I'm sorry if you don't like the necklace. But haven't you punished me enough already? No, Birdie, please don't lock me in the root cellar. It's so cold down there . . . so dark. Let me stay with you, here where it's light. You're so warm. Please!"

Persia felt sick and guilty. Whatever key she had turned had unlocked years of torture in this man's brain. But she couldn't stop now. She had to know his secrets, dark as they seemed.

"You may stay, Brother Cyrus, but only if you tell me the truth about the necklace."

He had been crouching against the far wall. But her words brought him upright. Suddenly he was on the offensive.

"If you don't like the necklace, you can go to hell! I thought you'd want it because it was hers. If you think I killed her, you're crazy! The Thugees did it. Everyone knows that. I'll admit I loved you enough then to kill for you. That pleases you, doesn't it? Ha! I thought you were so special—an angel, a saint! You were nothing but a scheming witch, Hannah!"

He came toward Persia with a threatening look on his face. When he spoke, he was imitating a woman's voice. " *'Do this, Brother Cyrus! Fetch me that! Brush my hair! No, I don't feel like it tonight. Don't touch me! Don't kiss me! Don't come near me!'* " Then his voice changed to a deep growl. "What kind of man do you take me for, Hannah? You have your duties to me as well as your duties to God! Damned if I'll be pushed away any longer!"

He lunged at Persia and caught her about the waist. They both went crashing to the floor. He struggled with her skirts, trying to get at her. She heard the fabric of her bodice rip. She tried frantically to fight him, but it

seemed there was nothing she could do. Then suddenly
another idea came.

"Go to the root cellar, Cyrus! You've been a naughty
boy again!"

He let go and eased away from her, looking terrified.
"No, please, Birdie. I won't do it anymore!"

Persia slid away from him and rose to her feet, pointing across the room. "Then go sit in that chair. And
don't you move or you know what will happen!"

He hurried to the chair and sat, seeming to draw up
into himself.

"Now, Cyrus, I want you to tell me *everything!* I
want to know about the necklace, about Hannah's death,
about the ships, all of it."

His whole face crumbled. Tears ran down his hollow
cheeks. He was shaking all over. When he could control
himself enough to speak, he said faintly, "Please, Birdie,
if I do what you want, will you play the game with me?
But you aren't going to tell on me, are you? Mother gets
so angry. And last time, Papa used his razor strop on
me. They think it's *my* fault. They don't know that you
thought up the game."

Persia frowned. What on earth could he be talking
about? She decided to go along with him. "Yes, we'll
play. And I won't tell them. But you have to explain
everything that I want to know."

"I'll tell! I'll tell!" he whimpered.

"The necklace?"

"I didn't know they were going to kill them. Honestly
I didn't! I paid them to *delay* Lord and Lady Spencer,
just long enough so I could convince Hannah to marry
me. I swear before God, I did not know what they were
planning! Then when I heard about it and they came to
me with the necklace, I took it. I had to get rid of it
before Hannah saw it. She would never forgive me.
Never, ever!" His voice trailed off into weeping.

"But you told me you gave it to her. Don't lie to me,
Cyrus!"

He curled into a fetal position, hiding his face in his
hands. "No, I didn't give it to her. She found it. I

should have thrown it into the sea. But it was so beautiful . . . worth so much money. I hid it and she found it.
She was going to tell the police! I had to do it. I *had* to!''

"Do what, Cyrus? What are you talking about?"

He looked up at her suddenly with a stern expression
on his face. "*You* know, Birdie! *You* helped me! The
poison was your idea. But it wasn't working fast enough.
What if that Cunningham woman showed up, snooping
around? She already knew Hannah was sick. If she'd
come again, she might have insisted on returning Hannah to Bombay to a doctor. So the fire was the only
way. Afterward, I told everyone I burned the shack to
keep her disease from spreading.''

Persia felt sick, and the full force of her terror was
returning. She knew almost everything now. Too much!
When Cyrus snapped out of it, her life would be worth
no more than Hannah's. Never mind about the ships.
She had to get away *now*!

She began edging toward the door. "Stay in the chair,
Cyrus! I'll be back in a moment. But don't you move.
Otherwise . . .''

"No, Birdie, no!" he screamed, lunging toward her.
"You can't go! It's dark and I'm scared. Hold me! You
said if I'd tell you, we could play the game. Please,
Birdie! You promised!''

"What game?" Persia asked as much to distract him
as out of curiosity.

"You know," he whined. "The one we play in your
bed when Papa takes Mother to visit the neighbors and
it's just you and me.''

A new kind of horror snaked through Persia. Surely
he couldn't be suggesting what it sounded like. *He and
his older sister Birdie?*

"Come on, Birdie!" He was tugging her toward the
brass bed. "You promised! You promised! There's nobody home—just you and me. They won't find out.''

For the first time with her, Cyrus Blackwell was gentle, loving, adoring. Although she struggled against him,
he refused to let her escape. And she found out that

night that Cyrus Blackwell's usual brusque and unfeeling sexual performance did not come from ignorance. He was actually very skilled in the ways to please a woman. Apparently, his older sister had been a competent instructor in the art of love.

But Persia experienced no pleasure in his knowing touch, his practiced kisses, or his skillful thrusts. She was too frightened, too disgusted, and sickened by hearing his voice close to her ear, whispering all the while, "Birdie, my sweet sister . . . my darling . . . my own!"

When *the game* was finished, Cyrus, for the first time, fell asleep beside her. Dawn was streaking the sky outside. It was the perfect time. Her thoughts were all of Zack now. She would slip out, find a boat, and get away to Bombay. There, she would lose herself in the teeming city until she could contact Zack. He would come for her. She was sure of it!

It was no wonder Persia's thoughts were on Zack. For weeks, as the ship sailed the long route to Calcutta, he had been unable to purge her from his mind and heart. Their parting made no sense to him. They *loved* each other! Hadn't they both decided long ago that their love was written in the stars?

Leaving Second Mate Stoner in charge of the ship, Zack headed overland from Calcutta to Bombay the moment the ice was sold. He would find her. He would get her back. Nothing else mattered in this life except his love for Persia and hers for him!

He arrived in Bombay on the same morning Persia had slipped out of the bungalow. His first stop was at Cunningham's office to find out if Persia was still with Blackwell. From the agent's wife, he heard stories about the missionary on Elephanta Island and how well his new wife had adjusted. Gossip had it that they were the happiest married couple on earth. He was like a young man again, and she was blossoming with good health and happiness.

"I shouldn't spread tales before the word has been officially handed down, Captain Hazzard," Grace Cunningham whispered over tea at her husband's office, "but I know the look of a woman with child. I tell you, Persia was absolutely blooming when I saw her yesterday. And I'm sure her husband must be as happy about it as she is."

"That's wonderful to hear," Zack answered through gritted teeth and a forced smile.

He couldn't bring himself to be pleased for the newlyweds. And the thought of Persia carrying another man's child was almost too much to bear. Maybe he was doing the wrong thing. Perhaps Persia was as happy as Grace Cunningham claimed. If so, it would be selfish of him to turn up, unannounced, and disrupt her new life. Persia deserved better from him.

Yes, maybe he ought to just head back to Calcutta at once. He was about to offer polite apologies and be on his way when Mrs. Cunningham's words once more grabbed his full attention.

"I suppose you've brought her things?" she asked, interrupting his somber thoughts.

Zack frowned. "Pardon me?"

"Well, only yesterday she gave me a note to post to you. She said she was writing to ask you to ship her some things she'd left on board. I assumed you'd anticipated her desires and made the long journey back to Bombay to deliver her things personally. I'm sure her letter passed you enroute. Mr. Cunningham, you did send Persia's note on, didn't you?"

"Certainly, my dear," the agent grumbled, not looking up from his desk.

Zack frowned. All thoughts of returning to Calcutta suddenly flew out the window. Persia had left *nothing* on board the ship. He had searched and searched, hoping to find something of the woman he loved. A glove, a handkerchief, anything tangible that would help preserve her memory and make him feel close to her again. But it was as if she had never been on board the *Madagascar*. So why would she write to him? And why would she give the letter to a near stranger—lying about its contents—instead of asking her husband to post it on one of his frequent trips to Bombay?

Zack excused himself. Suddenly, time seemed of the essence. And he had wasted enough of it already. He would hire a boat at the harbor and set out immediately for Elephanta. Persia needed him. He knew it with a painful certainty.

Persia needed someone—*anyone*! Escaping the bungalow and her sleeping husband, she had run all the way down the hill to the quay. No one was about. She had spied four small boats at anchor. But, hurrying down to the waterline, she discovered that each one was chained and locked to a metal rung in the pier.

Frantic, she sped to the nearest hut, seeking the aid of one of the natives. The people were all smiles and nods, but no help at all. She was greeted by the same treatment at every house.

The sun was high now. If Cyrus was not awake yet, he would be soon. She had to escape. But how? The cave! She could go there and hide out until she figured a way to get off the island. Although she had never been to the cave, she knew the way. Cyrus had pointed out the trail on one of their walks about the island.

She fought her way through the tall elephant grass. Briars ripped her skirt and stockings and tore at her legs until they bled. But nothing could stop her. She pushed her strength to its limits.

Finally, ahead of her, she spotted the cool gloom of the cave entrance. Only a few more yards. Once she was inside, she could rest and make her plans. She began to feel a deep sense of relief. She was almost sobbing with it.

"Safe," she gasped. "I'm safe."

"*Persia!* Sister Persia!"

The voice echoed down on her from everywhere and nowhere. She whirled on the path, trying to spot Cyrus. He was upon her before she ever saw him—grasping her arms, dragging her away from the cave's shadowy mouth.

"Where do you think you're going?"

She couldn't answer. The sun beating down on her, his hands binding her arms, the fear swelling in her heart, all worked together to make her weak.

"Didn't I warn you about the cave? You are a foolish woman!"

Gone was the whimpering half-child she had coerced into confessing last night. No vestige remained of the gentle lover who had held her in his dead sister's place only a few hours past. Vanished was the cringing weakling he had been. There was no need to threaten this man with the root cellar. This was Cyrus Blackwell—lord over all on Elephanta Island, owner of the woman he had married.

He dragged her back to the bungalow. She was beyond protesting. She knew his secrets. There could be only one fate left to her. It was too late to hope for rescue . . . too late even to pray for a miracle.

But it seemed to Persia that somehow the miraculous was still possible. As they neared the bungalow, she spied another man coming up the path from the docks.

"Zack," she wailed, but he was too far away to hear her.

"Yes, *Zack*," Blackwell hissed. "Your lover come to rescue you, no doubt. And you'd like to go with him, wouldn't you?"

Persia glared at the man still restraining her. "*Yes*," she said defiantly.

"As I thought. But I don't believe you will."

"You can't stop me!"

Cyrus laughed softly. "Are you so sure about that? See the clump of shrubs over there, Persia dear?" he asked, too pleasantly. "Note the way the leaves glitter with a certain blue-black gleam at about the height of a man's heart?"

She looked and saw the sun glint off a gun barrel. Her heart sank.

"Jammu can shoot out a cobra's eye from this distance easily. Should you give the slightest hint that you are unhappy here and wish to leave, I'm afraid your lover will be *terribly hurt*. Do you understand what I'm telling you?''

Persia, cold of heart and voice, answered, ''Yes, Cyrus. You've made yourself quite clear.''

When Zack arrived before the bungalow, he was greeted by a sight that both warmed his heart and froze his blood. Persia—beautiful, loving Persia—filled his vision. Her blue eyes sparkled, making him remember how she looked when they made love. But the missionary's arm clasped her waist possessively. Could it be that Mrs. Cunningham was right—that she had accepted this man as her husband after all?

''Persia?'' Zack called. ''I've come to take you home.''

A silence followed. Persia's throat felt tight and dry. She eyed the gun barrel poking out of the shrubs and felt Cyrus's grip tighten on her waist.

''That's kind of you, Zack, but I can't go.''

''Can't?'' he yelled back.

''*Won't!*'' Cyrus hissed into her ear.

''Won't,'' she answered, her voice quivering now.

''You don't mean that!'' He was starting up the hill toward her.

''Better tell him not to come any closer,'' Cyrus whispered harshly.

''Please, Zack, stay where you are!'' Persia tried to keep her voice calm, but there was an edge of hysteria to it. He was so close. Yet to have him come to her would mean his death. ''I won't go with you, Zack. My place is here . . . with my *husband*!''

''What about us?'' He refused to give her up so easily. She was everything to him!

''Us? That's over now,'' she called. ''I belong here! I'm *happy* here!''

''I don't believe you, Persia. I'm coming up there.''

She heard the click of the rifle cocking. ''No, Zack!'' she cried. ''Go away! It's over. Can't you accept that?''

No, he couldn't accept that. But something was very wrong here. He had a feeling Persia was trying to protect him from something. He glanced about but saw nothing, no one.

"Please go now, Zack."

She was crying, he could tell.

"Come with me, darling?"

"I can't!" she sobbed.

She watched him turn and start back down the hill, her heart tearing apart with every step he took. He would soon be out of Jammu's range. All she had to do was break away and run to him. She'd be free of this place and Cyrus Blackwell forever.

She was on the verge of doing just that when her husband said, "I thought for a moment there that Jammu would have to kill him. You did well, wife. You must love him very much. Perhaps I should have let you summon him and have one last kiss. Then you could have spent the rest of eternity together. It seems almost a shame to send you on ahead of him. But after last night, it can't be helped."

She pulled away from him, but he caught her arm.

"I was afraid you might try that. Go, then; but before you do, let me answer your question about the ships. You never let me finish last night. This very day a vessel will be putting in on the far side of the island. But this one will be *loading* cargo. Should you decide to run to your Zack, or disobey me in any way, I'll see that your precious Sindhu is taken to the slave markets with the other children I've selected. Do exactly as I say, and Sindhu will be spared."

Persia's first impulse was to sob hysterically. But knowing her fate was about to be sealed, a burning anger flamed to life in her heart. Yes, he would kill her! She had known that since last night. But she would not go with a whimper and a tear. And she would not see Sindhu sold into slavery.

"Well, *wife*, shall we go into the house now?"

She glared up at him. "You go to the devil, *husband*!"

CHAPTER TWENTY-NINE

ZACHARIAH Hazzard hadn't been fooled one bit by Persia's act. She might have told him to go in so many words, but her eyes also had talked to him. And the tone of her voice had spoken volumes to him of her despair and her need to escape. Even her posture had conveyed her terror. Something was *very* wrong on Elephanta Island!

Now, as he rowed silently across the stretch of water that separated the two of them once more, he strained his eyes and ears for the slightest hint of any danger that might be lying in his path. Not danger to his own life; he could handle anything that threatened. But danger that might keep him from rescuing the woman he loved. For tonight he would spirit her away under cover of darkness. And *nothing* would stop him.

The past hours in Bombay had been well spent. He'd finally backed Cunningham into a corner and made him talk about Cyrus Blackwell. The agent's earlier reticence had been due to his own involvement, Zack learned. Cunningham was not only working as agent to sell the crops grown on Elephanta—he was disposing of illegal cargoes as well, opium being the most profitable. Selling Indian children into white slavery ran a close second.

It seemed that in India when foreigners broke laws that involved the natives—in this case stealing children— often they were never prosecuted but wound up quietly murdered in their sleep. Cunningham, caught by his own greed and seeing no way out, was less than anxious to sip poison and partake of eternal slumber. But neither did the prospect of having Captain Hazzard's big hands around his throat delight him. He talked.

And Zack knew that if Persia had learned even a fraction of what he had just found out, she was in dire trouble. He only hoped he could reach her in time.

After Zack left the island that morning, Persia had expected her own death to come at any moment. Instead, Blackwell had forced her back into the house and ordered her to her room to bathe and change. When she came out, he was waiting in the parlor.

"Have a seat, won't you?" he offered quietly, almost cordially.

Persia sat, but on the very edge of the chair. Death, when it came, might be swift, but the waiting . . . the wondering . . . was a special kind of hell.

"I've had Indira fix you a drink. Please don't refuse it. This isn't going to be easy on either of us."

Persia stared at him. He was so different from the night before. How could he be one man one moment and another the next?

He took a long sip from his own frosted glass and smiled at her. "It's really too bad, you know. I think you and I might have been good together, Persia. But then it's too late for conjecture now, I suppose. I'm really sorry for what I have to do. But, of course, I have no other choice after last night."

"What about last night? What happened to you?" If she was going to die anyway, she was certainly going to find out a few things first.

He sighed deeply and set his glass down. When he

leaned forward—arms on his knees—he looked so casual, so very *normal*. "I don't want your pity," he began. "God knows I've had enough of that for ten lifetimes. Hannah smothered me with hers. And as for Birdie, she nearly destroyed me with it." He laughed cynically. "Well, with my sister, actually, it was a mixture of pity and guilt."

"I don't understand what you're trying to tell me."

He arched a brow and smiled sadly. "Don't you? You mean you don't know what happened last night? Come now, Persia! You're a bright woman. Don't make this more difficult for me than it already is. The *root cellar* . . . the *game*? You don't understand?"

"Only partly."

He sighed. "Where to begin? Birdie's mother died when she was very young. Our father remarried almost immediately. But it was a number of years before I was born. Birdie was in her late teens. Of course, like all men, my father had always wanted a son. He was overjoyed when I came along. He lavished his affection on me alone. I'm afraid my mother had turned him against Birdie even before that time. Mother was a beautiful woman—black hair, flashing brown eyes, lovely skin. And she had, let us say, a *winning way* with our father. Birdie, I learned, resented her terribly. The antipathy was mutual. There was little harmony in our household, until . . ." He paused and looked away from Persia.

"Yes, Cyrus? *Until?*"

"Until Birdie made up the game. I was always terrified of the dark when I was small. Birdie played upon that whenever she could. She took malicious glee in terrorizing me. Because of my mother, our parents were caught up in the social whirl of York County. They often left Birdie home to watch after me. She had no beaus, no prospects for marriage. She was a sharp-tongued old maid in the making. She hated the thought. And she hated me! To get her revenge, she would wait until Mother and Father were away, then she would lock me down in the root cellar. She threatened to do even worse if I dared tell my mother."

Persia could hardly believe it, but she was beginning to feel sympathy for the man. They had both suffered a great deal of pain at Birdie Blackwell's hands.

"One night when I was about twelve and Birdie had been left in charge by our parents, she burst into my room and found me naked, examining myself with some curiosity. I had just bathed and was getting ready for bed when the oddest thing happened to me. I knew it was evil to touch myself; Mother had told me so. But I did and it caused this strange swelling. I was terrified, sure that I would be bloated and dead before morning." He laughed softly. "You know how children are."

Persia remembered her terror at her first monthly bleeding and nodded.

"Well, Birdie came into my room and found me that way. I remember being more terrified of her at that moment than I was even of dying. I knew she would lock me away, and I didn't want to die alone in the dark. But instead, she came to me and knelt down and stroked me. I was crying, but she soothed my tears away, assuring me that everything would be all right."

Persia shuddered, imagining the scene.

"She took me to her bed . . . and, well, the game began that night. I know now that I was her first lover. And after that, whenever our parents were out, we played Birdie's game."

"Did your parents ever find out?" Persia asked almost timidly.

"No, not completely. But they came home one night to find me still in Birdie's bed. Both of us were asleep. But both of us were also naked. My father gave me a terrible beating. My parents never realized how attached we were to each other . . . how much we loved each other."

"But you left, Cyrus. You left Quoddy Cove and Birdie. What happened?"

His face lost its calm, and his eyes narrowed to dark slits. "Birdie found someone else. I can't explain the jealousy I felt at the time. I threatened to kill her. She laughed at me. In a fit of spite, I began seeing her suitor's younger sister. Birdie only laughed at my attempts to win her back. She told me I was a *foolish boy*. I hated her! Oh, how I hated her!" He smiled—a mad, vicious smile. "I plotted to get even. Finally, I came up with a plan. I would do away with the man. Then Birdie would be mine again. But the night I torched the house, only the mother and the girl I had been seeing were at home. Birdie's lover escaped. Still, I frightened her enough so that she stopped seeing him. But I had to go away. She said it wasn't safe for me to stay. The seminary, too, was her idea. She said no one would suspect me of the crime then. So I went, and here I am."

Persia had lost her fear. She was numb. "And Hannah?" she asked quietly.

"I loved her. She was the only woman I never compared with Birdie," he wailed, rubbing a hand over his eyes. "From the first moment I saw her, I knew I had to have her. She loved me, too, or so I thought. But her parents refused to allow us to marry. I wasn't good enough for her! She had to have a *prince*!" He lowered his voice. "Well, I should have let him have her. She was no wife to me. I worshiped the ground she walked, but she only scoffed at me. She threw herself into God's work; for that she cannot be faulted. But she wanted no part of being a wife. She would taunt me, tease me: 'Brother Cyrus, won't you please brush my hair?' " He closed his eyes and inhaled deeply. "I can still smell that raven-black hair—like passion flowers in the bright sun. It felt soft as the finest silk. She was so beautiful— almost as beautiful as my mother. But then when she found the necklace, it was all over. I knew I couldn't let her live, as much as I loved her."

He had tears in his eyes. Persia fought the urge to feel sorry for him. The man was a *murderer*, many times over! *And she was to be his next victim!*

He looked at her suddenly and there was a fierce light in his pale eyes. "Persia, why did you come here? You didn't need me, you had *him*! How could you have been so foolish? How could you have thrown away love and wasted your life so?"

She felt a moment of hope. "It isn't too late, Cyrus. I know the right path now. If you'd just let me go."

He stared hard at her, seeming to waver, seeming to try to make a decision. But finally he shook his head. "No. Had it not been for last night, we might have bargained. But when I took you then, you were everything to me that Birdie had ever been—everything that Hannah refused to be. It *is* too late. You are truly my *wife* now! I'm a jealous man, Persia. I *won't* let him have you! As for myself, I can live with the pain and the guilt no longer. I long for the comfort of death. But I would know no ease, even on the other side, if I left you here for him."

"What are you saying?"

"Indira!" he called suddenly. "Come and prepare Sister Persia. It is time for the *suttee*!"

"Cyrus, wait! Tell me what's going on," Persia begged.

He smiled at her sadly. "You wanted to see the cave. I will show you."

Zack was in the boat Cunningham had procured for him. Faintly, in the distance, he could see the outline of Elephanta's shore. He stroked hard, and soon the dark island was looming large before him. He could hear chanting and the wailing of many souls. Some sort of ceremony was in progress. He bent to his oars. He *must* make it in time!

All the inhabitants of Elephanta were gathered at the cave. Persia stared from face to face, trying to find a sympathetic eye. But all the dark eyes were downcast. Each face wore a mask of sorrowful acceptance. She now knew what fate awaited her. She was about to become a victim of the ancient rite of *suttee*—the burning alive of a widow with her husband's corpse.

Long shadows danced about the walls and ceiling of the cave, making the three fierce images of the *Trimurti* seem alive as they gazed down on the funeral pyre.

She stood beside Cyrus Blackwell—her hands bound—wearing a flowing white robe to match his shroud. Even in the humid warmth of the underground cave, Persia felt cold. It was the cold of death.

Wailing chants filled the cave. The pyre was ready, piled high with sandalwood. Nearby, another, smaller flame melted the butter that would be clarified into ghee, to be smeared on their corpses to purify them and send their souls on their way to whatever afterlife awaited them.

Persia was given a draft of bitter brown liquid to drink. She was beyond refusing. It seemed to her that death lingered already in the cave. There was no escape. The vultures from the Towers of Silence hovered near.

Cyrus kissed her cold cheek. "I will go before you and be waiting on the other side. Remember, physical pain is nothing. You will join me in an instant."

Whatever herb or drug Persia had been given had dulled her mind and senses. She was beyond fighting now. Cyrus's words were received and accepted.

She watched as two white-robed figures set torch to the pyre. She knew her husband was to die first. She did not know how. She heard a click, looked up. Jammu's rifle was aimed at Cyrus's heart. In another instant he would be dead, and she would be forced to join his body on the flaming pyre.

"No!" Persia cried. "No, you can't! *Please!*"

Suddenly, the sound of bells assaulted her ears. A great gust of wind whipped through the cave. The flames leaped higher and higher. She stared at Cyrus. Any moment now, she knew she would see the bullet strike him and a red blossom of blood spring from his chest. When that happened, it would be the end for her, too. She tried to remember the words of the Lord's Prayer, but they refused to come. The only thing that did come was a scream.

Zack was halfway up the stone steps that led to the mouth of the cave when he heard Persia's hysterical cries. He took the last of the flight in great bounding leaps. The sight that greeted him at the mouth of the cave froze his blood. Beneath the ancient idols carved into the rock, a crescent of dull-eyed natives stood watching as Cyrus Blackwell opened Persia's robe.

"We will know each other once more before the end," the missionary said.

She tried to pull away from him, but he held her in place.

Zack leaped at the man, knocking him away. Blackwell went sprawling, taking several of the spectators to the cave's floor with him. Without giving the missionary time to recover, he scooped Persia up and fled. She felt like a limp doll in his arms. And all the while, as he raced down the stone steps, she kept murmuring, "No, please, no."

"Darling, it's all right now," he said, trying to reassure her, but she seemed not to hear him.

By the time he placed her in the bow of the boat and shoved away from the stone wharf, he could hear other footsteps thudding down of the steep hill.

"I should have killed the bloody bastard," he said. But this was no time to waste breath on should-haves. He needed all of his wind and strength for rowing. It was a long way across to the mainland. And if he allowed their pursuers to overtake them, it would mean his death and worse for Persia.

Zack eased the boat into shore just as the first streaks of dawn were tinting Malabar Hill with feathers of gold among the green treetops. Persia had not spoken a word the whole time. She seemed in a daze of terror.

"Persia," he whispered, "do you think you can walk?"

She cringed away from him, wild-eyed. "No, don't touch me!"

"Darling, it's me—Zack. You're safe now, but we have to get away from here. Blackwell and the others are right behind us. They'll be here any minute."

"Zack?" Her voice sounded faraway, and she stared up at him with vague, unfocused eyes.

Hearing shouts as their pursuers' vessels neared, Zack pulled Persia out of the boat and thrust her up onto the bank. "Get out of sight! Quickly!"

The first of Blackwell's followers didn't wait for their boat to touch shore but dived into the dark waters and were soon rushing Zack. He fought the two men off—knocking the first out with a hard right to the jaw, then sending the second sprawling back into the water. Before the others could be out of their boats and on him, Zack rushed up the hill.

"Persia!" he called. But she was nowhere in sight.

Although dawn was breaking, the garden of the dead was still shrouded in deep, violet shadows. Zack stood still on the path for a moment, listening for some sound while he scanned the verge of the jungle for the white glow of Persia's robe. But she was nowhere to be seen. He hurried on toward the Towers of Silence.

"There he goes!" He heard Blackwell's voice from the landing. "You men fan out and find her. I'll take care of him."

Zack glanced over his shoulder to see a white-robed figure starting up the path. Cyrus Blackwell.

"Persia," Zack called quietly, hoping to flush her out of hiding before the others found her. "Persia, come to me. It's Zack, darling. You'll be safe with me."

The man passed so close to her that Persia could have reached out a hand and touched his boots. She wanted to leap up and run from him, but her flight through the thick vegetation on the hill had left her weak and breathless. All she could do now was huddle in the bushes and hope he wouldn't see her or hear her heart thundering in her breast. The sight of the flames, their singeing heat, was branded on her eyes. She would not be burned alive!

Who was the man? And why was he chasing her? Her mind reeled in a drugged fog of terror. She didn't know where she was or what was happening to her. She remembered only the cave and the fire and death waiting to consume her. There had been many men and women there—all staring at her, all waiting to see her die. She had been so afraid. She was still afraid. Her mind refused to function.

The man who had stolen her away moved on up the hill. Bending a branch out of the way, she stared after him. There, beyond his dark silhouette, looming like five glowing castle turrets in the first rays of the sun, were the Towers of Silence. How did she know what these buildings were called? She frowned. She had no idea. But she associated peace and rest and safety with the great structures. She felt suddenly drawn to them. Slowly, carefully, she made her way through the underbrush that bordered the path, edging ever closer to her sanctuary.

Cyrus Blackwell had Hazzard in sight. There was no need to hurry. There was no place he could go. As for Persia, his men would find her. Her purification might have been interrupted for the time being, but she would shed her many sins before the sun set on the peaks of Elephanta. She would enter Nirvana with him. Only then would her baptism be complete and her soul be one with that of the universe. She would be his wife at last.

"Come to me, wife!" he called. "This is our time. Your sins shall be purged and your spirit made holy. But only I can help you. He will only sink you deeper into the depths. But together you and I can enter heaven."

Both Persia and Zack heard Blackwell's words. Hypnotized by his voice, Persia stood erect in the garden and started toward the white-robed figure.

"No, Persia!" Zack yelled. "Don't listen to him."

He and Blackwell both spied her at the same instant. Seeing the other man head toward her, Zack charged into the jungle forest to try to reach her first.

But when Persia spied the two men rushing toward her, the terror gripped her with new force. She could trust neither of them. Death was waiting for her somewhere in the night. She would only be safe if she could reach one of the great towers. Forcing herself to run, she made her way up the hill—stumbling, groping, gasping. At last, she reached the smooth, white wall. She clung to it for a moment, trying to catch her breath. The surface felt cool and soothing against her fevered cheek.

"Save me! Oh, please, save me!" she moaned.

She opened her eyes and glanced up. Circling high above, dark against the dawn pink of the sky, great birds swooped on widespread wings. She could feel the powerful thunder of their strokes in her heart.

"Thank you!" she sobbed. "You've come."

Never taking her eyes from the black creatures wheeling overhead, she climbed the steps slowly. The birds swooped lower, eyeing her curiously.

"Come to me," she called, raising outstretched arms to them. "Take me away from here."

"Persia, no!" The man's voice seemed to come from far away.

She glanced down. He was only a dark speck below her, but he was still a threat. She must coax the great birds down to fly her to safety before he reached her. Then she spotted a second figure, approaching the man who had called to her. He held a heavy sandlewood log in his hands, raised over the other man's head. She knew that awful thing. It had come from her own funeral pyre. She couldn't watch.

With her eyes tightly shut, she stumbled on the steps and fell to the grate at the top of the Tower of Silence. She heard the flapping of wings just over her head. She could feel the wind of flight all about her. She smiled. Soon they would come to her. Soon now she would be free. No pain. No fire.

She opened her eyes one last time. The dark-clad figure lay stretched out on the ground far below. For some reason—she couldn't think why—the sight pained her. The man in white robes was nowhere to be seen. It didn't matter. She closed her eyes again. The wings were drawing nearer. It would be over soon. They would take her away.

"Get away, you filthy scavengers!"

Startled by the sound of the familiar and dreaded voice so near at hand, Persia sat up, staring. It was the man in white. He meant to hurt her. He lunged at her, but she scrambled away. She felt herself slipping through the grate and grabbed for something to hang on to.

When she gripped the edge of his robe, it tore away
from his body. He screamed in terror.

The Parsees' feathered morticians swooped lower. The
time was wrong for feeding at this place. Still, hunger
knew no hour. There was not the odor of decay about
the feeding area. Still, the food was there—uncovered—
only waiting to be devoured.

The instant that Persia's hand ripped the robe from
Blackwell's body, flinging him at the same time to his
back on the grate, the soaring birds of prey had their
signal. They swooped to the feast.

The largest of the creatures, attracted by his wide,
staring eyes, flew straight for Blackwell's face.

The next to the last sight Cyrus Blackwell saw was a
set of curved talons coming straight for his face. The last
was the unblinking red eye of the vulture, staring into
his, before the talons found their mark.

Screams of agony echoed down through the Towers of
Silence to where Persia clung to the robe, swinging
above the bone-strewn pit. The shock jolted her to her
senses. Over her head, black against the grate and the
early-morning sky, she saw Cyrus Blackwell's body,
being quickly stripped clean by the hungry vultures. For
a time she watched, aghast, as he jerked with weak
spasms of the life he now held to so tremulously. He had
planned to die, but not this way. Then she realized there
could be no life left in the few bloody shreds of flesh left
clinging to his bones. His death dance was caused by the
action of the vultures' tearing talons alone.

When his clean bones rattled down through the grate,
falling about her, she screamed.

"Zack! *Zack!* For God's sake, help me!"

She was shaking, shivering, sobbing. She had to hold
on to the robe. If she slipped, she would be in the pit
with *him*.

Suddenly, she felt herself being raised up. Closer and
closer came the sky, while a black form huddled over
her.

"It's all right now, Persia. It's over, darling."

"Oh, Zack!" she cried.

A moment later, she was through the grate and in his arms. His lips found hers, and he tried to reassure her tenderly. She was sure now of who she was and who he was. And she knew that she loved him with everything in her.

So why did she turn away from his kiss? Why did his body pressed to hers repulse her?

The strange terror that filled her took away her will to struggle against him. He took her lips and kissed her deeply. And finally, she surrendered to the weakness she had fought for hours, letting herself slip away beyond any man's reach.

Carefully, Zack lifted Persia in his arms and started down the narrow stairs of the Towers of Silence.

"Everything will be all right now, darling," he whispered, but she never heard.

PART FOUR

1848

CHAPTER THIRTY

*P*ERSIA stood at her window, staring out over Gay Street and feeling desperately lonely. A light snow was falling, clothing the village in the same pristine white that she now wore. The mellow voices of a group of carolers drifted up to her. It was Christmas Eve—a time of joy and peace and love. And it was the hour of her wedding to Zack.

Why did she feel so desolate—so removed from everything and everyone in the world?

She loved him; she knew she did. And she had waited a long, long time for this moment. But the old fear remained. She needed his tenderness, yet she withdrew from it. It wasn't that she wanted to turn away from him. During her time with Cyrus Blackwell, something had been taken from her. What she had offered Zack so willingly and happily before was no longer hers to give. It was almost as if the evil missionary had managed to take a part of her to the grave with him.

She had stalled Zack as long as she could, making him wait months after their return to New England before

she agreed to set a date for their marriage. She had
almost hoped the time would never come. No, that was
not true. Her real hope had been that things would
change before the time arrived. That she would be herself again.

But nothing had changed. She was as she had been
since the night in the cave on Elephanta Island, facing
the funeral pyre—empty, alone, cold, and terrified for
any man to come near her.

And now she must face her wedding night. She must
allow him a husband's rights. How could she bear it?
Something about Cyrus Blackwell had turned her away
from physical love. She had not even been able to let
her father kiss her upon her return home.

She jumped, startled by the knock at her bedroom
door.

"It's time, Persia," Europa called. "Everyone is waiting in the parlor."

"I'm coming," she answered with a sinking feeling in
her heart.

The parlor of the Whiddington home was decked with
holly and evergreens. A roaring fire warmed the large
room, casting its golden glow over the smiling faces of
the guests. Asa Whiddington beamed at his younger
daughter as he led her to her waiting groom. He thought
that there hadn't been another bride as lovely since he'd
married his own Victoria.

Persia wore the same gown her mother and grand-
mother had worn before her—all antique white satin and
point d'Angleterre lace. Asa thought back to another
wedding that seemed long ago. That had not been a
happy occasion like this one. This time there was no
black veil hiding the bride's beautiful face, only a diaph-
anous cloud of white cascading from a crown of pearls.

Then the bride's father frowned slightly. Maybe it was
the veil that made Persia's eyes look less than sparkling.
In spite of the fact that she now had the man she loved,
he had sensed some underlying tension between them
ever since their return from India. They had told him

nothing about the trip that could have cast a permanent
gloom over the two of them. Granted, losing First Mate
Barry had been most regrettable. But men died at sea. It
had always been so; it would always be. And the business with Blackwell had been shocking. But that part of
his daughter's life was all behind her now.

No, whatever was bothering Persia and Zack, it was
something far more personal and tragic. He knew she
had lived as the missionary's wife for a time. Blackwell's
death had been sudden and violent. But surely she could
not be mourning a man she hardly knew. She had loved
Zachariah Hazzard for a long, long time.

Zack, too, was aware of Persia's gloom on a day when
she should be shining bright. And he guessed the cause.
He had lived with it since that terrible morning at the
Towers of Silence—the first time she had turned away
from his kiss. It was almost as if she now existed within
the sheltering walls of her own personal tower of silence.

She had allowed him to take her to Calcutta, back to
the ship. And there had been no argument when he
declared that he still intended to marry her, as soon as
possible. But that had not been soon enough for him.
Even after they returned to New England, he had been
forced to wait—watching her carefully and treating her
with all the gentle patience at his command.

It was as if a part of her had died during the time she
was on Elephanta Island. Zack loved her still—more
than ever—but he was allowed to do so only from a
distance. His slightest touch made her shiver with dread.
An attempt at a kiss brought tears. And anything more
was beyond imagining.

She had been a very sick woman for most of the
voyage home. Whatever had happened during her time
with Blackwell had taken its toll on her. And the horror
she had been a part of at the Towers of Silence had all
but driven her over the brink. For a time, Zack had
feared that she would never be well enough to marry,
that she might not even live.

But once they returned to Maine—familiar surround-

ings and well-loved relations—she had come around.
She was almost herself again. She even set the date for
their wedding. But she had yet to allow Zack the slightest intimacy. She loved him well, but from a chaste
distance. And now they were about to exchange their
solemn vows, while upstairs the bridal bed awaited.
What would she do? And how would he handle it if she
refused him?

"Zachariah, my dear brother-in-law-to-be, won't you
join us?" The fetchingly plump Europa—ruffled from
head to toe in Christmas-plaid taffeta—brought Zack out
of his musings.

"Yes, I believe it is time," agreed the lanky young
minister who had taken Brother Osgood's place when
the old preacher passed on during the summer. "Please
join hands."

"Persia?" Zack whispered, offering his hand.

She hesitated for such a long time that a nervous
rustling passed through the parlor. Seton coughed, and
several of the young Holloways shuffled their boots
restlessly.

When Persia finally placed her fingers in Zack's palm,
her touch was so light that he could hardly feel it. Only
his long desire for contact and the chill of her fingertips
actually told him they were joined, flesh to flesh.

Her voice trembled the slightest bit as she made her
responses. She stared up into Zack's eyes the whole
time, her own brittle blue and wide with something akin
to terror. Zack both longed for and dreaded the moment
about to come.

"You may kiss the bride, Captain Hazzard," the minister intoned solemnly.

Europa bustled forward to lift Persia's veil. Zack stared
down into her face, caressing her tenderly with his dark,
troubled eyes. She was so beautiful—more so now than
ever. Her skin was like translucent china from all she
had been through and her long recovery afterward. He
watched her lips part as if she meant to speak.

"What, darling?" he whispered.

She closed her eyes and two tears squeezed from their

corners. He started to draw away at the sight of them, but she pursed her lips and lifted them bravely for his kiss. He met her pale lips gently, almost hesitantly. She offered no response. She neither kissed him back nor tried to refuse him. Suddenly, a coldness far more frightening than what he had felt before gripped him. Was this the way it would be? She would allow him to take, while she gave nothing in return? He couldn't live with that.

The supper reception stretched on and on. Persia acted bright and gay, but her eyes told another tale as Zack watched her closely. He guessed that she was playing the bubbling bride, trying to delay the hour that they would go upstairs to be alone together. Several times already he had tried to draw her away from the table, but she had chided him affectionately, pleading to stay with her family for "only a little while longer, Zack darling."

Finally, her own father put an end to Persia's charade. "Well, my dear, I think we should excuse you now. The Christmas bells will be ringing in the new day soon."

Everyone murmured agreement. Her father's words struck pain in her heart, but there was nothing she could do. She would have to go with her husband, up to the old canopy bed where she herself had been conceived on a snowy night much like this Christmas Eve.

After saying prolonged good-nights and thank-yous to everyone, Persia hurried from the dining room, not accepting Zack's offered arm. He followed her up the stairs and to the master bedroom, but she hesitated outside the door.

"You go on in, darling," she said to her husband. "I need to get some things from my old room."

His face grim at this new ploy, Zack answered, "Whatever you say, Persia, but don't be long."

"Only a moment," she promised.

But her moment stretched on and on. Zack shed his formal clothes and put on a dressing gown. He poured a brandy, lit a cigar, sat down, stood up, paced the room.

"Dammit, what's she doing?"

By the time she came through the door, he was on his way to fetch her.

"Persia, where have you been?"

"I'm sorry I kept you waiting, Zack." Her voice was a thin wisp of breathy fear. "I had trouble unfastening the buttons on my wedding gown."

He looked at her. She was dressed in a long night-gown that covered her, chin to toes, with another wrap-per covering that. So, she'd escaped to her own room to undress and smother herself in this shroud-thing—the perfect defense against him.

"You have a *husband* now to undo your buttons, Persia." He sounded angry and he knew it. But he couldn't help it. He was.

"Please don't be cross with me, Zack. It's been such a long, tiring day. Why don't we just crawl into bed and go to sleep?"

Disappointment gripped him—so deep and total that it left him feeling weak. He could not let her do this tonight. They had to set things straight between them . . . *now*. But he curbed his temper. He would have to be gentle with her.

Zack reached out and took his wife's hand before she had time to draw it away.

"Persia, come sit by the fire with me for a while. We need to talk."

She tried to resist. He would have none of it. He was determined to be gentle, but he would be firm as well.

"Zack, I really am exhausted."

He drew her down to the couch next to him and put a warm brandy into her hands. "Drink this. It will make you feel better."

He smiled crookedly, convinced that the only reason she accepted the brandy was so that she could take her hand from his.

"Well? What did you want to talk about, Zack?" she asked.

This wasn't going to be as easy as he had hoped. He didn't know how to approach the subject of her time as Blackwell's prisoner on Elephanta. He didn't like to think about what she must have been through, and certainly it wouldn't be easy for her to discuss. Undoubtedly she had been misused by Blackwell. But it had to come out in the open, they had to clear the air between them if they were ever to have a real marriage.

"Persia, I want you to tell me what's wrong. We're not in India any longer. You're in no danger. And anything you say will be strictly between the two of us."

She stiffened beside him. He could almost feel her guard coming up. He turned to read her expression, but a shadow had descended over her face.

"I don't even want to think about that time, much less talk about it. It's cruel of you to bring it up, Zack, especially on our wedding night."

"Are we going to have a wedding night, Persia?"

His point-blank question stunned her. She looked away from him, into the fire.

"I don't understand what you mean," she whispered.

He took the brandy snifter from her hand and set it on the table. Then he gently brought her palm to his lips—breathing over her flesh, kissing it, finally touching one throbbing spot with the tip of his tongue. Her fingers tensed in his.

"You know what I mean, darling. *I want to make love to you.* Am I going to be allowed that privilege?"

"Tonight?" she asked quietly, still not looking at him.

"Yes. Starting right this minute, in fact. I've been very patient, Persia. The last time we made love we were in Bombay. It was before—"

"No! Don't say it!" she cried, and suddenly she was sobbing.

He pulled her to his chest and tried to soothe her, but it seemed that all her pent-up emotions from months and years past were bent on release.

"It's all right, darling. Go ahead and cry," he soothed. "When you're finished, we'll talk it all out."

Even though his heart went out to her in her pain and grief, Zack felt a certain amount of elation that she allowed him to hold her. This was a first step, small as it was.

* * *

Persia was aware of his arms around her. She wanted them there. Suddenly her crying turned from pain to joy. For the very first time in so long, she didn't feel repelled by Zack's touch. She was frightened—yes!—but it was not the awful terror she had experienced for the past months. All the guilt and pain and fear of her time with Cyrus Blackwell seemed to be slipping away. Finally, her sobs subsided.

"Better?" he asked.

She wiped her cheeks and offered him a wan smile. "Yes. I think so."

"Can you talk about it now? You don't have to worry about shocking me. I know you were his wife. And I know that whatever you were forced to do, you had no choice in the matter."

Suddenly, she wanted Zack to hold her and to kiss her and—yes, glory be!—to make love to her. But she would have to make him understand first.

"I was never his wife. . . ."

He frowned, not understanding.

"I was his legal wife, yes. But there was no love between us. I've never been truly married until this very night. Someday I'll tell you everything. But not now . . . please, not now, darling." She looked down at their clasped hands suddenly, unable to meet his intense gaze.

"You mean he never forced himself on you?" There was an unmistakable note of relief in Zack's voice.

"Well . . . yes and no," she stammered.

"Persia, you're talking in riddles. He had you on that island for a long time. What did he do to you? Something terrible happened. I know because you've been so long coming out of it."

"Zack, you mustn't hate me." Her eyes pleaded with him.

He hugged her. "Never, darling! *Never!*"

"But what I have to tell you sounds so bizarre. I don't know even how to begin."

"Slowly, darling. We have all night . . . a lifetime."

She leaned back, letting him encircle her shoulders

with his arm. She tensed for a moment when his fingers touched her breast. But it felt wonderful. She relaxed and closed her eyes. She began at the very beginning and told him about everything—Cyrus and Birdie's game, his marriage to Hannah, his use of the servant Indira, his brutal attacks on her, the murders he had committed.

"He was not in his right mind. The night you came for me, he meant to kill himself and have *suttee* performed. I was to be burned alive on his funeral pyre," she explained. "For a time that night, I was totally under his control. It seemed I had no choice but to die with him."

"Persia darling, you've been through so much." Zack cradled her in his arms, never wanting to let her go, wanting to protect her from the world always.

"We all have," she answered quietly.

"And that's why you've pushed me away all these months? Because you couldn't bear thinking about the terrible things that had happened. Why did you turn me away when I came for you?"

"I had no choice. They had a gun on you. I had to keep you away. The thought of your being killed . . . It was just too awful! He also threatened to sell little Sindhu into white slavery if I made a false move. Thank God you're both safe from him now; you here, and Sindhu with a good family." She paused as if her thoughts were drifting. Then she shook her head and continued, "Afterward, it seemed that a barrier to love had come down. I couldn't do anything about it."

"And now?"

His hands were cradling her cheeks, and his lips hovered over hers, so close that she could feel his words on her face.

"Oh, Zack," she said softly, feeling her body warm to his. "Kiss me."

When he answered her demand, Zack found her lips parted and ready to accept him.

Persia felt no need to draw away. She answered his velvet probing with hungry thrusts of her own. A new need arose within her, but it was nothing to be feared. This longing was good and true and spawned by love.

Gently, he lifted her into his arms and carried her to the bed, holding his breath for fear she might protest. But she snuggled close to his chest, showering little kisses on his neck and sighing softly.

When he placed her on the bed, she cast aside her wrapper and asked timidly, "Would you help me with these little buttons?"

Zack's fingers trembled as he worked at the tiny things. And he felt a rush of need when she moaned as his fingers brushed her bare breasts.

When she lay before him, ready, he took great care to love her slowly, tenderly, throughly. And when he entered her, she clung to him, sighing his name and whispering her words of love.

Suddenly the world was filled with sound of bells. It was Christmas! The most wonderful Christmas Persia had ever known. She needed no carolers to serenade her; the song in her heart was the sweetest on earth. And there was no pretty wrapped gift that could be half as precious to her as the gift of Zack's love.

There was peace on earth and in her heart.

And there was love . . . *true love* . . . forevermore.

About the Author

BECKY LEE WEYRICH, a native Georgian, was born on Margaret Mitchell's birthday in a hospital that later became a library, and she is named for Daphne Du Maurier's *Rebecca*. So it seems only fitting that she should have become a writer.

Before taking pen in hand, she spent her early career as a professional navy wife and mother of two. For seventeen years, she moved with her pilot husband from base to base, living in such diverse locations as Maine, Florida, California, and Naples, Italy.

In 1969 she took a job on a Maryland newspaper, writing a weekly column. Since then, she has contributed to several newspapers and magazines. She wrote, illustrated, and published two volumes of poetry. She turned to fiction in 1978, and since then has written eleven novels, including six other Fawcett titles: RAPTURE'S SLAVE, CAPTIVE OF DESIRE, RAINBOW HAMMOCK, TAINTED LILIES, SUMMER LIGHTNING, and GYPSY MOON, winner of a Romantic Times "Reviewers' Choice Award" in 1986.

Becky Lee Weyrich now makes her home on St. Simons Island, Georgia, sharing her vintage beach cottage—Unicorn Dune—with her husband and son, one dog, and assorted cats. Her hobbies include golf, clogging, bowling, beachcombing, collecting Victorian antiques, and spoiling her two grandchildren.

THE ROMANCE CONTINUES WITH...

Becky Lee Weyrich